Traditional Tales from the Nutmeg State

LEGENDARY CONNECTICUT

David E. Philips

CURBSTONE PRESS

Cover design by Stone Graphics
Printed in the U.S. by Bookcrafters

Curbstone Press is a 501(c)(3) nonprofit literary arts
organization whose operations are supported in part
by private donations and by grants from the ADCO
Foundation, the J. Walton Bissell Foundation, the
Connecticut Commission on the Arts, the Lef Foundation,
the Lila Wallace-Reader's Digest Literary Publishers
Marketing Development Program, administered by the
Council of Literary Magazines and Presses, the Andrew W.
Mellon Foundation, the National Endowment for the Arts,
and the Plumsock Fund.

Library of Congress Cataloging-in-Publication Data

Philips, David E.
    Legendary Connecticut: traditional tales from the
Nutmeg State/by David E. Philips. — 2nd ed.
        p. cm.
    Includes bibliographical references and index.
    ISBN 1-880684-05-5: $14.95
    1. Legends—Connecticut.   2. Tales—Connecticut.
I. Title.
GR110.C8P48 1992
398.2'09746—dc20
                                    92-24532

distributed in the U.S. by
InBook
Box 120261
East Haven, CT 06512

published by
CURBSTONE PRESS
321 Jackson Street
Willimantic, CT 06226

To
Janet
my wife

To Evan and Sandi
Donald
and
Kimberly
my children

And to
Shady Nook
where it all started

This Volume is
Affectionately Dedicated

Contents

PART III— SUPERNATURAL LEGENDS

PART IV — COLONIAL LEGENDS ABOUT INDIANS

Acknowledgments

Although preparing a book like *Legendary Connecticut* is ultimately a lonely, demanding and sometimes frustrating business, my work has been encouraged and the burden of authorship eased by many people over the past few years. For their contributions and assistance, I would like to extend my sincere thanks to the following:

To The Board of Trustees for The Connecticut State Colleges for granting a sabbatical leave in the fall of 1979 which permitted me to complete most of the research for this book.

To Charles R. Webb, president of Eastern Connecticut State University for his faith and encouragement.

To David M. Roth, my colleague at E.C.S.U., Connecticut historian and director of the Center for Connecticut Studies, for his wisdom, support and friendship.

To the outstanding staff of the J. Eugene Smith Library at E.C.S.U., especially Dean Reilein, Nick Welchman and Jody Newmyer, for their friendly and able assistance on numerous occasions.

To Joan Jensen of the University of Connecticut Library, Margaret Perry of the Canton Public Library, Valerie Fidrych of the Stonington Free Library, the reference librarians of the Free New Haven Public Library, Yvonne Brown of Tolland and Margaret H. Talbot of Andover, for providing valuable research assistance.

To two generations of students in my folklore and Connecticut studies classes at E.C.S.U., many of whom I have acknowledged by name in the Bibliography of this book, whose projects have enriched the Connecticut Folklore Archive and whose enterprise and perseverance continue to astound their teacher.

To Regina Zenewitz and Eloise Farris, who typed my manuscript, for their unfailing skill, good humor and enthusiasm.

To my family: my father, for inspiring in me an interest in history and the passing parade; my wife, for her love, strength and understanding; and my children, for their willingness to give up their father for extended periods of time to the pursuit of the elusive Connecticut legend.

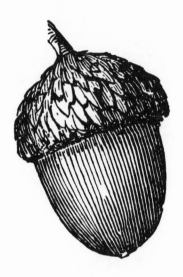

Introduction

Homer D. Babbidge, Jr.
22 February 1984

Its people seem to possess an uncommon attachment to Connecticut. When asked why they are so fond of their home, Connecticut residents are wont to respond with vague references to "the quality of life"; and when pressed to define this quality, their reply often embraces the equally elusive word "heritage."

So important does this heritage seem to us, that the late Governor Ella Grasso appointed a Task Force to preserve it. That Commission spent two years at work, with its effort largely devoted to defining the term. It was easy enough to identify the major components of Connecticut's important and prominent history, still in evidence in the form of natural landmarks, architectural monuments, strong institutions and annual celebrations. And yet I am not sure that anyone on the Task Force was satisfied that its definition was complete.

One reason for this is that the dimensions of our heritage are not unlike the stones that make up that unsurpassed symbol of Yankee tradition — the stone wall. They come in all sizes, shapes and textures. Some stand out in their grand regularity; others are notable for eccentric angularity. And the facets of our heritage are, like those stones, not only many and diverse; some of the most important are obscure and elusive. It is a fundamental rule of dry stone wall construction that innumerable small stones — "chinks" and "wedges" and "shims" — are essential to the balance and stability of the great stones that catch one's eye. These serve as the unnoticed mortar that holds the construct together.

Legends are prominent in this "small stones" category. They do not announce themselves as do fine architectural relics, saying "we are your heritage," and yet they are, in a very fundamental way, essential to that heritage.

Unlike the great political, economic and cultural cornerstones of the Connecticut Heritage, popular legend blends fact and fiction, wisdom and whimsy to create a tradition that supports the events and achievements of our collective experience; creating heroes, explaining mysteries, celebrating wonder and nurturing the imaginations of Connecticut residents for centuries.

Appropriate to their function, these little pieces of our heritage are neither uniform nor elegant. But their eccentricities — their character, if you will — gives them elements of charm and grace that are undeniable. Taken in the aggregate, they are essential to both the style and stability of our cultural foundations.

The stuff of legend is not limited to the past. It surrounds us even today, echoed in the names of our cities and towns, rumbling in the ground below Moodus, lingering in the mists above Thompson, and repeated in the ghost stories of teenagers. Legends persist because they hold meaning for today.

Many of the tales presented here are, often unconsciously, as much a part of our modern lives as shopping malls and home computers. The story of Israel Putnam, for instance, details the accomplishments and heroic traits of a national figure now reduced to the namesake of meeting halls and hotel ballrooms. His presence comes alive in legend, as do those of lesser known figures such as Mother Bailey and Jemima Wilkinson. Their heroism celebrates the Yankee characteristics of craftiness and pluck, courage and humor, while the talltale of Coventry farmer Lorenzo Dow simply delights in the unusual strength of a lovable local. Lillinonah's Leap in New Milford stands as a monument to heroism of another sort; the love of an Indian maiden and a white settler that survived cultural differences, separation and finally death.

We are indebted to Professor David E. Philips, who has sought out these legends like so many small stones. He has dug them up through extensive research, dusted them with the brisk brush of his intellect and placed them in this volume in the honored position they deserve. In *Legendary Connecticut* he has drawn attention, in a most delightful way, to the role of legend in the continuity of Connecticut life.

This Introduction may well have been Homer Babbidge's last public statement.

It reflects the warmth, the wit and the love of heritage which were always his personal hallmarks.

I am grateful that he found the time and the strength to lend a helping hand with our old stone wall of a book.

Thank you, Homer.

D. E. P.

(Homer Babbidge died on March 27, 1984).

Author's Foreword

When *Legendary Connecticut* was first published in 1984, the Author's Foreword outlined some of the reasons for writing the book. I spoke of the gap in our knowledge of Connecticut's folk narratives, which I hoped to fill with this collection. I mentioned the ways in which legends add another dimension to our understanding of the state's popular values and traditions, its "soul," so to speak. I even proposed that no study of Connecticut history would be complete without taking into account the perspectives offered by traditional stories. In his wonderful introduction, the late Homer Babbidge seemed to endorse that idea.

Now, while I still believe in the educational, historical, and social virtues of the tales in *Legendary Connecticut*, I have come more and more to feel that perhaps their greatest value lies in their capacity to delight. Though they may be Nutmegian in their settings and characters, these legends transcend the parochial. They please, simply because they are great stories!

That notion has been strengthened over the years by several things. First, the publication of *Legendary Connecticut* launched me on a modest career as a professional storyteller. As such, I have regaled audiences ranging from school children and Cub Scouts to local historians and retirement community residents with stories from this collection, during more than one hundred programs across the state. Everywhere, they have been warmly received.

In addition, I am delighted that so many parents have told me they have greatly enjoyed reading the book aloud to their children. Since I had made an effort to set down these legends in an informal, conversational style suggesting their origins in oral tradition, I have been particularly gratified to hear of the pleasure they have given to listening, as well as reading audiences of all ages.

The stories included in this collection are not — in the purest sense — folk legends, since (with few exceptions) they are not set down verbatim from the lips of live informants. Rather, they are tales which had their origins in oral tradition, but which came to my attention through their appearance in more than one hundred printed sources or in collecting projects by students in my folklore classes at Eastern Connecticut State University. The latter, including many audio tapes of folk storytellers, were archived in the J. Eugene Smith Library at Eastern and were a major source of both narrative material and inspiration.

When assembling a collection of tales such as these in *Legendary Connecticut*, the author was faced with a number of creative challenges, not the least of which was the problem of inclusion and organization. Surprisingly, Connecticut turned out to be a rich repository of legendary materials. And as my table of contents grew longer and longer, I finally had to call an arbitrary halt to any more tales beyond the 250 or so already selected. Moreover, I made it a point to include every sort of legend, from tales about heroes and memorable local events to stories of ghosts, witches, and the supernatural. Finally, I endeavored to present a representative, but by no means exhaustive collection of legends from every section of Connecticut.

An even greater challenge was posed by questions of form and substance. Folk legends by their very nature tend to be formless; a story would have a beginning and middle, perhaps, but no "literary" ending of the sort expected of written narratives. Also, typical of folk stories everywhere, the legends I wanted to include more often than not turned up in print, on tape, or both in more than one version. Details varied. Names and dates differed. Structures ranged from dramatic to none at all. Finally I decided to write the story as I would "tell" it, picking details from the variants I found especially interesting, enjoyable, or instructive, and whipping some rather untidy oral narratives into reasonable literary shape. Overall, the "voice" of each story was guided by the author's "feel" for the appropriate tone.

One criterion remained uppermost, however. I vowed to adhere to the narrative core of every tale, to respect the structural elements common to each legend, no matter how many versions my research uncovered. Thus, while the narratives in *Legendary Connecticut* are faithful to tradition, they have also been "reborn," dressed in the author's own style and literary fashion to become both old and familiar, yet fresh and new. I hope they bring to reader and listener alike as much enjoyment as they have brought to the author.

David E. Philips
Willimantic, Connecticut
October 1992

PART I
Personal Legends

An Introduction

THIS SECTION INCLUDES stories which focus on an individual regarded as legend-worthy by the folk and which, like all such tales, purport to tell the truth about that person. Some of these personal legends are attached to what might be called *culture heroes*, people like the Leatherman or Israel Putnam who were accepted by the folk as reflecting their values or beliefs. Such legends were often known and recounted over wide geographical areas, persisting in tradition for long periods of time. Other personal legends clustered about purely *local heroes*, Rufus Malbone or Elmer Bitgood, for example, figures familiar in a limited geographical region and much talked about by their fellow townspeople, but who never attained widespread folk celebrity.

Another kind of personal story included in Part I is the *anecdote*, a folk legend characterized by brevity, concentration on a single event — often extraordinary or exemplary — in the life of the central character and emphasis on the alleged personality traits of the subject. Anecdotes tend to be told either about figures of wide renown (George Washington, Noah Webster,) or about purely local characters, especially those representing favorite character types, like the miser (Phineas G. Wright), the clever rascal (Abel Buell) or the absent-minded minister (Rev. Bulkley). Anecdotal legends such as these are among the most popular forms of folk narrative. Undoubtedly they continue to circulate in colorful variety and profusion wherever people gather to exchange views or share experiences.

"The Old Leatherman"

*A*STRANGE, LONELY vagabond who wandered across the hills and valleys of western Connecticut and eastern New York State during the latter half of the nineteenth century is probably Connecticut's single most famous legendary figure. In his time, the man known as the "Old Leatherman" was a living legend, inspiring stories and rhymes, sales of large picture post cards and an invitation (declined, of course) to become a regular exhibit in a New York City freakshow, or "museum." After his death, his memory was kept alive by both ordinary folk and a succession of imitators, who, dressed in Leatherman clothing, took to the roads of southern New England in an effort to cash in on the fame of the original. According to most accounts, the Leatherman first appeared on the country lanes of Connecticut in the years just before the Civil War. Some have even pinpointed the place and time as Harwinton, on a misty April morning in 1858. That's probably close enough. From the time of his dramatic entrance on the stage of Connecticut legend until he died in 1889, he walked a regular circuit — always clockwise — from the Danbury area through Watertown and Middletown, down along the Connecticut River, westward through the Connecticut coastal towns to New Caanan, then into Westchester County, New York, before circling eastward again toward Danbury to retrace his steps once more. With each circuit, he covered a distance of 360 miles or more, walking about ten miles every day.

In each community he passed through, the Leatherman had identified a home or two where he knew friendly people would provide food whenever he appeared. A "host" family became accustomed to preparing a simple meal and setting it on the back doorstep for the eccentric tramp, every thirty-four days. For no matter what the season of year or the weather conditions, the Leatherman inevitably showed up — virtually at the same hour — according to that precise schedule, for a period of nearly thirty years! Only in his last few years did the schedule vary and the interval between visits increase, sometimes — as during the famous "Blizzard of '88" — to as many as forty days. But as late as 1884-1885 he made nineteen consecutive trips of exactly thirty-four days each. It was probably inevitable that such predictable behavior would make a lasting impression on folk living in the "Land of Steady Habits."

A striking sight he must have been, too. From the floppy, peaked cap pulled down low over his piercing, grey-blue eyes to the soles of his massive boots, he was dressed in clothing made entirely of leather. His suit featured a long jacket, with cavernous pockets, assembled from square, leather patches roughly sewn together with heavy leather thongs. The pants were made of the same rude construction, and resembled the padded coverings worn by ice hockey goalies today. Some waggish observers have said that this garb was peculiarly suited to the favorite folk hero of Connecticut. Because it was made of patches, it had a kind of continuous life. It was never new, but never completely worn out, either. When one patch wore out, the Leatherman went to work with palm* and needle and replaced it with another patch.

He frequently used a long, knob-ended walking stick and always toted a two-foot-square leather bag slung over his shoulder with two leather straps. In this satchel he carried a few scraps of food, extra leather patches, a pan from which he ate, a hand-made knife and hatchet, matches, tobacco and leather-working tools. Some people say that a few leather factories on his regular route were in the habit of placing good leather pieces on their discarded scrap piles whenever the Leatherman was scheduled to pay a visit. In any case, he never seemed wanting when it came time to mend cap, suit, bag or boots. And when the hot summer sun had dried out his leather ensemble, they say the reclusive hiker could be heard creaking and cracking in the distance long before he came into view.

When the Leatherman first began his legendary rambles, he must have aroused a certain amount of apprehension in startled witnesses to his comings and goings. But it wasn't long before their fears were quieted. Never, for

* A metal disk worn over the palm of the hand to push a needle through leather, canvas or other tough substances.

example, would he enter a home or barn, even to eat at a table or to escape the fiercest storm. During his long lifetime of tramping the byways of Connecticut and New York, he was never known to have paused to eat, rest or sleep under a man-made roof. He preferred, instead, the natural shelter provided by caves, mostly little more than overhanging rocks, or lean-tos made from fallen trees, branches and twigs.

To this day, the map of western Connecticut is dotted with "Leatherman's Caves," each with a tradition of having once been a temporary home for the homeless man. A few of these caves, especially those in the Meriden-Southington area and above Lake Compounce in Bristol, were known to be full of rattlesnakes. But because the Leatherman never seemed to be bothered by his venomous companions, some people believed that he possessed magical powers to charm the snakes and render them harmless.

Unlike other vagabonds who wandered the roads of New England in the nineteenth century, the old Leatherman had no interest in work or money. He never indicated a willingness to do chores for pay, like an ordinary tramp, and even though he would occasionally accept pennies offered him by children, he always returned the coins by placing them on a fence post or rock in the yard after finishing his meal. The children would then retrieve them and perhaps use them again when the Leatherman stopped the next time. He would accept gifts of food, of course, and sometimes matches or tobacco for the pipes which he left in many of the cave shelters he frequented.

In addition to his indifference to money, he had a positive passion for silence. Except for occasional noises which sounded to some like grunts and to others like phrases from a foreign language, the Leatherman never in thirty years spoke a recognizable word of English, not even a "good-bye" or "hello." He could make his wants known with a nod or a hand to his mouth, but anyone attempting to engage him in conversation or ask him a question was doomed to failure. In fact, such an effort always brought a cold reaction. One day when the Leatherman arrived at the Fenn home in Plainville, one of his regular food stops, the rap on the door was answered by Mr. Fenn, a farmer who had rarely been in the house during the wanderer's previous visits. "How are you?" asked farmer Fenn innocently. At that, the Leatherman drew back sharply, turned rapidly from the doorstep and never stopped at the Fenns' again, though he continued to pass the house for many years.

Eccentric and unconventional though his life-style was, the Leatherman's benign behavior and personal habits gradually calmed the fears and began to inspire the positive admiration of the hundreds of Connecticut people with whom he came into contact. While there were a few reported instances of harassment of the strange-looking tramp, by and large he was treated with respect by young and old alike. Once, at a tavern in Forestville, a few men grabbed him and tossed him into a horse trough in a fruitless effort to make him talk. On another occasion, in Branford, after the Leatherman had consumed a meal consisting of two cans of sardines, a loaf of bread, a pound of milk crackers, a quarter-pie, two quarts and two cups of coffee, a gill of brandy and a bottle of beer, someone, just for a joke, offered him a whole watermelon. He rose from the doorstep where he had been eating, walked off with his accustomed firm, springy step and never again stopped at that particular house. Such provocations, however, were apparently rare.

Over a period of time, the care and feeding of the Leatherman became a mark of distinction and privilege. People who lived along his route competed for the honor of providing his meals and the child who could boast that "my folks feed the Leatherman" was the envy of all his or her classmates in school. If there was an important event, such as a church social, scheduled on the day the Leatherman was due to come through, attendance was reduced because people who didn't stay home to feed the visitor might lose the honor next time around. Children, particularly, were strongly attracted to the eccentric walker and often accompanied him for short distances, he on one side of the road and they on the other.

As late as 1977 one 96-year-old Woodbridge woman who vividly recalled seeing the Leatherman when she was a child of four remembered the strong reaction of people in her neighborhood as he approached. Said Mrs. Mabel Hotchkiss Perry: "He looked strange, awful funny, but I wasn't afraid of him. Everything he wore seemed massive. He headed for the Judge house to get some food and the first thing I know, they were yelling from the kitchen, 'Here comes the Leatherman.' Then quick as lightening, three heads appeared in the doorway. Then he went back to the main road and went north toward Naugatuck."

Another elderly woman who, as a child, attended the little school on South Chippens Hill in Bristol, recalled that her teacher used the Leatherman as in incentive for the children to work for higher marks. Those achieving the best grades would be rewarded by being allowed to bring in something for the tramp on "Leatherman Day." On the inevitable day, when word was passed that the Leatherman was coming, the teacher dismissed the school and the children would line up outside. Then the child with the highest grade was permitted to step forward and offer the gift he or she had brought. The Leatherman would always come over, accept the gift without comment, nod his thanks and continue on his way. There are many who claim that in his time the old Leatherman was the best-fed, if not the most honored person in Connecticut.

The Blizzard of '88 and a case of lip cancer, probably contracted from years of over-exposure to the sun, combined to slow the Leatherman down. They say that in March of 1888 the celebrated vagrant was caught near Hartford in the worst snowstorm of the century. Found lying helpless in a snowbank, with both hands and feet frozen, he was reputedly admitted to Hartford Hospital. Here, his cancer was discovered. Despite his serious physical problems, the Leatherman soon departed the hospital in some mysterious fashion (he was supposedly under close watch) and headed once more for the open road. The blizzard and brief hospital stay caused him to be four days later than usual in making his rounds that spring.

Death, allegedly the result of injury sustained in a fall, finally slowed the old Leatherman down permanently on March 29, 1889. His body was discovered in one of his makeshift shelters near Ossining, New York, and buried without fanfare in the Sparta Cemetery in Ossining. The grave was originally marked only by an iron pipe driven into the ground, but in more recent times the site has been identified by a bronze plaque, suitably inscribed, unveiled during impressive ceremonies conducted by a group of interested citizens.

Although the secrets of the old Leatherman's origin, identity and motivation went with him to the grave, the folk imagination has worked overtime to explain them, often in fascinating (though totally unverifiable) detail. The most persistent legend goes something like this:

In the mid-nineteenth century there lived in the neighborhood of Lyons, France, a young man named Jules Bourglay (also rendered as Burgglay, Bengley, etc.), son of a woodcarver and himself an accomplished woodcarver. Since there was not a big demand for woodcarvings at the time, the family was very poor. One day Jules met and fell in love with the daughter of a prosperous Lyons leather merchant named Monsieur Laron, but because of their different stations in life, they could not be seen in public together. Their secret romance ended when Jules decided to admit his love and ask M. Laron for his daughter's hand in marriage.

As Jules expected, M. Laron first refused to permit his daughter to marry beneath her class, but the woodcarver's son was persistent and obviously intelligent — and eventually struck a bargain with the wealthy leather merchant. M. Laron would take Jules into his firm on a one-year trial basis. If, at the end of the year, the lad proved himself a successful businessman, M. Laron would give his blessing to the marriage of Jules and his daughter. If he failed, however, the eager suitor would have to leave France and never see his sweetheart again.

For the first few months, the new leather merchant was a world-beater. As the business prospered, Jules worked his way deeper and deeper into M. Laron's confidence. Indeed, the time soon came when the wealthy merchant gave young Bourglay carte blanche to speculate with M. Laron's money in the booming Parisian leather market. Unfortunately, just about the time Jules sank a large bundle of the firm's francs into what he thought would be a sharply rising market, the bottom dropped out of leather. As leather prices fell, Jules poured more and more Laron money into the market.

Finally, with leather prices having dropped forty percent from their peak, the market completely collapsed, leaving the Laron family business bankrupt and the unfortunate Bourglay minus one fiancée. They say that the shock of losing everything affected Jules' mind. Found wandering the streets of Paris, muttering curses upon himself for bringing down the house of Laron, he was committed to a monastery for mental rest and spiritual rehabilitation. Jules Bourglay remained at the monastery for nearly a year, then disappeared, never to be seen again in France. Somehow, so the story goes, he made his way to America, determined to walk off his guilt in silent penance, the burden of that guilt symbolized by the sixty pounds of leather goods which weighted down his body. And thus was born the old — or maybe not so old — Leatherman.

His death did not stop nor time dim the legend of the Leatherman. In a significant way it was perpetuated, as if by general consensus, by both private and public acclaim. Although he seldom "sat" for a formal photographic portrait, many photos of the leather-clad recluse, most of them taken without his knowledge, can be found today in family albums in scores of Connecticut homes. Considering the fact that the contents of nineteenth-century albums were customarily restricted to pictures of relatives and close friends, the number of collections in which the swarthy tramp is the only exception to that rule speaks volumes about the singular place he held in the hearts of "his people." In addition, his likeness graced numerous public places: on hundreds of souvenir postcards, a few of which can still be found stuck in mirrors or tacked to the walls of taverns or barber shops in towns along his route; in a large photograph prominently hung in the Derby Public Library; and in smaller photos displayed, among other spots, in the Bristol Public Library and, before it closed, in the Honiss Oyster House in Hartford. And for many years the story of the Leatherman was required reading for students at the Danbury State Teachers College (now Western Connecticut State University), since the education of future teachers in the public schools of Connecticut was apparently considered incomplete unless it included a thorough grounding in the legendary life of the state's favorite folk hero.

In a less "official" but equally important way, the legend of the Leatherman was continued, too, in folk tradition. In fact, several new tales began circulating within weeks after news of his death reached the people who knew him. One of the most widespread beliefs held that the eccentric itinerant had somehow, during his long wandering, amassed a small fortune which now lay buried in one of his caves. But a few treasure hunters scouring various caves for the alleged cache cooled the enthusiasm of other prospective hunters when they reported that the Leatherman's shelters were protected by his ghost. The experience reported by one Clematis Sorrel a farmer, while searching the Great Saw Mill Woods cave near Shrub Oak, New York, is typical. Returning to his farm long after midnight, the treasure hunter told his family in a quavering voice that while he had been trying to find his way out of the inky cavern, a cold, clammy breeze suddenly sprang up and snuffed out his torch. Then he saw the old Leatherman. The unmistakable figure carefully lit a pile of leaves and sticks, rose slowly from his squatting position and gestured for the intruder to leave at once. He did, running at full-tilt all the way back to his farm.

Although Sorrel may have been the victim of a prankster — Leatherman look-alikes were common on the roads of Massachusetts and Connecticut following the death of the original — similar reports by hunters seeking the treasure in other caves favored by the Leatherman were frequent enough to fix the tale of the ghostly protector firmly in tradition. Even today, when rural folk see unexplained fires glowing at night in the Taconic Hills of New York State or among the crags of Connecticut's Litchfield Hills, they say the old Leatherman has returned to his familiar haunts, doomed forever to pace off his penance in thirty-four-day cycles.

Israel Putnam

*I*F EVER CONNECTICUT produced an authentic folk hero, it was Israel Putnam, the fearless farmer from Pomfret, who, from his earliest years until the end of his active life, attracted legends as a magnet attracts iron filings. Although Putnam never quite attained the national renown of, say, Davy Crockett or Daniel Boone, in his own time — when the competition for hero status was fierce — his reckless courage, Yankee shrewdness, charismatic leadership and fighting spirit were known far beyond Connecticut's borders through the circulation of folk legends which celebrated his exploits.

The heroic stature Putnam attained was achieved with almost no assistance from contemporary media (i.e. popular biographies, newspaper sketches, almanacs, stage skits and the like), which played an important role in the manufacture of such heroic biographies as those of Crockett and Boone. In a nation which has generated few true folk heroes, Putnam was an exception. And emerging at a time in the nation's history when genuine heroes were needed by the folk to show them what to do or how to survive, Israel Putnam filled the bill admirably.

To some degree, the legendary life of Israel Putnam conformed to the life pattern of the archetypal heroic personality described by such writers as psychoanalyst Otto Rank in *The Myth of the Birth of the Hero* and folklorist Lord Raglan in *The Hero*. These commentators demonstrated that the legendary life of the hero, whether mythological or historical, universally revered or merely locally respected, European or American, tended to conform to a pattern with common elements: an unusual birth, a demonstration of special powers early in life, mature experiences exemplifying the ideals of the society and a death which suggests the possibility of some later "life" devoted to guiding the living. With the possible exception of the last element, Israel Putnam's legendary biography followed the archetype quite nicely.

In the first place, the circumstances surrounding his birth were, according to tradition, at once mysterious and unusual. Supposedly, Israel Putnam was born in Salem, Massachusetts, on January 7, 1718, into a family which had been among the earliest settlers in the Massachusetts Bay Colony. It is said that Israel's father, Joseph Putnam, was such an outspoken critic of the witchcraft persecutions which shook Salem in the final years of the seventeenth century that he earned the lasting disapproval of both relatives and neighbors. As a precaution against the time when he might be accused of being a witch (or a warlock), they say Joseph Putnam kept his musket loaded and a fast horse saddled at all times, ready for possible flight. Although Israel Putnam was probably born in Danvers, Massachusetts, this legendary association with Salem and a father who fearlessly spoke up for truth in the face of dark powers which sought to destroy him was entirely appropriate for the hero-to-be.

As a boy, it was reported, Israel hated the classroom but loved the great out-of-doors, where he excelled at hiking, hunting, and fishing, and became intimately familiar with all of Nature's ways. At an early age he showed his fighting spirit and defended his way of life, according to an often-recounted tale about an experience one day in Boston, where his father had taken him for a visit. Here, Israel was taunted unmercifully by a big-city boy because of his rustic clothes and rough country manners. The tough rural lad took it for a while, they say, but finally turned on his tormenter and gave him a sound thrashing.

Israel Putnam first came to Connecticut in 1739 and settled on a farm in the "Mortlake" district of the eastern Connecticut town of Pomfret. Although he was only twenty-one years old, he already had a wife and growing family, as well as several slaves to help him clear the land and operate the farm. Despite his well-managed spread and evident wealth, however, Putnam was not popular with his haughty Pomfret neighbors. Since the "rough Mortlake farmer" owned no pew in the meeting house, he sat on a rude bench near the entrance of the church, while the "peers of the parish" occupied slightly elevated pews looking down on him. Only after the episode with the wolf did his neighbors' attitudes appear to change.

A few years after he began farming in Connecticut — most agree it was sometime during the winter of 1742-1743 — young Putnam went to his barnyard one morning only to discover that seventy of his sheep and goats had been slaughtered during the previous night. When he found a number of large wolf tracks, with two toes missing on one paw, he knew that his animals had been the victims of an old she-wolf which had ravaged the area with her whelps each autumn for years. The farmers had usually managed to kill her brood, but the mother wolf had always evaded them. However, she had once left two claws in a trap before making her escape, so her tracks were immediately identifiable.

Angered by the slaughter, Putnam called together five of his neighbors who agreed to pursue the wolf until she was dead. The men took turns hunting in pairs, with two tracking ahead while the other four followed behind. All the first day they followed the wolf west until she doubled back toward the scene of the killing. After tracking her all night, the six hunters had reached an area only three miles from Putnam's farm by 10:00 a.m. the next morning. Then, seventeen-year-old John Sharp, who had run ahead of the other trackers, sent word back that he had followed the wolf to her den, where she was presently hiding. Word quickly spread that the old neighborhood nemesis was cornered at last.

All day long, Putnam and his neighbors tried to get the wolf out of the cave. Efforts to smoke her out proved futile. A hound sent into the den quickly came out howling, with such deep lacerations that no one else would risk a good dog in another try. Putnam attempted to order one of his slaves into the den, but the poor man was so paralyzed with fear that he was useless. Finally, Putnam took off his jacket and waistcoat and prepared to take on the wolf himself. After fashioning a torch from birch bark, he ordered a long rope tied around his ankles so he could be pulled back in case of trouble. Then he lighted the torch, entered the cave, and propelling himself forward with his arms and knees, began snaking along the yard-wide passage that ran some twenty-five feet into the side of a hill.

As he reached the end of the narrow tunnel, Putnam heard the ominous snarling of the cornered wolf and, moments later, his torch revealed the animal, fangs bared and eyes glowing in the torchlight. Deciding at this point to return for his gun, Putnam gave the signal to be pulled out of the cave. Mistaking the signal for a trouble call, his friends yanked him out so rapidly that his shirt was stripped from his body and he was painfully cut and bruised. Nevertheless, once he had caught his breath and loaded his musket, Putnam again entered the cave and began inching his way toward the wolf. Finally, he again came eyeball-to-eyeball with the snarling beast. Just as it prepared to attack, Putnam fired. The blast, they say, was deafening, while the cloud of smoke, dust, and dirt which followed, blotted out everything in sight.

This time his friends answered Putnam's signal for removal much more carefully. After allowing the smoke and dust to settle, he once more returned to the cavern to discover the results of his shot. When he got close enough to touch the wolf's nose with his torch without response from the animal, he knew the old scourge of the farmyards was dead. He grabbed the great head by the ears, kicked the rope and together, Putnam and the wolf were slowly dragged from the den, amid cheers from the crowd at the mouth of the cave. As they watched Putnam emerge grasping the dead animal's ears, a few late-arriving observers concluded that the young farmer had actually wrestled the wolf to her last, fatal fall. Stories to that effect circulated in the area for years.

The whole crowd then carted the carcass up and over the icy hill to Kingsbury Tavern, where it was suspended from a spike driven into an overhead beam for all to admire. They say that by midnight most of the farmers in Windham County had arrived to celebrate the end of the legendary beast and to toast the beginning of a legendary hero. In the years that followed the successful wolf hunt, a whole cycle of folk stories made the rounds which transformed the once-obscure Putnam into a kind of farmer version of Paul Bunyan. As the folk told it, he could plant faster, plow straighter furrows and mow wider swaths than anyone could imagine. He could also break and ride horses so wild that no mere mortal could even get near them, and drive a nail into a tree with a single musket shot, from a distance of a hundred yards or more. When the Connecticut legislature commissioned Putnam a militia lieutenant in 1755, they may have thought they were getting a one man army!

Between 1755 and 1765 Israel Putnam participated in campaigns against the French and Indians as a member of Rogers' Rangers, as well as with regular British forces. Promoted to captain in 1756 and to major in 1758, the farmer-soldier continued to burnish his legendary reputation with several extraordinary exploits during this initial phase of what was to become a long military career. They told, for example, about the time Captain Putnam single-handedly saved Fort Edwards from being blown up, when it was endangered by a burning magazine packed with three hundred barrels of gunpowder. With the fire apparently burning out of control, everyone in the military installation fled in fear. Putnam alone stuck to his post, eventually put out the fire and saved the fort, though he suffered severe burns in the effort.

A year later, on August 8, 1758, Putnam narrowly escaped another fire in a miraculous way. Captured by the Caughnawega Indians during a New York State campaign, the incredible Major Putnam was stripped and lashed to a tree. Then brush was arranged around his feet, as the warriors prepared to burn him at the stake. Just after the Putnam-roast began, however, a sudden cloudburst extinguished the flames before they even singed the soles of his feet. Undaunted, the warriors rekindled the fire with dry twigs. Suddenly, an ally of the Indians, a French officer named Molang, burst through the circle of braves, kicked the burning sticks away from the uncomfortable captive and ordered him released from the tree. Proclaiming his undying admiration for the courage of the American, Molang escorted Putnam to a nearby French encampment the next day, and on August 18, under a flag of truce, took him to Fort Ticonderoga. Two months later, under pretense of his being "an old man," Putnam was given his outright release. When details of this episode filtered back to Connecticut, his fellow citizens merely nodded their heads in appreciation. They knew "Old Wolf" was just too tough to burn.

Still another of Putnam's exploits during the French and Indian War illustrated the value of Yankee ingenuity. It seems that one day while campaigning with British General Amherst, the American officer came upon a large force of British troops whose progress had been halted because a French warship of twelve guns was patrolling a large lake they were supposed to cross. With no naval forces at his command, General Amherst admitted his men were blocked. Up spoke Major Putnam: "I'll take her," he vowed. When the British general asked how the American proposed to do the impossible, Putnam replied, "Just give me some wedges, a beetle [hammer] and a few men of my own choice, and those Frenchmen will be ours by dawn tomorrow." Having agreed to the odd request, General Amherst watched dubiously as Putnam and his men, under cover of darkness, rowed silently out under the stern of the troublesome gunboat, drove a few wooden wedges between the rudder and hull, then rowed back ashore. In the morning, all the British had to do was form a welcoming party on the beach as the French ship, sails flapping and out of control, came drifting aground. When the story of the warship captured with beetle and wedges got back to the Kingsbury Tavern in Pomfret, the knee-slapping could be heard for miles.

Of all the legends about "Old Put" that came out of his campaigns against the French and Indians, the one about his victory over an arrogant English officer in a tense war of nerves was probably the favorite back home in Connecticut. The incident reported in the story happened — if it happened at all — because of the mutual hostility, jealousy and suspicion which existed, despite their alliance in arms against a common enemy, between the regular

British officers and their colonial American counterparts. One day, during an early campaign, they say, a British major fancied that he had been insulted by Captain Putnam in some matter or other, and sent the American a crisp note, challenging him to a duel. Surprised but undisturbed, Putnam ignored the letter. Next, the major appeared in person at Putnam's tent, demanding a reply. Putnam responded cheerfully, "I'm but a poor, miserable Yankee who never fired a pistol in my life, and you must realize that if we fight with pistols, you would hold an unfair advantage over me." Instead, the colonial militiamen proposed an alternative. "Here are two powder kegs," he said. "I have bored a hole and stuck a slow match [fuse] into each one. If you would be good enough to seat yourself on that one, I will light the matches and then sit on the other. Whoever dares sit the longest without squirming shall be declared the bravest."

The other soldiers hanging around Putnam's tent were so pleased with the idea of this novel "duel," they forced the Englishman to agree. Putnam lighted the slow matches and both officers took their seats on the powder kegs. While the American puffed a cigar and looked cool, the Britisher tried not to watch, as the fuses grew shorter and shorter. The onlookers drew back as the sputtering fire came within inches of the holes in the gunpowder barrels. Finally, the major could stand it no longer. "Putnam," he cried, "this is willful murder; draw out your match. I yield." A smile lit Putnam's face as he took another long drag on his cigar. "Now, now, my dear fellow," said he, "there's no need to hurry. These kegs have nothing in them but onions." Without a word, the British major slid out of the tent, amid the taunts and catcalls of the delighted crowd of soldiers who had just seen the work of one Yankee who "really knew his onions."

With fifteen honorable combat wounds marking his body and memories of a hundred hair-raising adventures, the legend came home to Pomfret in 1765, hoping to find peace in farming the familiar acres, getting to know his eight children and socializing with old friends. While Putnam lost his first wife and a daughter shortly after his return from the wars, he was soon married again — to a wealthy and socially prominent widow whom he had known for years — and did manage to spend a relatively quiet ten years, farming in the grand manner and devoting himself to the many local offices with which his fellow townspeople honored him. But for a man like Israel Putnam, it seemed, there could be no permanent retirement from the limelight. So when the figurative powder kegs on which the British and Colonials had been sitting for so long finally blew up in April, 1775, folks might have predicted that "Old Wolf" (or "Old Put" as he came to be called in his later years) would be right in the middle of it.

At 8:00 a.m. on Thursday morning, April 20, 1775, a dispatch rider galloped into Pomfret with news of the attack at Lexington and a call to arms against the British. For years they told the story about what happened when Israel Putnam, then a colonel in the colonial militia, got wind of the "Lexington Alarm." When the word came, they say, he was way down in his back forty, plowing the straightest furrows in Windham County. Without a moment's hesitation, Putnam halted his oxen, mounted his horse standing nearby and blowing a kiss to his wife as he galloped by the house, rode off to summon the patriot militia into active service. The oxen, still yoked to the plow, were left standing in the field. More than two hundred years later, there are people in the Brooklyn-Pomfret area who can point out the very spot where that plow stood rusting in its furrow while the absent plowman made history, battling the "Lobsterbacks" around Boston.

A lot of Connecticut people thought that General Israel Putnam's heroic leadership at Chelsea Creek and Bunker (Breed's) Hill in the opening rounds of the Revolution had earned him, and not George Washington, the honor of supreme command. It was Putnam, they knew, who at Chelsea Creek had exposed his body to draw the fire of the British schooner *Diana* and coaxed her in close to shore where she could be raked and destroyed by the hidden Continental cannon. They also heard that it had been the wily old Indian fighter whose, "Don't fire 'til you see the whites of their eyes" had cause his men to shoot the British with such deadly accuracy on Breed's Hill. Although he did for a time exercise supreme command after the Continental Army removed from Boston to New York, he was replaced on April 13, 1776, by General Washington, the newly-named commander-in-chief. For the duration of the Revolutionary War, Putnam's duties were divided between active field commands and inspiring the recruitment of men, arms and provisions in his home state of Connecticut. As anyone who heard the tales of his successes could have predicted, "Old Put" performed in every instance above and beyond the call of duty.

Many were the stories told of General Putnam's incredible daring during the difficult Revolutionary War years. While in command of the Hudson Highlands, for example, he pronounced the death sentence on Nathan Palmer, a Tory spy who also held a British Army commission, after Palmer had been caught and brought to Putnam's headquarters at Peekskill, New York. Soon after learning of Palmer's capture, General Tryon, the ruthless British commander at New York, wrote to Putnam demanding the immediate release of his agent and vowing vengeance on the Americans if the spy were harmed. Putnam's reply to Tryon read:

"Sir: Nathan Palmer, a lieutenant in your service was taken in my camp as a spy: he was tried as a spy; he was condemned as a spy; and you may rest assured, sir, he shall be hanged as a spy.

I have the honor to be, etc. . . . . . .

Israel Putnam

To His Excellency Governor Tryon.
P. S. Afternoon. He is hanged."

Everyone heard, too, about how General Putnam narrowly avoided capture by the British when he was nearly trapped by an enemy raiding party at a house in Greenwich, on February 26, 1779. It seems that Putnam had come from his headquarters at White Plains, New York, to inspect some American positions in the Connecticut town. Early one morning, just as he finished lathering up for his shave, he suddenly caught sight of some Red-coats in his shaving mirror. They were sneaking through the door behind him, ready to pounce on the man who, for them, would have been a VIP (Very Important Prisoner). In an instant, Putnam was out the window, into the saddle of his horse and galloping away down a road leading to the edge of a rock cliff. With the British in close pursuit, Putnam had no choice when he reached the top of the precipice: horse and rider leaped over the edge.

As his pursuers watched in astonishment from the heights, the bold American general plunged toward the valley floor below, his horse slipping and stumbling every step of the way. The British marines took a few half-hearted pistol shots at "Old Put" as he descended, but the charmed Putnam merely laughed at the bullets and waved his sword in defiance. Since not a single Red-coat had the nerve to follow Putnam's plunge down the embankment, the daring American easily made good his escape. (Today, a bronze tablet at the top of the incline known as "Put's Hill" marks the spot on "Horseneck Heights," Greenwich, where Putnam took his legendary plunge.)

General Israel Putnam's last hurrah came at Redding, amid the suffering and dying of troops under his command, during the terrible winter of 1778-1779, in the encampment forever after known as "Putnam's Valley Forge." Here a contingent of Connecticut and New Hampshire volunteers somehow survived the hunger, cold and despair of that bitter bivouac only because their commander, suffering fully as much as his men, served as an inspirational model of courage and attention to duty. When a paralytic stroke struck down the heroic old soldier in December of 1779, forcing his permanent retirement from active duty, his troops wept openly as "Old Put" reviewed them for the last time. Then he went home to Windham County to live out his last ten years in a home that was always so full of veterans, friends, neighbors and notables that Mrs. Putnam suggested only half-facetiously that he "open a tavern so he could charge a little something to pay for the wear and tear on the furniture." The old soldier never faded away, but he died, according to the records, on May 29, 1790.

Having died in Brooklyn — the Putnam farm was located in a section of Pomfret that became part of the new Town of Brooklyn when it was incorporated in 1786 — Israel Putnam was buried in an above-ground tomb in the Brooklyn town cemetery. Above the grave, the family erected an impressive marble slab, with an epitaph composed by Timothy Dwight of Yale. Within a few years, however, the site became so overrun with hero-worshipping visitors anxious to go home with an Israel Putnam relic, that the badly mutilated marble marker was removed for safe keeping to the Capitol Building in Hartford. There it has been on display ever since, giving rise to the belief by many who have viewed it for the past two hundred years that Putnam's body lies beneath it, perhaps in a basement crypt.

As a matter of fact, Putnam's remains can no longer be found at the Brooklyn cemetery where they were first interred. In 1888 they were removed and placed in a sarcophagus built into the foundation of a monument newly erected on a plot of ground near the Brooklyn town green. Atop the monument stands a noble equestrian statue of Connecticut's greatest folk hero. There are some who say that the uncomfortable look on the frozen, bronze face of the mounted figure is the result of Israel Putnam's feeling insecure in body and spirit. For one whose body and spirit have been almost as restless in death as in life, the story has a valid ring. In any case, after two centuries the legends about his extraordinary life still keep alive the spirit of Israel Putnam in his beloved Connecticut.

Perry Boney

CRADLED BY GENTLE, well-rounded mountains with names like Candlewood and Green Pond, Mizzentop and Quaker Hill, there was once a remote, timber-rich valley stretching north of Danbury, known far and wide as the "Big Basin." Then, in 1927, a power company threw a dam across the Rocky River, and the little farms, the once-busy sawmills and the remaining strands of white oak scattered across the valley floor slowly vanished beneath the waters of the long, deep lake that formed behind the dam. As Candlewood Lake gradually flooded Big Basin, it not only drowned the last remains of what had been a lively folk culture, but it also destroyed an area which probably generated, over the years, more legends per square mile than any spot in Connecticut.

It is doubtful, for instance, that anyone lives today who can tell about the time Paul Bunyan himself worked in the Big Basin logging camps, when he stopped off to whale down some Connecticut oak and chestnut to keep in shape for his later efforts in the pine forests of York State and Michigan. Forgotten, too, no doubt, are the exploits of Charlie Munson, keeper of a legendary hilltop oasis known as the Sherman Light House. They used to say that Munson's secret-recipe corn beer and inspired square dance calls stimulated the local folk to perform feats of daring or agility unknown beyond the rim of the Big Basin. Even Cross-eyed Turner's annual pigeon-shoot-clambake-wrestling-match-square-dance parties have, in all probability, been lost to living memory. But curiously enough, considering all the "tall tales" that have swirled out of the hills and ravines of the Big Basin country of New Fairfield-Sherman, the legend which may have had the longest tradition of all was a "small tale," because everything about Perry Boney and the store he kept for years on the western edge of the Basin was considerably smaller than "life-size."

Nobody ever knew where Perry Boney came from. But one day, sometime back around the turn of the century, they say, there he was, a thin little man with a wild shock of hair and pale blue eyes who seemed always to be watching things invisible to others. Children who grew to know and love him were convinced that he could talk to the elves and fairies living by the pools along Greenwood Brook, and many believed that Perry himself was reared beneath a toadstool before emerging on some temporary assignment in the mortal world. In any case, though it seemed the elfin man could look right through a person and see what was on the other side, he never told anyone what, exactly, those china-blue eyes discovered. That was his secret — and certainly a part of his charm.

Perry Boney was the owner, manager and sole employee of a tiny general store that nestled down in the woods "like an acorn cap dropped into the forest," on a hillside near the New Fairfield-Sherman town line. Known throughout Big Basin country as "The Smallest Store in the World," Perry's mini-market was so small that it could hold no more than two children or one adult at a time — in addition to the owner, of course. A little gate with a tiny, tinkling bell to announce the approach of a customer marked the entry path leading to the Smallest Store. Perry had lined each side of the walk with a fence of dwarf brushwood trees to protect the petunia and candytuft beds which he planted every year.

At one side of his store stood a huge Salisbury-iron kettle, filled to the rim with rich soil and always bright in the summer with portulaca blooms on which Boney lavished special attention. They say that the portulaca was first planted there by Perry's sweetheart, but that she died before any blossoms appeared. Every year after her death, just before the seed pods burst, the small storekeeper carefully spread cotton netting over the kettle so the garden his departed lover had planted would continue to grow. Every spring when the seedlings appeared, Perry tended them gently with an odd little tool made of crooked wires that some Yankee peddler had left behind after visiting the store.

Inside, the world's smallest store was attractive, if a bit cramped. A tiny bell, like the one on the front gate, announced the entry of a customer, and when Perry reached beneath the counter to pull out a cash drawer that looked like a pullet egg carton, a set of delicate chimes rippled the air with music. On the shelves behind the low counter, Perry always kept a stack of goods that he knew his regular customers wanted: two kinds of snuff, one in a red box, the other in a yellow, for the Swedish woodchoppers, or a box of his "specials," long, blue shotgun shells that produced such a powerful recoil, local hunters seldom bought more than one box. Since Perry was not keen on hunting, they say he sold these "specials" to minimize his customers' enthusiasm for the sport. Hanging on the back wall and dominating the interior was Perry's prized possession, a sign advertising rye whiskey, featuring a full-color, oil painting of "Custer's Last Fight." The owner and his customers admired the garish piece of commercial art as if it were a Rembrandt, and all agreed that it gave a needed touch of class to the Smallest Store.

Whenever Perry's stock ran low, he took a little covered market basket and walked the three or four miles over to the general store in Sherman to replenish his shelves. When he got back to the Smallest Store, he never took a mark-up on the goods he resold, always charging his customers exactly what he had paid for them in town.

Folks in Sherman never tired of telling about the curious relationship between Perry Boney and the town's mascot, a semi-tame raccoon. Every time Perry came into Sherman for supplies, the coon came scampering out of the field to meet him. Then, as the little storekeeper spoke to the animal with strange, low whistling sounds, the mascot followed him up the steps of the general store and waited outside, washing its paws and admiring its masked face in the ice cream sign, until Perry's shopping was done. When the little man set off for home, the raccoon immediately fell in, exactly ten paces behind him, and followed him up Greenwood Hill and down the other side, all the way to the Smallest Store.

Just as mysteriously as Perry Boney had originally appeared in the Big Basin country, he disappeared. Some say Charlie Munson was the first to notice. Having given up the sale — but not the consumption of his famous corn beer, Charlie had turned to hauling logs for a livelihood. Since his route took him past the Smallest Store a couple of times a day, the teamster became accustomed to seeing Perry puttering around outside his store. He always waved to the little storekeeper as he rumbled by. Then, for three days running, according to Charlie's story, he failed to see Perry, and noticed the door of the mini-market was just swinging open and shut, open and shut, on its leather hinges.

On the fourth day, Charlie decided to investigate. While the corn beer king claimed that he found Perry Boney's lifeless body lying beside the kettle of portulaca, a faded blossom in his hand, most people discounted the story.

They say Charlie just made that up to justify removing "Custer's Last Fight" from the back wall of the store and selling it for some quick cash money to an "insect" (Charlie's name for any York-stater). Charlie admitted that he had, indeed, taken the remarkable painting and "skinned an 'insect' good" for it. But, then, who's going to take the word of a man who never drew a completely sober breath in his life?

No, most of the people in Big Basin who knew Perry Boney accepted the notion that when the little shopkeeper finally found whatever it was he was looking for, he just closed the Smallest Store and walked back into wherever it was he came from, no regrets and no looking back. For years after, folks who hunted and fished in the wilderness areas west of Candlewood Lake could prove Perry Boney had not died. He was still out there somewhere, they knew, because on many a moonlit night they could hear the sweet, distinctive notes of the tiny flute he used to play in the evening outside the entrance to the Smallest Store. Only newcomers and "insects" scoffed, sniffing, "Why, that's only the wind whistling down the draw on Greenwood Mountain." But believer or skeptic, everyone who ever heard the legend of Perry Boney and The Smallest Store in The World had to admit that it held a lingering and haunting fascination.

Chauncey
Judd

*A*STORY WHICH enjoyed great currency during the American Revolution and for years afterward had all the ingredients of a grade-B Hollywood western and featured, as the unlikely hero, a sixteen-year-old boy who had the misfortune of being in the wrong place at the wrong time, after a too-late date with his sweetheart.

It all began in the early morning hours of March 15, 1780, when the bad guys — seven heavily-armed men, all notorious Tories — broke into the Bethany home of one of the good guys, Capt. Ebenezer Dayton, a dedicated patriot militiaman. Led by a renegade American soldier, the villainous gang had nothing more on their minds that night than stealing as much of Dayton's money and property as they could get their hands on. Later, they intended to make their getaway across Long Island Sound to British-held territory on Long Island.

Now, the robbery itself went just about as planned. The housebreakers knew that Capt. Dayton and some friends who had lived with him had brought a lot of money with them to Connecticut, when they recently were forced to flee Long Island because of their American sympathies. They also knew that the patriot officer was away in Boston on business, leaving the house to the protection of his wife, Phebe, their three small children and two young black servants. About midnight, the Tory seven burst through a window into Mrs. Dayton's bedroom, passed on through her chamber and tore open the door of the room where they apparently expected to find Dayton's Yankee friends, asleep. Luckily, the patriots had left the day before.

Meanwhile, Phebe Dayton rushed to a front window and, screaming at the top of her lungs, tried to alarm her close neighbors, the Rev. Hawley, the parish minister, and Dr. Hooker, the town physician. The next day, both of those worthies said they had heard the shouting, but couldn't tell where it was coming from! Anyway, Phebe's screeching did bring the robber gang on the run. They bound her in a chair with torn sheets, gagged her, placed one of her infants in her lap, and while one thug held a gun to her head for two hours, the others ransacked the house from attic to cellar.

Altogether, it was said, the thieves found about £450 in gold and silver belonging to Dayton, while they gleefully smashed other valuable goods — things like china and furniture — which they could not easily carry away with them. According to reliable estimates, the total value of property either carried off or destroyed that night came to £5000. But when they left with the loot about 2:00 a.m., the most successful part of their caper was behind them, because from then on it was a downhill roll for the Tory "gang that couldn't shoot strait."

Their first real problem popped up soon after they left the Daytons' house. As they were making their way toward a section of Middlebury known as Gunn-town, where they were scheduled to hide out in the cellar of a home owned by British sympathizers, they were suddenly startled by a figure hurrying along the woods path towards them. Enter Chauncey Judd.

The son of Isaac Judd, a prosperous Middlebury farmer, Chauncey had taken "Ditha" Webb, his steady girlfriend, to a quilting bee earlier that evening, and by the time he had finally seen her safely home, it was later than he thought. So he decided to take a short-cut home — along the same little-used road on which the band of burglars was fleeing the scene of their crime.

As Chauncey moved aside to let the furtive men pass, he made the mistake of bidding a "good evening" to one of them whom he recognized, David Wooster, a young Tory neighbor. Quickly the thieves surrounded this young man who might identify them, and, after conferring briefly, decided they would have to make him a prisoner and take him along on their flight. So, with his hands tied behind him, blindfolded and gagged, Chauncey Judd was forced to stumble along the path to the gang's first hideout.

The little band and their unfortunate prisoner spent the next two days and nights in a barn near the home of Jobannah Gunn. Here they mostly occupied their time arguing about whether or not to kill Chauncey, interrupting their deliberations occasionally to punch or kick the plucky lad. The gang leader, a man named Graham, a deserter from George Washington's forces now employed by the British as an army recruiter, was all for shooting young Judd on the spot. Others did not want the boy's blood on their hands, and finally persuaded their vicious chief not to add murder to the robbery and kidnapping charges already accrued. Thus, when they finally moved on to their next refuge, Chauncey was still alive, but barely kicking.

Since Graham's gang was not the brightest group ever to come down the pike, another mistake could be expected momentarily. And that's exactly what happened. The Middlebury place in which they planned to hide until the heat died down was the home of David Wooster, the gang member recognized on the night of the Dayton robbery not only by Chauncey Judd, but also, as it turned out, by Phebe Dayton. When the thieves arrived at the Wooster home, they were told that they could hide in the cellar kitchen; but when they asked Mrs. Wooster if they could hang Chauncey down the kitchen's well, she refused to permit it. He would spoil the drinking water, she said. So they all hunkered down on the stone floor of the cellar to await developments.

They didn't have to wait long. Before they could make themselves comfortable, they heard a banging on the Woosters' front door, followed by angry voices and the sound of heavy boots on the floor above their heads. Enter Capt. Dayton and a search party. It seems that Dayton had returned from Boston earlier than expected, found his house in a shambles and his money stolen, and learned from his wife that the robber gang had included David Wooster. No fool, the patriot officer settled on the Wooster house as the first place to look for the Tory terrors.

As the searchers fanned out through the house, the cellar-dwellers scrambled for a place to hide. Finally, they all piled into a dark fruit cellar and silently shut the door behind them. His gag removed, Chauncey tried to shout for help, but one of the men kept a hand over his mouth so tightly that he could hardly breathe. The fruit closet proved to be an effective hiding place. The search party came right up to a little opening in the wall of the hideaway, but darkness prevented Dayton's men from seeing it or the men huddled behind it. Chauncey's heart dropped lower than the bottom of the kitchen well when he heard the search party finally go back up the cellar stairs and out the front door.

Though they hadn't been discovered, their brush with Dayton's posse convinced the bad guys that the sooner they left the area where their identities were known, the better for their health. So, throwing their bags of money over their shoulders and once more binding and gagging young Chauncey, the thieves sneaked out of the Wooster home early in the morning and hastened to their next stop, the tavern operated by David Wooster's father. Here, for the rest of the night, they sat around a dining table in total darkness (they dared not show so much as a single candle), plotting future strategy.

Unwittingly, the group created yet another problem for themselves with their noisy discussion. Although they were not aware of his presence, a slave who worked for the tavern owner had been hiding in the building that night and overheard every word the kidnappers said. Long abused by Mr. Wooster, the black man vowed to blow the whistle on this Tory crew which included the son of his hated master.

So, after absorbing all he could of the gang's plans, exit the eavesdropper. Unseen, he hurried into the sleeping village and quietly spread the word about the hideout of the men who were fast rising to the top of patriot Connecticut's "most wanted" list. Unfortunately for Chauncey Judd, however, once more Graham and his cohorts in crime eluded capture. When a hastily-assembled search party entered Wooster's tavern, they found it empty.

While the robbers had so far managed to evade their hunters, intelligence about their escape plans obtained from the black informer made things easier for their diligent pursuers. The last reel of this classic melodrama — including the mandatory chase scene — was about to unwind. Even though they did most of their travelling at night and in an area where Tory sympathies ran strong, seven men toting clinking bags and leading a gagged and blindfolded teen-aged boy could not forever go undetected by patriot eyes. Especially was this true now that every American sympathizer within a thirty-mile radius of Middlebury was following the story and promising as a patriotic duty to capture the outlaws and rescue poor Chauncey.

Things really began to come unglued for the bad guys as they passed through Derby on their way to Stratford and the sea. They were spotted by some alert, early-rising Yankees, who notified local militia officers Capt. William Clarke and Capt. James Harvey, commanding a search party in the area. Pointing down the Housatonic River toward Stratford, the informants told leaders of the posse, "They went that way" — and the chase was on in earnest.

As they followed a path along the river, the bad guys' luck held until they reached a place in Stratford just above the point where the Housatonic meets the Sound. Then they looked back and suddenly realized that the patriot pursuers, joined now by a very angry Capt. Isaac Judd, were hot on their trail — and gaining. They decided that the jig would soon be up unless they could quickly find a boat in which to cross Long Island Sound. Since they didn't have much choice, they piled aboard the first boat they found big enough for eight men, shoved off — and nearly sank, before they had rowed more than a half-mile. Their getaway whaleboat leaked like a sieve!

Meanwhile, back on the shore, Captains Clarke and Harvey managed to secure two seaworthy whaleboats, hand-picked their strongest men as crews and set out after their quarry, whom they could make out at some distance ahead, alternately rowing and bailing furiously. Chauncey Judd was to say later that if he hadn't been so badly needed as a bailer, the panicky kidnappers probably would have tossed him overboard to lighten ship and divert the pursuers. Anyway, when by an almost superhuman effort the Tories managed to reach the Long Island shore without sinking or being overtaken, Chauncey was still alive — and more hopeful than he had been since becoming a prisoner.

The robber gang landed on Long Island in a cove where they were screened for a time from their pursuers' view. They unloaded their bags of loot, hauled the old whaleboat behind a clump of alders and, as quickly as they could after such an exhausting voyage, made their way to Bailey's Tavern in Brookhaven. The tavern was immediately behind British lines; so when they were all safely inside, they congratulated themselves for finally making what they thought was a successful escape.

Their celebration, however, was premature. Just as Graham and company were hoisting a second round of toasts to the king, their weary arms barely able to lift the mugs from the table, the American forces burst through the front door of the tavern. Facing the loaded muskets of the patriots and drained by their frantic row across the Sound, the outlaws had no fight left.

That evening as the sun sank in the west, the prisoners, manacled and chained, were led down to the shore to await transport back to Connecticut, for trial. And bringing up the rear of the little procession, walking arm-in-arm, were Capt. Isaac Judd and his son Chauncey, tired and scratched, but otherwise not much the worse for wear.

Now, this was a story with a happy ending for everybody, with the possible exception of gang leader Graham. He was tried, convicted of desertion and spying, and hanged. In those days before plea-bargaining, the rest of the group, along with tavern-keeper Wooster, were all convicted of the serious crime of robbery and sentenced to four years in the hell-hole of New-Gate Prison. It is said, however, that all of them managed to escape from New-Gate before their time had been served, and flee to Nova Scotia.

As for Chauncey Judd, the "stolen boy of the Revolution" returned home a hero. Not only was he pointed out on the streets of Middlebury as the young fellow who bravely survived the terrible Tory abduction, but he later received $4000 compensation from some unknown source — possibly money confiscated from the Woosters or other British sympathizers. Oh, yes, he eventually married Ditha Webb, the girl he squired to the quilting bee on the night he was kidnapped. While he never tired of retelling the story of his youthful adventure, in his later years Chauncey claimed that he had been crippled by the gang's mistreatment, and blamed his chronic poor health on the incident. Folks were always inclined to take Chauncey's complaints with a grain of salt, though. After all, they said, he did manage to father eight children and live to a ripe old age. He couldn't have been all *that* handicapped!

Gurdon Saltonstall

*T*HOUGH THE COMPANY of Puritan divines must have contained a fair share of crusty characters, popular tradition suggests that none could hold a candle to Connecticut's Gurdon Saltonstall. As minister, businessman, one of the founders of Yale University and governor of the colony from 1708 to 1725, he was obviously one of early Connecticut's most important movers and shakers. But as sometimes happens with powerful people, Saltonstall was not one to hide his light under a bushel — or even a hogshead. To the contrary, he liked nothing better than to dress up like a French dandy and, shouting orders to the servants, set forth upon the country roads in his magnificent carriage, so common folk could see a real gentleman and be uplifted by the sight.

Originally a New Londoner, Saltonstall became interested early in the eighteenth century in the already thriving iron works by the shores of a lake which the Indians called Lonotononket ("Tear of the Great Spirit"), but which the less romantic Yankees named Furnace Pond, lying between Branford and East Haven. This interest was heightened and Saltonstall's opportunity to play the grand lord was improved when he married the heiress to the Roswell estate. On the ancestral lands of his bride — which included much of the shore of Furnace Pond — Gurdon Saltonstall erected a magnificent, rambling manor house, with lawns sweeping down to the shores of the lake. Now he could live in the manner to which he would like to become accustomed, right next door to the bog iron works with which he wanted to be associated.

During this period, it should be noted, Furnace Pond had become the favorite resort of all the geese within what must have been a hundred mile radius. Over a period of time, the massive gaggle apparently became discontented with merely commanding the waters of the lake with their raucous honking and flapping presence and took to coming ashore to squabble among themselves and forage over the lakeside farmlands. Gurdon Saltonstall's carefully manicured lawns and gardens soon were recognized by the goose population as the best picnic spot in the area, much to the detriment of the landscape and the temper of the landlord. Common folk used to come for miles around to take a gander at the pompous lord of Saltonstall manor as he battled the feathered invaders. Much to the amusement of his neighbors, Saltonstall often left the field of combat in ignominious defeat, his fine clothes in disarray, his voice hoarse and his beefy face scarlet with rage. Not surprisingly, the goose-war became the principal subject of conversation wherever the good folk of East Haven and Branford gathered to gossip.

Down that way they are still talking and chuckling about what might be called Saltonstall's last stand in the war against the geese. After what happened at Chidsey's ferry, they say, the high and mighty Gurdon Saltonstall lost all his lust for goose feathers. The whole incident took place at Stony Creek, where a man named Chidsey operated a grist mill. However, at high tide the river above the mill became so deep that ox-carts and carriages on their way to the mill were unable to cross. At such times Deborah Chidsey, wife of the miller, operated a one-woman ferry service at the fording-place so that customers could reach the mill and the Chidseys could turn a few extra pennies in the bargain.

One fine day when the tide was rising in Stony Creek, who should rumble up to the river bank in his elegant coach but Gurdon Saltonstall, a vision of sartorial splendor. After some haggling, Dame Chidsey agreed to ferry the overbearing squire across the stream so that he could make an important business meeting in New Haven. Now, nobody ever knew for sure exactly how it happened, but through accident, clumsiness or malice, the ferry-woman managed to ground out her raft — right at mid-stream. As she unsuccessfully tried to pole the ferry off its perch, her passenger began to huff and puff and turn beet red. "What are you going to do?" screeched the angry Saltonstall, "What are you going to do?" "Do?" answered the feisty ferry-woman, gathering her skirts. "Wait for the tide or fall or" — stepping over the thwart — "do as I do." So saying, she stepped into the water and began wading ashore, petticoats billowing around her, honking wildly as she splashed and flapped her elbows like the wings of a goose.

Many a gale of laughter rocked the village when word got around that old Gurdon Saltonstall, unwilling to wet his fine boots or to take them off, sat all day and half the night on the stranded ferry, until the next high tide at last released him. As if that story were not enough to bring lasting fame to the name of Saltonstall, years later they gave his name to the lovely lake where once he fought the geese. So it remains on the map today. Maybe the self-important Saltonstall had the last laugh, after all.

Abel Buell

*T*HE JEKYLL-AND-HYDE-LIKE story of Abel Buell, one of the most fertile and imaginative minds ever to come out of Connecticut, has been told and retold so often that it has become a favorite part of the state's legendry. Born in the isolated, rural town of Killingworth in 1742, Buell early in life, so they say, exhibited an extraordinary taste in things artistic and a precocious skill in fine metalworking. At a tender age the boy was apprenticed to Ebenezer Chittenden, a talented goldsmith in whose shop on Killingworth's main street was crafted ware of gold and silver which enjoyed wide favor among affluent families, locally as elsewhere in the colony. It is said that Buell's proven talent for designing and creating works of unusual beauty made him a favorite with his master, and Chittenden advanced him rapidly in the business. At nineteen, the young metalsmith found himself sufficiently secure to ask his sweetheart for her hand in marriage. Rarely could a young couple have begun life together under more favorable circumstances — or so it seemed.

Scarcely a year after their marriage, however, the Buells' world suddenly turned upside down. It all began when neighbors passing the Buell home late at night noted that a light in a second floor window burned, night after night, until the wee small hours of the morning. Since "early to bed and early to rise" was a universal practice in colonial America, the late-burning light became an object of curiosity in the neighborhood. Finally, so the story is told, one observer could stand the mystery no longer. Late one night this nosiest of neighbors set a ladder against the side of Abel Buell's house and climbed up to have a peek through the lighted window. As he surveyed the scene in Buell's upstairs room, he could scarcely stifle a gasp of surprise.

There in the flickering candlelight was the town's most promising young artisan bent over a table holding an engraved plate, ink and bundles of paper currency, busily altering five-pound notes of the colony into those of larger denominations. Making money was never a crime in Connecticut, the prying neighbor knew, but making big ones out of small ones late at night on a homemade press in a private upstairs mint was something else again. The following day, when the authorities knocked on Buell's door and asked to search his home, they were doubly amazed at what they found. They were shocked to learn that the description they had received of counterfeiting by one with Buell's spotless reputation was, sadly, only too accurate. And they were awed by the superlative quality of the workmanship in the altered banknotes. Why, the raised notes from Buell's plate could only be detected by comparing them with stubs on the colony book!

Counterfeiting, or forgery, as it was called in Buell's case, was an extremely serious crime in colonial New England. Penalties imposed on felons convicted of the crime were generally harsh, indeed. However, Abel Buell's youth, demeanor and previous exemplary conduct argued strongly for leniency. And Matthew Griswold, then the King's Attorney who conducted the prosecution, and later governor and renowned statesman, pressed the case as lightly as possible. As a result, Buell's conviction was followed by what, for those days, was a light sentence. He was condemned to be imprisoned, cropped and branded.

Once more, something about the talented young man aroused the sympathies of the authorities, and the cropping and branding imposed by his sentence were carried out in the kindest way possible. Instead of cropping his entire ear, officials cut off only a small piece. This bit of flesh was kept warm on the tip of his tongue until it could be replaced on the ear, where it soon grew back again as good as new. The branding was done high up on Buell's forehead, where the mark might later be covered by hair. Here a hot iron shaped like the letter "F" (for forger) was held against his skin until the convict could say "God save the King." Buell's blessing was said to have come almost simultaneously with the touch of the brand.

While the young man from Killingworth did spend a short time in a Norwich prison, influential friends soon secured him the limits of his home town. Buell improved his condition by inventing a lapidary machine, said to be the first ever made in America. With the new device, the clever craftsman produced a beautiful ring, set with a large central stone surrounded by smaller gems, which he presented to Matthew Griswold, the attorney who had sent him to jail but went easy on the prosecution. They say that this unique gift brought Buell a swift pardon, for soon after Griswold received it, the artisan became a free man.

Shortly after gaining his freedom (about 1770), Buell moved to   New Haven, probably to begin a new career where his past was not known. Here he quickly found employment with Bernard Romans, the earliest American map-maker, then engaged in preparing his map of North America. Before long, Romans dispatched Buell to the west coast of the Florida peninsula, at the time entirely unknown and under strict Spanish rule, to survey and draw maps of the area. Thus began yet another adventure for the Killingworth native.

As Buell later told the story, the Spanish governor at Pensacola received him coldly and seemed very suspicious of his mission to Florida. Quietly, as the map-maker learned later, the governor laid a trap for him. One day a merchant of Buell's recent acquaintance paid him a visit. After expressing admiration for the young man's skill and dexterity, the visitor asked Buell to show him how he might break the seal on a letter from the Spanish governor, open the letter and then reseal it in such a way as to escape detection. The unsuspecting Buell complied with the request, whereupon he was arrested on the spot as a spy and shipped off to a coastal island prison. Somehow the inventive Connecticut native managed to build a boat, and, accompanied by an island boy, succeeded after a voyage of several days in reaching a friendly southern port. From there, according to his own account, he slowly made his way back to New Haven, his sketches of the Florida coast tucked into his pack.

During the Revolutionary War, the map of North America was finally published at New Haven. Not only was it engraved by the recent returnee from Florida (with the help of Amos Doolittle), but since British type was unavailable because of the war, the type used in printing the map was cast in America's first type foundry, an operation employing some twenty boys and established by none other than Abel Buell. It is said that his work on the map led the legislature to restore his civil rights. Then, after the close of the war, Buell turned nearer to the kind of work that had gotten him in trouble years before. But this time it was all legal. Having invented a minting machine capable of turning out 120 copper coins a minute, Buell was hired by the legislature to create the state's official pennies.

Impressed with Buell's skill in making the best of bad situations as well as his inventive genius, the state legislature next sent the former forger to England early in 1800. Supposedly he was on a copper-buying mission for the mint, but in actuality, so the story goes, he was employed to steal information about some textile machinery which had recently made a successful debut in

British mills. Once, while passing through one of the inland mill towns on some errand or another, Buell found local officials in a state of agitation because a new iron bridge over the river had been rendered useless by some fault in its construction. The crafty Connecticut visitor stayed on for a few days in the town, examined the balky bridge, suggested to the builders a few changes which solved their problem and was given a reward of a hundred guineas for his advice. Finally, with an ample supply of copper, abundant information on weaving machines and a smuggled Scotch mill expert, Abel Buell returned to New Haven, where he directed the construction of one of the first cotton mills in Connecticut.

During his long and adventurous life as goldsmith, forger, lapidary, jewelry designer, engraver, surveyor, type manufacturer, mint master, bridge engineer, industrial spy and textile miller, Abel Buell must have seen money enough to make him rich beyond his wildest dreams. It was his misfortune, however, never to hold on to any of it, even the stuff he made himself. When he died in 1825, the inventive genius of so many varied enterprises was a pauper, resident of the old New Haven almshouse. He died as he lived — on the town.

"Mother" Bailey

*D*URING THE WAR of 1812, a number of naval engagements and minor maritime skirmishes in New England coastal waters kept people in the port towns in an almost continuous state of watchful agitation. This was especially true in the Groton-New London area, where there were many still living who remembered those terrible days of September, 1781, when British forces under Benedict Arnold took them by surprise, captured Fort Griswold in a bloody battle and then burned and sacked New London. They knew that the enemy was perfectly capable of doing an encore performance.

So, when in June of 1813, two British men-o'-war suddenly hove into view in the Sound off New London, both consternation and calm resolution ran swiftly through the Thames River towns. Only a few days earlier, Commodore Stephen Decatur and his small fleet of American ships had taken shelter in New London harbor, dodging hot pursuit by a superior British naval force. Now, everyone thought, the *Orpheus* and the *Ramilies*, commanded by Sir Hugh Pigott and Commodore Hardy, respectively, were going to stand into the harbor — to get Decatur. As word spread rapidly of an impending attack, once again volunteers climbed the heights behind Groton to man the guns at Fort Griswold, while many terrified elderly citizens packed their household goods into carts, and with numbers of women and children, fled to inland villages and farms.

Meanwhile, up at Fort Griswold, the men who were feverishly preparing the ancient cannons for action against the British ran into a serious snag. They informed Major Smith, their commanding officer, that there was an acute shortage of gun wadding on hand, and that unless a lot more of the flannel cloth used to load the cannon could be found immediately, the guns would be next to useless. Smith quickly formed a search party and ordered the men to scour Groton for anything they could find in the way of yard-goods to use for wadding. But since the hour was late, all the stores were closed and most of the homes, whether occupied or not, were locked up tight.

Finally, however, a couple of searchers knocked on the door of a house on Thames Street where Anna Warner Bailey lived. Mrs. Bailey actually answered the frantic summons and listened intently as the men quickly explained their mission. No sooner had they reached the urgent plea for cloth — any kind of cloth — to stuff the guns at Griswold, than the feisty Bailey dropped her red flannel petticoat to the ground at their feet, exclaiming, "Give this to the British at the cannon's mouth. There are plenty more where this one came from." The men did not wait, however, for more samples of Mrs. Bailey's patriotic spirit, hastening back to Fort Griswold with the scarlet undergarment held high in triumph.

Soon Mrs. Bailey's "Martial Petticoat" was hoisted on a pikestaff and planted on the ramparts by the troops, their morale lifted by the lady's unique contribution to the war effort and their resolve hardened by her fighting spirit. As it turned out, the soldiers' petticoat fever was spread in vain, because fortunately, no cannon had to be fired this time around. After several days of sailing about menacingly in Long Island Sound, the British ships apparently thought better of entering the harbor and dropped from view below the horizon.

Within a very short time, the story of Mrs. Bailey's lowered petticoat had raised the Groton lady from obscurity to stardom. With her slip on everyone's lips, Anna Bailey not only picked up the affectionate nickname "Mother," but she was also the guest-of-honor at a gala ball given by Commodore Decatur to celebrate the American "victory" in the non-engagement with the British. By the end of the war, hardly a soul in the United States had failed to hear of Mother Bailey's generous gesture.

Over the years no politician, from selectman to President, could pass through Groton without paying his respects to the intrepid matron. And come they did: President James Monroe, General Lafayette, on his tour of the United States, and President Andrew Jackson, to present an iron fence for the west side of her house as a token of appreciation. If there had been TV in those days, Mother Bailey would have been interviewed on all the talk shows, maybe even invited to the White House, such was her lasting fame. Apparently all the adulation agreed with her, because Mother Bailey lived to a ripe old age; she died in 1851 at age ninety-two.

Elmer Bitgood

STORIES ABOUT MEN who possessed extraordinary physical strength have been a staple of oral folk tradition since the days when Hercules worked as a stable hand, Atlas carried the weight of the world on his shoulders and blind Samson toppled tall buildings with a single tug. In Europe, legend cycles attached to strongmen frequently circulated so widely and over such long periods of time that natural features ultimately blended with supernatural elements to create truly national culture heroes, demigods who could dispatch a fire-breathing dragon, rid a nation of snakes or pull an embedded sword from a rock, as the need arose.

Such Old World epic heroes as Beowulf, St. Patrick and King Arthur, however, have few counterparts in native American folklore. Most of the "heroic" strongmen who have stirred the popular imagination of Americans across the land have been inventions of professional writers, ad men or cartoonists. Their exploits have seldom, if ever, passed into folk tradition. Foremost among such "fakelore" musclemen, is, of course, the giant logger, Paul Bunyan. Originally promoted as authentic "tall tales" told by lumbermen in the Minnesota woods, the stories of Bunyan and Babe, his blue-eyed ox, were actually the creations of one W. B. Laughead, an advertising man who worked for the Red River Lumber Company in Minneapolis. Written as advertising copy, the Bunyan tales bore very little resemblance to the oral legends of the men who worked the lumber woods from Maine to Minnesota, and were, apparently, unknown in nineteenth-century logging camps.

Despite the fact that Paul Bunyan bears about the same relation to living folk tradition as a character in a television commercial, there is no denying the lasting hold that strongmen figures like him have retained on the popular imagination. Thus, literary creations like Washington Irving's Bram Bones, cartoon characters like Li'l Abner, Popeye and Superman and sports figures like Babe Ruth — all of whom may be seen to demonstrate the superiority of brawn over brain — continue to muscle their way into America's popular symbolism.

While truly national strongman-heroes are rare in the United States, many regions of the country have spawned anecdotal legends — short, oral tales — about individuals who have performed remarkable feats of strength and who have gained, because of their prowess, a lasting place in the folk legendry of their own group and locale. New England, in particular, has generated a rich collection of anecdotes about such local characters. Their exploits have found their way into numerous town histories and, in some cases, have been kept alive in oral tradition by generations of admiring local storytellers. Characteristically, however, the fame of such strongmen-heroes has seldom spread beyond the confines of their native stomping grounds.

One example of the local strongman-hero about whom an impressive number of anecdotal legends has clustered is "Tall Barney" Beal, the huge lobsterman of Beals Island, Maine. Although "Tall Barney" died in 1899, several professional folklorists, notably Richard M. Dorson, have collected and published ample evidence of the continuing vitality of Barney Beal stories in the oral tradition of the Jonesport-Beals Island area of the Maine coast. Another local character who possessed extraordinary strength was Barney Beal's contemporary and fellow State-of-Mainer, Jonas Lord, a machine shop worker in Wayne, Kennebec County. As late as the 1930s, anecdotes about Lord's feats of strength (he was so strong he would never wind his own watch lest he'd wind the stem right off) were still circulating in oral tradition in the Wayne area. Yet another typical New England strongman whose feats were preserved in the folk legendry of a limited area was Geoffrey Hazard, known as "Stout Jeffrey" among his family and neighbors in South Kingstown, Rhode Island. "Stout Jeffrey" even had a muscular sister who figured in some of his exploits. It is said, for example, that brother and sister would occasionally astound the local folk by alternately lifting — "in playful sport" — a full barrel of cider (31 gallons) by the chimes and holding it up to drink at the bung. Drinking from a full cider barrel lifted to the lips was apparently an achievement much admired by New England villagers. At least one account of such a feat can frequently be found among the region's strongman anecdotes.

While samples of local strongman legends have been collected and recorded from all over Connecticut, the number and variety of such anecdotes told about Elmer ("Li'l Elmer") Bitgood in the Voluntown-Plainfield area of eastern Connecticut put Elmer in a class by himself. One of three brothers, Elmer was born in Voluntown around 1870, grew up on the family's Crooked Hill Road farm and then moved away, sometime around the turn of the century, to follow an itinerant life as a logger, sawmill hand and jack-of-all-trades, from Plainfield into western Rhode Island. Although his brothers, Paul and Doane, are usually dismissed by local storytellers as "not strong at all," Doane also earned some reputation as a strongman and figures in a number of the tales about Elmer. Paul gets very little respect from local legend-swappers; he became a physician. If he is recalled at all by keepers of the Bitgood flame, he is referred to, stiffly, as "the doctor."

Although Elmer Bitgood died in 1938, his deeds have been kept alive in the Voluntown-Plainfield area by several generations of storytellers. As recently as 1971, a folklore student collected almost twenty different anecdotal legends about Elmer's exploits and personal habits from a few living informants in Plainfield. If the occasional published scraps of Bitgood lore were combined with the "Li'l Elmer" stories still told by such old-timers as the ever-changing "gas house gang" at Cliff's Gas Station in Plainfield, the Bitgood legendry might approach in richness, if not in range of dissemination, the "Tall Barney" Beal repertory.

It seems that the Voluntown strongman earned at least a regional reputation for extraordinary strength at quite an early age. They tell the story, for instance, about a stranger who rode up to the Bitgood farm one day, looking for Elmer. When the visitor spied an obviously strong young fellow *pushing* a plow through a field by main force, he called out, "You must be Elmer Bitgood, the strongman." "Oh, no," came the reply. "I'm Doane, his brother." Then, lifting the plow from the furrow and holding it out with one hand like a pointer, he said, "That's Elmer over by the barn."

If that stranger thought Doane was big and strong, he was probably awed when he finally met his brother. Even at an early age, everyone said, Elmer was *very* large and *very* strong. A retired Voluntown farmer, whose father had been Elmer's friend and co-worker around the turn of the century, recalled the strongman's impressive physical appearance for the student folklorist in 1971:

God, he was a big man! His arms reached past his knees. Or down to his knees. When he was walking, his arms were long enough to bend down to his knees. I'm gonna tell you, he was a big man.

The same informant estimated that Elmer in his heyday weighed "350-something pounds," and several others confirmed that estimate. His arms, they agreed, were like "legs of mutton."

Another Plainfield resident, a teacher in his thirties, told the folklore student how he first heard about the giant woodsman:

Oh, I was just in grammar school then, maybe ten, eleven or twelve years old. In those days we used to go to school in a taxi and the taxi driver was a great big fellow. He was six-foot-four or better and weighed 250 pounds or more, maybe 275. He was huge. He was so huge that when he sat behind the taxi wheel, he used to have a big wide leather belt around his waist so that the steering wheel, when it rubbed there, wouldn't wear a hole in his clothes. Now that's a pretty good size boy... He was a huge fellow. And I don't know how the conversation came about, but one day we must have been talking about tug-of-wars or something, and he said, 'Did you know we used to have a tug-of-war championship here in Plainfield?' And we were joking and we said, 'No. I suppose you were the anchorman, you're so big?' And he said, 'No, not me. I was the small man on the team.' We said, 'You, the small man on the team, as big as you are?' And as I said, he was six-foot-four or better and 250 or better. And he said, 'Yeah, old Elmer Bitgood, he was the anchorman.' And he weighed 350 or better and I didn't measure as to any height, but kind of lean towards a figure of six-foot-eight, because he said that he [Elmer] used to tower over Herman [the taxi driver]. Herman was six-four or six-five, or somewhere around there. And he said that he [Elmer] was the anchorman. So that's the first I heard about the Bitgood boys.

Given his enormous size, it is not surprising that anecdotes about Elmer Bitgood's capacity for food and drink are local favorites. The retired Voluntown farmer interviewed in 1971 spoke on several occasions about the Bitgood boys' traditional Sunday dinner. Every Sunday, he said, Mother Bitgood used to cook forty-five pounds of beef for her sons, but by the time Elmer had helped himself to the meat, there was hardly enough for anyone else in the family. The Sunday dinner always ended in a fight between the Bitgood brothers "because only one of them was going to have any meat to eat." "They were supposed to have forty-five pounds of beef cooked," the storyteller marveled, but "I still don't believe that, either." If there's any truth at all to the story about Elmer's original "Big Beef" dinner, there may also be some truth to the traditional story that Mrs. Bitgood had to prepare her boys' meals in a washtub.

Another popular story about the Bitgood eating habits has been collected from several different sources. As the Plainfield teacher recalled it:

Well, in those days, well it's still about sixteen miles from Plainfield to Norwich, but once a month the boys [Elmer and Doane] would hook up the horse and do their monthly shopping — and they'd get a barrel of crackers. Well, in those days I guess they came in bulk, and the cracker barrel was, I guess, about a 55-gallon barrel. I guess that's what they were, and they were full of crackers. And on the way back, they opened the barrel and by the time they got half way back, maybe a little further, the barrel would be empty. So it's a pretty good indication that they ate well.

Then, there's the legend about Elmer's consuming passion for Connecticut fresh milk. A retired farmer, whose father had gone to school with the Bitgoods in Voluntown, reported that his father told him often about how Elmer "was supposed to drink a ten-quart can of milk, up by the schoolhouse, when I was going to school." But he added skeptically, "I didn't see him do it." However, the ten-quarts-of-milk-at-a-gulp anecdote has been collected from others. According to one version, Elmer went one day to a local farmer, said he was a mite thirsty and asked for a drink of milk. The farmer pointed to a full ten-quart milk can and told Elmer to help himself. Much to the dairyman's astonishment, the huge man lifted the can to his lips, drained the contents without taking a breath and asked the farmer if there might be more available.

Such was the Bitgood boys' reputation for eating, they say, that during the years when Elmer and Doane worked in the area, none of the churches around Plainfield dared publicly advertise their fund-raising suppers. The churches had learned from sad experience that a visit from the Bitgoods to one of their "all-you-can- eat-for-fifteen-cents" ham-and-bean suppers spelled financial disaster for the event. Whispered invitations always ended with the warning, "Don't tell the Bitgoods." Nevertheless, word-of-mouth news occasionally reached the Bitgood ears. Once, according to legend, Elmer and Doane showed up at a baked bean supper, and each paid for five meals. After polishing off the huge helpings they had paid for, the lads emptied every platter in sight and topped off their meals by consuming the contents of a six-quart bean pot. The Bitgoods gave poignant meaning to the term "eating up the profits."

They also tell the story about the time Elmer was working with a logging crew over in the woods around Rice City, Rhode Island. Since he was going to be in the area for a spell, he rented a room in town at a boarding house operated by a Mrs. Love. Elmer warned his hostess that he had a hearty appetite and insisted on paying her board for two people. The one thing he asked in return was that there be no house restrictions at the dinner table.

Since Elmer Bitgood lived in the days before the advent of specialty clothing stores catering to oversized men, his outfits had to be specially tailored to fit his mountainous frame. But because he never wore anything but "a blue shirt and a pair of overalls," only the overalls required major modification. According to one informant, Elmer used to buy the biggest bib-overalls he could get, at a country store in Oneco. Then he'd get his mother to split them at the seams and sew in a big, V-shaped gusset in the rear. Last, he'd take a second pair of suspenders and put them on the back, to hold the whole ensemble together. Even so, since the bib in front "would just about reach his belly-button," Elmer took to wearing the overalls backward, for comfort rather than modesty, probably. Elmer also preferred to go barefoot most of the time, never wearing shoes except when the winter snow was deep. He always "worked in the woods barefooted, right in the briars, anywhere," until the snows came. But as soon as early spring arrived, off came his boots — until the snow piled up the next season.

From the days of his youth until he passed middle age, "Li'l Elmer" Bitgood was known the region 'round for the extraordinary weights he could lift or throw and the heavy loads he could pull. One of the favorite anecdotes about the former activity has to do with Elmer's exhibition of rock-lifting and tossing. It seems that after Elmer and Doane had moved to Plainfield and gone to work in the woods, a large number of spectators would gather at the sawmill site every Sunday to watch the strongest men around try to compete with Elmer in a kind of primitive weight-throwing contest. The weights: 375-pound stones, in which stout iron rings had been secured. According to tradition, Elmer always prepared for the stone-toss by hefting a smaller, 300-pound rock in one hand and pumping it up and down to "warm up" for the major event, much as an on-deck hitter in baseball swings a weighted bat before going up to the plate to hit. Finally, Elmer would grab onto the ring, lift the 375-pound boulder off the ground with one hand, slowly swing it back and forth to gain momentum, and then let it fly. Needless to say, Elmer's ten to twelve-foot heaves were never really challenged; so the rock-throws were more exhibition than contest. Except for brother Doane, none of the other men even managed to lift the 300-pound "warm-up" stone off the ground!

Although the legendary stone-tossing seemed to dominate the Sunday gatherings in the woods clearings, there are many traditional anecdotes about other weight-lifting feats performed by Elmer (and sometimes Doane) during those recreational outings. These exploits frequently took place in a barn located near one of the mill sites. One such marvel was reported by an eyewitness, who used to join the crowd of spectators when he was a child of ten or so:

They [Elmer] *had a big bag of sand made out of a big heavy canvas and both ends were sewed right in it so there wasn't no place to get out of it. Must have weighed 175 pounds, or something like that. [Then] they used to lay down and set it up on end, and lay down on the floor, and tip it over on their back and get up with it. That bag of sand was, oh, gosh, I guess it was about that big around. It was all sand. And a big canvas bag so you couldn't get a finger in it nowhere. And they'd lay down on the floor, lay down on the side of it, and tip it over on their back, and roll it up on their shoulder, then get up with that bag. He did. After he rolled it on himself, he'd get up with it! That was in that barn, too, when I went there.*

Still another extraordinary feat of weight-lifting which took place in the barn at the sawmill was recalled by the same eyewitness:

Well, then, they [Elmer] had a — I don't know what you call it — a trapeze, or what it was, in the barn. And all kinds of belts up there and everything, you know, where they used to go. And they had a calf picked up by the teeth, or something [i.e. Elmer would hang from the "trapeze" and lift the calf with his teeth by means of a belt attached to a strap girdling the animal.] *Brought it on the floor and they picked that* [calf] *up! Then he* [the calf] *got bigger, and he had to lift that! They* [Elmer] *had to lift that cow up when she got to be — I don't know how much she weighed.* [i.e., Elmer continued to lift the animal with his teeth until the calf had become a full-grown cow.]

Apparently both Elmer and Doane Bitgood were proud of their reputations as strongmen and delighted in their exhibitions of strength from the time they were boys in Voluntown until they were nearly middle-aged men. This meant, of course, that in order to perform up to expectation at the regular public exhibitions in the woods, both had to keep in shape and stay "in training" between performances. Since they lived, of course, before the days of "fitness centers" or YMCA exercise rooms, that meant constructing and using their own apparatus.

One such rig — probably good for improving leg and shoulder tone — was developed, according to one informant, before the boys moved to Plainfield. It consisted of a platform, raised just high enough off the ground so the Bitgoods could crawl under it on their hands and knees, upon which they loaded 2400 pounds of fieldstone. Then Elmer and Doane would scramble underneath and slowly rise up. "They just lifted the legs off the ground, that's all they did," said one storyteller.

Once the Bitgoods had moved to Plainfield, Elmer regularly worked out on some makeshift barbells which he constructed out of 55-gallon barrels of sand attached to each end of some shafts discarded from the sawmill. Depending upon the amount of sand in the barrels, each "barbarrel" might weigh anywhere from 1000 to 1800 pounds, according to an eyewitness to the Bitgoods' work-out sessions. It is said that Elmer used to warm up with a 1275 pound "barbarrel," "lift it right over his head," before moving to the more challenging 1700-1800 pound apparatus. However, they say it didn't take

Elmer much more exertion to press the heavier weights than it did the lighter ones.

In addition to his lifting huge rocks, sand bags, "barbarrels" and cows, they say Elmer Bitgood also hoisted a host of other impressive weights. In fact, if the hangers-on at Cliff's Gas Station in Plainfield are to be believed, there was scarcely a heavy object for miles around that Elmer didn't have his way with at one time or another. Take the time he picked up the steam boiler out at the sawmill, for instance. In those days, the steam-run sawmills were set up wherever the logging crews worked in the woods. One day they needed to lift the mill's huge boiler, to hitch it to a wagon. After several tries failed to move the tank, Elmer was called in. He stuck a railroad tie right into the fire-box, put his shoulder under it, lifted the whole boiler right off the ground and held it until it was secured to the wagon.

Another time, at Danielson, so the story goes, he lifted a railroad freight car off the tracks and refused to put it back down again until he got his price for the performance (Elmer was not above taking money for his feats). Then, of course, there was the business with the flour barrels. It seems that one day on the return trip from Norwich with a load of supplies, the Bitgoods' wagon got so bogged down in the mud that the horses couldn't pull it up the steepest hills. So, every time they came to a grade, Elmer would lighten the horses' load by pulling two full flour barrels off the wagon, tucking one under each arm and climbing up the hill with them. When Doane and the wagon reached the top of the hill, he'd hoist the barrels back onto the wagon — until they reached the next incline.

Only one of Elmer Bitgood's reputed weight-lifting accomplishments — picking up a Model T Ford — seemed unimpressive to a principal source of Bitgood anecdotes:

That's nothing. I've done that myself. I took a Model T once by the front end and set it on its back and tipped it up like this. They weren't that heavy. That's when I was strong. I used to be able to pick a Model T up by the crank [the starter-crank in front of the car's hood] *when I was a young fellow. Take the crank, pick it up and set it right on its back. Turn car. You know how a turn car was made? Set it on the end. Set it right straight up and down.*

Since Elmer Bitgood's ability to play "turn car" (or even to pick up a Model T and carry it around) was one of the few weight-lifting deeds which apparently could be matched by other reasonably strong young men in the Plainfield area, his Model T exploit never seemed much worth passing along.

What was worth telling others about, however, besides the remarkable weight-lifting stories, were descriptions of Elmer's weight-pulling feats. While there may not be as many of the latter as the former in current oral tradition, the ones that are often make up in quality what they may lack in quantity.

Probably the most frequently-heard anecdote concerns the Bitgood boys' unorthodox plowing activity. One member of Cliff's "gas house gang" recalled it this way:

God, them fellas [Elmer and Doane] *had some kind of harness. They used to plow the garden with a harness. One* [Elmer] *would pull the plow and one* [Doane] *held the plow. Sure, they used to do that.*

Frequently the anecdote about Doane plowing the field hitched up to his brother Elmer in harness is completed with a variant on Doane's plow-pointing episode:

Somebody went by one time and they [Elmer and Doane] *were plowing and they asked them where Beach Point was. And* [Elmer would] *pick up the plow right by the handles and* [point it] *towards Beach Point and* [say]: *'That's where Beach Point is.'*

Another informant, somewhat younger than the one just quoted, tended to play down the plow-pointing accomplishment, but finally admitted to some admiration for the feat:

Those [stories] *were kind of hard to believe, like, you know, picking up the plow* [when someone] *asks, 'How do you get to Norwich?' and he* [Elmer] *picks it up and says, 'That way.' Well, this is probably so because in those days they were small, relatively small, wooden plows with the iron sheer. So, actually, the weight of those things weren't too much. The problem there would be the balancing at the end of the wrist, you know? That's a lot of weight, once you string it up there about six feet.*

One day Elmer's experience with pulling a plow came in handy, when a Model T Ford full of out-of-towners got mired down in mud at the foot of a steep hill, right in front of his house. They say he never hesitated a moment. He just pulled down his plowing harness from its peg on the wall, hitched himself up to the sunken car and pulled it to the top of the hill, astonished passengers and all. He wouldn't take a cent for his troubles, either.

Another story about Elmer's weight-pulling prowess and his pleasure in performing before crowds of admiring friends and neighbors is associated with the horse-pulling events at the local country fairs in eastern Connecticut. Back in the early part of the century, everyone used to go to the agricultural fairs, where the horse-pulling contests were among the most popular attractions. Farmers for miles around would enter their best teams of draft horses in a competition to see whose team could haul the heaviest load a given distance in the shortest time. A sled piled high with rocks served as the traditional "pull." The old-timers around Plainfield swear that it became the "in" thing to do at these events to wait until the sled was so heavy that no team of horses in the contest could even move it. Then "Li'l Elmer" would appear with his harness, they'd hitch him up in front of the draught-team and he'd wow the crowd by pulling the horses *and* the sled full of rocks over the approved distance.

Perhaps the greatest number of anecdotes recalling Elmer Bitgood's weight-pulling activities was generated by his participation in the local rope-pulls or tug-of-wars. As noted already, Elmer was always in demand as anchorman on the Plainfield teams that challenged all comers, in town and out, in what was probably the favorite kind of athletic contest in the rural Connecticut towns of the early 1900s. One informant whose memory goes back to those halcyon days said that two men, sometimes the Bitgood brothers, sometimes Elmer and another strongman, like Herman, the taxi-driver, always challenged five men on the other side — and were never known to lose. It is said that before a five-man team was scheduled to pull against a two-man team anchored by Elmer Bitgood, they practiced by tugging on a rope tied firmly to a large oak tree. This way, they said, they gained a "feel" for what it was like to pull against the huge woodsman. Elmer's opponents always believed that if they could uproot the tree, they might have a chance to win the tug-of-war. Tradition has it that neither the oak nor Elmer ever swayed an inch. As one old-timer put it, "Elmer got that rope around his back, and they never set him up, never. He got that rope around him and got his feet around that rag [a wet rag used to mark the middle of the rope] — and that was it."

For all of his size, strength and pleasure in showing off his prowess as a strongman, Elmer Bitgood had the reputation of being a taciturn, not overly-ambitious person. Legend has it that an embarrassing speech impediment rendered him unusually quiet, while his casual approach to hard work caused his mother no end of annoyance. If his mother sent him out to the woodpile for wood to stoke the fire, so one story goes, Elmer would always return to the house with "one or two [sticks], no more." And, they say, the neighbors found it unwise to hire him to do more than one day's work. Not only was he inclined to take his time with the chores, but he ate so much that they couldn't afford to keep him on the job any longer than that.

Like most very large, very strong men, Elmer was also rather easy-going and slow to anger, according to tradition. He probably realized instinctively that he could easily kill or maim someone in a fight, so he generally kept his temper under control. However, there were limits to the giant's patience, as illustrated by one anecdote still treasured by the gang at Cliff's Gas Station in Plainfield:

Then another one that tickled my fancy was way back in those days, Plainfield was a pretty good-size town, and they used to have these traveling shows [carnivals] come in. And, naturally, the whole town would go see these shows because, you know, actually it was the center of amusement at the time. One time they had this wrestler there, and offered $50 for anybody that would get in the ring with him for three minutes, you know? And, naturally, everybody was afraid to get in there with this big wrestler. He was about six-foot-two, according to the old-timers. And they finally coached [coaxed?] old Elmer to get up there, and he didn't want to go in there. They finally got him up there and the promoter says to Elmer, 'Don't worry, he won't hurt you.' Elmer says, 'Okay, I won't hurt him.' But anyway, something went wrong. I guess the guy tried to throw Elmer down, you know, because he had to pin him in three minutes, or lose $50. And in those days $50 was quite a bit of money. I guess he tries to throw Elmer down and maybe hurt Elmer a little bit, or something. Because what I heard from the old-timers, Elmer just got a little p.o.'d and picked this old guy up and bounced him off the floor and sat on him for the rest of the time, which was about two-and-a-half minutes. Just sat there, 350 pounds or better, sitting on the guy and the guy couldn't move. So the promoter was a little perturbed because he lost $50, and Elmer was $50 richer, I guess.

Folklorists who specialize in the collection and study of personal legends have noted that the longer anecdotes about local strongmen circulate in oral tradition, the greater the chance that supernatural elements will creep into the descriptions of their exploits. And now that some seventy or eighty years have passed since the heyday of Elmer Bitgood, such appears to be the case with his legendry. How else can the following anecdote be explained?

As the story goes, Elmer found himself in his middle years working in a woolen mill. One of his main jobs was hoisting huge bales of wool from the floor of the storage shed into a loft three stories above the floor. This was kind of a tricky business, because it not only required great strength, but a nice sense of balance as well. Then, one day Elmer got a little too close to the edge of the gallery, lost his footing and plunged toward the floor, fifty feet below. On the way down, however, realizing that this would be his last fall if he hit the floor, he saw a way to save himself. As he passed the second story level, he glimpsed out of the corner of his eye an open door on the first floor. Behind the door he could see great mounds of soft wool lying around on the floor, awaiting the loom. Quick as a wink, Elmer made what might be called a "mid-course correction," flew right through that open door and landed safely in the pile of wool. No question, he was some strong man!

An interviewer once asked one of Elmer's relatives who remembered him well if the anecdotes about her kinsman were true. "Why, you know how stories grow," replied Miss Annie Bitgood of Oneco. "You start with a feather in the mornin', and by night it's a feather bed." And as long as the Elmer Bitgood feathers fly, there will probably continue to be feather beds at night. But at least those feathers have been plucked from a real creature. In Connecticut, anyway, who needs Paul Bunyan?

"Old Gard" Wright

*P*HINEAS GARDNER WRIGHT was the kind of harmless eccentric who used to be as much a part of the New England scene as stones in the pastures. "Old Gard," as he was always called by his fellow townspeople, was born in Fitzwilliam, New Hampshire, in 1829, but his family moved to Putnam when he was still a child, and he spent the rest of his life in that northeastern Connecticut town, much to the frequent amusement and occasional amazement of its citizens. When he died in 1918, he was buried beneath a distinctive granite marker which he designed himself, in a grave specially created to his specifications.

The Wright gravestone features not only an impressive bas-relief bust of the deceased, but also an inscription which sums up with precision and economy his philosophy of life — and death: GOING, BUT KNOW NOT WHERE. "Them's true words," Old Gard used to tell anyone who would listen, "but there ain't many folks got honesty and courage to say the same thing." Today, those passing the gravesite, near the front of the Grove Street Cemetery in Putnam, can clearly see Gard's frowning face, the deep, piercing eyes gazing stonily over the real world he found so baffling and into that "other" world he deemed so mysterious.

According to the stories still circulating among the old-timers in Putnam, Gard Wright had a healthy respect for money from a very early age and was known all his life as a subscriber to Poor Richard's admonition to "waste not, want not." Some of his neighbors thought he was probably the stingiest man east of the Connecticut River. Others, less kind, called him a miser. In any event, folks claim that his reputation for being close with a buck got him in trouble early, when he was employed, as a young man, by George Morse, Sr., at the old Bundy brickyard in Harrisville. It seems that some of Bundy's best bricks kept turning up missing. Naturally, suspicion fell on young Phineas. When he couldn't prove his innocence, they say, he was sentenced to attend Sunday School through the summer months — barefoot.

Maybe Old Gard's dedication to the dollar was a reaction to his father's deserting his family to join the California gold rush. Anyway, his father died a pauper in Stockton, California, in 1849, leaving his son to provide for his mother and sister when Gard had scarcely reached his maturity. Or maybe his sense of thrift was only a more highly-developed example of the New England conservative conscience at work. Whatever the case, Old Gard worked hard all his life to make ends meet for himself and his family. To all outward appearances that struggle seemed always about to be lost, but there were a few observers around town who harbored a sneaking suspicion that underneath his rough exterior lay a hoard of pure gold. Given Old Gard's ways, they said, he just might be the richest man in town.

Legend had it that he was "disappointed in love" when he was in his twenties, so he never married. In fact, everyone knew that Gard became a confirmed woman-hater. He reportedly wrote reams of verse on the perfidy of the female sex, and he frequently used to shake his head and say, "Never beat by a man, but by a woman." Ironic this was, too, because during his entire adult life, Old Gard was beholden to women. He lived for years with his widowed mother and a sister, and after they both died, he spent his last years in the modest family house, ministered to by a niece who served as a kind of nurse-house-keeper. It was she who cut his hair, shaved him, trimmed his beard and washed his face and hands. The final irony in all of this became clear when the old misogynist died. Not only did he confirm the rumors about his hidden wealth, but he left his entire estate — estimated at $125,000 — to a woman, his niece-housekeeper. At least that final "beating" by a woman was apparently self-inflicted.

There is little question that his niece's extraordinary inheritance had been amassed, literally, penny by penny. The man who listed his occupation in the Putnam City Directory as "having no business but minding my own" actually spent a lifetime at hard, manual labor. But the various jobs — hod-carrier, railroad hand (he claimed he broke the first earth for the old "Air-Line" railroad), pig farmer, garbage collector, woodsman — seldom earned him more than seventy cents a day. Obviously, it took a positive passion for pinching pennies to build an estate of 125,000 real, 1918, pre-tax dollars. Certain concessions, sometimes regarded as peculiar by the rest of Putnam, had to be made.

His life-style, for instance, reflected nothing so much as crushing poverty. During his years as a pig farmer, he was always seen driving about town in a dilapidated wagon drawn by an ancient, sway-backed horse, seeking garbage to feed his swine. His horse, they say, had to survive on hay retrieved from the roadside where it had dropped from passing hay wagons or on grass plucked by Gard from meadow and swale. His clothing, too, was a veritable declaration of destitution. His unwashed body was covered by tattered and fragrant overalls, and on his head perched an old straw hat, held on by a cord that once belonged to a bathrobe. In summer he always went barefoot, perhaps harking back to his boyhood Sunday School "sentence."

If Old Gard had one habit that might be called out of character, it was drinking. Under his buggy seat he was known to secrete a little brown jug which he occasionally uncorked and tipped to his lips. He always drove up to Webster, Massachusetts, to get the jug refilled, though. He refused to buy liquor in Putnam, after some of "the boys" in his home town pulled sort of a mean trick on him. Old-timers recall that the hangers-on at a local saloon got fed up with Gard's incessant requests to "set 'em up" at the bar, with never a reciprocal offer from the frugal pig-farmer. So one night they set him up so frequently that he passed out cold. In fact, when he sobered up early the next morning, he found himself laid out in a coffin, packed in ice.

As thrifty as Gard Wright was, though, cost was apparently no consideration when it came to planning his final resting spot, a project which was said to have occupied much of the last fifteen years of his life. First came the grave, a much more spacious hole than the ordinary, complete with a floor and brick walls on all sides, fashioned by Windham County's best mason. Old Gard told people that he planned it that way so the earth wouldn't crowd him and he "would have plenty of room to turn over and move about." They say he was also thoughtful enough to leave several demijohns of whiskey and gin on the floor of the grave — dug fifteen years before it became permanently occupied — so that those who finally buried him might freely drown their sorrows.

Most of Gard's pre-burial planning, however, was directed toward his gravestone, especially the bas-relief bust of himself set in an arched alcove cut into the center of the large slab, directly over "them true words" he lived and died by. People still recall the trouble Old Gard had getting that bust just right. First, after the sculptor had completed the likeness, and the marker was ready to be set in place at the gravesite, Gard was said to have had a dream in which he was denied entry into heaven because his beard was parted. Realizing that he had never done much in his life to endear himself to the Keeper of heaven's gate, and not wishing to take any more chances with possible exclusionary rules, Old Gard had the sculptor chisel the offending part out of the beard. They say it cost the notorious skinflint $400 to form the chin-whiskers into an unparted state.

But that wasn't the end of it. Before the marker could be erected, Gard happened to overhear two villagers who had come around to admire the stone, comment about the length of the beard. Why, the beard was much too long, they agreed, and really should have been trimmed to a "decent" length. After they left, Old Gard examined his bust with a newly-critical eye — and decided the visitors were dead right. Again the stone-barber was recalled. This time, they say, it set the old man back over $1000 to have the beard chiseled down and shaped to a seemly size.

At last the startling image was completed to the subject's satisfaction, the fitting slogan was cut into the stone, and the granite marker was set in place by the brick-walled tomb, to await the fatal day. On May 2, 1918, Putnam's favorite miser, atheist and general non-conformist, a man who had spent eighty-nine years going he knew not where, finally went.

Lorenzo Dow

BECAUSE THE REV. Lorenzo Dow belongs as much to the national folklore treasury as to that of his native state of Connecticut, it is impossible to associate the hundreds of stories which clustered about him with Nutmeg tradition, alone. Still, many of the legends about the itinerant Methodist preacher did originate in the area where he began his career. Later, though, these and many new ones circulated in any number of places along the Atlantic seaboard where he appeared in the pulpit.

In his *Connecticut Historical Collections*, John Warner Barber published the following brief account of Dow's life, only two years after the minister's death:

Lorenzo Dow, a celebrated itinerant preacher, was born in this town [Coventry], about two miles south of the Hale house [Nathan Hale Homestead], Oct. 16, 1777. He was distinguished for his eccentricities and labors. He commenced preaching in the Methodist connexion. He travelled through the United States, from New England to the extremities of the Union, at least from 15 to 20 times. Occasionally he went into Canada, and once to the West Indies. He also made three voyages to England and Ireland, where he drew crowds around him. 'It is thought, and not without reason, that during the 38 years of his public life, he must have travelled two hundred thousand miles.' He wrote a number of books, besides his 'Journal', or Life: the titles are usually as eccentric as their author. He died at Georgetown, (D.C.) Feb. 2nd, 1834.

For all his passion for objectivity, even historian Barber could not avoid commenting (twice) on his contemporary's spectacular eccentricity — and for good reason. For if ever there was a man who feverishly rowed his boat through the waters of life with only one oar in the water, it was "Crazy Lorenzo" Dow.

Yet, there was another side to the Rev. Dow, one that comes through in Barber's brief biography, when he talks about the preacher's "labors" and the monumental mileage which Dow ran up in the cause of saving souls. There can be little question that along with his bizarre, legend-inspiring personality, the evangelist was totally committed to his mission, absolutely indefatigable in the pursuit of it and brilliantly ingenious in devising effective methods of bringing it to the fallen world through which he travelled. In truth, the Lorenzo Dow legends probably circulated as widely and as long as they did because people secretly admired the man more than they publicly ridiculed his behavior. If all this suggests that Lorenzo Dow was one of America's most talented and effective travelling salesmen, then so be it.

Dow apparently began his roving ministry while still in his teens, and made his first reputation as a charismatic, hell-fire-and-brimstone orator in areas near his birthplace, like the Hope Valley, in those early years of riding the circuit in eastern Connecticut, where he was one of the first evangelists. It is entirely possible that here he began developing some of the tricks of showmanship for which he became world-famous. Such was the one, for example, reported by the noted humorist Charles F. Browne, better-known as "Artemus Ward:"

On one occasion he [Dow] *took a text from Paul, 'I can do all things.' The preacher paused, took off his spectacles, laid them on the open Bible, and said, 'No, Paul, you are mistaken for once; I'll bet you five dollars you can't, and stake the money.' At the same time putting his hand into his pocket, he took out a five-dollar bill, laid it on the Bible, took up his spectacles again, and read, 'Through Jesus Christ our Lord,' 'Ah, Paul!' exclaimed Dow, snatching up the five-dollar bill, and returning it to his pocket, 'that's a very different matter; the bet's withdrawn.'*

As odd in his appearance as he was in his behavior, Lorenzo was described by almost every eyewitness to his preaching as not only uncouth in his person, but endowed with a harsh, raspy voice and hard, jerky movements and gestures. Someone who saw him preach in Ridgefield when Dow was about thirty years old wrote, "He was thin and weather-beaten, and appeared haggard and ill-favored, partly on account of his reddish, dusty beard, some six inches long...." Despite his unattractive qualities, however, he had a remarkable, intuitive understanding of the tastes, prejudices and weaknesses of common, country people; he possessed an unerring knack for adapting his speaking style to such audiences.

A tall, bony stork of a man, not unlike Washington Irving's Ichabod Crane, he affected oddity in almost every aspect of his life. He liked to appear unexpectedly, surprising his audience into attention, and on a number of occasions, having made an appointment to preach a year in advance, he would suddenly materialize, like an apparition, at the very minute set. He often used scraps of Biblical text, extracting from them (as in the example of Paul, cited above) an unexpected meaning or startling point, by a play upon words. And if an audience seemed unable to follow the logic of an argument on some moral question, he was always able to pull an illustrative anecdote from his full memory-bag. He knew a story could be more effective than argument with unlettered people — and he was a master storyteller.

Examples of his unorthodox actions can still be collected from Connecticut informants whose families have passed the stories along from one generation to the next for over a hundred years. One tells about the time he finished one of his four-hour-long performances, snapped his Bible shut with a bang and jumped out an open window directly into the saddle of his waiting horse, before galloping off down the road to his next engagement. A similar story is told about his departure from home before he left on one of his trips to England and Ireland. On the appointed day, Lorenzo was said to have suddenly stood up from the breakfast table, called to his wife, "I shall return in a year," and then taken his leave — through the kitchen window. Even in private life, "Crazy Lorenzo" had to keep up his image!

There are so many characteristic legends about Lorenzo Dow that it is difficult to decide on where to begin — and when to stop. Two stories, however, have been repeated so often, both orally and in print, that they could be called "classic" Dow-isms. They bear one more recitation here. Both have been collected from numerous locations throughout the preacher's enormous circuit (they are frequently localized) and indeed, became so well-known that they were often told about evangelists other than Dow, in complete innocence of the original source.

The first, generally called "How Lorenzo Dow Raised the Devil," went something like this: Once there was this crazy preacher named Lorenzo Dow who was travelling in the northern part of Vermont, when he got caught in a terrible snowstorm. He managed to make his way to the only light he could see. After repeated knocking at the door of the humble log house, a woman opened it. He asked if he could stay the night. She told Dow her husband was not home and she could not take in a stranger. But he pleaded with her and she reluctantly let him in. He immediately went to bed, without removing his clothing, in a corner of the room separated from the main living quarters only by a rude partition with many cracks in it.

After he had slept for just a short time, the preacher was awakened by the sounds of giggling and whispering from the main room. Peering through a crack in the partition, he saw that his hostess was entertaining a man not her husband! No sooner had he taken this in, when Dow heard a man's drunken voice shouting and cursing outside the front door, and demanding to be let in. Before admitting her husband (for it was he, returned unexpectedly), the wife motioned her lover to hide in the barrel of tow, a coarse flax ready for spinning, beside the fireplace. Once inside, the suspicious husband quickly sensed that his wife had not been alone, and demanded to know who else was in the house. When the quick-witted wife told him about the Rev. Dow, sleeping in the corner, he was not satisfied. After all, he was not so drunk that he would take his wife's word for the identity of the houseguest.

"Well, now," roared the husband, "I hear tell that parson Dow can raise the devil. I think I'd like to see him do it — right here and now." Before the devil could shut up her boisterous husband, he had pulled the famous preacher from his bed, where he had pretended to be sound asleep. "Rev'rend," he bellowed, "I want you to raise the devil. I won't take 'no' for an answer." Seeing that he would have to perform, Lorenzo finally said, "Well, if you insist, I will do it, but when *he* comes, it will be in a flaming fire. You must open the door wide so he will have plenty of room." The husband opened the door. Then, taking a burning coal from the fire with the tongs, Dow dropped it into the tow cask. Instantly the oily contents burst into flame. Howling in pain from the fire which engulfed him, the flaming figure of the man hidden in the barrel leaped out onto the floor and, just as quickly, darted out the open door, trailing ashes and smoke. He ran down the snowy road as if pursued by demons. It is said that the sight of all this not only sobered the drunken husband immediately, but permanently cured his taste for booze. And *that* was certainly one of the Rev. Dow's major miracles!

Another story about the canny preacher has been told almost as often as the "raising-the-devil" yarn. Usually called "Lorenzo Dow Catches a Thief," the legend has been widely collected from oral tradition and has been printed and reprinted in newspapers and books, sometimes with varying details, but always with the same basic narrative line. One version goes this way:

While passing through some dense woods one day, on his way to a scheduled revival meeting, Lorenzo Dow came on two men cutting wood. Mounting a large stump, he announced, "Crazy Dow will preach from this stump six months from today, at two o'clock P. M." Six months later, as a huge crowd awaited him at the appointed spot, Dow encountered a man in great distress on the way to the scene of his sermon. After inquiring what the matter was, the preacher learned that the unhappy man was a poor woodsman whose axe, his only means of making a living, had been stolen. Dow promised the wretched fellow that if he would attend the services scheduled to start shortly, he would locate the axe for him. Before Lorenzo continued on, he leaned down, picked up a stone and put it in his pocket.

In the midst of his powerful sermon, the fiery minister suddenly interrupted his flow of words, reached in his pocket and pulled out the rock. "Brothers and sisters," he rasped, "There is a man in this audience who has had his precious axe stolen. There is also one among you who stole it. I am going to rear back and throw this rock, here, right at the thief's head." So saying, he pretended to throw the stone with all his might. When only one man in the crowd ducked his head down, Dow went over to the fellow and said, "You have the man's axe." And so he had. The thief returned the axe to its owner and never again robbed anyone.

Despite his unattractive physical appearance, his eccentric behavior and his wandering ministry which kept him from home for long periods of time, Crazy Dow was married at least twice and made his permanent (if that's the correct word for it) home, at various times in his life, in Hebron and in Montville. He apparently married his first wife when they were both quite young, but though she died after only a few years of marriage, he seemingly held her in great esteem. For it is said by persons in Hope Valley who should know, that when his first wife died, he had her body wrapped in "cut after cut and fold after fold" of woolen cloth and then buried her without a coffin and standing bolt upright in the grave, so she could the more quickly and surely reach heaven. The epitaph on her gravestone reads: "Peggy Dow. Shared Vissitudes of Lorenzo." The latter is probably a gross understatement.

After Peggy died, they say, he became acquainted with a young woman named Sally, from the Colchester area. One night he took her for a buggy ride and tried to get her to accept his marriage proposal. He had already made arrangements with the Rev. John Whittlesey to marry them as soon as the girl said "yes," no matter what time of day or night his proposal was accepted.

Lorenzo popped the question about 11:00 p.m., as they rode up Bean Hill: "What do you say we get married?" "Oh, Lorenzo, don't talk such foolishness," she replied. But he was persistent. "Come on," he urged, "we've waited long enough." Although Sally finally agreed, she said, "We can't get married tonight. Let's wait 'til tomorrow." But, of course, the shrewd preacher was "hot to trot," which they did — straight to the Rev. Whittlesey's home, known as the "Red Cottage," in Salem.

As the buggy pulled up to the front door of the Red Cottage, Lorenzo called out, "Hey there, parson, wake up. It's Lorenzo Dow and I'm here to get married." Soon the minister and his wife, still dressed in nightclothes, appeared at the upstairs bedroom window. Although Sally once again balked at the thought of getting hitched to the odd man at her side, she finally relented, vowing to "be a thorn in his flesh and a sword in his side." "Get on with it," shouted Lorenzo. So, as he leaned out the window over the couple below, the Rev. Whittlesey performed the simple service while his wife witnessed it. When it was over, the minister tossed down the marriage certificate, Lorenzo grabbed it before it hit the ground and Mr. and Mrs. Lorenzo Dow trotted off happily down the moonlit road to a new life together. It should be added that Sally Dow never kept her pre-marriage vow, for she was Lorenzo's constant companion on his wandering journeys, listened without complaint to his long, rambling sermons and proved to be the one true friend he had for the rest of her life.

Capt. S. L. Gray

L IBERTY HILL IN Lebanon, Connecticut, is the final resting place
of Capt. S. L. Gray, master mariner, whose death, manner of burial
and family circumstances all inspired stories, some of which are
still remembered by local residents today. The inscription on his headstone,
now pocked by age and toppled by vandals, reads:

Capt. S. L. Gray
died on board ship James Murray
near the island of Guam
March 24, 1865
Age 51 years, 4 mo.

Captain Gray was master of the whaling ship *James Murray*, which sailed
from her home port of New London on what turned out to be a tragic voyage,
just after the outbreak of the Civil War. Aboard — in addition to the usual
crew, of course — were Sarah Gray, the captain's wife, and their 16-year-old
daughter, Katie. It was not unusual in those days to find the wife and even
the children of sea captains accompanying a husband and father on whaling
expeditions, most of which lasted from two to four years. Mrs. Gray, however

was not a frequent companion to her husband on such voyages and was much better known for her domestic accomplishments back home in Lebanon than for her maritime ventures. It was said, however, that Katie had been with her father on all his whaling trips.

Before his vessel cleared New London, Capt. Gray had been warned that he should be on constant lookout for Confederate raiders, not only along the southern coast of the United States but also in the whale fisheries of the southern and western Pacific, the *James Murray's* destination on this particular trip. But alert as he undoubtedly was, Capt. Gray was on deck and vulnerable on the day his whaler was engaged by the famous southern raider *Shenandoah*, in waters near the island of Guam.

They say that an early shot from the Confederate ship mortally wounded Capt. Gray. And while the officers and crew of the *Murray* somehow managed to avoid being sunk or captured by the *Shenandoah* and were able to get their wounded skipper into a harbor on Guam in a reasonably short time, Capt. Gray died aboard his beloved ship on March 24, 1865. It also might be mentioned that there were some who claimed that Capt. Gray did not die as the result of wounds received in the naval action, but from diphtheria, one of the most dread diseases of the nineteenth century. Whatever the cause, however, there seemed to be little doubt that the master of the *James Murray* was dead.

Although it was customary to give an ocean burial to sailors who died at sea thousands of miles and many sailing months from home, Sarah Gray would not hear of delivering her husband's remains to Davy Jones' locker. Instead, she ordered the crew to open a barrel of rum from ship's stores, place Capt. Gray's body in the spirits and then seal the cask — permanently. And so it was that when the James *Murray* finally returned to New London, the makeshift coffin holding the "pickled" body of her late master was removed to Lebanon, where it was buried — rum, Capt. Gray and all — in the family plot at Liberty Hill Cemetery.

Katie Gray outlived her father by only four years. When she died, she was buried near Capt. Gray and next to the graves of five brothers and sisters, each of whom had died, under somewhat mysterious circumstances, before or around their second birthdays, while their father and oldest sister were away at sea. While no one knew the cause of the deaths of the five Gray infants, some people believed that Sarah Gray had some sort of hand in their early demise. They said that Katie survived as long as she did only because her father took her to sea with him. Their suspicions were strengthened when Katie passed on after living for four years with her widowed mother. Some who knew Sarah Gray well were of the opinion that her cooking could have been a major contributing factor in snuffing out her children's lives. Whatever the case, Sarah outlived her husband and all her children by more than twenty years. Last of the legend-provoking family, she lies with them forever in Liberty Hill Cemetery.

Jemima Wilkinson

MANY STRANGE TALES have emerged from the southeastern section of Ledyard, Connecticut, where descendants of the Rogerine Quakers settled in the eighteenth century, and where religious zealotry and Sabbathday clamor were for a long period an established, if troubling, way of life. While it is not entirely clear whether she had any direct connection with the small band of "quaking" fanatics organized by John Rogers of New London in 1674, Jemima Wilkinson was surely a product of the region's fervent religious climate, her legend a monument to its very fundamentalism.

Born in 1752 into a large Quaker family, Jemima grew up on her fathers marginal farm in Cumberland, Rhode Island. Although she had little formal education, he is reputed to have been an enthusiastic reader from a very early age. Her favorite childhood books were weighty volumes on Quaker theology and history, and, of course, the Bible. In fact, they say she was so well versed in the Good Book that she was able to spout long passages of scripture almost verbatim, and even her ordinary speech was so laced with biblical phrases that it came out modified King James.

Sometime between her early teens, when her mother died, and her mid-twenties, Jemima made her way to Connecticut — no one knows why or under what circumstances — and came to live in the town of Ledyard. Little is known about this phase of her life, except that she seems to have been regarded by her neighbors as more than a bit eccentric (maybe it was the biblical lingo), a young woman with a mind of her own who was inclined to do her duty as she saw fit, and devil take the hindmost. Jemima Wilkinson was apparently well on the road to anonymity, when at the age of twenty-four, sorely troubled, they say, by the area's bitter religious strife, she took a positive step that would change her life: she took sick and "died."

Following her untimely "demise," Jemima was dutifully laid out for burial and relatives, friends and neighbors gathered around the coffin to pay such last respects as they could muster. The hand-wringing and tears of the mourners were said to have been copious — and, according to some who were present at the services, richly insincere. Then, so the story goes, just before the pine box containing Jemima's body was to be lowered into the ground, a friend lifted the lid so that the funeral guests could gaze one final time upon the face of one whom most were secretly pleased to see pass on to another world. No one could have predicted what would happen as the cover opened.

Instead of a pallid face in sweet repose, what should appear to the wondering eyes of the huddled crowd but the slender figure of an obviously vital Jemima Wilkinson rising from the coffin, a blush upon her cheeks and exultation in her voice. If she was going to be buried today, Jemima vowed, she alone would preach the interment sermon. But, she intoned, she wasn't about to be buried, this day or any other day soon.

As the startled mourners drew back in awe, the now animated lady stood bolt upright in her casket and launched into a colorful explanation of her astonishing return from the dead. "Yes," she said, "I have passed through the gates of a better world, and I have seen The Light. But they asked me to return to you, my brothers and sisters, a second Redeemer, to show you the way to salvation." In impassioned tones she described the heaven she had visited, the mission she was about to undertake, the souls she would save. The day of her resurrection, Jemima assured her stunned audience, would mark the beginning of a moral regeneration for the whole world.

Finally, she begged her listeners not to be afraid, for they had, indeed, witnessed the death of Jemima Wilkinson. "The Jemima Wilkinson ye knew is truly dead and buried," she cried. "My rebirth has endowed me with a new name. Henceforth, brothers and sisters, I shall be known as the 'Publick Universal Friend,' for such will I be to all in this sinful world." Whether Jemima had gone through what today would be called a "near-death experience," undergone a true mystical vision or induced in herself a kind of catatonic trance, few who heard her resurrection speech were unimpressed with its sincerity and persuasiveness.

Well, you can imagine that it didn't take long for word of Jemima Wilkinson's unexpected return from the dead to spread through southeastern Connecticut — and beyond. Farmers and their families rode into Ledyard village by the wagonfull to see for themselves the living, breathing proof of the miracle in their midst. And she gave everyone who came within earshot plenty of the gospel according to Jemima. Tinkers and tradesmen, peddlers and woodsmen, soldiers and drovers began to swell the congregations which gathered to hear her preach. For weeks, she was the leading attraction in southeastern Connecticut, and she might have gone on forever if the whispering campaign hadn't started.

"She always was a little queer," they began to say. "Damned work of the Devil," others muttered. "An obvious trick to make fools of us all" still others claimed. The debunking of Jemima Wilkinson grew more insistent as the weeks passed. Finally, the born-again evangelist decided that the time was ripe for seeking greener pastures. Having convinced a small group of loyal followers to pack up their worldly possessions and set out with her into the sunset, the "Publick Universal Friend" and the "Jemimaites," as they were first called, decamped for westward places yet unknown, their hopes high, their zeal undiminished.

The historic annals report that the Jemimaites settled for a brief period, probably in the early 1780s, in New Milford, where, according to a contemporary account, a number of persons in the northeastern part of the parish were attracted to their fellowship. Although they built a house of worship, they soon sold the church and their private properties and removed with their leader to the wilderness of Tioga County, in northeastern Pennsylvania. Perhaps the reason for this final move out of New England had something to do with the continuing hostility shown by the conservative Puritans toward Jemima and her followers. Tradition reveals that in New England, at least, the charismatic leader's name was synonymous with fraud and delusion.

While the Pennsylvania settlement lasted only a few years, it seems to have been successful in attracting additional believers to the "Jemimakin" (as it was then called) circle. But once again the need to spread Jemima's word struck the activist sect, and once more the little colony pulled up stakes, moving *en masse* to a new vineyard. This time, Jemima decreed that the promised land lay nearly a hundred miles to the northwest, through country which was virtually a trackless wilderness. In order to show their respect for their leader and also to reduce the wear and tear on her person from what promised to be a difficult journey — the Jemimakins constructed for her traveling comfort a magnificent sedan chair complete with well-padded seats, a garish paint job and the initials "P.U.F." emblazoned on each side. Jemima was loaded aboard and, carried by her adoring proselytes, she led her followers through the woods, all the way to the northern shore of Lake Keuka in Yates

County, New York. "We will set down our roots here," declared the Publick Universal Friend, "and we shall call this place 'The City of Jerusalem.'" And so it was that in the year 1787 the wandering Jemimakins found what would prove to be their final harbor.

Given the circumstances surrounding the extraordinary "birth" and dynamic life of Jemima Wilkinson, Publick Universal Friend, it is not surprising that a lively legend tradition followed in the wake of her 43-year preaching career — and flourished long after it ended. While never as widely known or as varied as the anecdotes about Lorenzo Dow, her male counterpart and contemporary, nevertheless, the Jemima legends were told and retold for generations in the regions through which she passed, from her native Rhode Island to her final home in New York State. In the manner of true folk narrative, the settings for the various stories changed according to the individual storyteller. They were always localized, since identifying a place known to the audience added an important note of "factual truth" to the legend-teller's tale.

Probably the anecdote most frequently associated with Jemima Wilkinson was the one about walking on water. Told in every region where her ministry was remembered, the story has been associated with many locations where it was supposed to have taken place, including several rivers and ponds in Rhode Island, the Housatonic River near New Milford, the Schuylkill River above Philadelphia and Keuka Lake in New York State. And while the legend typically varied in other details as it spread in oral tradition, the most common version was remarkably stable. It went something like this:

Challenged by many skeptics and some unabashed non-believers to prove that she had the divine power she claimed for herself, Jemima Wilkinson agreed to duplicate in public Christ's feat of walking on water. A time and place for the performance were agreed upon and advertised as widely as possible, for Jemima knew that the effectiveness of miracle-working was directly proportional to the number of people worked. Once a satisfactory crowd had gathered at the appointed hour, near the designated body of water, Jemima materialized, dressed in her customary long,flowing robes, and launched into a vigorous sermon on faith, frequently punctuated by the question, "Do ye have faith?" But at the end of her long exhortation, the question and response having been built to a near-frenzy, Jemima would suddenly stop. With her shining eyes fixed directly on the audience, she then posed the critical question: "Do ye have faith? Do ye believe that I can do this thing?" "We do. We believe," screamed the crowd. "Ah, it is good," Jemima declared. "If ye have faith, ye need no other evidence." With that, she gathered her robes about her, turned with a flourish — and departed.

Another legend frequently (but not exclusively) associated with the Publick Universal Friend involved her alleged ability to raise the dead. Like the walking-on-water story, this one recounted an event staged to impress critics, suggesting that in patriarchal, Puritan New England, anyway, miracle workers, especially if they happened to be women, were constantly called upon to give proof of their divine powers. Further confirmation of this may be gained from the fact that the same raising-the-dead story was sometimes connected with Mother Ann Lee, the Shaker prophetess. Nevertheless, since the legend does bear some relation to the story of Jemima Wilkinson's own "rebirth" in Ledyard, it was perhaps natural for the folk to make her the usual central figure in the anecdote. A common version went this way:

In order to demonstrate her ability to raise the dead, Jemima Wilkinson persuaded one of her faithful followers to pretend to be dead. The "deceased" was wrapped in a winding shroud, placed in a coffin and taken to a cemetery, ready for burial. Again, since the demonstration had been widely advertised, a good crowd had assembled to bear witness to the miracle. Just as Jemima was about to reach the dramatic climax of her performance, an army officer stepped out of the crowd, interrupted her sermon and asked if he could put his sword through the corpse prior to resurrection — just to make sure the subject was dead. As he pulled the sword from its scabbard, the "corpse" jumped out of the coffin and beat a hasty retreat, his winding sheet flowing out behind him like a flag of surrender.

One final legend told about Jemima is probably typical of a whole cycle of off-color yarns about her which once circulated in folk tradition. Since most of them were a bit too racy for print, they have been lost in time. But surviving stories like the following lend further credence to the belief that the New England suspicion of the Publick Universal Friend was related as much to her sex as to her alleged miraculous powers:

One day Jemima Wilkinson was called upon to pay a visit to Judge William Potter, a prominent citizen of Kingston, Rhode Island, who was feeling poorly and in need of spiritual comfort. The Judge's wife, who had been away when Jemima arrived at the house, came home unexpectedly and found the Universal Friend in her husband's bedchamber, in rather intimate proximity to the ailing jurist. When Jemima attempted to explain the nature of her ministry, Mrs. Potter cut her off abruptly. "Minister to your lambs all you want," the angry woman was supposed to have said, "but in the future, please leave my old ram alone!"

In the final thirty-two years of her life, Jemima Wilkinson apparently ministered very successfully to her "lambs" in the City of Jerusalem, New

York. As a matter of fact, her reputation in Yates County as a "sincere, kindly, benevolent woman" (so different from her New England image) was such that the town she founded beside Lake Keuka grew and flourished. In later years, long after Jemima's passing, when the first post office was pending for the City of Jerusalem, the federal government asked the residents if they would be willing to rename their settlement: something shorter, perhaps, with a less biblical ring to it, but appropriate, of course. Since everyone in town had originally followed Jemima Wilkinson from Pennsylvania or Yankee Connecticut, they agreed to call their town "Penn Yan." Thus Penn Yan, New York, was born and officially registered in Washington, D.C. It is said that the redoubtable Jemima Wilkinson retained her hold on the hearts and spirits of her followers until the day of her second — and permanent — death in 1819. And while no vestige of the religious order of Jemimakins remains today in the lovely wine country around Lake Keuka, the town of Penn Yan remains to this day a permanent monument to a remarkable and resolute woman, who rose from the dead in Ledyard, Connecticut, captured the imagination of thousands in her time and conquered both a natural and spiritual wilderness.

"The Old Darn Man"

*I*F WESTERN CONNECTICUT and New York State had their Old Leatherman, eastern Connecticut and bordering sections of Massachusetts and Rhode Island in the nineteenth century had their share of wandering eccentrics, as well. None, of course, could match the man of leather for fame or fable, but the characters known as the "Old Dog Man," "Old Blue Bag," "Jerry Blue Bag," "Old Eggelston" and the "Old Darn Man" intrigued generations of Connecticut families who watched them make their rounds and preserved their legends in letters, diaries and oral tradition.

The Old Dog Man had a relatively short career tramping through such towns as Hampton and Pomfret in Windham County on no particular schedule, picking up stray dogs along his route and sometimes selling them, his only visible means of earning a living. Sometimes when a family pet disappeared, suspicions were aroused that the Old Dog Man had been around, but he was never found to be dealing in anything but genuine strays. Strangely enough, there seem to have been two different itinerant vagrants with the same identifying quirk: carrying their possessions in a blue cloth bag slung over their shoulders. One, familiar to Windham County residents, was a regular visitor known simply as Old Blue Bag. A harmless sort, he always completed some household chore, such as filling a woodbox, before waiting around for a food handout. He had a reputation for being extraordinarily clean for one of his calling and, they say, frequently washed his clothes in local brooks and then laid them over bushes to dry. In wet weather he even went barefoot, either to save his boots or to keep them clean.

Another blue-bagger, who seemed to have restricted his movements to the Norwich area, had a less savory reputation than his colleague to the north and east. Thought by the people of Norwich to be a rogue Irishman, Jerry Blue Bag, as he was called, was not above removing from unwary households objects not nailed down. Some say Jerry was especially fond of wayward children, and not a few Norwich mothers were known to have suggested to an unruly child that further disobedience might lead to being bagged by old Jerry. Accordingly, youngsters made themselves scarce when he showed up in the neighborhood.

Old Eggleston (which might or might not have been his real name) was another piece of work altogether. A seasonal visitor — spring and fall only — to homes in Windham County, he was more honest than Jerry Blue Bag of Norwich but much dirtier than Old Blue Bag of Hampton and Pomfret. He was thought to have come from a good family, but an early bout of scarlet fever had affected his mind. His favorite question was, "I am not to blame for being a fool, am I?" One winter Old Eggleston froze his feet, came to a Hampton home in pitiful condition and was nursed through the winter by the family. Later, he returned to his benefactors' house and paid them by saying, "You are the only Christians I have ever met."

But for all of the local fame of these odd beggars, none came anywhere close to the Old Darn Man for longevity, length of circuit or legend-inspiring capacity. Certainly he was the only eastern Connecticut itinerant whose story approaches the Leatherman's in complexity and curiosity. The Darn Man apparently began wandering about Windham and New London Counties in Connecticut and into adjacent portions of Massachusetts and Rhode Island sometime in the 1820s, perhaps when he was in his early twenties. From that time on, he moved from place to place on an uneven route and roughly a six month schedule for more than half a century.

Like the Leatherman, the real name of the Old Darn Man is unknown, not, in his case, because he never revealed it, but because he apparently gave different people different names at different times. For example, Louise Watrous of Clinton, writing in the 1930s about the Old Darn Man from information provided by a 94-year-old Centerbrook resident who saw the vagrant in the 1850s, gave his name as Frank Howland and said he was a direct descendant of John Howland, a *Mayflower* Pilgrim. On the other hand, a vivid portrait written in October 1860, by a young Hampton man, William Henry Bennett — as the Old Darn Man sat before him in the parlor of the

Bennett home — states with great certainty that the visitor's name was George Thompson, and that he was a former merchant and native of Taunton, Massachusetts. There is also some tradition for George Johnson and other quite diverse names. However, whether he was a Howland, Thompson, Johnson or something else, one consistent thread runs through all the traditional stories about his true identity: he was a man of good breeding, advanced intelligence and great talent (especially as a violinist). Whether these qualities were derived from personal information divulged by the Old Darn Man or originated from repeated observations of his appearance and behavior — or a combination of these sources — is impossible to say.

Also like the Leatherman, the Old Darn Man was distinguished by his costume. The suit consisted of a long, double-breasted jacket with the kind of split "tails" familiar in formal wear even today, and close-fitting trousers with straps at the bottom. A long, brocaded vest hung down below the coat in front, and from the old-fashioned watch pocket dangled a gold fob, which made him look like a fine gentleman. On his head he wore a tall, bell-crowned hat, which may originally have been white, but which time and the dust of many country roads eventually turned to a dingy gray. The suit was said to have been made of the finest navy-blue broadcloth and it must have been so, because in all of his sixty years of wandering, he always wore the same outfit.

The Old Darn Man's passion for keeping his clothes in good repair gave rise to such names as Darn Coat, The Darned Man or (most frequently) The Old Darn Man. The first thing he would ask the resident of a house he had just entered for food or shelter was, "May I have a needle and thread to mend my clothes?" When these were produced, he always folded his tall, gaunt body into a chair and set about stitching up tears or worn spots in the suit fabric. He always refused offers from sympathetic housewives to do the mending, saying, "Thank you, Madam, but I must refuse. These are my wedding clothes and they are sacred. My bride will be here soon..." In time, of course, the strange, formal clothes, once so unblemished and perfect, came more and more to resemble shabby, crazy-quilts of stitchery. But never did a hole or tear long remain or a spot go unremoved from the Old Darn Man's garments.

Over the long years, the wanderer's dignified, once-athletic body became stooped, his jet black hair grew white and his hands trembled as he darned his clothes, but always his steel-blue eyes remained piercing, his answers to questions ambiguous and his habits consistent. He travelled only in the warm months of spring, summer and fall, returning, they say, to his "mansion" during the colder months. He almost always took only one meal in a house — either breakfast or supper but seldom both — and almost never spent more than a single night at any one home, not wishing to take too much from "my dear friends." On those few occasions when he was persuaded to stay a few days, he paid the family by reading to them aloud from books or newspapers, playing his violin or doing light housework, sometimes while singing to himself a song with the repeated line, "she sat under the green willow tree." To all appearances he was a gentle, well-read, dignified gentleman with a sad, lost air and some sort of endless, unfulfilled mission in life.

Based upon little more evidence than they had in the Leatherman's case, relying mostly on a few hints dropped through the years and conclusions reached from observing his habits, the folk who knew him and loved him fashioned a story explaining the Old Darn Man's way of life.

As a young man, they all said, The Darn Man had been a good athlete with a fine physique, blessed with a brilliant, well-ordered mind, and destined to go to Yale to prepare for a law career. But because he studied too long and hard, he was struck with a near-fatal illness, which he survived only because of his strong constitution. After some months of recuperation, he took a job near the salt water — as a teacher in a school near New London — to help speed his recovery. It was while teaching there that he met, fell deeply in love with and became engaged to the lovely young daughter of a New London sea captain.

Then the young man's fiancee made a journey that began in joy and ended in tragedy. Having determined to buy her wedding trousseau in New York City, she made the first part of the trip successfully, but while returning by ship to New London, drowned with many others when a sudden storm came up and capsized the vessel. Although the prospective bridegroom had managed to survive his recent fever, his mind did not wholly survive the shock of the untimely death of his wife-to-be. He was unable to attend her funeral services and sank into a long period of withdrawn depression. When he finally came out of it he could no longer remember anything except that his betrothed had left for New York City to purchase clothes for their wedding. Since she had failed to return, so the story concludes, the anguished young man put on his wedding suit and set forth to find her. Thus driven by unrequited love, the youth searched for almost sixty years for the lost bride, transformed by the process from a young man of infinite promise into the legendary Old Darn Man.

The story of the Darn Man's death is also the stuff of legend. They say that one night when he was staying with a family by whom he had been given meal and shelter for many, many years, the ancient vagrant was unusually silent and distracted. Finally, he went outside to sit in the moonlight under a tall elm tree he loved, where his troubled spirit had found rest in the past. As he glanced up through the branches of the tree at the glorious June moon, he was heard to whisper over and over, "My bride will come tonight. Surely she will not disappoint me. Come, my beloved little bride."

Suddenly, through the stillness came the sound of carriage wheels at the top of the hill and voices, including the rippling laughter of a young girl. Rising from his seat beneath the elm, the Old Darn Man moved rapidly to the picket fence bordering the road that passed the house. As the horses and carriage rushed down the hill toward the Old Darn Man, he suddenly opened the gate and darted into the road. "Here I am, my little bride," he cried in agony. "Long have I been waiting, do not pass me by..." As he held out his arms toward the oncoming carriage, the horses became frightened at the sudden apparition and lurched suddenly toward him. Before the driver could control them, the animals had knocked the old man down and the wheels of the carriage passed over his body. Though loving hands carried him inside, he died that night.

When the time came to bury the Darn Man, the womenfolk refused the conventional shroud brought by the undertaker. "No," they said, shaking their heads, "he would not feel comfortable in that. We will clean, press and mend his own clothes." And so, somewhere in Plainfield or Sterling, they say, the Old Darn Man was laid to rest in the same wedding suit he had worn for sixty years as he searched in vain for his lost bride.

Rufus
Malbone

*T*HE STORY of Rufus Malbone really begins before the American Revolution in Newport, Rhode Island. There Godfrey Malbone, a wealthy Tory aristocrat and merchant, built what was then regarded as the most beautiful mansion in colonial New England. However, he and his family were never to live in their new home. On the very night of the great mansion's housewarming party, the house became very warm, indeed; it burned to the foundation. Depressed by this disaster and what were said to have been severe financial problems brought on by the loss at sea of several of his trading ships, Godfrey Malbone decided to leave Newport and make a new life for himself in the Connecticut wilderness. He moved to Brooklyn, Connecticut, in 1766, bringing with him all that was left of his worldly possessions, including a number of Negro slaves.

Since slaves frequently took their owner's family name, Rufus, the son of one of the blacks Godfrey Malbone had brought from Newport, became known as Rufus Malbone. Born into slavery in February, 1824, Rufus became a familiar sight on the rural roads of northeastern Connecticut after he moved to the Putnam area a few years after the end of the Civil War. On a pleasant hillside on Rt. 44, just on the Putnam side of the Pomfret-Putnam town line, the independent black man built himself a crude dwelling, and for a period of sixteen years he made a precarious living by selling and bartering farm produce. Incidentally, his house, located on a property today known as the Davis Farm, no longer stands, having been destroyed by fire some time between 1884 and 1892.

Even to this day there are people in the Putnam area who can recall stories, passed down from generation to generation, about Rufus Malbone's incredible physical strength and his deep attachment for his horse, "Dolly." It is said, for example, that he could lift a whole barrel of cider off the ground, pull out the bung, take a long drink from the bung-hole and replace the stopper before gently setting the barrel on the ground again.

Another legend concerns Rufus' confrontation with a crowd of village loafers in Putnam. It seems that some men were standing around on a downtown street corner one day when the black man chanced to come by with a wagonload of vegetables drawn by "Dolly," his beloved horse. One idler called out in a loud voice, "Looks like a dark cloud coming up." Another shouted, "Seems to me it might be a black crow." Well, Rufus reigned in "Dolly," rather deliberately hitched her to a nearby post and approached the small knot of men still chuckling over their comments. Rufus asked quietly which one in the crowd had made the loud remarks so obviously directed at him. When none of the men would confess, the muscular merchant waded into the group, beat all of them painfully and left them lying in the gutter.

In the end, however, Rufus Malbone's strength not only failed to save him, but his reliance on it may have contributed to his death. In early October of 1884, Rufus and "Dolly" were driving to the Bartholomew farm with a full load of cider apples, when a wheel came off the old wagon. The 60-year-old man lay down beneath the cart, so they say, jacked up the heavy vehicle with his legs and feet and, while thus employed, somehow managed to reattach the loose wheel to the axle. Unfortunately, the exertion was too much for the aging Negro: he burst a blood vessel in his forehead and fell unconscious. Two men who had been following Rufus with their own wagonload of goods came upon the stricken man, carried him to his little house and put him to bed. Although he regained consciousness from time to time, he never recovered from the accident and died ten days afterward, on October 12, 1884.

They say that on his deathbed Rufus thought only of "Dolly" and what would become of her after he was gone. She was really a very fine horse, fast enough, some believed, to be a race horse, although Rufus would never race her and thought her far too good for a racetrack. She was quite intelligent and since he had raised her from a colt, no one else had ever driven her. Finally, as Rufus realized that death was near, he told his neighbors that he wanted "Dolly" buried in the same grave with him so that she would be as close to him in death as she had been in life. He said, "See that nobody ever holds the reins over "Dolly."

After Rufus' death, "Dolly" did become a neighborhood problem. Nobody owned her, nobody could drive or sell her and everybody fed her. Finally, after several meetings to discuss the horse's disposition, Rufus' nearest neighbor volunteered to dispatch "Dolly" and carry out her late owner's instructions for burial. He refused to use chloroform, the usual agent for humane killing of animals, but did agree to shoot her. On the appointed day, Rufus Malbone's

grave was reopened and enlarged, the neighbor called "Dolly" to the edge of the pit and she came "running across the field like a colt," they say. A single bullet did the trick. So, just thirteen days after her master's burial "Dolly" toppled into the grave beside his plain board coffin. It is reported that a much larger crowd assembled for "Dolly's" funeral than had attended the final rites of Rufus Malbone.

Over the common grave they soon erected a tall, slim, marble shaft, inscribed according to Rufus' instructions and completely paid for by him, prior to his death. On one side is carved "Rufus G. Malbone, Died Oct. 12, 1884, Aged 60 years, 7 months and 20 days." On the opposite face are the words, "Dolly, His faithful Horse, Died Oct. 25, 1884."

Even though the burial site is today in the middle of the side lawn on the Davis farm, it is excluded from the deed to their property. The small plot of land sacred to a former slave and his horse is also completely surrounded by a high fieldstone wall through which there is no opening. It is just as Rufus Malbone wanted it: he said that he "wanted to be alone with 'Dolly,' forever."

Uncas

*T*HE EARLIEST YEARS of the English settlements in Connecticut were enlivened by almost continuous conflict between two Indian tribes, the Narragansetts and the Mohegans, over territory claimed by each group. The area first called by the English "Nine-miles-square" and now known as Norwich formed a kind of boundary to lands controlled by each tribe, the Mohegans to the north and west and the Narragansetts to the south and east. Thus, it was a principal battleground for the skirmishing nations.

Given the fact that both tribes were led by aggressive chiefs whose courage, skill and boldness would have made them fit subjects for hero stories even under ordinary circumstances, it is not surprising that the years of conflict gave rise to many legends about Uncas, the Mohegan sachem and Miantonomo, chief of the Narragansetts. It is also interesting to note that the white settlers perpetuated these legends long after the Indians had disappeared from the area, which just goes to show that bigger-than-life heroes, scenes of one-on-one combat, extraordinary physical feats and exciting chases apparently know no bounds of time or race.

Some of the most interesting traditional tales describe a series of events leading up to the defeat of Miantonomo's forces by the tribe of Uncas, followed by the capture and execution of the Narragansett chief. Although some of the circumstances described in the legends were eventually transmitted to Governor John Winthrop and recorded in his journal, most of what is known about the conclusion of the warfare between Uncas and Miantonomo has come down through oral transmission, sometimes recorded by English chroniclers and sometimes unrecorded. Separate legends about individual events form an almost continuous narrative, something like the following account, and have, with the passage of time, been accepted as the closest thing to reliable history as can ever be discovered.

* * * * *

Although Miantonomo and Uncas had struck a 1638 agreement with the English in Hartford not to carry on hostilities against each other before first checking with them, the Indians' mutual dislike and territorial jealousies soon made them forget their pact with the white man. Apparently sparked by some incident, maybe Uncas' slaying of Sequassen, a Connecticut sachem and relative of Miantonomo, the flames of open war were crackling once more in the summer of 1643.

At that time Miantonomo secretly gathered about him a party of some five or six hundred Narragansett warriors and set off for the land of the Mohegan, hoping to catch Uncas by surprise and finish him off for good. Unfortunately for the Narragansett sachem, Uncas was on the alert. With his scouts in place all along the most obvious route that any Narragansett raiding party would take to reach his camp, Uncas was aware of Miantonomo's little "surprise party" by the time the aggressors crossed the Shetucket River at a fording place near the junction of the Quinebaug. As the Narragansetts streamed through the woods and over the long hill that overlooks the valley of the Yantic River, Uncas quickly gathered his troops about him and then boldly advanced to meet the foe.

When Uncas' men reached the area called the Great Plain, they learned that the Narragansetts were all ready to pounce on them from rising ground to the south. Sizing up a situation in which he knew his forces were badly outnumbered, Uncas quickly devised a strategy, halted his braves on high ground at the northern margin of the plain and explained his plan to the Mohegan warriors. When the strategy session broke up, Uncas sent a messenger to Miantonomo requesting a powwow with the Narragansett chief. When Miantonomo agreed, the two fierce sachems strode toward one another across the Great Plain, between their watchful armies. When they finally met face-to-face, Uncas proposed that their differences be settled in single combat between themselves, thus sparing the lives of many warriors on both sides. Said Uncas, "Let us two fight it out: if you kill me, my men shall be yours; but if I kill you, your men shall be mine."

Miantonomo would have none of it, however. Fearing some kind of trick by the Mohegan sachem, he replied, "My men came to fight, and they shall fight." As soon as he heard Miantonomo's answer, Uncas threw himself flat on the ground before the startled Narragansetts, a pre-planned signal to the Mohegans that all bets were off and that it was time to loose the arrows already in place in their bows. Under the shower of arrows, whooping and yelling, the Mohegans came charging across the field, tomahawks raised on high. Uncas, meanwhile, had quickly picked himself up and run over to his forces to lead the charge.

The Narragansett braves were taken completely by surprise. While their chief was parleying with Uncas, they had been standing around sharpening their tomahawks (or whatever), never dreaming the Mohegans would actually come out and fight a force so superior in numbers to their own. After a very brief engagement, the Narragansetts took off in the direction from which they had originally come, with Miantonomo leading the panicky pack and Uncas' company close on their moccasined heels. They say that many fleeing Narragansetts were so crazy with fear that they set new cross-country records in reaching the fording place on the Shetucket on their way back to their own territory to the southeast. One of them, so the story goes, was even found many days later "swimming" through bushes and underbrush lining the river, still so bewildered by fear and excitement that he thought he was *in* the water.

While one group of rapidly retreating Narragansetts went home via the old familiar path, another group led by Miantonomo took a less fortunate route: in their reckless haste they suddenly found themselves on the steep cliffs overlooking the falls of the Yantic. Many fell to their deaths in the rushing waters below, but their chief somehow managed to reach the other side with no more than a broken leg to show for his effort to leap across the Yantic from the cliff on one side to the equally high cliff on the other.

However, when the pursuing Uncas arrived at the top of the same gorge moments later and saw Miantonomo hobbling away into the woods on the opposite side, determination and hatred for his enemy gave wings to his feet. With a fast, running start, Uncas hurtled high over the Yantic rapids — and landed safely on the high bank opposite. This astounding leap permitted him to catch up with the injured Miantonomo within a few minutes. As soon as the Mohegan sachem touched the Narragansett chief's shoulder, Miantonomo stopped and, silent and unresisting, permitted Uncas to take him captive. Surprised at the ease with which he took Miantonomo, Uncas asked why he did not speak. "If you had taken me," he said, "I would have begged you for my life." The sullen Narragansett gave no response, choosing to die rather than ask Uncas for mercy.

At the request of his white friends in Hartford, Uncas brought Miantonomo up to the English settlement, where the victorious Mohegan willingly gave over his captive to the English government and agreed to abide by their decision on how to dispose of Miantonomo's case. Although the sachem of the Narragansetts had a nasty history of threatening Uncas' assassination, making war against the Mohegans without English permission and vowing to exterminate the white settlements, the Commissioners of the

United Colonies who tried his case hesitated to pass the death sentence. In their dilemma, the Commissioners turned to ecclesiastical counselors, five principal Puritan ministers of the colonies, for advice. The church fathers were unanimous in their opinion: for the public good, Miantonomo must be executed.

Having proclaimed the death sentence, the Commissioners decided that Uncas should have the pleasure of carrying it out. They thereupon directed Uncas to take Miantonomo "into the next part of his own government and there put him to death: provided that some discreet and faithful persons of the English accompany them and see the execution, for our more full satisfaction." So, accompanied by two English witnesses, Uncas led Miantonomo to the nearest Mohegan lands (probably somewhere in the present East Windsor or East Hartford area), split his skull with a tomahawk, sliced a large piece of flesh from the dead man's shoulder and, in savage triumph, ate it. The date was September 28, 1643.

Uncas thought it appropriate that Miantonomo be buried near the place where he had originally been captured and that a small pile of rocks be placed as a marker on the gravesite. So the Mohegans buried their fallen foe in a place on the western bank of the Shetucket River, north of the present village of Greenville, and marked the spot with stones, as Uncas ordered. And as years passed, the little memorial on the place called Sachem's Plain grew larger and larger. For being on an Indian route much traveled during the seventeenth century, it was visited by warriors from many tribes, both friends and foes of Miantonomo's people, who added to the pile as they passed by. It is said that no true-hearted Narragansett ever failed to throw a stone upon the heap with much wailing and moaning, and no Mohegan ever passed without hurling a rock with a howl of joy and exultation.

Sometime in the late eighteenth century, long after the Indians had passed from the land and the English settlers had come in numbers to the Norwich area, a farmer found a large mound of rocks on his newly-acquired acreage. Not recognizing its significance, apparently, he used the stones to build a foundation for his house and barn. There was nothing left to remind posterity of the spot where a fleeing Narragansett chief had been captured and ultimately buried until July 4, 1841. On that date a few citizens of Norwich erected a granite monument where once the pile of stones had been and dedicated it in dignified and solemn ceremonies. The simple inscription read:

MIANTONOMO
1643

"First Lady of Connecticut"

*A*N HISTORIAN ASKED to nominate a "first lady of Connecticut" might well come up with the name of Lady Alice Boteler Fenwick. Bride of Colonel George Fenwick, governor of the infant Saybrook colony from 1639 to 1644, Lady Alice was not only the first English noblewoman to risk the rigors of life in primitive Connecticut, but also the first white woman to alter the course of the state's history. For after her untimely death in 1648, Colonel Fenwick lost all interest in developing Saybrook as a baronial refugee center for Oliver Cromwell and his aristocratic Puritan cronies, and went back to England, never to return to the place where his young wife lay buried. Cromwell never made it to Saybrook.

On the other hand, almost any resident of contemporary Connecticut asked the same question about a female "first" would probably name Ella T. Grasso — and rightly so. As Connecticut's first female governor and the first woman in the nation ever elected a state's chief executive in her own right, Governor Grasso won for herself a notably high place in the history of Connecticut and in the hearts of her fellow citizens.

However, anyone familiar with the legends of the Nutmeg State might be inclined to pick as Connecticut's "first lady" one "Goody" Barber, a woman virtually unknown to history. Heroine of a traditional story which was recalled for more than two hundred years, the remarkable Barber stands as a prototype, a fitting symbol for the many extraordinary women whose varied feats have inspired and enlivened our folk narratives from the first settlement right down to the present day. Indeed, it might be concluded from her story —

and the evidence of a large body of Connecticut legend — that the role of women in the state's lore has been such that had Ella Grasso not finally emerged historically, the folk would ultimately have invented her anyway.

Be that as it may, the legend of Connecticut's first lady of folk tradition bears retelling here, both for its characteristic flavor and its claim on history, since several historians have cited it as proof that Wethersfield was Connecticut's first truly *settled* town.

It all happened back in the spring of 1635, when a small group of Puritans from Watertown, Massachusetts, set out in a small pinnace to sail around Cape Cod, into Long Island Sound and then up the Connecticut River, to establish a settlement at a great bend in the river known to the Indians as Pyquag ("the dancing place"). The previous fall, nine Watertown men had come to Pyquag — probably at the urging of rogue Puritan, John Oldham — to set up a few huts and try to make it through the winter. They were to pave the way for the 1635 settlers.

Traditions (and their later activities) tell us that the men of the 1635 company were a pretty quarrelsome bunch. As a matter of fact, members of this second Watertown group were little more than itchy-footed squatters who lacked the religious leadership so important to the success of other early Connecticut settlements. Right from the beginning of the voyage to Connecticut, so the story goes, the males squabbled among themselves about one thing or another, making the trip uncomfortable for everyone aboard.

Finally, after many days at sea and several more on the long, tidal river, the little ship arrived at Pyquag. Excitement grew as the captain laid the bow up on the shore in an area which today is Wethersfield Cove. Then, true to form, a great argument broke out among the men in the company about which of them would have the honor of being the first one ashore. Just as several of the angry males were about to come to blows, out sprang Ms. Barber. Nimbly, she vaulted over the ship's rail into the shallow water and, petticoats billowing, waded ashore. When the first white woman who ever set foot on Connecticut soil clambered onto dry land, she turned to the now silent men lining the ship's rail above her and gave them an unmistakable gesture of triumph. There, on the Indians' "dancing place," "Goody" Barber had cut a caper for sisterhood which would echo down through Connecticut legendry for generations to come.

The Rev. Bulkley's Advice

WHEN HE GRADUATED from Harvard College in 1699, John Bulkley was recognized as one of the two or three most brilliant scholars yet produced by America's first college. Regarded as especially strong in solidity of judgment and strength of argument, the young man quickly began to fulfill his promise after he became the first minister of the Congregational Church in Colchester. Within a few short years of his ministry, he had earned great respect from his peers for his tracts on matters of law, medicine and theology, and a widespread reputation among common folk for his wisdom and counsel in all manner of popular dispute. In fact, his mail became so heavy with requests for his advice that he sometimes had difficulty sorting them all out. And at least once, his confusion led to a mistake which was talked about for years and amused several generations.

As the story went, there was a church in the Colchester area that for some time had been torn apart by a disagreement. Finally, unable to solve their own problems and on the verge of falling apart completely, the various factions agreed to submit their grievances to the Rev. Bulkley for his resolution. To make sure that his advice would not be misunderstood, the squabbling congregation asked the Rev. Bulkley to reduce his reply to writing. He agreed to do so. Now, it so happened that the sage minister owned a farm on the outskirts of Colchester which was worked by a tenant farmer. Apparently, at the very time that he was pondering the difficult church feud, the Rev. Bulkley received a message from his tenant, asking his advice on certain questions of farm management. The farmer asked his landlord please to reply in writing, since he wanted to make no mistakes with his boss' property.

After due consideration, the Rev. Bulkley carefully composed replies to the church and to the farmer — then dispatched each piece of advice to the wrong party. The letter designed for the church went to the tenant, and the one for the tenant to the church. There was considerable puzzlement, therefore, when the expectant congregation listened as the moderator read aloud the advice which would solve all its problems: *"You will see to the repair of fences, that they be built high and strong, and you will take special care of the old black bull."* At these words, most of the congregation looked at one another with blank expressions and shrugged shoulders, but at least one member of the congregation thought he understood the counsel contained in what he took to be the catchy metaphors of the message.

The clever interpreter arose before his friends and neighbors, and spoke as follows: "Brethren, this is the very advice we most need; the directions to repair the fences is to admonish us to take good heed in the admission and government of our members; we must guard the church by our master's laws, and keep out strange cattle from the fold. And we must in a particular manner set a watchful guard over the Devil, the old black bull, who has done so much hurt of late." The members of the congregation all nodded in agreement at this masterful explanation of the Rev. Bulkley's mystical counsel, realizing that the learned minister with the big reputation had not failed them, after all. Moreover, they all agreed to abide by his wise advice and resolved to be governed by it in the future. Harmony had been restored to the long-afflicted church. Unfortunately, no one ever found out what advice the tenant farmer received or what effect it had upon his barnyard management.

George Washington's Horse

WHILE THE WADSWORTH stable in Hartford (now removed to the Lebanon Green) was at one time famed as a place where George Washington's horse slept, the Pixlee Tavern in Bridgeport was even better known throughout early Connecticut as the spot where Washington's horse nearly dined on a take-out order of fried oysters. Tradition, incidentally, does not reveal whether the same steed was involved on both occasions.

Anyway, according to the widely-circulated legend, General Washington was en route to Cambridge to join the Continental Army sometime in the late fall of 1775, when he found himself passing through Bridgeport just about supper time. Having come a long way on a cold day with very little to eat, he reined in his horse at the Pixlee Tavern, dismounted, handed the reins to the parking attendant — or stable hand — and, assured that the animal would be well cared for, proceeded to enter the popular Boston Road eatery and grog shop.

Unfortunately for the commander of the Continental troops, he had picked an unusually busy night to dine at the Pixlee. There was a large crowd bellied up to the bar, enjoying what was Bridgeport's most famous colonial happy-hour, and every table in the main hall was filled with diners tucking away large quantities of the house specialty — oysters, fresh from the local waters of Long Island Sound, fried according to an original recipe known only to Mrs. Pixlee. A shipment of the succulent shellfish had arrived only that afternoon, and the word had spread rapidly through town that the Pixlee menu would feature the seafood treat that very evening. So the tavern was jammed, standing room only, and not much of that, either.

Now, it chanced that on this particular trip General Washington was not only travelling alone, but he was also dressed in rather seedy-looking civilian clothing, perhaps to avoid detection while moving along the Tory-infested Connecticut shoreline. So, when he pushed his way through the front door of the tavern, the man whose face and fame would soon be known throughout a new nation went completely unrecognized by the Pixlee's patrons. In fact, hardly anyone even looked up as Washington stood just inside the entrance, gritting his wooden teeth and listening to the noisy crowd discuss such things as the outrageous price of imported ale or the box score of the latest Yankees-Redcoats encounter in Boston.

Then, grimly determined to find himself a seat and order some much-needed food, Washington shouldered his way over to a particularly desirable table, right next to the cheery, roaring fireplace. After he had stood hopefully nearby for a time, watching while several platters of fried oysters disappeared down the gullets of the seated guests, it finally became obvious to the hungry soldier that no one was about to move and make room for him. The general decided to take strategic action.

"You know," said Washington, casually addressing a florid-faced patron who had just finished off a third helping of oysters, "my horse is crazy about fried oysters. We've had a hard ride today, and I'll guarantee you, the old fellow would be mighty pleased to find some of those oysters in his feed-bag right about now."

At that, everyone at the fireside table stopped eating, wiped their sleeves across their lips and turned their eyes suspiciously toward the tall, bewigged stranger hovering over their dining board.

"Did I hear you right, Mister?" said the red-faced man, his jowls bobbing in disbelief. "Your horse will eat fried oysters? Why, I've never heard of such a thing."

"Yes, sir," replied Washington, "down in Virginia, where I come from, we practically raise our horses on Chesapeake Bay oysters. They make for a lively gait and a sleek hide."

In the excited discussion that followed this exchange, another one of the diners offered to wager that "no horse ever lived who would eat oysters."

"Very well," said Washington, seizing the opening, "why don't you folks just prove it to yourselves. Take some of your oysters there, go on out back to the stable and see what my horse does with them. I tell you, he'll make short work of them."

Immediately, all the guests jumped up from the table, heaped up a dish with the savory shellfish and headed for the stable. As they disappeared out the back door, Washington quietly removed his cape and cap, slid into a chair at the now empty table and, with a smile of satisfaction on his face, placed his order for the jumbo-size fried oyster platter. They say that by the time the disappointed guests straggled in from the barn, the father-to-be of our country was about half-way through a second serving of Pixlee's prides.

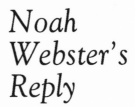

Noah Webster's Reply

*A*LTHOUGH NOAH WEBSTER was born and raised in West Hartford, the man who has been called "the father of his country's language" did most of the work on his great *American Dictionary of the English Language (1828)* while living in New Haven. Known by his contemporaries for his disciplined concentration, massive intellect and vast learning, Webster may have been the subject of many stories created by awed but iconoclastic fellow citizens and designed — as these kinds of tales usually are — to exploit the popular image of The Famous and to bring the god-like a bit closer to earth. While Noah Webster anecdotes may have disappeared from oral tradition, the following example of the genre should not be permitted to die.

It seems that among the servants in the New Haven home of Noah and Maria Greenleaf Webster there chanced to be a pretty young upstairs maid. One day, Maria Webster wanted to give some instructions to the servant girl, but couldn't find her anywhere. The only room in the house where she hadn't looked, of course, was Noah's study, because she certainly didn't want to interrupt her husband at his scholarly work. Finally, in desperation Mrs. Webster decided to check her husband's room. She opened the door quietly and discovered the maid all right: she and Noah were engaged in a rather passionate kiss! Maria Webster gasped and cried out, "Why, Noah, I am... surprised." Her husband turned slowly toward the door, releasing his grip on the girl, if not on his faculties, and replied, "I beg to differ with you, my dear. *I* am surprised. *You* are astonished."

PART II
Local Legends

An Introduction

The legends in this section are traditional stories which are closely associated with a particular place, especially those which incorporate *a place-name etymology* or celebrate an unusual *local historical event*. The people who know and tell these stories almost always believe them to be purely regional creations. But as professional folklorists have come to realize, many of these anecdotal legends are really localized versions of migratory tales, legends that move about from place to place through oral transmission, stopping in one spot only long enough to take on local features. Even a legend generated by a particular Connecticut event or geographical feature has a way of spreading outward, changing and being localized as it moves.

While a great number of the local legends in Part II are peculiar to Connecticut places, a significant number have counterparts elsewhere in the United States. Among the former group, the legends of the Charter Oak, the Windham "frog fight" and the "Dark Day," to name a few, have provided important symbols in which the folk take pride and with which they shape an identity. And among the latter group, such stories as the origin of Bride's Brook and the description of Litchfield's "church stove war" — with their parallels in other places in the United States — have permitted Connecticut people to participate in the folk culture shared by many Americans.

Perhaps the greatest number of local legends having counterparts all over the United States are those which explain folk etymologies of such places or geographical features as lovers' leaps, treasure islands, bottomless lakes (complete with marine monsters) and devil's dens. I have included only a few of these in this collection, although they may be easily collected by those wishing to add to their funds of legendry. In any event, all the place-name legends are gathered into a separate section of Part II.

Another section of Part II is devoted to the local historical legend. Since folk legends celebrating such things as incidents of war, sensational crimes, natural disasters, memorable accidents and tragic love affairs — as well as possibly unique local events — have been sadly neglected by collectors of legendry, I have included a large and representative sampling of the genre. Some have speculated that local historical legends have been disregarded either because folklorists have been preoccupied with other kinds of lore or because too often these legends have been regarded as "garbled local history" of little value to students of either folklore or history. Thus, the Connecticut local historical legends in this book are designed to expand the record. If readers are also entertained or instructed along the way, so much the better.

Silver Hill

SILVER HILL (also known as Mine Hill) in Roxbury takes its name from the mine on the heights west of the Shepaug River which was worked for its iron ore as early as 1724. Actually, the Silver Hill name was based more on wishful thinking than anything else, because precious little of the metal was ever taken from the mine, as far as anyone knows for sure. But as the early miners hacked away at the unyielding rock for the available spathic iron, they always hoped that plain old Mine Hill might really turn out to be Silver Hill, after all. At one time, in fact, no less a celebrity than Ethan Allen, the Green Mountain Boy from Connecticut, bought an interest in the mine, speculating, like others before and after him, that some miraculous alchemy would turn the base iron to precious silver.

Then one day, the hearts of Roxbury citizens leapt up when a mysterious German speculator hinted that there was, indeed, silver in their hills. He told them that he would be only too happy to sell them some stock in the local mine, at rock-bottom prices, of course. He did a land-office business for a while, too, especially when he displayed for the skeptical a suitcase full of metal bars that certainly looked like silver. One day, however, an observant prospective investor noted that some of the silver was peeling from the bars in the salesman's bag — and the scam was promptly terminated by an angry mob.

But this was not the end of the dream for Roxbury silver. For as the German con man was being unceremoniously hustled out of town, never to return, he dropped a suitcase, and several metal bars fell out of the hastily-packed contents. Tests on those bars proved without a shadow of a doubt that they were made of solid, one-hundred-percent, pure silver. It was enough to make any Roxbury citizen stop and wonder.

Rhodes' Folly

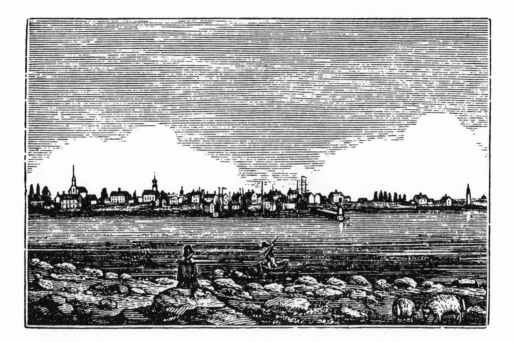

RHODES' FOLLY IS a small island in Fisher's Island Sound, off the town of Stonington, with a colorful history and an appropriate name. One of the remarkable features of the island was that in the era following the Revolution, the state lines of three different states, Connecticut, Rhode Island, and New York, were said to meet on the island. This unusual circumstance was surely the thing that attracted a canny entrepreneur named James Rhodes to buy the island in 1785, for this was a time of prohibition and Rhodes was a man with a plan to sell liquor to sailors, without fear of prosecution.

Rhodes' idea was to construct a large saloon on the very spot where the three state lines came together. If Connecticut officers entered on the Connecticut side of the room, Rhodes thought, he could quickly move his bar, booze, tables and chairs to Rhode Island, or New York, in another part of his establishment where they had no authority to arrest him. Or, if he were raided by officials from Rhode Island or New York, again, he could hastily carry his stuff into another state. The island seemed made to order for Rhodes.

For a while, it looked as if old Jim had surely bought himself a goldmine. Since there was no end of maritime traffic passing by his front door, there was no end to the number of thirsty seamen stopping by for a slug of rum before heading for the "dry" land or the open sea. Oh, the authorities from each state tried to bust Rhodes from time to time, but as soon as he saw them at one door or another, he quickly moved his operation into a safe state, in another part of the saloon.

One day, however, the sea-washed "line-house" was finally put out of business for good. That was the day, of course, when the frustrated prohibition agents from Connecticut, Rhode Island, and New York got together and came through all the doors at once. Ever since that fateful moment, the little island has been known as Rhodes' Folly.

Bride's Brook

THROUGH THE NIANTIC section of what is now the town of East Lyme flows Bride's Brook, a small stream which took its name from an unusual, romantic episode that occurred sometime in the winter of 1646-1647. At that time, according to tradition, a young man named Jonathan (sometimes Thomas) Rudd was in great haste to marry his sweetheart of long standing. For one reason or another — some say a blizzard came up, others that the magistrate was away on business — the official who was scheduled to perform the wedding service was not available when Rudd needed him. Since the law then required that one must wed in his home parish, the eager bridegroom searched the jurisdiction high and low for a minister or magistrate, but could find none.

Hearing that John Winthrop, later Governor of the Massachusetts Bay Colony, was visiting in nearby New London, Rudd appealed to the man from Massachusetts for resolution of his problem. But since New London was then under the jurisdiction of the Massachusetts Bay Colony, Winthrop had no authority to marry the couple outside his zone of authority. Finally, however, the wise Winthrop saw a way out of the dilemma. While the bridal party stood on the west bank of the brook known by the Indians as Sunkapung ("cold water"), in the couple's own parish, Winthrop stood on the east bank, within his New London jurisdiction, and there, across the babbling brook he united the happy pair in holy-and legal-matrimony. From that day forward the stream was called Bride's Brook.

Interestingly enough, Bride's Brook later figured in a dispute that inspired some fanciful stories. It all began when the people of Lyme questioned the legality of the brook as a boundary with New London. In order to save the expense of an appeal to the courts in Hartford, it was agreed by both towns that they would abide by the results of a bare-knuckle fight between two representatives from each town. Since the boys from Lyme proved more accomplished free-style brawlers than the New Londoners, the boundary was moved east to the Niantic River.

Lantern Hill

NEARLY 600 FEET above sea level, its summit of bare granite flecked with quartz crystals glittering in the sun, Lantern Hill (or Tar Barrel Hill, as it is also called) in North Stonington has served as both landmark and lookout since the first peoples came to this region where the continent meets the sea. Tradition says that it has served fishermen and deepwater sailors as a day-beacon, guiding them safely into the eastern Long Island Sound ports like Mystic or Stonington, from the earliest days of maritime activity on the coast. Since the shimmering, white summit can be seen from many miles at sea on a clear, sunny day, the landmark tradition probably has a sound basis in historical fact.

By the same token, on a clear day observers on the gleaming peak of Lantern Hill can see five states — New York, Connecticut, Massachusetts, Rhode Island, and Vermont — as well as more than a hundred miles of coastal waters. Sassacus, the fierce Pequot chieftain, was said to have stood on the summit many times, squinting seaward, eternally watching for the approach of enemy war canoes, or landward, seeking signs of hostile Narragansett campfires.

But it was an incident that occurred during the War of 1812 that finally gave this unusual height of land the names it is still known by today. Fearful of enemy naval attacks along the Connecticut coast, the people of Stonington had maintained a round-the-clock watch from the top of Lantern Hill since the troubles with England began. Then, in April of 1814, several hundred British sailors and marines had landed at nearby Pettipaug Point (Essex) on the Connecticut River and systematically destroyed an estimated $200,000 worth of property, including some twenty ships. When word of the Essex raid reached the Stonington area a short time later, the vigilance of the lookouts on Lantern Hill intensified and a system of warning the eastern shoreline villages of impending attack was implemented.

Huge hogsheads of tar — the same kind used to preserve manila lines aboard ship — were hauled to the summit of Lantern Hill. If a lookout spotted any sign of enemy sail, the men on watch were to put a torch to all the tar barrels, as a warning of imminent danger. The flames from such "lanterns" could, of course, be seen for many miles around. On the bright night of August 11, 1814, the tar barrel lanterns on top of the hill began to flicker. Immediately, the people of Stonington went into action. Women, children and the elderly quickly packed a few personal belongings into wagons and carts and hurried inland that very night, to seek refuge with friends or relatives in the country. The able men and militia headed for the waterfront to prepare the cannon for firing. When the dawn revealed a large British fleet standing into the harbor, apparently ready to land troops for a raid, the little village was ready, thanks to the timely warning.

For two days the British naval vessels milled about in the harbor, pounding the coastal defenses with an estimated sixty tons of cannon balls and shot. But the expected landing never came. When the enemy realized that their softening-up bombardment was having little effect on the Americans (who seemed only too well-prepared to defend themselves), the English broke off their attack, set sail for open sea and disappeared below the horizon.

Ever since frustrating the British raid at Stonington, its citizens have taken understandable delight in poet Philip Freneau's lines on the battle:

> It cost the King ten thousand pounds
> To have a dash at Stonington.

And ever since, the place from which the crucial early warning was flashed has been called Lantern (or Tar Barrel) Hill.

Devil's Den

NEAR THE CENTER of the town of Sterling, there is a large and curious cave with features so strange that residents from the time of the earliest settlement called it the Devil's Den. Situated within a rock ledge, the cavern had a circular area almost one hundred feet in diameter. Early explorers who tried the acoustics in this enormous main room came out to tell stories about the place being fit for the King of the Underground. Some whispered and many of those devout Puritan settlers believed them — that they had actually seen the Prince of Evil seated upon a natural throne in the cavernous den, thundering orders about the disposition of the souls of sinners.

The rock of Devil's Den is also split in two places (just like the Devil's cleft hoof) and these cracks form fissures fifty feet deep. Through one bubbled a small stream of water. The other served as an entryway to a room about twelve feet square, in which there was a depression like a fireplace, and above it, extending through the rock to the outside, an opening about three feet square — a perfect, natural chimney. In the cavern, too, was a natural staircase, winding down along the rock wall of the room, from top to bottom. The folk imagination worked overtime explaining how the Devil used that staircase from above and the fireplace below.

Despite the stories about the Devil's activities in the cavern, Devil's Den was notable during all seasons of the year for the extraordinary chill which permeated the place. In the cold months, a constant stream of water entering the room with the fireplace through the "chimney" would build up a massive iceberg, which often never completely melted, even during the hot months of summer. The sun, of course, never reached the icy underground recess. All of this is ironic, of course, in light of the Devil's reputation for preferring hell-fire and brimstone!

Devil's Hopyard
(and other
Diabolical Places)

*I*F CONNECTICUT PLACE-NAMES give any sort of an accurate indication, nobody ever beat the Devil for leaving a calling card all over the map of the state. With a half-dozen or so such geographical locations, there are legends explaining that the name came about because the Devil either visited or lived there, while for the rest, the devilish address seems to have stuck because they look like spots where the Evil One would feel right at home.

But those who know Connecticut history will understand where in the devil such an extraordinary number of diabolical designations really came from. For no people ever had a more devil-may-care attitude than those zealous old Puritans who trooped out of the Boston area in the 1630s to establish a worldly paradise in the Connecticut River valley. Those founders and the true believers who followed them were convinced that the Devil might really be lurking behind every bush — and that it paid to advertise his presence and power.

Give or take a few places — it's easy to overlook the Prince of Darkness — there appear to be some thirty-four Connecticut locations which either bear the Devil's name or nick-name (no pun intended), or are identified with his traditional home stomping ground. Leading the list of places named for the Devil are *Dens* with five, followed closely by *Backbones* with four, and *Footprints, Rocks and Kitchens* with two each. The entire list includes:

Devil's Den (Plainfield,* Weston, Monroe, Franklin, Sterling)
Devil's Backbone (Bethlehem, Plymouth, Bristol, Cheshire)
Devil's Footprint (Montville, Branford)

* See separate chapter in this book.

Devil's Rock (Old Saybrook, Portland)
Devil's Kitchen (Burlington, Thomaston)
Devil's Hopyard (East Haddam)
Devil's Meditation (shared by Middlebury and Watertown)
Devil's Island (in the Quinebaug River above Danielson)
Devil's Gap (Brookfield)
Devil's Gorge (Weston)
Devil's Jump (Derby)
Devil's Plunge (Morris)
Devil's Pulpit (Hamden)
Devil's Mouth (Redding)
Devil's Wharf (Deep River)
Devil's Dripping Pan (Branch Brook)
Devil's Belt (all of Long Island Sound girdling Connecticut)

When two *Satan's Kingdoms* (New Hartford, Bethany), a *Satan's Ridge* (New Hartford), a *Tophet Ravine* (Roxbury), a *Hell Hole* (Simsbury), a *Hell's Hollow* (Plainfield) and a *Purgatory Brook* are added to the roll of satanic spots, it becomes pretty obvious that in Connecticut's topography, anyway, the Devil never took the hindmost.

Of all the places in Connecticut bearing the Devil's name, the one with the greatest variety of legendary etymologies is the 860-acre state park in East Haddam known as the Devil's Hopyard. Here, the combination of booming Chapman's Falls, pothole-scarred rocks, the unearthly quiet in the dark glen below the falls and the steep, cave-pocked cliffs flanking turbulent Eight Mile River makes a likely setting for the growth and development of legends. Then, too, the "hellish" appearance of the Hopyard's gorge was probably enhanced for the early English settlers by local Indian tribes, which are said to have used Devil's Hopyard for religious rites and powwows. It probably wouldn't have taken much to convince those devout Puritans that the Indians they saw dancing around a midnight campfire were really evil demons paying their respects to the Head Man.

The "hopyard" part of Devil's Hopyard evidently has solid foundation in historical fact. At some time prior to 1800, there was a malt house near a small tributary of Eight Mile River called Malt House Brook, on the farm of one George Griffin. Although the malt house was abandoned prior to 1814, during the period of its operation, Griffin grew hops in a small clearing — the "hopyard" — beside the road running through the area now called Devil's Hopyard. But the Devil's presence in this hopyard is not so easily explained.

The most widely-circulated legend tells of the many times Satan has been seen, sitting on a huge boulder at the top of Chapman's Falls, playing his

violin while the evil witches of Haddam stirred a "hell broth for a charm of powerful trouble" in the cauldron-like potholes formed in the rocks below. Another story reports that a lone traveler, while walking through the Hopyard one night, saw some weird, shapeless forms leaping from ledges and trees near the falls. Later, these phantoms accosted the terrified man, who then beat a hasty retreat to the nearest tavern, where he related his experience to anyone who would listen. Some say that the traveler had spent too much time at the tavern *before* he took his ramble through the Hopyard.

Another story, one which demonstrates the folk inclination to rationalize the unexplainable through legend-making, claims that the "Devil" portion of Devil's Hopyard is a corruption of the surname Dibble. According to this still-lively tradition, there once was a hopyard located along Eight Mile River operated by a man named Dibble, who had a farm near Chapman's Falls. Dibble, they say, was a notorious bootlegger, who combined his home-grown hops with many secret ingredients to make a potent but illegal brew. This he sold to thirsty locals, including any teenager who asked.

It is said that one Haddam mother who found her young son in a drunken stupor induced by too many draughts of Dibble's delight called the brewmaster "a devil" for keeping the boy supplied with spirits. Also, Dibble had a reputation for throwing festive, if not riotous parties at his home, where young and old alike helped the generous host reduce his inventory of bathtub beer. As a corruptor of youth, then, he was in the same league as Old Nick, and "going down to Dibble's hopyard" came to have a connotation which local parents understood all too well. The fact is, however, there is no record of anyone named Dibble ever having lived within thirty miles of the Devil's Hopyard.

Yet another diabolical story connected with the Devil's Hopyard concerns the wayward son of a Congregational minister in Millington, the nearest village to the Hopyard reserve. Although the remarkable saga of Abraham Brown was apparently concocted in the fertile imagination of Judge Hiram Willey (his "romance" appeared in four successive issues of *The Connecticut Valley Advertiser,* in the summer of 1909), it has circulated so long in oral tradition that it now qualifies as a true folk legend. Today, those who relate the tale, originally entitled "Weird and Romantic Devil's Hopyard, A Story of Religious Bigotry A Century and A Quarter Ago and When Witches Hovered Near," are probably unaware of its literary origin. Anyway, today's legend-tellers give every indication that they believe Judge Willey's fiction to be historically accurate, and offer it frequently as an explanation for the "Devil's" presence in "Devil's Hopyard."

According to this well-known story, there once was a Millington parson named Obadiah Brown, who lived north of the Devil's Hopyard. He had two sons: Rufus, a paragon of Puritan virtue, and Abraham, an unholy terror because he did not fear God and professed a kind of fatalistic belief. "If I am foreordained to be damned," said Abraham Brown, "I shall be damned. And if I am foreordained to be saved, I shall be saved — and nothing I can do will prevent one or the other."

Conducting his life on the basis of that creed, Abraham developed early into quite a free spirit. He sat in the Millington meeting house during Sunday services and, with motions and grimaces, imitated his father in the pulpit, much to the delight of the children in the congregation. Once, he was observed spitting down from his front row seat in the gallery upon the bald head of a deacon. He even broke into the church one day, stole the sheepskin cover off the pulpit Bible and wore it under his clothing to protect his backside from floggings administered by the schoolmaster.

Since the church had been securely locked, it was thought at first that the theft of the sheepskin had been the work of the Devil. In fact, one parishioner said that on the night the sheepskin disappeared, he had seen in the moonlight a strange-looking creature fly from the window over the gallery. "It looked very much like Granny Whipple," said the observer, referring to a local woman with a reputation for being a witch. But the investigation into the theft finally came to an end when the missing sheepskin fell out of Abraham

Brown's britches one day, during a particularly vigorous thrashing by his teacher.

Convicted of stealing the holy coverlet, Abraham was sentenced to a year in jail. Here, so that he might finally learn to read and redeem his soul at the same time, he was given a primer which illustrated each letter of the alphabet in a pious little precept:

A In _Adam's_ fall / We sinned all.

B Thy life to mend, / God's _Book_ attend.

However, after Abraham had completed his prison term, the jailers found written on the wall of his cell a bit of graffiti which suggested that the youth may have learned well how to read and write, but that he had not been completely rehabilitated:

All men sinned in Adam,

Some in Hell and some in HADDAM,

The chief end of man —

Keep all you've got and get all you can.

When Abraham came home from jail, his father was anxious to hear about his son's jailhouse redemption. Instead, Abraham told the stern minister that he had enjoyed reading the silly catechism and Bible stories to the Indians who shared the lockup with him. Moreover, he said, he agreed with the Indians' opinion of Puritan doctrine: "Ugh," they said, "heap big lies." Abraham also told his father that he thought the Indians' concept of a happy hunting ground was far superior to his father's vision of Hell and that the Indians' ideas about the future life, in general, were more rational than those of the framers of the Westminster Catechism. Upon hearing such heresy, Obadiah Brown turned Abraham out of his house, ordering him never to return.

Abraham sought refuge in the home of a neighbor, Squire Robert Shaw. Here he met a man from Cuba who was about to leave for Havana. When, the Cuban offered to take Abraham with him, the homeless youth accepted his offer. Before they departed, however, the Cuban suggested that he and Abraham have one parting bit of fun with the Rev. Brown. So, having obtained from Squire Shaw a bull's hide with the horns still attached, the Cuban wrapped it around him and, with young Brown beside him in the wagon, drove furiously past the house of Obadiah Brown, shouting and whooping wildly.

Since Abraham disappeared shortly thereafter, the legend became current that the wayward lad had finally been taken by the Hopyard devil and carried off to the nether regions, there to fry forever for his sins. Not only did the story carry a clear warning to all the secret sinners in the area, but it also proved to the superstitious local farmers that the Devil was alive and well — and waiting, in _person_ — down at the Hopyard.

While the place-name legends about Devil's Hopyard dominate Connecticut's traditional devil lore, they are by no means the only tales about diabolical locations which circulate in the state. For example, they tell the story down around Portland about the young Mattabasett Indian who incurred the wrath of the Evil One by constantly disrupting the powwows with his incessant bragging and mockery of the gods. It seems the Indians held their powwows in a meadow beside the Connecticut River, near a spot in the river where there was a "blow-hole." Sometimes the water just seemed to blow up from the bottom of the river through the hole, throwing a great geyser into the air.

Well, one day during one of the Mattabasetts' gatherings, the boastful brave was again making fun of the gods. And even though a chief warned him to stop lest the Evil Spirit come and snatch him away, he refused. He also told the old man that the young Indians no longer believed in spirits, good or bad. He even ordered the elder to stop talking such nonsense! At that the Devil exploded. Furiously angry at the young man for no longer believing in him, the Evil One came roaring out of the blow hole and grabbed the proud brave. The youth squirmed in his grasp, but the Devil jumped back into the water with him, and they both disappeared down the deep hole in the river. So hot with anger had the Evil Spirit been, they say, that his burning foot left a scorched print in the rock from which he had jumped. The Indian braggart never returned, but the Evil Spirit's cloven footprint can still be seen today on the boulder they call Devil's Rock.

Devil's Footprint in Montville, located a few hundred feet behind the old Mohegan meeting house, is a rock with an imprint similar to the one on Portland's Devil's Rock. But the story explaining its origin is different. According to an old Mohegan Indian legend, the Evil One, who used to live in the Montville area, occasionally felt a need to leap over Long Island Sound to Montauk on Long Island, to visit his numerous subjects there. He used the Montville boulder, a rock several feet high and three feet across, as a handy launching pad, but because such force was exerted as he lifted off, he gradually dug in the rock a crevice about ten inches deep, in the shape of a cloven hoof — the Devil's footprint. Incidentally, this story is true, because over at Montauk there is a similar boulder with an identical imprint. It's obviously the spot where the Evil Spirit began his return trips to Connecticut.

A "footprint" in a stone found in the Weston valley called Devil's Den has given rise to several origin-legends. One tradition has it that when the Devil walked the earth in that area, he stepped on soft clay, leaving a footprint-like indentation too large to have been made by man. When the clay hardened into stone, they say, the footprint was permanently preserved. However, another legend claims that the Devil's Den valley of Weston was once so full of snakes, wolves, bears and other frightful creatures that colonial settlers in the area associated the place with the Devil's menagerie — and fearfully told their children to avoid the place at all costs. Both versions of the story are still known today.

Unlike the traditions associated with places named for the Devil, legend and history blend together in the accounts which explain the origin of Satan's Kingdom and Satan's Ridge, both in New Hartford. According to legend, Satan once used the rocky gorge of the Farmington River bearing his name as his exclusive playground. Here, he and his band of lesser demons gamboled away their days and nights, until the day finally came when the Angel Gabriel blew them all away with one blast from his golden trumpet. Gabriel and the good angels had decided that the rugged area was just too lovely to be cluttered up with demonic denizens.

Whether the tale of Gabriel's environmental beautification program is true or not is hard to say, but according to the historical record, the Satan's Kingdom district did, in fact, once serve as a refuge for a scattering of human beings who might easily have been mistaken for devils. Either attracted by the place's name, or — more likely — its isolated and inaccessible location, a notorious group of "Indians, Negroes and renegade whites" settled in the Kingdom, in the last years of the eighteenth century.

Using their settlement as both home and hideout, the inhabitants ranged the region far and wide, begging, robbing, vandalizing and stealing anything that wasn't nailed down. Before the nest of thieves was finally cleared by law enforcement officers — Gabriel was not available — they say that Satan's Kingdom had grown so evil that it was even giving the Devil a bad name. Anyway, the raid may have marked the beginning of the end for the Devil in Connecticut.

Silver Lane

O N THE WAY to join Washington's forces in 1781, The French Main Army under General Rochambeau marched in four divisions through Voluntown, Plainfield, Canterbury and Windham before settling down for an extended period in the town of East Hartford. The elegant French soldiery was followed day after day by sturdy baggage wagons and carts, bearing chests of silver heavily guarded by special elite forces. When the troops reached their main quarters in East Hartford, the silver was stored in the James Forbes House, where the army paymaster drew on the hoard, so tradition says, to pay the soldiers.

For the people of colonial Connecticut, where a silver coin was as rare as a Roman Catholic prayer book, the sight of all those Frenchmen spending their silver wildly in the community inspired commemoration of a permanent sort. So a main road near the center of Rochambeau's encampment was called Silver Lane — and so it remains today. Incidentally, as testimony to the free-spending ways of the French soldiers, silver coins dating to the time of the encampment have reportedly been unearthed from time to time in the vicinity of Silver Lane, even in recent years.

Sachem's
Head

O NE MIGHT GUESS that Sachem's Head, the rocky promontory (or "headland") jutting into Long Island Sound two miles west of Guilford harbor, took its name from an Indian chief (or "sachem") who once lived there. Not so: the legendary derivation of the name is much more complicated — and interesting than that.

They say that the place recalls an incident in the bloody warfare between English and Mohegan forces led by Capt. John Mason and Chief Uncas, respectively, and the Pequots under their chief, Sassacus. After the Pequot massacre at Mystic, the small band of surviving tribesmen was pursued and harassed by the English-Mohegan forces as they fled westward toward Fairfield along the Connecticut coast. Although most of the pursuers went from the fort at Saybrook by water, a number of soldiers with Uncas and his warriors scoured the shores near Long Island Sound, lest any of the Pequots seek shelter in the caves and inlets. Not far from the shallow harbor at Guilford, they spotted a Pequot sachem (not Sassacus) with a few Indians, whom they chased enthusiastically. The Pequots went onto a long, narrow point of land at the south side of a small, deep harbor, hoping their pursuers would pass them by.

Uncas, however, knew Indian craft, and ordered some of his men to search the peninsula. Seeing that they were about to be discovered, the frightened Pequots jumped into the water and swam across the mouth of the narrow harbor. But they were not quick enough. As each climbed from the water, he was taken prisoner by the Mohegans. The sachem was sentenced to death, then and there. Uncas put an arrow through his heart, cut off his head and stuck it up in the crotch of a large oak tree near the harbor. Here the grisly trophy of war sat for many years, gradually bleaching to a silver-white in the sun. It also gave a name to a rather pretty seaside overlook.

Town of Bozrah

AUTHORITIES ON PLACE-NAMING have been struck by a paradox: as Puritan religious fervor declined in New England, Biblical place-names became more numerous. In Connecticut, where this phenomenon was particularly noticeable, especially in the naming of towns, the Biblical allusions may have been the result of Puritanism retaining its hold on the folk longer than it had in less conservative New England states. But there is also some suspicion that names like Goshen (1738), Canaan (1738), Sharon (1738) and New Canaan (1801) were chosen more for their advertising value than for their religious association, suggesting, as they would for those who knew the reputations of the Biblical originals, images of fertile valleys flowing with the milk and honey of an abundant life.

The naming of the southeastern Connecticut town of Bozrah, however, seemed to constitute such a jarring anomaly in this pattern that the folk have accounted for it with an amusing story. It is possible, of course, that the name conveyed a vaguely pleasant image of happy sheep making joyful noises within a safe enclosure, as mentioned in Micah: 2, 12: *"I will surely gather the remnant of Israel; I will put them together as the sheep of Bozrah, as the flock in the midst of their fold; they shall make a great noise by reason of the multitude of men."* On the other hand, Bozrah's citizens also had to face the terrible threat of Jeremiah:

49, 13: "*I have sworn by myself, saith the Lord, that Bozrah shall become a desolation, a reproach, a waste, and a curse.*" However, neither Micah nor Jeremiah was the source of the town's naming, according to a persistent legend. Rather, Bozrah was derived from yet another Biblical text, applied under unusual circumstances by the Connecticut General Assembly. The following account explains how the informal, early name "New Concord" became the accursed "Bozrah," when the town was incorporated.

First settled as part of the original "Nine-miles-square" of Norwich and of the Parish of West Farms, Bozrah was set off as the Parish of New Concord or the Fourth Society of Norwich in 1737. So it remained until 1786, when the citizens sent a request to the General Assembly that New Concord be incorporated as a separate town. Their choice for the new town's name was Bath, after the famous spa and watering-place in England (note, again, the promotional value of the preferred name). The member of the society elected to carry the parish's request to Hartford was a man of somewhat eccentric manner and taste, according to the story. When the rustic petitioner finally appeared before the legislature to represent his town's case, he was dressed in loud, parti-colored homespun so exotic as to cause the amused legislators to remember the query of Isaiah: 63, 1: "*Who is this that cometh from Edom, with dyed garments from Bozrah?*" Overcome by the particularly fitting note of this text, the Assembly thereupon completely overlooked the rather conventional "Bath," and approved the incorporation of the town, with the name of "Bozrah."

Although the citizens of the quiet, agricultural community have ever since had to live with the same name as the desolate, desert town in Syria, they have perhaps been able to find consolation in the fact that their town could be confused with no other in the United States. While the Concords and Baths have been repeated with some frequency from state to state, Bozrah, Connecticut, stands alone in the American gazetteer. It is curious to note in passing, especially in light of the prophesy of Micah (quoted above), that the Second Congressional District of Connecticut is presently represented in Washington by Sam Gejdenson, born of Jewish parents in a German displaced persons camp following World War II, who came to America with his family in 1950 — and settled on a dairy farm in Bozrah.

The Charter Oak

*O*NCE UPON A time more congenial than our own to the
thoughtful contemplation of history and traditions, every
Connecticut school child was familiar with Hartford's Charter
Oak and the stirring legend which planted the venerable tree firmly at the
center of the state's cultural symbolism. Indeed, with the possible exception of
the one more lovely than any poem Joyce Kilmer thought he would ever see,
the Charter Oak was probably America's best-known, best-loved tree. For this
was, after all, no spindly, robin-haired specimen, suited for nothing more
memorable than a poet's doting rhymes, but a veritable forest monarch,
destined to play a pivotal role in saving a young colony from tyranny and
preserving her people's freedom. Undoubtedly it was the tradition of the
Charter Oak which the noted historian George Bancroft remembered when he
wrote, "There is no state in the union in whose early history, if I were a
citizen, I could find more of which to be proud." Thus, while the legend has
been repeated countless times before, no collection of Connecticut legendry
would be complete without it.

There can be little doubt that the great white oak stood taller than other
trees in the forest long before circumstances rooted it deep in the colonial
history of Connecticut. Ancient — perhaps 400 years old — at the time of
Columbus' voyages to America, the tree had been an object of veneration by
generations of Indians, who had traditionally held their councils beneath its
expansive boughs. In 1614, during the earliest European voyage up the

Connecticut River as far as Hartford, Adrian Block and his men were so impressed with the stately oak that the Dutch explorer took special note of it in the log of his journey.

Then, when English settlers came to the land of the Indian sachem Sequassen in the 1630's, the old tree became the property of Samuel Wyllys, one of the first landowners in what would come to be the city of Hartford. But according to tradition, as Wyllys was busy clearing away the forest around his homestead and getting ever closer to the white oak, he was visited by a delegation of Indians fearful that their revered tree had been scheduled for destruction with all the rest. The Indians begged him earnestly to spare the tree, explaining that it had originally been planted as a token of peace by a great sachem who had brought his people from the west to the Connecticut River valley, and that the appearance of its first leaves in spring had been, since time immemorial, a sign from the Great Spirit that the days were propitious for the planting of corn. To the relief of the Indians — and, as it later turned out, the people of Connecticut — Wyllys left the ancient tree standing.

Even as legends clung to the early history of the massive oak, so, too, did they mark the original story of the Connecticut Charter. It has been said that back in the reign of King Charles I, the crown had no more faithful supporter in colonial America than John Winthrop, governor of the Massachusetts Bay Colony. However, John Winthrop's grandson, popularly known as "Winthrop the Younger" to distinguish him from his grandfather of the same name, had early left Massachusetts to cast his lot with the Connecticut Colony. So, after the restoration of the monarchy in 1660, when Connecticut decided to request a charter of liberties such as the other colonies had, Winthrop the Younger was chosen to carry the petition to Charles II, son of Charles I, who had been beheaded by Cromwell. The feeling was that the Second Charles might be especially generous with those who had been loyal to the First, and, thus, because of the family connection, Winthrop might be looked upon with special favor by the new king.

In order to remind Charles II of his father's close ties with the elder Winthrop, Connecticut's Winthrop brought with him as a royal gift a magnificent ring, which Charles I had once bestowed upon the Massachusetts Bay Colony governor as a token of their friendship. But as influential as the ring must have been in currying the King's favor, it was as nothing, according to contemporary court gossip, compared to the good accomplished by Sequassen's deed and the covetous Duchess of Castlemain. It seems that among the mementos which "Young" Winthrop had brought with him from Connecticut was an exotic-looking parchment covered with queer totems, the document by which Sequassen had signed away his birthright lands to the

English settlers at Hartford. They say that when the Dutchess of Castlemain, Charles II's current mistress, caught sight of the "savage" deed, she instantly fell in love with it and vowed to have it for her own.

Promising to entice all kinds of exceptional charter provisions from her royal boyfriend in exchange for the novel parchment, the Dutchess finally persuaded the Connecticut emissary to give it to her. Actually, Winthrop was well aware that the life of a favorite's fancy was likely to be fleeting; so he could expect soon to have the deed returned to him through the efforts of certain confidential servants. Anyway, whether it was the ring or a mistress' honeyed entreaties which did the trick is hard to say, but Winthrop the Younger did secure from Charles II such concessions to the Connecticut colonists' home rule that the Charter, signed and sealed on April 26, 1662, became the most liberal guarantee of rights enjoyed by any British colony in America, with the exception of Rhode Island. So unusual was it, in fact, that within twenty-five years — during the reign of Charles II's successor, James II — the crown decided to scrap it altogether. In that effort, the Connecticut Charter and the majestic white oak at the bottom of Samuel Wyllys' garden were forever joined in legend.

Trouble began brewing for the Connecticut Colony in 1687, when King James II, in contempt of their chartered rights, appointed Sir Edmund Andros, then governor of New York, as governor of all the New England colonies. The monarch was upset by the number and variety of rights granted to the people by their separate charters, and wanted to bring all of the colonies together under a consolidated patent which made it unequivocally clear that the word of the King of England was law. The colonies would be "encouraged" to give up their charters to the crown. They would then be revoked. For this difficult and demanding job, James had chosen the right agent, for Andros was arrogant, aggressive and tough, with just enough meanness thrown in to make him thoroughly unlikable, but very, very difficult to say "no" to.

Andros began putting pressure on Connecticut by sending messengers into the colony, demanding that the precious Charter under which the people had lived more or less happily for a quarter-century be surrendered to the crown. When Governor Treat (in effect) told Sir Edmund's deputies to take a flying leap into the Connecticut River, they returned, after delivering Treat's reply to the New England governor, with a potent threat from Andros: hand over the Charter immediately or else Connecticut would be officially exterminated. All of the colony's lands east of the Connecticut River would be annexed to Massachusetts, while territory west of the river would become part of New York. Although Sir Edmund was beginning to worry them a bit, Connecticut officials again refused to surrender their Charter.

Andros decided that he had had enough. He would have to unleash the ultimate weapon — himself. He would go to Connecticut and personally demand that the Charter be delivered into his hands. Having warned the colony's officials that he would be in Hartford on October 26, 1687, and that he would address the Assembly on the meaning of treason at Moses Butler's Tavern that evening, he prepared to depart from Boston. They say that never before had the people of Connecticut seen a gaudier show of armed force than Andros' procession across the colony, by way of Norwich, to Hartford. Mounted on a "steel gray horse with tapering ears and crested neck," the New England governor rode at the head of a column of seventy soldiers and two trumpeters, whose scarlet coats and gleaming guns and lances fairly blinded the eyes of the mournful citizens who lined the route. By the time Sir Edmund reached Hartford, according to eyewitnesses, the sullen crowds and long ride had put him in a nasty temper; his always short fuse was burning close to the explosion point.

The showdown at Butler's Tavern made for a striking scene. The falling dusk cast the meeting room in shadows which the flickering candles in two seven-branched candelabra did little to dispel. Governor Treat hunched in his deeply-carved chair at one end of the conference table, while down one side, on backless stools, perched members of the colonial Assembly. Facing them across the board were Andros' minions, their uniforms glowing pink in the candlelight. At the end of the table opposite Treat sat the crown's head man in New England, a cavalier hat with wickedly curling plumes set on his carefully curled locks and a fire that was not reflected candlelight in his beady eyes.

When Andros finally rose to speak, a silence like cold mutton fell upon the assembly. He minced no words. As the duly appointed governor of New England and agent of His Majesty James II, he had come for the Charter. Since James was their king as well as his, Andros said, it would be treason to refuse any longer to surrender the document. He would have them produce it — and quickly — or Connecticut would suffer the consequences of deliberately committing a treasonous act. When Andros was through, Governor Treat seemed to recognize the gravity of his words. He signalled Captain Joseph Wadsworth to fetch the precious charter from its hiding place in a blanket chest at the Wyllys home nearby.

In Wadsworth's absence, a heated debate broke out among the representatives of the Connecticut colony. As Governor Andros watched in stony silence, one after another, members of the colonial Assembly rose to argue the merits of giving over the Charter, or holding on to it, while those in disagreement with each speaker's position shouted insults from their seats. However, when Captain Wadsworth shortly returned and handed the Charter

case over to Governor Treat, the stage was
set for an act so dramatic that it has
lived on in legend to this day. But
whether the action was the result of
careful planning or a lucky accident will
never be known.

James II

As the "conspiratorialist" version of
the story has it, Governor Treat's opening
the box containing the Charter was a
prearranged signal for Guilford's Andrew
Leete to jump to his feet and launch into
a loud tirade against surrendering the
Charter. As he waxed more and more
eloquent, so this story goes, he was to
wave his arms in sweeping gestures and, with a final, convincing swipe, knock
over both candelabra on the table and plunge the chamber into darkness. On
the other hand, the "accidentalist" rendition of the legend says that Leete was
a sick man when he came to Hartford for the meeting with Andros, but, weak
as he was, he felt an obligation to attend and to speak his mind, if the occasion
presented itself. That opportunity arose, they say, just as Governor Treat
received the Charter from Captain Wadsworth. In measured and solemn tones,
the ailing Leete delivered a moving speech in opposition to giving up the
colony's cherished guarantee of rights. But as he voiced the deathly prophetic
warning that "measures obtained by force do not endure," Leete suddenly
clutched at his chest and toppled forward, unconscious, upon the table before
him, tipping over the candles as he fell.

All versions of the story agree on what happened following the loss of
illumination. Taking instant advantage of the darkness and confusion,
assemblyman Nathaniel Stanley seized the Charter and passed it through an
open window behind him to Captain Wadsworth, who had been observing the
scene from outside the tavern when the lights went out. With the priceless
scroll under his arm, Wadsworth raced back to the Wyllys house, where the
Charter had previously rested, and conferred breathlessly with Ruth Wyllys
about where to conceal it anew. They both thought it foolish to hide the
document in the house, for Andros' men would surely search the place where
they knew the Charter had been kept earlier.

Finally, Mistress Wyllys thought of the huge white oak on the hillside
below her house. It was a forest remnant, she told Wadsworth, twisted and
distorted by time and wind, with a crevice near its base large enough to
accommodate the charter case, with room to spare. Stuff the parchment in the

hollow, she urged, and none of the King's men would ever be able to find it. And so, wrapped in Captain Wadsworth's coat, the Connecticut Charter was hidden in the ancient tree, never to be recovered by the tyrant Andros. As it turned out, once he got over his rage at the disappearance of the Charter from the blacked-out room at Butler's Tavern and the fruitless search which followed, Sir Edmund decided to take over the government of the colony, even though he had been unable to lay his hands on the document. And until William of Orange succeeded James II on the throne of England, the people of Connecticut lived daily under the heavy hand of oppression.

Meanwhile, back on Wyllys Hill, the Charter Oak seemed to take a new lease on life, perhaps, some thought, because of the responsibility thrust upon it by the treasure in its bosom. The tree, which in 1687 seemed on the verge of collapse, continued to put out new growth for almost 170 years thereafter, until it was finally destroyed by a great storm on August 21, 1856. Then did the city of Hartford, indeed, all of Connecticut, begin a period of civic mourning. On the day the Charter Oak fell, an honor guard was placed around the remains, Colt's Band of Hartford played a funeral dirge, an American flag was attached to the shattered trunk and, at sunset, all of the bells of Hartford sounded in mourning knell.

From far and near the people of Connecticut came to gather even the smallest fragments of the oak, to hold and to pass along to posterity as precious reminders of their heritage. At least three chairs, including the one used today by the Speaker of the House in the General Assembly, were fashioned from the wood of the Charter Oak, while acorns dropped by the tree were gathered and planted, to produce in time a forest of trees directly descended from the historic oak. In fact, so many relics were said to have come from the fallen tree that Mark Twain insisted they could be lumped together and used as supports for the Connecticut River bridge bearing its name. Given the feelings of affection and respect which have traditionally been accorded the Charter Oak and its dramatic history, the author of *The Adventures of Huckleberry Finn* was probably telling the truth — without "stretching" it at all.

Dudleytown, Cursed Village

O N A HILLY plateau surrounded by four 1500-foot mountains, and overlooking the village of Cornwall Bridge, in Connecticut's northwestern-most corner, there once was a thriving community which seemed — at least for a time — to have all the advantages. Here, long before the white man came, Mohawk Indians hunted the gentle deer and gathered wild herbs for medicinal teas or a tangy root beer, made in the full moon of May or June. Among the great stands of oak, maple and chestnut, the owls which were to give the lasting nickname of "Owlsbury" to the village, hooted mournfully, from the heavy shade of noon to the darkest hours of the night.

As part of the general movement inland from the coastal regions of Connecticut, the first English settlers began to arrive here in the middle years of the eighteenth century. In 1738 Thomas Griffis was the first to take title to real estate on this high land in the southern part of Cornwall township, but he was soon followed by others, families with names like Jones, Carter, Porter, Patterson, Tanner, Rogers, Dibble and others, some of whom would one day find fame in various pursuits.

Not until 1747 did the first Dudleys arrive. Brothers Abiel and Barzillai Dudley, soldiers home from the French and Indian Wars, were joined a bit later by Gideon and Abijah Dudley. Along with other early arrivals, the

Dudleys cleared the land, planted buckwheat, killed deer for their winter food supply and established their farms on the irregular upland plain. Not only were the industrious Dudleys destined to give their family name to the growing community, but also — in the certain estimation of many they were responsible for the "curse" which a century or so later would help transform the thriving village into a crumbling ghost town.

For a hundred years Dudleytown expanded and prospered, thanks to the hard work, strong constitutions and versatile skills of the thirty to forty families who lived there through many generations. During the last quarter of the eighteenth century, many of them prospered from the booming iron industry centered around the great furnace on nearby Mt. Riga. During the Revolutionary War, almost every Dudleytown family augmented its farming pursuits by cutting and burning wood for charcoal to stoke the many furnaces in the area, while some even operated their own backyard smelters, fed by locally-mined ore and heated with local "wood-coal."

By 1800, Dudleytown had its own town hall and meeting house; improved thoroughfares, like Dudleytown and Dark Entry Roads, to accommodate the heavy traffic of horses and riders; and a growing number of quite substantial houses. There was no visible·sign then that the village would ever be anything but permanent and prosperous, its future assured by the abundance of nature and the character of its inhabitants.

Indeed, during its green years, Dudleytown produced an extraordinary number of citizens who went on to achieve fame or to build distinguished careers in Connecticut and elsewhere. For instance, Mary T. Cheney, a native of Dudleytown, went away to teach school and later became the wife of Horace Greeley, founder of the New York *Tribune*, advocate of a western youth movement and unsuccessful presidential candidate in 1872. The village had an even closer brush with the White House when Samuel Jones Tilden, grandson of Dudleytown's Major Samuel Jones, received one less vote than Rutherford B. Hayes in the 1876 electoral college balloting. No one, then, blamed the Dudleytown jinx.

Other Dudleytowners had eminent careers in education, the ministry or the law. Deacon Thomas Porter, churchman, militia captain, selectman and member of the Cornwall School Board, moved north in his later years and became a Vermont Supreme Court judge. His son, Ebenezer, born in Dudleytown, gained national recognition as president of Andover Seminary. He is said to have turned down several offers to become a college president because of a chronic pulmonary ailment. The sons of Andrew Andrews, who moved into Gideon Dudley's place after Gideon's death, became prominent Connecticut lawyers. Benajah practiced in Middletown, while his brother

Andre was Connecticut's State's Attorney, before moving to Buffalo, New York, where he died of cholera. Among Nathaniel Carter's grandchildren was David C. Carter, who became an Arkansas newspaper editor, Chief Justice at the Cherokee Nation and an important figure in national Indian affairs. And one of General George Washington's trusted advisors, General Herman Swift, was an early Dudleytown resident who later removed to another section of Cornwall before finally sitting on the bench of the Litchfield County Court.

Yet, despite the steady rise of Dudleytown and the worldly success of so many of its sons and daughters, dark forces, too, seemed to be operating in "Owlsbury." Something — some malevolent spirit, some terrible ill-fortune — dogged the village's every step forward, until, in the period following the Civil War, that unknown "something" began to catch up with the little town. None could reverse — or adequately explain — the decline and fall of the once proud village at the end of the nineteenth century.

Gradually, the descendants of the original settlers moved away or died, often under tragic circumstances. With no new families moving in to occupy the abandoned homesteads, the houses that had stood for a hundred years crumbled, their massive, hand-hewn beams collapsing into dank cellar-holes, to decay among the shattered shards of vital life, beneath protective blankets of wild tiger lilies. Untrimmed brush and vines turned Dark Entry and Dudleytown Roads into little more than tangled hiking trails, as high in the foliage of the second-growth trees that cast the remains of Dudleytown into perpetual gloom, the inevitable owls pronounced melancholy judgment on the passing scene below.

Grave historians have explained that the death of Dudleytown came as a result of "natural" causes: the opening of great expanses of farmland in the West; improved means of transporting western products to distant markets; the cutting over of the area's forests and the depletion of its soil; the development of the Bessemer process for making steel; the gradual growth of modern industry in urban centers, which caused young people from places like Dudleytown to seek economic opportunity elsewhere. While there may be some truth to the historians' analyses, there are many old-timers in Cornwall today who are convinced beyond the shadow of any academic's doubt that Dudleytown's demise can properly be assigned to only one cause — the "curse of the Dudleys." They will cite chapter and verse (if they will discuss it at all with strangers) to support their belief that from the very beginning, Dudleytown didn't have a chance.

They say that the trouble really started way back in the reign of England's despotic King Henry VII (1485-1509), when some early ancestors of the Dudleys who first came to America met untimely ends. In the early years of the sixteenth century, one Edmund Dudley had his head chopped off on orders of the King, after he made himself a general nuisance among favored members of the court circle.

Later, Edmund's son, John, Duke of Northumberland, plotted to take over the throne from Edward VI by trying to engineer the marriage of *his* son, Lord Guilford Dudley, to Lady Jane Grey, who had been proclaimed queen for a brief time after Edward died. Some say that Northumberland even had a part in hastening the death of the king. In any event, the elaborate plot failed, and both Dudleys and Lady Jane literally lost their heads over the matter.

While all of this was going on, Lord Guilford Dudley's brother returned home from a campaign in France, bringing with him a case of the plague which he promptly passed along to his own troops, killing most of them, as well as thousands of hapless British citizens. To say that the Dudleys were extremely bad news in sixteenth century England would belabor the obvious. The Dudley curse was obviously working overtime!

Still another of Guilford Dudley's brothers, the Earl of Leicester, became a favorite of Queen Elizabeth and never lost his head, but even he finally felt obliged to leave England, under mysterious circumstances, never to return. It was Leicester's direct descendant, William Dudley, who was the first to come to Connecticut, settling in Guilford (where else?), on the shores of Long Island Sound. Three of William Dudley's great-grandsons were the ones who gave their family name to their new home in the Cornwall hills, when they moved there from Guilford in the mid- 1700s.

People say that the curse transported by William Dudley across the Atlantic to Connecticut lay dormant for a while after his descendants moved to Dudleytown. But not many years passed before one of the Dudley brothers, himself, was touched by the family jinx. The victim was Abiel Dudley, who lived on in the village long after his brothers had departed. He was doomed to spend his declining years as a mentally-enfeebled public charge, his properties managed by a custodian named by the town, his failing body farmed out to the lowest bidder at the annual pauper auction. "Old Biel," as he was called, died at the age of ninety, a pathetic pauper.

William Tanner, a neighbor and contemporary of "Biel" Dudley, lived even longer, but for many years before his death at the age of 104, they say he was "half-crazy," and completely dependent upon the constant care of his widowed daughter. Everyone knew that Tanner was never quite right in the head after the murder of Gershorn Hollister, which took place in Tanner's home and generated a lengthy investigation, wide publicity and plenty of small-town gossip.

Bearers of the legend of the Dudleytown curse are even more enthusiastic about the terrible trials of the Carter families than they are about the Abiel Dudley or William Tanner tragedies. Around 1700, one Robert Carter had left his native Bristol, England, and migrated, like William Dudley, to Guilford, Connecticut. In the course of time, two of his sons, Adoniram and Nathaniel, found their way  to Dudleytown, there to raise their families, they hoped, in peace and comfort. Unfortunately, the Carters came to the wrong place.

Nathaniel Carter probably set the curse in motion by purchasing the house formerly occupied by Abiel Dudley and owned by "Biel's" brother, Barzillai, when he moved to Dudleytown in 1759. Married to Sarah Bennett twenty years earlier, Nathaniel had already sired a large family by the time he reached the Cornwall community. Although one of the children died and another married shortly after their arrival in Dudleytown, Nathaniel and Sarah Carter still had five children at home during most of their four-year residence in the old Dudley place.

Then Nathaniel made a fateful decision: in 1763, he and his wife, their daughters, Sarah and Elizabeth, their son Nathaniel and an infant son left Dudleytown to settle near Binghamton, New York. For some unknown reason, their thirteen-year-old son, Nathan, was left behind in Dudleytown. Ironically enough, Nathan turned out to be the lucky one! Anyway, the Carters built themselves a log house in the "Forks of the Delaware" wilderness, and settled down to live happily ever after. Alas, it was not to be.

In October, 1764, while the elder Nathaniel was away from home, a band of hostile Indians swooped down upon the Carter homestead, split the mother's skull with a tomahawk, dashed the baby's brains out against the log walls of the cabin, burned the house to the ground and carried off the three remaining children into captivity. Not long after, Nathaniel Carter was killed and scalped as he returned to the scene of his family's massacre.

The three Carter children were led by their captors into Canada, where Sarah and Elizabeth, with the help of some British officials, were eventually ransomed and returned to Connecticut. However, neither ever recovered from their terrible ordeal. According to historical annals, Sarah was "a stark mad thing until her death," while her sister eventually married, but remained a semi-invalid for the rest of her life.

Young Nathaniel, on the other hand, took to the Indian life, becoming a member of the Cherokee tribe, marrying an Indian woman and living with a branch of the Cherokee nation for the remainder of his days. Although Nathaniel never returned to Dudleytown, it was his son, Ta-wah, christened David C. Carter when he attended the Indian Mission School in Cornwall, who later became the editor, jurist and advocate of Indian rights mentioned earlier.

Meanwhile, during all the misfortunes of the Nathaniel Carter family, things did not go well back in Dudleytown for another branch of the Carter family. In 1774, just ten years after the Indian massacre in New York State, a horrible but unidentified epidemic struck the Dudleytown household of Nathaniel's brother, Adoniram. Before medical assistance could be obtained, Adoniram Carter, his wife and only child were wiped out. It just went to show, they say, that whether people remained in the village for a brief period or a lifetime, there was no escaping the Dudleytown curse.

Through the early years of the nineteenth century, the jinx continued to take its toll in the unfortunate town. An epidemic in 1813 was far worse than the one that struck down the Carters, with fatalities numbering in the scores, including several in the pioneering Jones family. Later, one of Dudleytown's greatest celebrities, Revolutionary War hero Gen. Herman Swift, became half-demented in his old age, especially after one of his several wives was struck and killed by lightning. There are also folks willing to blame the curse of their Dudleytown associations for the political misfortunes of Horace Greeley and Samuel Jones Tilden. They will also make a point of noting that Dudleytown native Mary Cheney Greeley died only a week before her husband was disastrously defeated for the presidency by U. S. Grant, and that Greeley himself died soon afterward.

By the end of the nineteenth century there was very little left of Dudleytown for the malevolent curse to work on. Nevertheless, it had a few gasps left. One of the last people to feel its sting was a solitary farmer, an immigrant from Poland, who saw in the abandoned farmland and deteriorating homestead of the former Rogers estate an opportunity to make good in his adopted country. He worked hard at pasturing sheep, but within a few years, they say, he became discouraged, gave up the farm and went elsewhere to seek his fortune. His departure left only one family living in Dudleytown: Patrick Brophy, an Irish laborer, his wife and two sons. They didn't last long, though. The boys were discovered stealing some sleigh robes down in Cornwall and rapidly left the area, just ahead of the law. Their mother worked too hard, ate too little and died of tuberculosis soon after her sons' flight. Finally, in 1901, after his house burned to the foundation, Brophy threw in the towel: he left Dudleytown forever. And then there was none.

Well, almost. Although the last resident of Dudleytown came to the deserted and overgrown village only in the summer, his story is in many ways the most bizarre of all. His name was Dr. William C. Clark and he was a prominent physician with a busy practice in New York City and a professorship at a city medical college. One day while he and his wife were scouting Litchfield County for a piece of property on which to build a country retreat, fate brought them to the old ghost town high above Cornwall Bridge. It was love at first sight.

Dr. Clark bought a great tract of land hard by Dark Entry Road, cleared a pleasant lot on a shady hillside, laid pipe to an icy, ever-flowing spring at the crest of the hill and built a rustic cabin from the hemlock he had cleared from this land. Although he may have wondered why he was unable to employ any local labor to assist him in constructing his dream hideaway, Dr. Clark enjoyed the hard physical labor — and never asked questions. Finally, down by the brook at the foot of his hill, he prepared a swimming pool, with banks of thick, green moss and crystal water which he was delighted to share with the gleaming brook trout which swam there. When it was completed and his beautiful wife joined him for a first satisfying splash, the Clarks agreed that this was as close to heaven as either of them was likely to come. Even the owls high in the overarching trees seemed to share their delight.

For many summers, as local residents waited for the old Dudleytown jinx to show itself, the Clarks found nothing but peace, rest and happiness at their camp in the woods. Then one day, quite unexpectedly, it happened. Dr. Clark was called back to the city on some medical emergency or another. They say that as he and his wife waited at the station for the train which would take him away, Mrs. Clark clung to him tightly, begging him to return to her at the earliest possible moment. Witnesses reported that as the train pulled out, the doctor's wife stood for a very long time, looking down the track toward the departing train, before slowly moving to return to her lonely "Owlsbury" cottage.

Dr. Clark completed his business in New York in short order, returning to Cornwall within thirty-six hours. But when nobody met him at the station, he hurriedly walked to the opening at Dark Entry Road and plunged into the shadowy woods. Except for the hooting of owls, all was quiet as he entered the clearing where his summer cottage stood. No sign of life greeted him as he ran, terrified, across the lawn to the cabin. But as he pushed open the front door, which had been left slightly ajar, he heard a sound that he would never forget. From an upstairs room came the maniacal, uncontrolled laughter of one who had taken leave of her senses. During his absence, his wife had gone quite mad.

Some seventy years have passed since Dr. Clark put a padlock on the last inhabited house in Dudleytown and returned to the city. No one today remembers the exact location of the old farmhouses or the graves where so many heroes and victims lie buried. An occasional curiosity-seeker will make his or her way along the overgrown rocks that mark the last vestige of Dark Entry Road, poke around in some cellar holes full of decaying debris, take a few snapshots that somehow never come out, because even at high noon on a sunny day it is too dark in Dudleytown. But the folks who live in the shadow of the ghost town on the hill know that the only thing permanent about the place are specters from the past, the mourning owls, and, of course, the legend of the Dudleytown curse.

"Swamp Yankee"

*T*HE WORD "SWAMP" used in combination with another word to form a derisive term is well known to students of American language. For example, one leading authority on the origin and use of names has recorded such terms of disdain as "swamp angel" (for a member of a Reconstruction-era anti-black group); "swamp Democrat" (for a rustic follower of Jacksonian politics); and "swamp rat" (for a Southern backwoodsman of the 1860s) — all expressions familiar over broad regions of the country during various periods in our history. On the other hand, there was also "Swamp Fox," the admiring nickname attached to Gen. Francis Marion, the famed American guerilla leader who gave the British fits when he struck from South Carolina swamps during the Revolutionary War.

But the origin and meaning of "swamp Yankee," a term often applied with mixed tones of disapproval and grudging respect to a type of rural Connecticut character, have stumped even the experts. One reason for such puzzlement may be that the expression has never had very wide distribution. In fact, "swamp Yankees" seem to be almost unknown outside of Connecticut, especially eastern portions of the state, and some areas of adjoining Rhode Island. But within the confines of that region, the term is known by almost everyone who has lived there for any length of time. Newcomers to the area who may have lived previously in every section of the United States have been particularly intrigued by the evocative term, since they have never heard it before moving to the Nutmeg State. Over the years, their questions about the significance and source of "swamp Yankee" have sent historians and linguistic geographers thumbing through notes or reference books — with rather uncertain results.

There does seem to be some agreement about the kind of person generally tagged as a "swamp Yankee." In doing some personal research on the subject, *Hartford Courant* columnist John Lacy asked a number of people to explain their understanding of the expression and reported a few responses in an April 30, 1982 feature. A newspaperman who grew up in Rhode Island told Lacy the term was applied to "Anglo-Saxon farmers in South County there." A New London journalist believed it referred to "a Yankee from poor origins, who had to really hack it out of nothing," while a librarian said it described "a person who lived in woodland swamps and who became fiercely independent, stubborn, obstinate and uninformed of what was going on in the outside." Fair enough.

There is also good reason to believe — because of the curious parochialism of the term — that "swamp Yankee" was born in Connecticut over two hundred years ago, in the wake of a little known incident which took place in what was then the northern parish of Killingly and is now the town of Thompson. Though the event had certain parallels with the celebrated Windham frog fight episode, unlike the latter situation, there were apparently no storytellers or poets around at the time to spread the legend. Thus, about the only thing that has been handed down from the Thompson incident is the elusive "swamp Yankee" expression. But what an enduring tradition that has been!

They say that the summer of 1776 was a terrible time for the people of New England, generally, and the citizens of Connecticut, in particular. Having made very heavy commitments of men and arms to the Continental forces fighting in the New York City area, the people back home in the towns and villages of the Nutmeg State were shocked when tidings reached them of the disastrous defeat at Brooklyn and the withdrawal of the American army from Long Island.

Eastern Connecticut soldiers in the Continental Line had suffered particularly heavy losses, and in August, General Washington had ordered to the field most of the remaining home militia units to serve as replacements or to help regulars cover the retreat. But for many of these men, too, the fighting around New York City would prove their last, as hundreds were killed, wounded, captured or felled by disease. News of these continuing calamities cast a pall over Connecticut towns when it inevitably reached the folks back home.

As summer passed into fall, each mail delivery brought new word of tragedy home to Connecticut — and mounting tension. Captain Nathan Hale had been hanged as a spy. Brave leaders like Ashford's Col. Thomas Knowlton and Thompson's Capt. Stephen Crosby were killed in action, leaving a total of fourteen children fatherless and home towns plunged into mourning. Letters from men in the retreating Continental army inevitably carried news of friends or relatives killed, rotting away on British prison ships, suffering from grievous wounds or dying from the diseases rampant in the crowded army camps. To many, it seemed that the American cause was teetering on the brink of disaster.

Along with the bad news arriving daily from the field, the domestic rumor mills were churning out loud alarms. The victorious British, they said, would sweep unmolested through Connecticut, since virtually every able-bodied man between sixteen and sixty was away with the fighting forces, leaving only aged men, invalids, women and children to defend the towns. In Thompson, the word was passed that some fifty slaves owned by Godfrey Malbone, the powerful Tory of nearby Brooklyn, had joined with remnants of the Nipmuck Indian tribe and were coming toward town, burning homes and slaughtering every hapless soul they found on the way. British regulars, even Hessians, people thought, might listen to reason, but only butchery might be expected from heathen blacks and savage redskins!

As fear approached panic on Thompson Hill, two ordinarily innocuous incidents triggered a strange stampede. First, an insolent boy in neighboring Dudley, Massachusetts, was knocked down in a fight with a suspected Tory. At about the same time, a dispatch rider with urgent messages from Boston galloped through town, in too much of a hurry to answer any of the anxious questions shouted at him as he flew by. In the pressure-cooker atmosphere which prevailed at the time, only one conclusion could be drawn: the Tor-ies were coming, the Tor-ies were coming! With no fighting men around, no guns and no ammunition, it now seemed to some of the first families of Thompson that their only salvation lay in flight — into the great, dismal swamp nearby, where no Tory, or British regular, or black or Indian would dare follow. So, a young boy was quickly sent forth to urge all citizens to head for the marshes.

To be honest, the lad's call to the swamp fell on a few deaf ears. Down at Larned's store, Rebecca Larned, wife of an absent militia officer, who had been left to tend both home and business, refused to flee in the face of the impending invasion. Instead, she built a huge fire in the kitchen, filled the fireplace with kettles of water and every iron tool she could find and said she would stand off the invasion with scalding water and hot iron, if necessary. Her mother-in-law, "Old Granny" Leavens, widow of the first William Larned of Thompson, kept an equally stiff upper lip. Having survived two husbands and several Indian attacks, "Old Granny" was not about to be moved by British, Tories, blacks or Indians. She just lay back in the chimney corner and snorted, "If I *am* to be killed by the Tories tonight, why then I *shall be; so* I'll just stay with Becky."

They say that at least one other Thompson family refused to rally in the swamp that day. Joseph Gay, seventeen-year-old son of Deacon Gay, had seen his father and four older brothers called to active duty and leave for the front. Left to protect farm and family, Joseph thought that hot irons, swamps and even muskets were pretty feeble instruments of defense. So when the call came to retreat to the marshland, he calmly harvested through the day, completed his chores and then, having gathered his large family in the kitchen for the usual evening prayers, read them "many comforting words" from the great family Bible, which had always proved their mightiest weapon against adversity. No Gay left the farm that night.

But, according to tradition, with the exception of the Larneds, the Gays and maybe a few other staunch souls, the folks around Thompson Hill heeded the swamp call in unseemly haste, "a most forlorn and panic-stricken company." "You tell Becky Larned that hot irons will never do for the British," the women warned, as they approached the damp and dismal dark. And poor, lame, old "Uncle Asa," hobbling along on legs crippled by gout caused by too much flip-drinking, was heard to complain to the woman assisting him, "Thithter, I've forgot my plathter. My plathter, I say." But she only muttered back, "Hurry up, there Asa, or you'll never dress your knees in *this* world again." When the pathetic congregation finally reached their destination, they found the swamp so moist and unpleasant that all could join old "Aunt Nabby" in her heartfelt offer to "give a wedge of goold [sic] as big as my foot for just one little dram right now." However, for Nabby and the rest, there would be little comfort of any kind that night.

Everyone knows, of course, that neither Thompson nor any other Connecticut settlement was invaded by marauding British or their sympathizers in that autumn of 1776. When the sun shone bright on the day after the retreat into the swamp, it burned away the fogs of terror that had blanketed most of Thompson's citizens for weeks. In little groups of two and three, the chastened refugees emerged from their dark hiding place, covered with mud and bramble scratches, and straggled back to their homes and farms.

They say, however, that almost none of the fugitives managed to reach home without being bombarded by the laughter and shouted barbs of those who had remained behind.

"Look at them swamp Yankees," went one cry. "Swamp Yankees, for a fact," echoed another. And so it went, until the fright and flight and ridiculous sayings of the original swamp Yankees were known all over northeastern Connecticut. And when the stories were repeated in letters to the troops in the field, they brought forth about the only real laughter heard that fall in the grim camps of Gen. Washington's battered army.

The Church Stove War

*H*ARD AS IT may be to believe it today, one of the hottest controversies to stir up the congregations of many colonial Puritan churches had nothing at all to do with theology. Rather, the question of whether or not to install a stove in the meeting house to warm worshippers during winter services got the good people of New England all steamed up. Apparently, pro-stove factions won a few eighteenth century victories — The First Church of Boston was said to have ordered one of the earliest in-house heaters in 1773 — but since creature comfort was widely believed to interfere with the Lord's message, most New England congregations piously froze through the lengthy services well into the nineteenth century. As one anti-stover put it, "Good preaching keeps me hot enough."

Though the best story about a church-stove battle has been told about a number of New England congregations, there is pretty good evidence to support the belief that it originated in Litchfield, during the ministry of the fiery and famous Rev. Lyman Beecher. At any rate, his son, the equally-renowned Rev. Henry Ward Beecher, always attributed the legend to the Litchfield society when he recounted it, as he often did.

It seems that there had for years been growing support for the introduction of a stove in the old Litchfield meeting house. However, the conservatives were stubborn, and efforts to persuade the congregational society to purchase a stove continued to be unsuccessful. As the verbal warfare between pro- and antistovers grew more and more intense, seven young men of the congregation decided to take things into their own hands. Between them, they purchased a stove and, after much difficult negotiation with the committee of elders, received permission to place it in the meeting house — strictly on a trial basis. This was done on a Saturday afternoon. The following day, the youthful pro-stovers gathered early to watch the reactions to their new installation.

Sunday dawned rather warm for a November day and by the time the first worshippers arrived for services, the sun had been shining brilliantly for some time through the church's naked windows. As people slowly entered, they paused and stared at the stove, set squarely in the middle of the broad aisle. Then, as they took their seats in the pews, they watched in wonder at the various responses of the more rabid pros and antis. Old Deacon Trowbridge, one of the worthies who had been persuaded to give up his opposition to the infernal combustion device, nevertheless shook his head as he felt the heat reflected from it, and gathered up the hem of his ancient greatcoat as he passed up the aisle to the deacons' seat.

Uncle Noah Stone, a wealthy farmer from the west end of the parish, who sat almost next to the stove, scowled and muttered at the effects of the heat, but waited until the noon intermission to voice his complaints over nut-cakes and cheese. Mr. Bunce, editor of the local newspaper and a leading pro-stover, lingered conspicuously beside the stove as he passed up the aisle, and, with obvious satisfaction, rubbed his hands together over the heater while carefully keeping the skirts of his greatcoat between his knees so they would not burn. But the climax of the whole spectacle came in the middle of the post-nooning services. The congregation watched in amazement as Mrs. Peck, a notorious anti-stover who had been perspiring and fanning herself for hours, finally fainted dead away from the heat.

Only then did the original instigators reveal the secret they had kept since installing the stove the day before. When they invited members of the congregation to step up and actually place their hands on the burner, the worshippers were shocked to learn that it was stone cold. Because of the warmth of the day, no fire had ever been set in the controversial stove! Needless to say, that Sunday marked the final day of Litchfield's great church-stove war.

The
Dark Day

*A*BRAHAM DAVENPORT, A long-time Councillor of the colony and later of the State of Connecticut, was a man distinguished by his vigorous understanding, uncommon firmness of mind and Christian integrity of character. A resident of Stamford, he was the grandson of the Rev. John Davenport, one of the founding fathers of the New Haven colony and a man who had played an important role in the "Great Shippe" disaster. Abraham Davenport was the central figure in two stories celebrated in literature and legend and traditionally cited to illustrate the constancy of Connecticut character.

As a matter of fact, one of the Davenport tales, the story of Connecticut's "Dark Day," has become so much a part of the state's lore that the event's bicentennial was remembered by special ceremonies in the House of Representatives of the Connecticut General Assembly on February 27, 1980. Although the memorial occurred somewhat prematurely because the legislature would not have been in session on the actual anniversary date, legislators were reported to have listened in hushed fascination as House Speaker Ernest Abate of Stamford recounted the legend of his illustrious fellow-townsman from an earlier time.

They say that during the first two weeks of May in 1780 the skies over much of New England had been so dark that people had difficulty conducting their daily affairs because of reduced visibility, even during the sunniest days. Many of the good Puritan folk saw in the lowering heavens a sign of God's displeasure. While the actual cause of the unnatural lack of light has been lost to history, both widespread and unchecked forest fires spreading their leaden smoke over the land and a complete eclipse of the sun, especially on the ultimate "Dark Day," have been cited by chroniclers as possible sources of the phenomenon.

Be that as it may, as the Connecticut General Assembly began their deliberations on May 19, 1780, the chambers of the State House in Hartford grew so dark that it seemed as if the sun had been turned off. Reports came from those who had been outside that the streets of Hartford, too, had been reduced to inky blackness. In many homes candles flickered in windows, birds were silent and disappeared, and fowl retired to their roosts. To many members of the legislature, devout Puritans as they were, it appeared that the promised Day of Judgment was at hand.

Probably as much out of general consternation as out of inability to conduct business in the dark, the House of Representatives adjourned. In the Council, however, it was a different story. There, advice on how to proceed under such trying circumstances was sought by the members from their most respected colleague, Abraham Davenport. With scarcely any hesitation, the worthy Stamford lawmaker answered: "I am against adjournment. The day of judgment is either approaching, or it is not. If it is not, there is no cause for an adjournment; if it is, I choose to be found doing my duty. I wish therefore that candles may be brought." That settled it. The candles soon dispelled the dismal gloom, deliberations continued, and a bill amending an act regulating the shad and alewife fisheries passed the Council that very day.

Needless to say, news of Colonel Davenport's decisive words received wide circulation. Not only did their repetition become a source of pride for his fellow citizens in Connecticut, but they also inspired John Greenleaf Whittier, one of New England's best-loved poets, to celebrate them in verse many years later, thus perpetuating the legend well beyond its time of origin. The final lines of Whittier's "Abraham Davenport" (1866) summed up the sentiment attached by the folk to Davenport's speech that black day:

> And there he stands in memory to this day,
> Erect, self-poised, a rugged face, half seen
> Against the background of unnatural dark,
> A witness to the ages as they pass,
> That simple duty hath no place for fear.

Revered throughout Connecticut for his courage and foresight during the famous "Dark Day" episode, Abraham Davenport spent his final years as Chief Justice of the Court of Common Pleas. In this capacity Davenport once again affirmed the value of devotion to duty, even under dire circumstances.

As the story goes, the venerable Chief Justice was "struck with death" (i.e. suffered a serious heart attack) while hearing a case in Danbury. Since the trial was only well-started at the time of his illness, the judge refused to be relieved from the bench until the case went to the jury. While in obvious and severe pain, he heard a considerable portion of the trial, gave the charge to the jury and even called the jury's attention to an article in the testimony which had escaped the notice of lawyers on both sides of the case. Once he had discharged his judicial obligations, however, Justice Davenport immediately retired to his chambers, lay down on a couch and died. The people of Connecticut would not soon forget the example of Abraham Davenport.

Laddin's Leap

*F*OR FOUR YEARS after the first Dutch and English families began to settle Greenwich in 1640, they had a terrible time with the Indians (and vice-versa). In part, the problem was the result of a comparatively large population of native Americans who called Greenwich home. Altogether, it has been estimated, between 500 and 1000 members of the Miossehassaky, Petuquapan, Asamuck and Patomuck tribes permanently occupied the southern portion of the present Town of Greenwich. Here they fished the Sound or the Mianus River, hunted the mountains far away to the north and raised their children in small villages scattered from Cos Cob to the Byram River. Since they rather enjoyed their pleasant life-style, the Indians were understandably reluctant to stand around and cheer as Europeans, in increasing numbers, cleared and built houses on their ancestral lands.

Another reason for the "Indian troubles" was the very considerable consumption of rum by the native population. The "cussed firewater," as the Indians allegedly called it, was sold to them by the Dutch in New Amsterdam, always to the advantage of the sellers and the detriment of the buyers. Not only did the Dutch city-slickers build a lucrative furs-for-rum business for themselves, but the liquor also made the Indians so crazy that they were easily "skinned" in business deals or, often enough, robbed of their valuables while under the influence. The story is told, for example, of one Greenwich Indian who was hastily stripped of his prized beaver-skin outfit, after two Dutch

160

traders had plied him with rum until he fell unconscious. This time, however, the red man had the last laugh. After he sobered up, he tracked down the Dutch fur thieves, planted his tomahawk in each of their heads and then fled to a distant tribe.

But the most significant contributor to the bad blood between whites and reds was neither European encroachment nor New Amsterdam rum. Rather, it was William Kieft, the governor of New Netherlands, a pantalooned dictator who prided himself on his ability to outsavage the "savages" any day of the week. Unlike his good-natured predecessor, Wouter Von Twiller, who took a live-and-let-live attitude toward the natives, Kieft was cruel and revengeful in the extreme. Having selected a half-dozen like-minded advisors, director Kieft dealt with Indians in somewhat the same way as Hitler handled Jews.

The high point of Kieft's career probably came in 1643, after the Mohawks from upper New York State attacked two of the small Hudson River tribes, killed their warriors and forced the survivors to scatter in utter destitution to find food and shelter among the Dutch of New Amsterdam and vicinity. Secretly, the governor called his advisors in and together they plotted a proper welcome for the starving Indian refugees in their midst. Dutch soldiers were sent out in the dead of night to locate as many sleeping Indians as possible and to bash their heads in with clubs before they knew who or what hit them.

Kieft's caper was enormously successful. Not only were more than a hundred Indians sent to the happy hunting grounds, but also the massacre was conducted so secretly and with so much strategy that the Indians believed for some time that the Mohawks had carried out the cold-blooded killings. Even the Dutch population was, for a time, so deceived. However, public misconceptions about who was responsible for the bloody affair did not remain for long.

Within a week or so after the mass slaying, local tribesmen learned that at the time of the murders, no Mohawks had been within a hundred miles of New Amsterdam. It soon became evident to the Indian population that whites, not reds, were behind the mindless massacre. The Indians reacted with a vengeance. With incredible speed, warrior pledged to warrior, and clan to clan, revenge against the white man. Within a very short time, an army of 1500 Indian fighting men, representing a confederation of eleven Connecticut and New York tribes, was prepared to search out and destroy their common enemy, wherever he or she could be found. Then, from Manhattan to Stamford and from Long Island to the Hudson River, a fierce war raged. Coastal Connecticut was ravaged, as Dutch and English alike answered for the genocidal act of Governor Kieft and his bully-boys.

The 1643-1644 warfare spawned many stories, of course. They recounted with depressing sameness incidents of housewives murdered while their children watched; children abducted or brutally killed; white men tortured, scalped and slain; houses and worldly possessions reduced to smoldering ashes. Everywhere, the accounts added up to the same story: the Indians were rapidly evening the score with the hated paleface. However, as frequently happens when people are in desperate need of a hero to give them hope when the tide seems to be running against them, the bad times on the southern Connecticut shoreline generated just such a figure, in a legend that has been passed down from generation to generation, with widely varying details, for more than 300 years.

While the hero's name was really Cornelius Labden and he was known as "a rough old Dutchman," the tale of his extraordinary adventure with the Indians was told so often by English-speaking folk that the Anglicized name *Laddin* became standard wherever the legend was known. In fact, in the version which follows — an adaptation of the legend which appeared in the *Stamford Advocate* in 1854 — the Dutchman has actually become an Englishman! But as always with folk narrative, such details are of no consequence. Now, to the story.

Soon after the Dutch first settled New York, a few English families migrated from other parts of Connecticut into an eastern section of Greenwich. Here they began a settlement on high ground which commanded an extensive view of the shoreline and Long Island Sound. The names of those pioneer settlers have long since been forgotten, with the exception of a man named Laddin, who, with his wife and lovely sixteen-year-old daughter, had located a short distance easterly from the main settlement. For a time, people in the little hamlet lived in peace and security, but only a few years passed before their quiet life was seriously disturbed by hostile Indian neighbors, stimulated by the Dutch to deeds of violence and revenge against the English.

One day, when Laddin was off clearing and cultivating a field away from his farmhouse, he was surprised to see dense clouds of smoke rising from the area where the village was located. He knew Indians had struck. Realizing that they would not rest until every house in the area was torched, he dropped his plow and ran, sometimes stumbling in his haste, back to his own home, prepared to defend it and his family to the last breath.

Scarcely had Laddin rushed inside, barricaded the doors and loaded his trusty musket, when the Indian war party arrived. Their passions aroused by the English blood already spilled that day, they surrounded the house, yelling and whooping, expecting to watch with great delight the easy destruction of yet another white man's home and family. But they didn't count on the fierce determination or the splendid marksmanship of the English farmer.

As Laddin blazed away at the Indians from one front window, they hung back in momentary confusion and even huddled to plan their next move. Finally, one of their fiercest warriors began a stealthy advance toward the house, a lighted torch in his hand. When he was only a few feet away, Laddin dropped him with one shot from his musket. The torch fell harmlessly to the ground and went out.

But the Indians would not be denied the satisfaction of seeing more palefaces writhing in flames, as their burning home crumbled around them. Another warrior volunteered to follow in the footsteps of his fallen comrade. With one shot Laddin sent him reeling backward, with a heavy groan, upon the body of the first victim. Another quickly followed, then another, and another; all shared the same fate. Finally, with unearthly yells, the remaining warriors charged the intrepid farmer's house *en masse*. When a half-dozen finally reached the house, they banged away at the barricaded door with frenzied screams and unbridled fury.

In the midst of the incredible confusion, Laddin's wife and daughter begged him to save himself and leave them to the mercy of the Indians, but he refused, saying he preferred death with them and for them to a possible life without them. Finally, though, Laddin was persuaded to make an escape attempt, believing that there was a faint chance the Indians would respect the women and spare their lives, if he were not there with them.

As the Indians began to move the barricade at the front door and Laddin's wife and daughter struggled to brace it against the onslaught, he realized that the back door was momentarily unguarded. With extreme reluctance the despairing man sprang softly through the rear entrance, making his escape, just as the front door gave way to the savage attack of the Indians. Then, while Laddin watched from hiding in nearby undergrowth, the Indians dragged his wife and child from the house by their hair, tomahawked and scalped them. There was nothing he could do to help.

Quickly, Laddin made his way to his horse, which he had concealed a short way off in an alder thicket, and mounted, ready for flight. However, in some confusion about what direction to take, he waited too long to spur his steed and was spotted by the Indians running from the scene of the massacre, after setting fire to his house. With despair etched on his face, Laddin suddenly turned the horse's head toward the high, sheer precipice which fell away below the smoldering remains of the village, resolved to deny the pursuing warriors the satisfaction of one more white victim — or die in the effort. Boldly, he galloped into the grove of trees which concealed the edge of the steep precipice below. Finally he stopped, as if to dare the fast-closing Indians. Turning toward them he shouted, "Come on, ye foul fiends, I go to join your victims." Then he dug his heels into the horse's flanks — and plunged over the brink.

Before the Indians realized that they had been lured to the summit of a hundred-foot drop, it was too late. In their lust for English blood, four of the pursuers followed Laddin off the high cliff and crashed to their deaths on the rocks below. They say that a fifth pursuer managed to grab a tree at the fifty-foot level and thus save his life.

Despite what he had just been through, however, Laddin knew exactly what he was doing when he dove over the edge of the rock wall. Since he knew the cliff intimately, he had at the last second urged his horse far to the left, where he could expect to land on soft, swampy ground rather than on ledge and boulders. While his mount was killed, Laddin did survive his daring leap, although many of his bones were broken and, according to some who knew him, his mind was permanently affected by the fall.

Thus, it remained for the one Indian survivor of the incident to return to his tribe and tell the story of the crazy white man who jumped off a hundred-foot cliff and, in so doing, helped in a small way to even the score with his enemies.

Yankee Doodle Dandies

*I*N 1756 A call went out for volunteers to form a Yankee brigade which
would be attached to British forces fighting the troublesome French
and Indians in the on-going wilderness war. From the villages and
farms of Connecticut, the eager young recruits straggled in to the advertised
place of assembly, the Norwalk home of the group's commanding officer,
Colonel Thomas Fitch, son of Connecticut Governor Thomas Fitch. As the
Nutmeg irregulars finally gathered in Col. Fitch's yard prior to setting out
for Fort Crailo, across the Hudson from Albany, New York, to join the British
regulars, they were about as unmilitary-looking a group as had ever been seen
in America.

Dressed in the clothes they wore when they left their farms, mounted on
horses only recently released from plowing duty and armed with muskets
designed more for shooting game than Frenchmen and Indians, the ragged
little band awaited their marching orders. But before they pulled out,
Elizabeth Fitch, Col. Fitch's sixteen-year-old sister, and some other young
women who had come to bid them farewell, became appalled by their motley
appearance. Crying, "You must have uniforms of some kind," Elizabeth led the
girls into the Fitch chicken yard, where they gathered enough feathers for all
hands. "Soldiers should wear plumes," insisted Elizabeth as she and her
friends distributed the chicken feathers and ordered each rider to put one in
his hat band.

When the curious Connecticut cavalry finally swung proudly into Gen.
Abercrombie's headquarters at Fort Crailo, the British soldiers were wildly
amused. Nothing seemed more ridiculous to the spit-and-polish regulars than

the thought of having to fight at the side of these colonials whose only distinguishing uniform item was a chicken feather.

"Dudes! Dandies! Popinjays!" called the fine, red-coated soldiers as they gathered about the new arrivals in camp. Dr. Shuckberg, a British army surgeon, was overheard to exclaim, "Why, stab my vitals, they're macaronis!", sarcastically applying the London slang of the day for fop, or dandy, and even provincial troops from Massachusetts and Rhode Island picked up the refrain: "Macaronis! Macaronis, for certain!" As the lads from Connecticut joined in the general merriment which their arrival had created, they heard young Dr. Shuckberg begin to sing the words to a little jingle he had made up on the spot to celebrate the occasion and set to the tune of an old, familiar folk ditty called "Lucy Locket Lost Her Pocket:"

> *Yankee Doodle came to town*
> *Riding on a pony.*
> *Stuck a feather in his hat*
> *And called it macaroni.*

So much for legend. The rest, as they say, is history. The nonsense song caught on like no other in American history. It not only survived the French and Indian War, but became the rallying song for colonial troops during the Revolutionary War and Union Army forces during the Civil War. American soldiers in World Wars I and II carried it to international fame. It helped to disperse the Yankee tradition across the northern section of the nation and ultimately made the term "Yankee" synonymous with "American."

While he might overstate the case a bit, historian W. Storrs Lee has also seen "Yankee Doodle" as a peculiarly representative Connecticut contribution to the field of culture and the arts. "Yankee ingenuity," Lee concluded, "did not flow in the direction of sublime artistry.... The Connecticut creative artist was droll, whimsical, original, but he shied away from the pretty and the elegant as he would from idolatry." In other words, making a "macaroni" out of a rough farm lad with a chicken feather might not have been an act of sublime art, but it may have been a profound expression of the creative spirit of Connecticut. Perhaps some subconscious realization of this inspired the Connecticut General Assembly, after years of petty wrangling, to agree finally in 1979 to make "Yankee Doodle" the official State Song.

Legends of Pirate Gold

FROM STONINGTON (Lambert's Cove) to Milford (Charles Island) — and a score of shoreline sites between — they have searched with spade and pick, following the dream. Along the Connecticut River, too, they have gouged and plumbed the storied spots from Old Lyme (Lion's Rock) to Windsor (Clark's Island), caught in the spell of the old stories handed down from generation to generation. What force has sent so many forth with tools in hand and spines atingle to probe the margins of Connecticut's tidal waters? What else but the lure of buried treasure, the legacy of the legend of Capt. William Kidd and his fabulous pirate hoard.

Never mind that their labors have not been in tune with history, for tradition ever scoffs at historical fact and often transcends the limits of common sense. For the record has proved time and again that despite his reputation, the redoubtable Kidd accumulated little booty from the time he began his buccaneering in New York harbor around 1698 until he was captured and permanently put out of business in the summer of 1699. Moreover, such treasure as Kidd did have — twenty four chests full of it — was all brought ashore on Gardiner's Island, off eastern Long Island, carefully inventoried and, with the permission of John Gardiner, feudal lord of the island, buried in a swamp there. Gardiner's itemized receipt to Kidd, dated July 17, 1699, listed precisely 1371.625 ounces (85.73 pounds) of gold, silver and precious stones.

Before he sailed off, never to be seen again, Kidd warned Gardiner that if he ever revealed the burial site, he would "answer with his head." However, that proved an idle threat, for Capt. Kidd was captured soon after leaving Gardiner's Island; and from the time of his arrest until he was hanged in London in 1701, he was always in safe custody. Meanwhile, the governor of the

Massachusetts Bay Colony sent messengers to Lord Gardiner, claiming Kidd's treasure for the state. Once Gardiner was convinced that Kidd was secure in a Boston prison and could not come for his head, he reluctantly showed the colony's officials the spot where the chests were buried. All of the treasure was then dug up and returned to Boston. Wrote John G. Gardiner, over a hundred years later, "There has been much digging here upon this island for Kidd's money, even within half a dozen years, all along the coast. But I think it doubtful whether there was ever any buried except that which was buried here [i.e., on Gardiner's Island]."

Despite the testimony of the Gardiner family and the records of the Massachusetts Bay Colony, the dream of pirate gold has never died along the Connecticut shore. And in a way, there is more reason to believe the old tales of buried treasure here than in the rest of New England, for Capt. Kidd and other less noted buccaneers did, in fact, cruise Long Island Sound. And if they chose to secrete any ill-gotten goods, what better places could be found than the coves or islands of Nutmegian waters? And so the old legends persist at Milford, where town records say Capt. Kidd visited on at least two occasions, once striding boldly through the coastal town, tipping his hat in courtly fashion to the ladies who came to gape. Some say that he later wrote a letter to one lovely Milford maiden, while others claim that he made the mistake of leaving part of a treasure map with a local woman named Ann Smith, who betrayed him to the authorities.

Most of the Kidd-talk in Milford, though, has insisted for years that the fabled pirate buried treasure on Charles Island, perhaps under a huge boulder called Hog Rock. So many have searched in vain for the storied swag on Charles Island that its surface has been turned into a many-pitted wasteland, where no vegetation grows. Still, the dreamers dig on, paying no heed to the well-known story of the two treasure hunters who once uncovered an ironclad chest on Charles, only to abandon it in terror when they saw a shrilly whistling, headless body, wrapped in a flaming sheet, plunge toward them from the heavens as they lifted the box from its hiding place. Feeling the next day that they must have been out in the sun too long, the treasure-seekers returned to the site of the discovery, only to find no sign of the chest, the burial hole or the shovels they had abandoned in their flight. Some legends maintain that the spirits of Paugasset Indians, who once used Charles Island as a summer resort, beheaded the pirates for desecrating their land and made invisible any treasure buried there.

Way up-river in Windsor, too, the traditions live, swirling about Clark's Island, where once Kidd's sloop *San Antonio* was anchored, while her skipper and crew came ashore with a huge chest, bulging with gold. Those who tell the story say that the moon was dark and fog hung low over the Connecticut River as the shadowy figures went to work preparing a hole for their precious hoard. Once the treasure was safely deposited, the pirates were seen gathering around their captain, to draw lots to determine which of their number would stay behind permanently to guard the site. The man who drew the short straw was promptly shot and killed, his body was lowered onto the sunken chest and both were covered with six feet of earth. Tradition says that the murdered pirate's protective shade guards Kidd's treasure yet. No one has ever found it, anyway.

Over the years, reports have circulated among those who live along the Connecticut River — and near the mid-section of the Connecticut shore — that on dark and foggy nights they have seen a great ship pass by, flying the pirates' skull-and-crossbones emblem. Since popular belief holds that ghosts of those who have stolen money during their lifetimes but have not returned it must forever wander the earth at night, they say the phantom ship is the *San Antonio*, with Capt. Kidd at the helm, searching for lost and nearly forgotten treasure troves. Find the booty, the believers say, and Kidd can "pass over" in peace.

If such be the case, his ghost will surely stop at old Wethersfield landing, where searchers after his casks of gold have been frustrated for years by horrible noises and once, according to a terrified digger, by the ghost of a sailor killed with a water bucket wielded by Kidd in a fit of anger. He may also drop a spectral anchor at Haddam Neck, where legend says that his men buried two chests in a hill, under an overhanging ledge, west of Clarkhurst Road. And while he is in the neighborhood, perhaps Kidd's shade will visit Haddam and Lord's Islands, where, according to the old tales, rich chests were buried long ago.

Then, on to Branford's Thimble Islands the spectral ship will sail; Kidd's ghost will find on Money Island that his precious gold is still there. And so it remains, too, under the great rocks on Coburn's Island in Clinton, near Hammonassett Beach. But when he reaches Pilot Island off Norwalk, the old pirate's ghost may be disappointed. For after the Civil War, it is said, Captain Joseph Merrill dug up a hoard of Spanish coins, after he had three dreams revealing the exact location of the treasure. As recently as the 1930s, a few old-timers in Norwalk could still recall childhood memories of Merrill, telling the story of his find and even showing them some gold doubloons.

If the Norwalk cache was really Kidd's — who knows who hid it there? — it would be, in fact, the only one ever found since old John Gardiner gave over those twenty-four casks to the Massachusetts Bay Colony. Thus, the ghostly pirate ship must sail on in its endless guest, while along the shores of

Connecticut waters the legends still whisper to the adventurous to take up their shovels and follow the gleaming lure.

But wait! No survey of Connecticut pirate treasure legends can be complete without recounting the tale of what might have been the richest buried treasure ever recovered in the Nutmeg State. Given all that digging along the shores and all the speculation about Capt. Kidd, it is both strange and ironic that the discovery was made more than thirty miles inland from the nearest tidal waters, and had nothing to do with the ubiquitous Kidd. For this is the legend of Blackbeard's booty, buried in a granite-walled excavation in Hampton, and discovered — or was it? — less than sixty years ago.

Before he died in the fall of 1939, a man named Cady owned a property in the Howard's Valley section of Hampton long known as the Jewett homestead. In his final days, Cady was fond of telling the tale of a stranger who came to his house one evening in 1938. Although Cady lived alone and was somewhat wary of strangers, there was something about his visitor that inspired trust, the homeowner said, and so he asked him in. The stranger, who gave his name as Barney Reynolds, proceeded to tell Cady a remarkable story. Reynolds was, he said, a direct descendant of the notorious Capt. Edward Teach, known wherever sailors spun their yarns as "Blackbeard," the meanest, most ruthless pirate who ever sailed the Spanish main. Cady's visitor said that he had recently inherited a treasure map, handed down from Blackbeard himself, which unquestionably placed a buried hoard somewhere on Cady's property.

When Reynolds spread the yellowed map upon the Hampton man's dining room table, Cady said he could scarcely believe his eyes as the stranger showed him landmarks etched on the parchment which pointed to the exact location of the buried treasure: in the dooryard of a house, a stone shaped like a horse's head; following a line southeast-by-south across the road, a boulder, perhaps chipped purposely, resembling a dog's head, pointing south; and, across a small brook, on a line bearing right, a fish's head, the eye, realistically placed on the low stone, looking directly at the treasure pit, just twenty paces due south. Cady's heart beat faster, he said, for he immediately recognized them all! They were, indeed, on his land.

Reynolds then proposed a deal. If Cady would provide him with the proper digging tools and promise not to bother him until he had excavated the site where Blackbeard's treasure was buried, he would split the hoard with the landowner, fifty-fifty. Cady agreed, and the following morning Reynolds tramped off across Cady's land, headed for the boulder with the fish's eye. Two days passed, the Hampton man said, and he began to wonder how Reynolds was doing. After a third and then a fourth day went by with no word from Blackbeard's relative, Cady's curiosity got the better of him. Even if it meant giving up his share of the booty, he had to find Reynolds and check his progress.

Quickly he followed the trail marked on the old map, until he reached the place where he knew Reynolds was working. But when he got there, an astonishing sight met his eyes. There was a pit fully eight feet deep and about five feet square, the walls lined with large slabs of smooth granite too perfectly placed to have been naturally formed. Over the pit lay timbers rigged in such a way as to hoist a flat capstone which topped the vault and lay on the ground nearby. All around the in-ground vault Cady's tools were scattered, as if dropped in haste. There was even a pair of muddy boots at the bottom of the hole. But most alarming of all, Cady recalled, there was no sign of Reynolds. And, indeed, the owner of Blackbeard's map was never seen again. "No one ever knew whether he found the treasure or where he went," Cady said.

Why were pirates so far inland? And what was Blackbeard doing in Hampton? Cady had a theory. Between 1713 and 1718, Capt. Teach was known to have pirated West Indian shipping. He may well have anchored off New London, unloaded his portable booty and made his way northward over the old Nipmuck Indian trail, either to reach Boston by way of an overland route, or more likely, to evade pursuers. Near the "Canada settlement" in Hampton, Cady theorized, the pirate party crossed easterly to reach the North and South Road, later the King's Highway, which, in turn, led to the Connecticut Path to Boston. Or, if he were so inclined, he could have doubled back to New London by the east route, originally the old Tatnick Trail, from Worcester to Norwich. The Cady home was just off the Nipmuck Trail, near a place where many paths intersected. Thus, Blackbeard, wishing to lighten his load before heading for Boston or back to New London, designed the elaborate burial pit, made the map and buried his treasure. And there it lay, Cady thought, until Reynolds took it away. But, then, like everything else connected with pirate gold, this is only the way the story goes.

The Phantom Ship of New Haven

THE REPUTATION AND worldly wealth of the Rev. John Davenport, Samuel Eaton, Edward Hopkins and others from the city of London who were determined to establish a "plantation" in New England in the mid-1630s were such that the people of the Massachusetts Bay Company sought their presence with unabashed enthusiasm. But, while Charlestown made them "large offers," and Newbury offered to give them the whole town, the Rev. Davenport's congregation wanted to plant a distinct colony. Thus, in the spring of 1638 a very distinguished group of Englishmen arrived at the head of the shallow harbor formed by the confluence of the Quinnipiac, Mill and West Rivers and began a settlement soon to be known as New Haven.

Although the original colonists were shortly joined by others from the general London area, the New Haven colony did not flourish according to the great expectations of its founding families. Competition in trade from the high-powered merchants of Boston to the north and the canny Dutch of New Amsterdam to the south sapped the wealth of the New Havenites. As a spiritual leader of the colony, the Rev. Davenport prayed fervently and often for an improvement in their fortunes and as political leader sought to enhance the colony's competitive position by a 1644 order that all males between the ages of sixteen and sixty spend four days shoveling mud out of the harbor to increase the channel depth for larger, deep-draft ships. But in those early years the economic path lay mostly downhill, despite all the efforts of God and man in New Haven.

Finally, in 1646 a group of New Haven merchants, banded together as the Shippe Fellowship Company, engaged a Rhode Island builder to construct a ship which they hoped would reverse the colony's trade decline. By January, 1647, the 150-ton cargo vessel had been loaded heavily with about all the tradeable goods the people of New Haven could scrape together; more than a half-dozen of the colony's most prominent citizens were aboard for the trip; and the maiden voyage of "The Great Shippe" was ready to begin. But because the members of the company were better businessmen than they were sailors, the obstacles in the way of a successful journey began before the ship left the dock.

In the first place, January was probably the worst month of the year in which to venture forth on the North Atlantic. In fact, the vessel was iced in so solid at her pier that a three-mile channel had to be hand-chopped through the ice before the "Great Shippe" could reach the open waters of Long Island Sound. Worse yet, the ship had to be towed stern-first through the ice, causing near-mutiny among crew members, who universally believed that beginning a voyage backward was a bad omen.

Worst of all, once the vessel finally reached the choppy waters of the Sound, it had a disconcerting tendency to roll at a frightening angle. Even the ship's master, George Lamberton, an experienced mariner, predicted many times that the "walty" (unstable) ship would "prove their grave." But, despite all the errors in judgment and signs of doom, the "Great Shippe" finally sailed into the icy mists of Long Island Sound, the tears and fears of the large group gathered to see them off echoing only faintly astern. After all, crew and cargo were under the protection of Divine Providence, to whom the Rev. Davenport had raised his glorious voice in prayer as the ship weighed anchor: "Lord if it would be thy pleasure to bury these our friends in the bottom of the sea, they are thine; save them!"

With the fate of the New Haven colony — not to mention the lives of many of her most influential citizens — riding on a successful voyage, little wonder that news of their trading ship was awaited with the keenest anticipation by the people of New Haven. Each new arrival from England was questioned anxiously, but the winter months passed, spring moved toward summer and no tidings of the vessel's fate reached the Connecticut settlement. As a contemporary chronicler said, "New Haven's heart began to fail her: This put the godly people on much prayer, both publick and private, that the Lord would (if it was his pleasure) let them know what he had done with their dear friends."

Then, on a humid June day, some six months after the "Great Shippe" had departed, New Haven was struck by a very heavy thunderstorm that rolled in from the northwest in the late afternoon. An hour before the late June sunset, the storm had passed and the air was calm, but the towering thunderheads still hung over the harbor mouth and the Sound to the south of the village. Soon, a rumor spread which turned New Haven into a joyous community of thanksgiving: their lost ship had been sighted emerging from the clouds in the harbor and driving toward the settlement with all sails set and flags flying. Scores of people rushed to the waterfront to witness this miraculous answer to their prayers.

The goodly assemblage watched in hushed awe as the full-rigged vessel, riding a sea of clouds, sailed majestically toward them, a strong wind billowing her sails — even though she was evidently running *into* the prevailing northwesterly breeze. Then, as the vessel came as close to shore as the water depth allowed, the main topmast seemed to break off, fall and become entangled with the lower sails. As dusk approached, it appeared to the spectators that other spars, masts and sails began to carry away, until the specter ship became little more than a derelict hull. Many said that they saw a human figure on the bow of the vessel, sword raised and pointing toward the sea, just before the ship finally rolled over on her side, shuddered once and disappeared into the mists that surrounded her.

From the time of the ship's first appearance to her evaporation in the fog, perhaps thirty minutes had elapsed. Since all of the remaining clouds dissipated and the atmosphere became clear before complete darkness set in, the mystified onlookers sought some sign of wreckage or debris in the now calm waters of the harbor. They found none.

All who bore witness to the events in New Haven harbor agreed, however, that the ship they had seen was, indeed, their own "Great Shippe" and that God, in his inscrutable way, had explained to them what her fate had been. While the Rev. Davenport exhorted his congregation to rejoice and thank God for the "extraordinary account of his sovereign disposal" of their friends and relatives, the loss of the "Great Shippe" almost rang a death-knell for the infant New Haven colony. A hundred years passed before the Connecticut plantation could bring itself to build another trading vessel for trans-Atlantic commerce.

The Winsted Wild Man

MOST PEOPLE IN Connecticut would never associate the fabulous, giant man-beast made famous by wilderness legends from around the world with their own heavily populated, highly urbane state. Unlikely as it may seem, however, reported sightings of a creature much like the "Abominable Snow Man" (yeti) of the high Himalayas or the elusive "Bigfoot" of the Olympic Peninsula in Washington have a long tradition in the Nutmeg State. And since these reports have for almost a hundred years, now, concentrated on the Winsted area of Winchester, the mysterious, man-like monster has been dubbed "The Winsted Wild Man."

One of the earliest published accounts of the wild man appeared in the August 21, 1895, edition of the Winsted *Herald*. Written by editor Lou Stone, well-known in the area for his fund of tall stories about unusual events, the article described what happened on one recent day to Selectman Riley Smith when he went to Colebrook on business. Along the road, according to Stone, Smith stopped to pick blueberries and "his bull-dog, which is noted for its pluck, ran with a whine to him and stationed itself between his legs. A second afterward, a large man, stark naked, and covered with hair all over his body, ran out of a clump of bushes, and with fearful yells and cries made for the woods at lightning speed, where he soon disappeared." Selectman Smith estimated that the odd creature was at least six feet tall and ran upright, like a human.

While the wild man may have made intermediate appearances between 1895 and the early 1970s, he again attracted press attention in late July, 1972, when reports came from Winsted that a strange, man-like creature had been spotted early one morning by two young men, on the Winchester Road near Crystal Lake Reservoir. It seems that Wayne Hall, 19, of the Winchester Road, and his friend David Chapman, 18, were at Chapman's house, sitting up late and talking, on the night of July 24. Early the following morning, the young men were startled by "weird noises outside." "It sounded like a frog and a cat mixed together," said Hall, "a real weird sound like when a frog blows up and makes a lot of noise."

The two friends looked out the window in the direction of Crystal Lake and at some distance saw what both described as a figure "about eight feet tall and covered with hair." Because of the distance and the dim light, however, they could make out only arms, legs and a head. No face was visible. As the two youths watched from the window, the wild man came out of the thick woods from the area of Crystal Lake, crossed the road and entered the shadows near a lighted barn where Albert Durant of Winsted kept race horses.

"It was kind of stooped," Hall reported, "but more upright. It was hairy; I would say black. It never crouched down; it was always upright. Once in a while, it would reach up and scratch its head." Asked if it might have been a large, black bear, he replied, "It was no bear." Chapman and Hall observed the monster for almost forty-five minutes as it alternately entered and emerged from the shadows around the Durant barn. Finally, it went back across the road and into the dark woods toward the lake.

A little more than two years later, in late September of 1974, the Winsted Wild Man was spotted again, this time when he came out of the woods early in the morning of September 27 and struck terror into the hearts of two couples who had been parking near the Rugg Brook Reservoir. Press accounts of the sighting quoted Winsted patrolman George Corso, who, while cruising about 2:30 a.m. on Main Street, had been flagged down by two obviously agitated Harwinton men and told about their very recent encounter with a six-foot, 300-pound creature covered with dark-colored hair, at the edge of the reservoir. "They were terrified," Corso reported, and when one of them persuaded the police officer to return with him to the spot where the wild man had been seen, the young man insisted that all the cruiser doors be locked before they left town for the three-mile drive to the reservoir. Although Corso thought that a creature as large as the one described could rip off the cruiser's doors whether they were locked or not, he humored the Harwinton youth anyway. "He was really shook," Corso explained.

As they drove toward the reservoir, the informant told the policeman that earlier in the evening, he and his friend and their dates had decided to park for a time by the lake. It had been a bright, moonlit night. After they stopped, one of the men got out of the car. Suddenly, he saw the creature emerge from the nearby woods and start to walk toward the car, its eyes eerie in the reflected moonlight. The young man leaped back into the car and the badly frightened foursome beat a hasty retreat.

When the squad car finally reached the reservoir embankment where the monster had last been seen, the young man suddenly shouted, "There it is now. Don't stop." Corso quickly turned the cruiser around, and though he carefully searched the area to the water's edge with his spotlight, saw nothing. Although he finally gave up the fruitless night search, after sunrise Corso returned to the scene of the sighting, along with a newspaper reporter. Neither could find any sign of what the couples had witnessed, not even a giant footprint in the brush-covered, hard-gravel surface of the reservoir bank. The police concluded that the parkers had probably seen a black bear, but everyone agreed that they *had* seen something very unusual. Winsted desk sergeant David Gomez remembered that the young man who made the initial report told him, before returning home to Harwinton, "I will never in my life go up there again."

Hoax? Hallucination? Black bear? Escapee from a zoo or circus? Perhaps. But one thing is sure: no one who has claimed to have seen the Winsted Wild Man seems able to forget it.

The Hessian Husband Kidnappings

WHEN THE BRITISH under General "Gentleman Johnny" Burgoyne surrendered to the Revolutionary Army troops at Saratoga in 1777, it proved to be both a crucial victory in the Revolutionary War and, a short time later, a lesser-known but delightful victory for some lonely maidens in Canton and Simsbury. Now it so happened that among the forces that had fought their way from Montreal to Saratoga with Burgoyne were some 4000 Hessians, German mercenaries hired by the British to assist them in stamping out the Colonial rebellion. After this huge group was taken prisoner at Saratoga, the victorious Americans decided that the best way to dispose of "the Hessian problem" was to march them on over to Boston, where they would be loaded aboard ships and sent home to Germany.

So, in small detachments of twenty or so, the Hessians were herded toward Boston along the old North Road through Connecticut, guarded, some say, none too carefully by their captors. As the captive soldiers trooped through Canton and Simsbury, they fell under the approving inspection of some of the young women of the villages. Remember, for quite a long time these and other New England maids had been living in places where most of the young men were either away fighting the redcoats or had gone west to settle new territory. So, when a whole army of able young men suddenly appeared at their very doorsteps, the eager women saw them not as foreigners and former enemies, but as highly eligible bachelors on the hoof.

Tradition has it that at least twenty percent of one particular Hessian detachment had mysteriously disappeared by the time the group decamped from Simsbury for Boston. Rumors circulated for years that the German lads had been spirited away at night by the most love-crazed ladies in the area and, what's more, the kidnap victims had put up very little resistance. There may be little truth to this story, but in later years, the peculiar popularity of sauerbraten and dumplings in Canton and Simsbury made people wonder.

Barkhamsted Lighthouse

SOMETIME AROUND 1740, give or take a few years, there lived in the town of Wethersfield a full-blooded Narragansett Indian who went by the unlikely name of James Chaugham (probably pronounced "Shawm" or "Shawn"). Born on far-away Block Island, the young man had somehow found his way to Connecticut's second oldest community, adopted the ways of his white neighbors and, through hard work and a pleasing personality, established himself quite well in their regard. If he fancied the English-sounding name "Chaugham," they said, why not let him use it?

During this same period, there was growing up in a proper Wethersfield family a young woman named Molly Barber. Like some teenagers from time immemorial, Molly provided her family with almost more headstrong personality than they could handle, particularly when it came to men in her life. One day she announced that she was planning to marry a young man whom she knew her father was not too fond of. As she expected, Mr. Barber denied his daughter permission to marry the man of her choice, whereupon Molly threw an old-fashioned temper tantrum. Among other things, she vowed that if she could not wed her current boyfriend, she would henceforth marry the next fellow who asked for her hand, no matter what kind of person he was or — and she knew this would get to her father — what his racial origins might be.

Well, since Molly promptly began broadcasting her availability around town, it didn't take long for the word to reach the ears of young James Chaugham. One thing led to another, as they say, and before Mr. Barber could do anything about it, Molly and James were united, privately and secretly, in holy matrimony. Then, maybe to avoid her father's wrath or ostracism by a disapproving community, or perhaps just to find privacy for their new life together, the newlyweds left Wethersfield and headed north into the howling Connecticut wilderness, up around the Massachusetts border.

Some say that they first moved in with some Indians who lived in a little cabin on top of one of the hills above what is now the Barkhamsted Reservoir. But it is more likely that they picked out a homesite on the side of Ragged Mountain, overlooking the West Branch of the Farmington River, about two miles south of Riverton, in an area which today is part of the Peoples State Forest. In this remote country, with not another permanent neighbor within miles, the Chaughams cleared a plot of land and built themselves a log cabin. It was said to be the first home in the town of Barkhamsted. In this place, the Wethersfield emigrants raised eight children, six of whom grew up, married and continued to live nearby their parents' house, in what became a veritable village of Chaughams.

From the beginning, they say, the original log dwelling served as a welcome landmark for the occasional travelers passing along the desolate north-south trail which followed the West Branch of the Farmington. Not only did the house have a number of windows, but it was also not very tightly chinked; so the cooking and heating fires burning day and night, winter and summer, glowed so brightly through the various openings that passers-by began to refer to the lonely cabin as the "Barkhamsted Lighthouse."

In later years, when the Hartford-Albany turnpike was built along the Farmington River, it passed directly below the Chaugham cabin. With the increased interstate traffic, the fame of the Lighthouse spread, because drivers on the stages making their way south over the toll road would always watch anxiously for the light streaming through the walls of the Chaugham cabin, and when they finally saw it, they would shout to the passengers, "There's Barkhamsted Lighthouse; only five miles more to New Hartford the end of the route."

Apparently Molly and James got on well with folks in their region, even though their nearest neighbors were probably down in New Hartford. In fact, they say that James Chaugham would always light a signal fire on the top of Ragged Mountain, up behind his cabin, whenever he learned that the New Hartford settlement was under threat of Indian attack. Then the New Hartford residents would gather in the fortified house they had built to protect themselves from the occasional sorties by hostile Indians out of Satan's Kingdom, and wait for the Indians to appear or the danger to pass. The people of New Hartford had great affection for the keepers of the Barkhamsted Lighthouse.

Sad to say, the reputation of the Lighthouse as a welcoming or warning beacon in the northern Connecticut darkness failed to survive after the death of Molly Chaugham — known and loved in her last years as "Old Granny" Chaugham — at the age of 105, in 1820. While the descendants of James and Molly lived on for several generations in and around the Barkhamsted Lighthouse, the "Lighthouse Tribe," as they were called, turned out to be a wild, rough and roistering clan, with an appetite for booze, brawling and burglary. One tradition even suggests that local folk believed that the Chaugham posterity had somehow mysteriously disappeared and that the Lighthouse had been taken over by a bunch of robbers who committed numerous acts of violence in the region. When the alleged robber gang later disappeared as well, rumors spread that ghosts of the Chaughams had returned to avenge themselves on those who had turned the Lighthouse site to such evil purposes. One dark and moonless night, so the story went, the spirits killed and scalped every one of the wicked bandit band.

More than likely, however, the Lighthouse Tribe and the legendary criminal gang were one and the same. An 1854 article on the Lighthouse colony gave a vivid account of the depths finally reached by descendants of the romantic Wethersfield refugees. Four or five shelters still remained, reported the *Mountain County Herald*, "built after an architecture about halfway between a wood pile and a rail fence." The inhabitants, the report went on to say, "have a look of utter desolation and destitution. Around this place are about twenty-five half-clad human beings of every possible race, from that of the African to the Anglo-Saxon and Indian. All during the year, winter and summer, some of these may be seen peddling baskets and brooms and receiving food and clothes in return." Another nineteenth century commentator added: "Some of the Chaugham posterity have become civilized enough to try the old game of wrestling with a whiskey bottle, and with the same result — to get thrown — and they are not the only natives of this town who have seemed to try to see how poorly and meanly they could live, and had great success follow their efforts."

Obviously, the chances for long-time survival of the Lighthouse Tribe were pretty dim, and, to the relief of everyone and the surprise of no one in Barkhamsted, the last vestiges of the Chaugham presence had completely disappeared by the 1920s. So ended the luminous legend of the interracial lovers which had begun nearly two hundred years before in Wethersfield.

Escape from
New-Gate
Prison

*T*TWO YEARS BEFORE the first shots of the American Revolution were fired, the Connecticut General Assembly decided that what the colony needed most was a good, heavy-duty gaol (this was before the days of j-a-i-l-s). Up to that time, the county gaols had been the only places available for the confinement of convicted criminals. But these filthy lock-ups were always filled to overflowing, despite the fact that many cells were periodically emptied as inmates died in droves from the insect or rodent-borne diseases then rampant in them. In their wisdom, the legislators decreed that any new prison would have to meet certain specifications. It would have to be fairly close to Hartford; absolutely escape-proof; self-supporting (i.e., inmates would have to be "profitably employed"); and — most important of all, then as now — cheap to build and maintain.

Next, some lawmaker had a brainstorm. He remembered that up in what were known as the "Turkey Hills" of northern Simsbury (now East Granby) there were some abandoned copper mines which had been sporadically dug with disappointing results since early in the century. Maybe one of those old mines would fit the requirements for a gaol specified by the General Assembly. Since this seemed like a fine idea, the legislature immediately appointed a three-member study commission to "view and explore the copper mines at Simsbury... and consider whether they may be beneficially applied to the purpose of confining, securing and profitably employing such criminals and delinquents as may be committed to them." So, off went the commissioners, into the Turkey Hills.

When they filed their report with the Assembly a few months later, it was obvious that the study group had been mighty impressed with the prison potential of a many-shafted mine that ran deep under a mountain called, appropriately enough, Copper Hill. Only eighteen miles from Hartford, the mine boasted at least one cavern, twenty feet below ground, large enough to accommodate a "lodging room" sixteen feet square. There were also lots of connecting tunnels where prisoners could be gainfully employed by having them pick away at the veins of copper ore located there.

Better yet, according to the report, the only access to the mine from outside came from two air shafts: one, twenty-five and the other, seventy feet deep, the latter leading to "a fine spring of water." Still better was the £37 total estimated cost of mine-to-gaol conversion: £17 for the underground room, and £20 for the "doors" to cover the outside access holes. But best of all, the commissioners crowed, "When completed, it will be next to impossible for prisoners to escape." Why, concluded the legislature, this old mine was almost more suitable for "beneficial" prison application than they could believe!

By October of 1773, the government had obtained a lease from the landowner at Copper Hill, carpenters had built the lodging room and workmen had fitted a heavy iron door into the twenty-five-foot air shaft, six feet beneath the surface. In the same month, also, the General Assembly designated the place as "a public gaol or workhouse, for the use of this Colony"; named it "New-Gate Prison," after London's dismal house of detention; and appointed a Master (or Keeper) and three Overseers to administer the gaol. In addition, the legislature was thoughtful enough to provide for a "skillful miner or miners," to be named by the Overseers and paid out of prisoners' wages, to "instruct or assist the prisoners in their work." Once John Viets had been approved as New-Gate's first Master, and despite a disturbing (then, as now) £74 cost overrun, Connecticut's answer to the infamous "Black Hole of Calcutta" was ready for business — just in time for Christmas, 1773.

Now, the General Assembly did not establish New-Gate as America's first state-run gaol just to provide secure confinement in a temperature-controlled environment for Connecticut's run-of-the-mill "criminals and delinquents." Only men (never women) who had been convicted of the most dastardly crimes known to the colony — burglary, robbery, counterfeiting or passing funny money and horse-stealing — were eligible for a one-way trip down the twenty-five-foot hole in the ground into the state's dank, dark "prison-without-walls."

Chosen for the dubious honor of being New-Gate's first prisoner was one John Hinson, a twenty-year-old man about whom — considering his historic, "ground-breaking" status — surprisingly little is known. Convicted for some unrecorded crime and remanded to New-Gate by the Superior Court on December 22, 1773, Hinson spent exactly eighteen days in the "escape-proof" gaol, before departing quietly for parts unknown, apparently during the early morning hours of January 9, 1774. Although no one saw him leave, obviously, there was some evidence that he had used the seventy-foot well shaft to climb out of the mine, a difficult but not impossible feat, given Hinson's youth, diminutive size (5'6") and compelling motivation.

Immediately after discovering that their one and only charge had flown the coop, the prison Overseers contacted the General Assembly with the startling news. Naturally, the legislators were incredulous. How could Hinson have escaped so easily and speedily? Hadn't the original study commission predicted that breaking out of New-Gate would be "next to impossible"? Didn't the General Assembly spend top dollar (or pound) to make sure that criminals who were sent down that hole in the ground, stayed down there? Tough questions, but the prison officials were equal to the challenge: the legend of the "evil-minded" accomplice was born.

Since there was no wall or enclosure of any kind around New-Gate's grounds at the time, it was a simple matter, so the story ran, for someone to walk up to the deep but coverless well shaft, drop a rope down and pull the prisoner out of the underground gaol. Since the natural barriers were so forbidding, the argument continued, no man could have escaped without some sort of "outside" help. Therefore, concluded the Overseers, Hinson must have had assistance in his climb to freedom and subsequent disappearance. But who would do such a dangerous thing? Back came the age-old answer: *cherchez la femme*, especially one who would risk all for love.

So compelling was this romantic, though fanciful, scenario that as it received wider and wider circulation, it began to be repeated as fact. Not only was the heat gradually shifted from the prison administration to the legendary "dark lady of New-Gate," but the tradition of John Hinson's shadowy accomplice gained a firm hold on the folk imagination. Indeed, as the tradition continued, variations on the legend evolved. One of the more interesting variants attributed the "dark lady's" motivation not to love, but to "scruples against solitary confinement!" Thus, as this story went, the woman accomplice acted as a matter of conscience: "it was not good for man to be alone."

As a consequence of the successful escape of John Hinson and, three months later, three more New-Gate prisoners, probably by the same route, the Connecticut General Assembly reluctantly came to the conclusion that two holes and an underground mine do not necessarily a prison make. So they ordered a series of modifications that included, in 1802, the erection of a high stone wall around the prison. Despite all the new security arrangements, however, those who were confined at New-Gate never tired of making strenuous efforts to leave. Few were successful after the improved security measures were taken, but a number of them were said to have happily died trying.

Finally, in September, 1827, after almost fifty-four years of operation, during which well over 800 prisoners were committed to its clammy subterranean dungeons, New-Gate Prison was abandoned and the remaining inmates were transferred to the new state prison at Wethersfield. Significantly enough, the last escape attempt occurred on the night before the move to Wethersfield, when a prisoner fell back into the well — and drowned — as he tried to emulate old John Hinson, of sainted memory. Coming when it did, at the bitter end of the facility's long, dark history, the death was a tragic, but somehow fitting reminder of New-Gate's most enduring legend.

Legends of
Mt. Riga

L IKE SO MANY other things in the wild, mountainous area around
Salisbury, in the northwestern-most corner of Connecticut, the origin
of the name of Mt. Riga has remained a mystery — and inspired a
legend. Some authorities claim that the 2000-foot elevation north of Salisbury
village, once the location of America's most important iron furnace, was
named by Swiss or Russian immigrants who arrived in the years before the
American Revolution to work as charcoal burners and forge hands in the
Holley and Coffin works at Forge Pond, near the summit of Mt. Riga.

Here they labored beside native Yankees to turn the local brown hematite
ore from the pits of Ore Hill or Lime Rock into iron of great tensile strength,
suitable for implements of farm and home and, later, cannon and musket
barrels to help free those farms and homes from British rule. It was the Swiss
workers, some say, who first dubbed their mountain workplace "Rhigi"; while
others, just as certain, maintain that the Russians, perhaps remembering the
port city on the Baltic Sea from which they had departed their homeland, were
responsible for giving Mt. Riga its name. Still others are satisfied to let the
naming remain an enigma, in keeping with the area's reputation for
nourishing the unexplainable.

Whatever the case, Mt. Riga's furnace for almost a hundred years
provided the Salisbury area with a strong economic base, unprecedented in a
community so small and remote. Here, during the Revolutionary War era,
were forged the cannon that frustrated the British fleet at Stonington; the
sabers swung by Sheldon's Horse, Salisbury's elite fighting unit; and the great
anchor of the frigate *Constitution*, so heavy that it took six yoke of oxen to drag
it away from the slopes of Mt. Riga. Even after the war was won, the boom
begun by munitions went on in the Mt. Riga region, fueled by the endless call

for hoes and scythes, axe blades and bell clappers, rifle barrels and plows — all the wrought metal goods needed to tame a wilderness and settle a new nation.

As the "woodchuck holes" grew deeper and deeper in the hills around Salisbury, area furnaces annually poured more than two thousand tons of iron into the national manufactory — and countless golden dollars into the pockets of the local iron masters. The story goes that Salisbury has no central green because the founders were too busy making money at their ore pits and furnaces to bother planning one. And when the first minister was invited to the settlement, they say, he had to sleep for some time in the corner of a blacksmith shop, until his parishioners could find enough time away from their forges to build him a parsonage.

As the nineteenth century began, however, a combination of factors began to spell the slow decline of the industry that made Salisbury the "Pittsburgh of Early America." Since it took 250 bushels of charcoal and three tons of ore to produce a ton of cast iron by the primitive methods then employed, there came a time when the area hardwoods were depleted and the ore pits cleaned out. Hauling both charcoal and ore up the side of a mountain became clearly uneconomical. The forge on Riga closed for a time.

When new owners took over, they found that the steam pumps which had for so long kept water out of the pits were no longer serviceable. However, just about the time the new electric pumps recommended by works superintendent John Monohan were ready to operate, an underground river apparently opened up, flooding the pits and nearly drowning workers who had to scramble for their lives. Monohan blamed "The Spirit of Riga" for the disaster. Said he, in despair, "There's a million dollars' worth of new machinery down in the bottom level of them woodchuck holes!"

Whether it was the disappearance of natural resources, the economic demands of a changing market or, as John Monohan believed, some evil spirit at work, there can be little doubt that the perfection of the "Bessemer process" of making steel was the straw that broke the sagging back of the Salisbury iron industry. Ironic this was, too, because one of those instrumental in developing the steelmaking process in American was Alexander Lyman Holley, a Salisbury native! Finally, in 1847, the fire that had cast its glow over Forge Pond for nearly a century was banked for the last time. The thriving village beside the pond near Mt. Riga's summit began to empty and crumble, soon to be reclaimed by nature. By mid-century the blue smoke which had hung low over the Salisbury hills for as long as anyone could remember, was seen no more.

Even before the collapse of the region's iron industry, the proper people of Salisbury began to take notice of a strange, dark breed of short people who inhabited tiny farms and isolated shacks scattered through the many little glens on the lower slopes of Mt. Riga. No one really knows where they came from — or when — but because they were said to speak a gutteral-sounding language and live in ways alien to the native Yankees, the belief was widely held that they were Hessian deserters from the British army, stragglers from Lafayette's forces or York State Dutchman (or a blending of all three ancestries).

During the heyday of the Mt. Riga iron works, these mountain people worked as wood-cutters, charcoal burners, ore carriers and forge hands. They associated only with one another, apparently intermarried, tended their tiny farm plots and minded their own business. Because of such strange behavior, the "Raggies," as they were called by the affluent Yankees of Salisbury, were regarded by the townspeople with suspicion, spoken about in whispers and even thought to have supernatural powers. The possibility that these dark people were somehow in touch with unearthly forces seemed to be confirmed by the persistent rumors floating around Salisbury that the Raggies and other residents of the slopes of Mt. Riga had frequently seen ghosts flitting through their isolated glens, especially on still, moonlit nights.

The presence of the supernatural at work in Raggie-land was further confirmed in 1802 when several buildings up in Sage's Ravine were involved in a mysterious stone bombardment, or lithobolia, which amazed the neighborhood and frightened residents for years to come. The strange phenomenon began between 10:00 and 11:00 p.m. on the bright, moonlit night of November 8, in S. Sage's clothier's shop. A man and two boys were in the shop, with the boys having retired to rest, when a block of wood came flying through a window, noisily shattering the glass. After that came pieces of mortar, until the man in the shop became so concerned, that he sent the boys to the owner's house nearby to inform him of the situation. After Sage arrived, he was alarmed to see the glass in his windows occasionally break, as if struck by some object; but though the night was bright with moonlight, he was unable to discover the source of the objects striking his store, try as hard as he might. At daylight the bombardment ceased, but it began again at 9:00 p.m. the following evening and lasted until midnight. For two more days it continued, starting and stopping a bit earlier each day.

On the fourth day, the phenomenon moved about 100 rods north to the home of Ezekiel Landon. Here the Landon family was treated to on-again-off-again glass breakage, both day and night, for a period of several days. Finally, the bombardment ceased altogether. The objects thrown into the Sage shop included wood, charcoal and stone, but mostly pieces of hard mortar of a sort never seen in the area before or since. The Landon house was struck only by stones, the first of which came through the door. Altogether, thirty-eight panes of glass were smashed in Sage's shop and eighteen in the Landon home. Several times persons in both places were struck by the unidentifiable flying objects, but injuries were slight.

As news of the ghostly bombardment spread, hundreds of people, including many ministers, were said to have come to Sage's Ravine to observe the stone and mortar barrage. What made every witness wonder was the fact that nothing could ever be seen coming toward a window until the pane actually shattered, and whatever passed through the window fell directly down on the window sill, as if placed there by human fingers. Frequently, pieces of mortar or charcoal were thrown through the same hole in the glass in rapid succession.

Many explanations were offered by those who observed the mischief, but none ever took satisfactory account of all the abnormal characteristics of the flying missiles. Eventually, the shower of stones was attributed by many — including some clergymen — to witchcraft or diabolical hands. Unlike the violent lithobolia inflicted upon the Walton family of Portsmouth, New Hampshire, in June of 1682, however, the Salisbury missile bombardment was never attributed to a specific witch or stone-throwing imp.

The population of Raggie-land was greatly increased after the failure of the iron industry in the Mt. Riga region, as the victims of technological unemployment came down from the village at Forge Pond and scattered individually and in small groups into the valleys and shallow mountain hollows on the lower slopes of the mountain. Gradually, as they were assimilated into the earlier Raggie culture, they formed a kind of "lost tribe" left over from the boom period in the Salisbury area. Existing in rude cabins and tar-paper shacks, a dozen men, women and children sometimes crowded into ill-heated rooms; intermarrying (if they married at all); drinking from springs often contaminated by human wastes; eating preserved woodchuck, jacked deer or suckers from local brooks, the Raggies were said to have had a mortality rate exceeded only by the fertility rate of the women. A typical Raggie farm, according to the disapproving townspeople of Salisbury was "a half acre of land, the rest just Creation."

But despite all of this, they were a proud people. Seldom in serious trouble with the law, skilled in the art of surviving on the bounty provided by nature and beholden to no one, the Raggies survived as a distinctive folk culture with their own beliefs, customs and entertainments well into the twentieth century. The good folks of Salisbury village may even admit that vestiges of Connecticut's "lost tribe" can still be found today in the back country around Mt. Riga.

Because it explains something of the Raggie spirit, one of their folk tales bears repeating here. The story was passed to the "civilized" world in the 1930s when fishermen from outside the immediate Salisbury area began to catch fair numbers of sockeye salmon in Twin Lakes, two bodies of water on the edge of Raggie country. Since the sockeye is native only to the Pacific Northwest and was previously unknown east of the Rockies until large schools began to appear in the Connecticut waters, conservation scientists of both state and federal agencies were puzzled by the extraordinary occurrence. No one ever tried to stock Twin Lakes, yet there was the sockeye. So important was this discovery that the press services carried the news, along with speculation from fisheries experts as to how they got there, to the outside world. Through it all, according to several sources, the Raggies just smiled. Not only had the so-called "golden trout" been on their menus for several years, but they had an answer to the origin riddle incorporated in a tale they told to anyone who would listen.

Since time immemorial, the Raggies knew, kingfishers had been instrumental in maintaining the fish life in the ponds which both birds and men depended upon for sustenance. Sensitive by instinct to changes in the ecology of a pond, kingfishers stocked those waters in which certain species seemed endangered, thus introducing new blood and improving the breed's chances for survival.

One early spring day, so the Raggie story goes, a gigantic kingfisher was seen hovering over the Twin Lakes. So large was the bird that it darkened the sun, small birds retired to their roosts and the owls at Owlsbury (Dudleytown) appeared to make the hills echo with their mournful cries. A few brave Raggies who dared look up at the kingfisher reported that it appeared very tired, and that its long beak was splintered and worn stubby at the end. Finally, the huge bird lit in a giant oak tree near a cranberry bog, bending the tree like a small bush under its enormous weight.

As several Raggie observers watched, the monster kingfisher was joined by a native bird of the same species and the two cousins seemed to engage in an animated conversation. Some of the bird language was overheard by a retarded youth who smiled in seeming understanding. But when questioned about the kingfishers' chat, all the boy could offer was a prediction: "There'll soon be good fishin' in the lakes!" At that, the giant kingfisher flew from the oak tree and, on wings which again darkened the sun, flew westward.

Many months later, according to the legend, the huge kingfisher returned to Twin Lakes, but this time he stayed a little longer than before, attended by numbers of local birds which seemed to be helping him in some task. According to old man Wilcox and other Raggies who happened to be picking cranberries nearby, they saw great numbers of sockeye salmon dropped into the Twin Lakes by the fisher birds that day. And within a year, they say, the boy's prediction had come true. Raggie fishermen were pulling all the "golden trout" they could eat from the Twin Lakes, although several more years would pass before outsiders caught the fish and revealed its presence to a wondering world.

The giant kingfisher was never seen again after the day of the great sockeye stocking. But a short time later, Raggie berry-pickers on Bear Mountain, Connecticut's highest peak, reported the discovery of a massive swath of fallen timber half-way up the mountainside. When they examined the area closely, they said, they found large bundles of blue and white feathers "with quills as thick as a man's wrist" scattered among the fallen timbers. They reckoned that the big bird must have miscalculated his altitude and crashed in a fog, as he tried to wing his way back to Oregon or Alaska for another load of sockeye fingerlings to stock the waters of Twin Lakes.

X Y Z

*D*EEP RIVER WAS a bustling little Connecticut River town during the last quarter of the nineteenth-century. Boasting a world-famous ivory piano-key factory, numerous businesses catering to the maritime interests on the river and a lively commercial block, the community easily supported two banking institutions, unusual for a town so small. Thus, while criminal activity was even then associated in the public mind with the larger cities, the people of Deep River became convinced that their town could match New Haven or Hartford anytime, because something approaching a crime wave began in 1874. After all, thieves always go where the money is, and Deep River was rolling in it.

The Deep River National Bank was the intended target of robbers who tried to break in that year, but for one reason or another, the attempt failed. Over the next few years other efforts to crack the National Bank were also unsuccessful. Then, early in 1899, Asa Shailer, president of the town's other bank, the Deep River Savings Bank, received a letter from the American Bankers Association which contained disquieting news. According to A. B. A. intelligence sources, a band of burglars was being assembled for the express purpose of robbing banks in Connecticut. "Your bank and the Deep River National Bank are mentioned as institutions upon which attack is contemplated," the letter added, ominously.

Given Deep River's past record of bank robbery attempts, Shailer took the warning seriously. Though previous break-in efforts had been unsuccessful, the town banks could ill afford to press their luck too far. The Savings Bank president called the bank's directors into emergency session and at the meeting it was decided that for the first time in the institution's 48-year history, it would have an armed night watchman. A bank employee sent to the Winchester Firearms Corporation in New Haven to buy a weapon for the guard returned with the company's newest riot gun, a rifle reportedly able to kill two people with one blast. The watchman hired to carry the fearsome weapon was Harry Tyler, a Deep River man who had earned a reputation for cool courage under fire when he had foiled an attempted hardware store robbery in the town.

In February, 1899, Asa Shailer received another letter from the A. B. A. with more unsettling news. "Burglars are contemplating an attack on a bank in Deep River," the message warned, "when the moon has waned and the nights have grown darker." Harry Tyler and his Winchester were ready, but the moon waned (and waxed) many times before the expected burglar "attack" was launched. In the early morning hours of December 13 a dog's bark alerted Tyler that something was up. Sure enough, as he peered through the window in the Board Room at the rear of the bank, the guard saw four men approaching stealthily. When two of them began to jimmy the window, Tyler noticed that one of them carried a revolver. That convinced the watchman that these were no pranksters but the long-awaited, genuine bank robbers. Tyler stepped back slightly into the shadows, put the riot gun to his shoulder, aimed carefully and pulled the trigger.

After the blast, a makeshift posse quickly formed on Main Street to hunt for the three would-be robbers who had run from the scene of the shooting. But for the fourth bandit there would be no more running. His body was found crumpled beneath the bank's north window, a fair portion of the left side of the head removed by the shot from the Winchester. The corpse was removed to a local funeral home where, for several days, it was viewed by people from both near and far in the hope that someone could make an identification. But no one knew him and since his companions were not caught, there seemed no choice but to give him decent, if anonymous, burial. After the founders of the Fountain Hill Cemetery donated a plot, the hapless burglar was laid to rest in a short ceremony witnessed by a few curious townspeople. His grave was unmarked.

For several days the thwarted robbery and slaying of the unidentified man received wide publicity in the press from Boston to New York. The Deep River Savings Bank was flooded with letters praising the bank's effective security system and the courage of Harry Tyler. But as Tyler bathed in the tide of admiring letters, he came upon one note that struck a different chord. Written in what he took to be a woman's hand, unsigned, and delivered in an envelope bearing an illegible postmark, the brief letter asked that the unknown bank robber's grave be marked with a monument inscribed with the last three letters of the alphabet. Although there was no explanation for the strange request and no way to judge its seriousness, Tyler complied. Over the grave of the man he had killed, he placed a wooden marker with the roughly carved inscription "XYZ."

As the sensational events of December 13 began to fade from local memory and investigation of the case failed to produce a single clue as to the identity of any of the would-be-robbers, Deep River gradually turned back to the business of earning a living, the late XYZ all but forgotten. At this point, however, the mystery deepened and the legend took another curious turn. For it became obvious after a few years had passed that at least one person had not forgotten the anonymous victim of Harry Tyler's Winchester. People began to notice that each December 13, a woman dressed all in black rode into Deep River on the train. Always alone, she would leave the station platform and walk out along the tracks to Fountain Hill Cemetery, where she placed a small bouquet of flowers on the grave marked XYZ. In all the years she made her pilgrimage — annually, as far as people could remember — no one ever thought to question her identity or her association with the man buried in the grave she decorated. Her last recorded visit was made in 1947, when the *Hartford Times* published a "human interest" piece on the lady in black and the flowers found by the cemetery's groundskeepers.

Was the lady in black the author of the letter requesting the XYZ marker? Was she the widow or grieving sweetheart of XYZ himself? Or was she just a woman who had lost a loved one and singled out the XYZ grave for symbolic remembrance? When an officer of the Deep River Savings Bank takes down the old Winchester riot gun from its place of honor on the north wall of the Board Room — as happens on occasion down to this day — he probably ponders the answers to these and other questions which will never be answered.

The Irving-Johnson Murder

*J*UST OFF STATE highway 32 at the Bozrah exit lies the Bozrah
Rural Cemetery, where are located the gravesites of the principals in
a murder and suicide so sensational that details of the episode and its
aftermath are still subjects of controversy in the area after more than a
hundred years. In brief, on February 5, 1872, Jane Maria Johnson was brutally
murdered by William Irving, who then took his own life shortly afterward, on
the very same day.

Jane Maria was the beautiful, well-educated daughter of one of Bozrah's
leading citizens, Dr. Samuel Johnson. Still unmarried and living at home at
the age of twenty-six, she was the apple of her father's eye, but, according to
some not-so-admiring acquaintances, a bit soft at the core. William Irving was
a very handsome Irishman, whose Celtic charm and exceptionally good
physique made the hearts of many young Bozrah maidens jump when they saw
him. He was employed as a gardener and handyman on the Johnson estate.

There are still those who claim that William and Jane Maria had a
mutually passionate attachment which ended tragically when the Irishman,
recognizing their love could never be consummated in marriage because of
their vastly different stations in life, took Jane's life and then ended his own.
Those who hold this view point to the fact that at twenty-six, Jane was
considered an "old-maid," a fate almost worse than death in an age when early
marriage was regarded as a woman's only goal in life and a major badge of
distinction. Jane was getting desperate, so this line of reasoning goes, and

encouraged the hot-blooded handyman's advances. He killed her, they claim, when he realized their love was an impossible dream. On the other hand, some see William Irving as simply another violent Irishman who murdered an innocent young woman when she firmly rejected his repeated, unwanted advances.

Whatever the motivation, the actual events involved in the murder and suicide were brutal and bloody. According to reliable reports, Jane was seated in the living room of her home when Irving entered with a muzzle-loading shotgun, walked up to her with the gun at the ready and fired point-blank. For some unexplained reason, however, the shot only injured her slightly. So, as a maid who had been attracted by the blast ran about the room shouting, "Murder. Murder," Irving knocked Jane to the floor and beat her to death with the barrel of the shotgun.

Immediately after the bludgeoning, Irving dashed to his quarters, where he grabbed a straight-razor. Then he went directly to Jane's bedroom, locked the door behind him, lay down across her bed and slit his throat from ear to ear. They say that the frantic Dr. Johnson had to scale a ladder and climb through the bedroom window in order to recover the body of his daughter's killer.

Jane Maria was laid to rest with impressive ceremony in the Johnson family plot near the center of Bozrah Rural Cemetery. Over her grave the family erected a fine, marble marker, inscribed with her name — and nothing else. It can be seen there today, slightly in the shade of the huge stone marking the grave of Dr. Samuel Johnson, who outlived his daughter by many years.

In the same graveyard there is another monument, much pitted with age and tilted at a crazy angle, marking the last resting spot of William Irving. This modest stone, however, lies in a very remote part of the cemetery, isolated by apparent design from all the other gravesites in the burial ground. The inscription reads:

WILLIAM IRVING
COMMITTED SUICIDE
FEB. 5, 1872
HE WAS THE MURDERER OF JANE M.,
ONLY DAUGHTER OF DOCTOR
SAMUEL JOHNSON

Even after more than a century, much controversy and speculation center on the Irving gravesite. Some say that the remote grave and the bitterly-inscribed stone are the products of Dr. Johnson's desire for permanent revenge on his daughter's killer. There are others who say that the Johnson family compounded the insult to Irving by seeing to it that his body was buried standing on its head, so that he would never know eternal rest. Still others concur in the insult by the victim's family, but insist the corpse was buried standing on its feet rather than upside-down.

There is also a current body of opinion that holds to a belief that the corpse of William Irving was never buried in Bozrah Rural Cemetery, either under the marker or anywhere else. This last group claims that a medical school was so anxious to get a body as perfectly formed as William Irving's for carving in class that it made the authorities an offer they could not refuse. And the marker? A spite-stone, they say, put up by the Johnsons, knowing full well that the body had gone to a hands-on anatomy lab. In fact, to this very day no one really knows what happened to the slightly damaged but still impressive remains of murderer William Irving.

The Lonely Death
of Capt. Smith

I N THE YEAR 1760, one Captain Simon Smith of New London was returning home from a campaign in the French and Indian War. Whether he had fallen ill before or after he mustered himself out of active service is unknown, but by the time he and his trusty horse had passed through Thompsonville and reached the tiny eastern Connecticut community of Andover, it was obvious to all who saw him that he was a very sick man. According to tradition, the youthful soldier stopped briefly at an inn in the village for a short respite from his long, difficult journey, but though the innkeeper tried to hold him there because of his sickly appearance, Capt. Smith insisted on getting on home without further delay.

Though he managed to ride a short distance south on the Gilead road, the New London soldier was mortally ill. No longer able to cling even feebly to his horse, he soon slid from the saddle onto the road, where his body was later discovered by passers-by, still attended by his loyal mount. The thought that Capt. Smith had died from smallpox, one of the most dread diseases of the eighteenth and nineteenth centuries, so terrified the inhabitants of Andover that they decided to bury Smith, along with his horse which they shot — and all his personal effects at a spot beside the road where he fell. Man and horse were given a hasty burial in a common grave, above which was placed a marker to his memory with the touching inscription: "Loved yet unattended. All Alone Sweetly repose beneath this humble stone ye last remains." Though worn by more than two-hundred years of exposure to the elements, the solitary marker has survived to this day.

The Moodus Noises

ONSIDERING THE VARIETY and longevity of the traditional
lore they have inspired, it is probably safe to say that no Connecticut
phenomenon has occasioned more wonder, imaginative speculation
and even scientific investigation than the mysterious underground rumblings
and accompanying earth tremors known collectively as the "Moodus Noises."
Apparently centered in an area which includes Cave Hill and neighboring
Mount Tom, near the place in East Haddam where the Salmon and Moodus
Rivers flow together, the Noises have awed and confounded all who have heard
them from time immemorial.

For the earliest inhabitants of this region, the people of the Pequot,
Mohegan and Narragansett tribes, the thundering and quaking around
Mount Tom were evidence of the living presence of the god Hobomoko, who sat
below on a sapphire throne and decreed all human calamity. The Indians
called the area "Matchemadoset" or "Matchitmoodus" — now "Machimoodus"
— meaning, literally, "Place of Bad Noises." Since Hobomoko's thunder was
sometimes loud and violent and at other times soft and gentle, it was said
that Connecticut's Indians depended upon the local Machimoodus tribe to
interpret the many voices of the evil deity. Living, as they did, in the shadow
of sacred Mount Tom, the pious men of the Machimoodus were thought by
others to have direct access to the raging spirit beneath its slopes.

Thus, when Hobomoko spoke, the resident medicine-men listened. Then, as chieftains from other tribes gathered with their offerings, the Machimoodus priests would engage in great powwows, finally emerging with the right formula for calming the angry god through sacrifice and prayer. They say that many were the times when the Machimoodus medicine-men were kept very busy consulting with visiting sachems and preparing offerings to the underground deity.

When the first white settlers came to the region in the 1670s, they were shaken by the Noises — in more ways than one. As might be expected, those devout Puritans were inclined to believe that the Indians' Hobomoko and their own Satan were one and the same being, and speculation about this possibility occupied much of their energies. Such notions appeared often in letters like the following, written by the Rev. Stephen Hosmer, Haddam's first minister, to a friend in the Massachusetts Bay Colony, and dated August 13, 1729:

As to the earthquakes I have something considerable and awful to tell you. Earthquakes have been here (and nowhere but in this precinct as can be discerned; that is, they seem to have their center, rise and origin among us), as has been observed, for more than thirty years.

I have been informed that in this place before the English settlements, there were great numbers of Indian inhabitants, and that it was a place of extraordinary Indian Powwows, or in short, that it was a place where the Indians drove a prodigious trade at worshipping the devil. Also I was informed, that, many years past, an old Indian was asked, what was the reason of the noises in this place? To which he replied, that the Indian's God was very angry because Englishman's God was come here.

Now whether there be anything diabolical in these things, I know not; but this I know, that God Almighty is to be seen and trembled at, in what has been often heard among us.

The Haddam ministry must have been an unusually challenging post for the Rev. Hosmer. Not only was he the messenger of God in the only parish around where the Devil lived right underfoot and constantly made threatening noises, but he was also spokesman for the God who was responsible for keeping the Indians' resident evil spirit all stirred up. Indeed, Pastor Hosmer had reason to tremble!

As time passed and the Indian influence waned, other causes for the Moodus Noises were noted in the records of East Haddam's inhabitants. For instance, during the years when the witchcraft mania swept southern New England, there was a popular belief in the neighborhood of the Noises that they were the sounds of violent battle — between the good witches of Haddam and the bad witches of Moodus, engaged in unending and inconclusive warfare.

In 1816 and 1817, during a period of earthquakes so violent they were felt in a band stretching from Boston to New York City, the Noises were attributed by some to "mineral or chemical combinations exploding at a depth of many thousand feet beneath the surface of the earth." Others suspected the explosion of subterranean gases powerful enough to move large boulders beneath the earth, but not strong enough to open fissures at the surface.

All of these notions pale, however, in comparison with the imaginative theories inherent in the legend of Dr. Steel and the "carbuncle." As the story went, there arrived in East Haddam sometime in the 1760s a mysterious stranger who claimed that his name was Dr. Steel. They say he was an Englishman possessed of strange and magical powers, who had been sent to Connecticut by King George to lift the curse of the Moodus Noises, which had lately been reported to the monarch.

The learned and aged physician built a crazy-looking house in a lonely spot on Mount Tom, near a cave that some said gave direct access to the realm of Hobomoko. Dr. Steel had determined that if he could find and seize the "great carbuncle" — a pearl of gigantic size — which blocked the mouth of the cavern, the Noises would temporarily cease and the countryside would have peace, at least for a time. After he retired behind the walls of the house, closing every window, crack and keyhole behind him, Dr. Steel and his research became mysteries as deep as the Noises themselves.

While no one was admitted to the odd little building on Mount Tom, curious observers were intrigued by the clang of hammers issuing from the house all night, the endless showers of sparks from the chimney and the sulphurous odors emitted from within. Then, one night, all activity ceased. Dr. Steel emerged from his house and, walking along a path marked by a faint light which moved before him, made his way to the closed entrance of the singular cave.

They say that as the ancient alchemist fell to his task of digging at the immense pearl that lay across the mouth of the pit, loud grew the Moodus Noises that night. Finally, with near superhuman effort, Dr. Steel pried the carbuncle from its resting place and removed it from the cavern mouth. What followed would be long remembered by astonished witnesses. From the depths of the cave a blood-red light shone forth, streaming into the heavens like a crimson comet or a spear of the northern aurora. It was, they believed, the flash of the great carbuncle, and all who looked through it said that the stars beyond appeared dyed in blood.

When the sun rose the next day, the people of East Haddam discovered that both Dr. Steel and the monstrous pearl had departed earlier that morning on a ship bound for England. Later, news reached Connecticut that the magnificent stone had continued to bring evil to its surroundings, for the galley carrying the pearl and Dr. Steel had sunk in mid-ocean, with the loss of all hands. Ever since, so they say, from the depth of a thousand fathoms the crimson rays of the carbuncle have occasionally shone forth, lighting up a morning sky and striking fear into the hearts of sailors who have seen it.

But in East Haddam, the residents were pleased that Dr. Steel's prophecy had come true. Before he sealed himself away in the funny house on Mount Tom, he had told the people that removal of the offensive carbuncle would quiet the Moodus Noises for years to come. And so, indeed, it did. Even decades later, when the sounds and shocks occasionally recurred — and the Indians said the mountain was trying to give birth to another stone — things never were as bad as they were in the days before Dr. Steel delivered them from evil.

With the arrival of the scientific age, traditional talk of evil gods, magic carbuncles and subterranean gas explosions began to be drowned out by scholarly discussions of such things as gneiss and mica schist, disturbed metamorphic strata, fault lines and seismic stress. Oh, a few exceptions to such scientific arguments persisted. One early nineteenth-century journalist said in print that the Noises were due to "pearls in the mussels in the Salmon and Connecticut Rivers" — undoubtedly a survival from old Dr. Steel's carbuncle theory. And one Sunday evening in 1852, a church congregation was led to believe that a horse caused the Noises.

It seems that villagers had gathered for worship in the East Haddam Congregational Church at Little Haddam, when the services were suddenly interrupted by what people first thought was a horse and carriage striking the side of the meeting house and scraping noisily along an outside wall. Believing that a horse harnessed to one of the wagons parked in the rear carriage shed had broken loose, men of the congregation rushed outside to capture the runaway. But they found nothing amiss; all the horses and wagons were still tethered. Later, having compared notes with their non-churchgoing neighbors, the ear-witnesses to the puzzling incident had to conclude that their equine visitor had really been the Noises, up to some of their old tricks.

Nowadays, of course, the mysteries of the Moodus Noises have all but disappeared, lost to the calculations of modern seismologists, using the latest sophisticated instruments and guided by advanced geophysical research. As recently as October 19, 1981, for example, a triumphant headline in the *Hartford Courant* proclaimed "Seismic Detective Solves 'Moodus Noises' Mystery," while the story beneath trumpeted the scientists' discovery that shallow "micro earthquakes" were the root-cause of the Noises.

It is certainly good that the geologists and seismologists have finally answered all the questions about the legendary Noises. And men of science have to be believed. Yet, despite all the learned conclusions, there are probably some folks down in the Haddams who still get a little thrill out of saying, "There's something mighty queer about them sounds." After all, it would go against human nature if people couldn't occasionally entertain the thought that maybe, just maybe, the medicine men of Machimoodus or old Dr. Steel knew what they were talking about.

The Atlantic's *Bell*

WHEN SHE WAS launched early in 1846, the steamship *Atlantic* was not only queen of the Norwich and Worcester Railroad fleet, she *was* the N. & W. fleet. Designed to improve the rail line's freight and passenger revenues by providing a comfortable sea link between Norwich and New York with the railroad's Boston to Norwich train service, the *Atlantic* was the last word in safety and comfort when she began regular service on August 18, 1846. Captain Isaac K. Dustan took pride in his $140,000 ship's structural soundness, powerful engines and luxurious accommodations. The sparkling saloons and staterooms featured what was reputed to have been the first gas lighting system in any steamship on the Atlantic coast. Skipper and owners were convinced that the *Atlantic* could put the Norwich and Worcester in the forefront of the highly competitive Boston to New York transportation business and could beat the odds that some fatal accident would overtake her, as it had so many other ships during this, the golden age of coastwise steamboating in New England waters.

For a few short months in the early fall of 1846, the *Atlantic* fulfilled her owners' dreams. But on a bitter cold Thanksgiving eve, as the steamer prepared to leave Norwich on her regular voyage to New London and New York, a savage storm was brewing. All day Wednesday, November 25, a chilly northeast wind had been buffeting the southeastern Connecticut coast, and by the *Atlantic's* scheduled early evening departure time, it was blowing at near gale-force. Occasional snow squalls made the oncoming night even more dismal. To make matters worse, the Boston train was late this evening. By the time the Boston passengers and freight had transferred from train to boat for the voyage to New York, it was after midnight. And as the *Atlantic* cast off from Allyn's Point to head down the Thames for a stop at New London, the wind velocity seemed to have increased even further.

The passage to New London was made without incident, but as the *Atlantic* prepared to depart the Whaling City and head for the open waters of Long Island Sound, at least one passenger was so concerned about the high winds and heavy seas which would be encountered that he left the boat in New London to await calmer weather. Capt. Dustan, however, was not frightened by the storm. He had a duty to perform, he was already behind schedule and he never doubted that his experience and his ship's capabilities would be more than a match for an angry Mother Nature. As Capt. Dustan ordered the lines cast off at New London, about forty-five passengers and sixty crewmen prepared somewhat apprehensively for a bumpy ride to New York.

As the *Atlantic* passed from the relative calm of the Thames into the waters of Long Island Sound, Capt. Dustan himself may have had second thoughts about leaving New London. Here the winds had whipped up twenty-five-foot seas and the northeaster howled at full gale-force. Intense cold and blowing snow added to the nightmare scene. Then, shortly after passing the light boat anchored five miles off the New London shore, the *Atlantic* was struck by two towering waves in rapid succession, while at almost the same moment, the passengers heard a "deafening and terrifying" explosion. Unable to withstand the extreme pressures imposed by the storm, the main steam pipe or "chest" had blown up, scalding some unfortunate members of the engine room crew, starting a small fire and, worst of all, leaving the ship dead in the water, at the mercy of the elements.

Nor were those elements kind. Almost immediately after the steam chest explosion, the wind suddenly changed direction. Instead of being blown along through relatively open waters by the northeast gale, the helpless boat was now being pushed by almost hurricane force northwest winds straight down upon the western end of Fisher's Island!

As daylight broke on November 26 it became obvious to all aboard the *Atlantic* that the ship's two anchors, ordered dropped by Capt. Dustan following the explosion, were finding no holding ground. By 10:00 a.m., when the surf on Fisher's Island became visible, blanket-clad passengers gathered in the saloon for prayers led by the Rev. Dr. Armstrong, followed by the donning of life preservers and the securing of some floating object: a board, a door or a shutter. Up on deck, to lighten the ship, Capt. Dustan had ordered the

Atlantic cleared of all loose objects. Coal, freight, and baggage went into the sea. To reduce wind drag, the *Atlantic's* smokestacks and upper deck-house were dismantled and jettisoned. With all possible preparations for grounding completed, passengers and crew waited for the end.

It was not yet to be. Providentially, the *Atlantic* missed the southwestern tip of Fisher's Island and was driven, anchors still dragging, into Fisher's Island Sound, only eight miles off the New London shore. Although it seemed at one point in the early afternoon that the anchors might hold, the wind suddenly increased in velocity and once more the *Atlantic* drifted, with ever-increasing speed, toward an eastern point on Fisher's. In the fading afternoon light, it soon became apparent to all on board that this time there would be no reprieve. Life-jacketed and bearing their doors and shutters, the passengers assembled on deck as the surf loomed ahead. On what was left of the upper deck, Capt. Dustan calmly gave orders and prayed. Someone overheard him say over and over, "If the *Atlantic* goes, I go with her."

She struck Fisher's Island stern first, at dusk. The anchor chains snapped. After four or five minutes of awful pounding by the huge breakers, the vessel swung around toward shore. Then, in the next instant, one extraordinary mountain of water swept her broadside upon the rocks of the island shore. As the returning wash from the gigantic wave swept away many passengers waiting on deck to take the desperate shoreward plunge, the *Atlantic* "split into atoms," her wreckage to be scattered and pounded for miles along the beaches of Fisher's Island.

The steamship *Mohegan*, out of Norwich, began rescue operations on Friday, November 27. Although the *Mohegan* had for a time stood by the drifting *Atlantic* on the previous day, sea conditions were such that no ocean rescue was possible. In an extra edition published at 6:00 a.m. on November 28, the Norwich *Evening Courier* told of the terrible toll in the Atlantic disaster. Of the fifteen bodies then lying in the temporary morgue at the railroad depot, only two were identifiable. The rest were so horribly battered that identification would be difficult, if not impossible. The crew of the *Mohegan* even reported that one body recovered from the debris on Fisher's shore was so mutilated that immediate burial on the island seemed appropriate. Altogether, officials estimated, forty-two passengers or crew members were lost that terrible night. Some bodies were never recovered, while many of those which were, could never be identified.

Among those who lost their lives in the wreck of the *Atlantic* were the Rev. Dr. Armstrong, the minister who had led the passengers in prayer, and Captain I. K. Dustan, whose dedication to duty may have exceeded his common sense. His battered corpse was returned home to Staten Island, where it was received with grieving tears by his aged mother, his widow and their five children. More fortunate than thirty fellow passengers who had been with him on the train from Boston Wednesday night and who had died in the *Atlantic* disaster was Daniel Webster, the famous orator and statesman, then serving as a United States senator. Webster, like several other New York-bound train passengers that fateful night, had decided not to risk the stormy sea passage and remained overnight at the American House, to resume his journey by land when the weather improved.

In the aftermath of the *Atlantic* catastrophe an eerie story began to circulate along the Connecticut shore. It probably began with crew members on the *Mohegan*, who reported that from the beginning of their rescue operation, they had been guided and somehow moved in their efforts by the tolling of the huge fog bell on the shattered wreck. Attached to a portion of the hulk still rolled by the tides and waves, the bell sent forth a peculiar shrill, clear note which could be heard for miles across the waters of Long Island Sound, tolling mournfully, they said, for the *Atlantic's* dead.

No one knows how long the funeral bell actually pealed its haunting knell from the dreadful shore, but for more than a hundred years there have been sailors, fishermen and landsmen, alike, who have sworn that when the time and weather conditions on Long Island Sound are just so, they have heard the solemn bell of the *Atlantic* reverberating across the waters from Fisher's Island. Those who have heard the sound regarded it as both memorial to those who died and warning to those who live. None needed ask for whom the *Atlantic's* bell tolled. The spirit of this ghostly legend is echoed in the lines inscribed on the New London memorial to Captain Isaac Kip Dustan:

> *Far, far o'er the waves, like a funeral knell,*
> *Mournfully sounds the "Atlantic's" bell.*
> *'Tis the knell of the dead, but the living may hear;*
> *'Tis a warning to all amid the opening year.*

The Sunken House
of Gardner Lake

*I*F YOU DROPPED anchor some still night at a certain spot in Salem's
lovely Gardner Lake, they say you can hear a haunting melody, played
on an old piano, arising from beneath the quiet waters. And if you
chose next day to investigate the source of the mysterious refrain by diving
with mask and tank into the depth of those dark waters, you might just find
yourself standing on the roof of a house with a piano in its parlor. For there is,
indeed, a full-size home resting on the lake bottom, inhabited now only by
creatures which breathe with gills.

The sunken house in Gardner Lake began its watery history sometime in
the winter of 1899-1900. The previous fall, the owner of the home had engaged
a constructing firm to move the house from its original lot on one side of the
lake to a lot he had recently purchased on the opposite shore. The contractor
determined that the most efficient way to move the building was to wait until
deep winter cold had frozen the lake solid and then to slide it from shore to
shore on the thick ice. Once the house was jacked up off the ground and placed
on giant runners, a team of oxen could easily accomplish the task.

Moving day finally arrived, but by the time the house had been prepared
for the sled, moved down to the shore and slid half-way across the lake,
darkness had fallen. The workers decided to leave the house resting on its icy

bed overnight and complete the move after daybreak. However, when they returned to the lake the next morning, they discovered to their chagrin that the extreme weight of the house resting on one spot for so long had been too much for the supporting ice. It had cracked under the pressure, leaving the house and all its contents listing heavily to port and threatening to sink altogether. Lacking the equipment to haul the structure from the water, all the contractors could do was go through the house salvaging such valuables as were portable and leave the building and its remaining contents to Mother Nature.

Surprisingly enough, even after the ice left Gardner Lake, the house stubbornly refused to sink. In fact, for several years it continued to float, half-submerged, on the surface of the lake. Here tourists came from as far away as Boston to view the remarkable floating house, and children from the area were said to have enjoyed rowing out to play in the still unsubmerged attic. Years after it finally settled to the bottom of the lake — at a point where water depths are said to exceed fifty feet — divers in scuba gear have enjoyed finding the sunken hulk and exploring its interior. As late as 1959, a doll and crockery were recovered from the damp domicile. Recent explorers have also reported that many of the larger pieces of furniture remaining in the house are still in a remarkable state of preservation. Especially is this true, they say, of the upright piano leaning against a parlor wall.

But even the divers can offer no explanation for the occasional stories that come from fisherman working the waters over the sunken house on certain warm, quiet evenings. More than a few anglers have come home at night to tell family and friends about the echoing piano melodies which have come faintly to their ears — as if from the water directly beneath them — and which, they claim, they just can't seem to forget.

Norwich's
Barrel Burning

*U*NTIL WELL INTO the nineteenth century, the biggest customary holidays in Connecticut were Election Days, Training Days and Thanksgivings, but in Norwich, the Annual Thanksgiving was anticipated by the residents of the town and all the countryside for miles around with more enthusiasm than any other day of celebration. Although its time-honored essential characteristic remained a stirring sermon in the old Puritan manner, Thanksgiving in Norwich somewhere along the way developed a unique adjunct to the traditional festivities called the "barrel bonfire" or "barrel burning."

In its earliest form this peculiar folk custom apparently involved nothing more than erecting a very tall pole, piling around it a pyramid of old barrels — large at the platform on the bottom, but a single, well-tarred cork forming the apex — and setting the whole arrangement on fire. The burning of the barrel pile was accompanied by revelry and great hilarity among the triumphant onlookers and was said to be considered by the young people of Norwich as indispensable to a finished Thanksgiving. When built upon the plain, one historian noted, "the whole valley was lighted up by the blaze, like a regal saloon." And when an elevated site was chosen, the flaming pyramid threw such a flood of light out over the woods, houses and streams below, that it created a truly picturesque effect.

As the popularity of the "barrel bonfire" increased, the construction of the contraption to be burned changed somewhat, apparently to improve the effect or to satisfy larger audiences. First, mast high poles were raised near the base of the high ground on each side of the Thames River, at the head of the harbor. Then tar-filled barrels were strung like beads on a rope that stretched between the poles and were hauled to the very tops. Then more barrels were stacked, pyramid fashion, around the base of the poles, and, after it grew completely dark, the whole monument was set ablaze. Various "teams" of local boys would fight for the best positions on the hills from which onlookers from all around gathered annually to view the celebrative spectacle. Watching the fire was accompanied by the drinking of much fire-water.

Perhaps it was injuries resulting from the keenness of the competition to secure prime viewing spots or maybe — as some reports have it — serious burns and even one death caused by the fires, but something finally snuffed out the Norwich Thanksgiving barrel burning. Possibly, as local industry changed, it was just a case of the old river town, once a major producer of barrels and staves, running out of the basic ingredient for the bonfire. But for years it was a flaming success.

The Tell-Tale Apples

THEY SAY IT all begin on a crisp November day in 1759, when a peddler arrived in a village in the "Nine-miles-square" of Norwich (now Franklin). On his back he carried a pack fairly bulging with notions dear to the hearts of colonial farmwives. Now, the arrival of any stranger in these remote parts was likely to cause considerable excitement, but a visit by a Yankee peddler was bound to be an especially festive event. "The Square," after all, was nowhere near the beaten path, and news from the outside world was almost as welcome as the opportunity to buy needed goods.

Word of the itinerant merchant's arrival spread quickly through the countryside. As the visitor unpacked his tinware, cutlery and yardgoods and arranged them for display, many were the housewives who gathered about to admire and to bargain. All day they came, on foot and horseback, until the sun fell low in the sky. By dusk, the peddler's once ample stock had been much reduced and his purse was heavy with silver. Before the last customer departed, the vendor inquired — in what some say was a heavy foreign accent — about a place where he might stay the night. An inn, perhaps, or a farmhouse with some accommodation for bed and board?

The lingering farmwives told him that there was no hostelry this side of Norwich town. Then, someone suggested that he might find lodging at the farm of Micah Rood, to the north, over the next ridge. So, with his remaining goods clanking loosely in his pack and his moneybag ajingle, the peddler set off into the growing dark toward the Rood farm. He was never seen alive again.

The next day news traveled fast that the battered body of the itinerant salesman had been found beneath an apple tree in Micah Rood's orchard. His head had been split open, as if by some sharp instrument, and his remaining goods lay strewn upon the ground, apparently picked over by the murderer. His purse, of course, was nowhere to be seen.

Suspicion immediately fell upon farmer Rood, known widely in the country 'round for his hermit-like ways and crotchety disposition. People remembered, too, that Micah Rood harbored a special grudge against all Frenchmen, since his father had been killed in the French and Indian War and his widowed mother, who lived with him, was a daily reminder of his father's untimely death. Some thought that Micah may have suspected the peddler was a French spy sent down from Canada to reconnoiter the area. After all, the peddler did have that strange accent, and when it came to foreigners, brother Rood could be pretty hostile.

Although authorities conducted a thorough investigation of the crime, they were unable to produce a single shred of evidence linking Micah Rood with the peddler's murder. No pilfered goods were ever found. No trace of the missing money ever surfaced. As might be expected, the leading suspect angrily denied any knowledge of the unsavory affair and withdrew further from the society of his neighbors. After a time, as other events began to push the murder into the background, the gossip and speculation about the peddler's death faded from local conversations.

However, when the long winter passed and spring finally came to the Rood orchard, passersby noted a strange phenomenon: instead of blooming white or pink as they always had, the blossoms on all the trees in the Rood apple orchard were streaked with red. More remarkable, the blossoms on the very tree beneath which the unfortunate peddler's body had been found the previous fall were almost uniformly scarlet. The more superstitious villagers began to fancy an explanation for the unnatural coloration, but not until the following fall, almost a year after the discovery of the corpse, did Mother Nature make believers of all the residents of Nine-miles-square.

Then the orchard of Micah Rood bore strange fruit, indeed. Every tree produced apples whose firm, white pulp was marbled through and through with rich, red streaks never seen before. And deep inside, close to the core of every apple from the "murder tree," people found tiny stains in the unmistakable shape and color of blood drops. The tell-tale apples, they said, were final proof of Micah Rood's guilt, the certain evidence of the dying peddler's curse upon his killer.

As the years slipped by and the family Rood grew and prospered on the eastern Connecticut land, details of the peddler's murder and accusatory spell faded or changed. But with each spring blossoming and every fall picking in Franklin's haunted orchards — even to this very day — the bloody apples bring a fresh reminder of that ancient, unsolved crime and a Yankee peddler's eternal curse.

The Windham
Frog Fight

W HETHER THEY CALL it the Battle of the Frogs, the Bull
Frog Fright or — by those leaning toward a little Latinate
alliteration — the Big Batrachian Battle, an incident that
almost literally scared the pants off the inhabitants of Windham Center in
1754 has been celebrated in story and song for more than 200 years. Because
the "singular occurrence" came at a time when the last French and Indian
War was getting underway, the scattered settlements in eastern Connecticut
were pretty tense and watchful to begin with. In Windham, the people were
especially anxious, since one of their most prominent citizens, Col. Eliphalet
Dyer, an attorney in civilian life, had just raised a regiment prior to joining
the expedition against Crown Point. With many of the town's able young men
already off fighting the "savages" with Gen. Israel Putnam, rumors of
massacres and assorted bloodletting regularly circulated among the folks back
home.

Then, on a dark, cloudy, steamy night in June, according to the most
reliable witnesses, it happened. After family prayers had been duly performed,
the residents of the settlement retired to rest, and for several hours all enjoyed
a period of well-earned sleep. Just after midnight, however, their peaceful

slumbers were abruptly ended by a noise so loud and hideous that they rose from their beds in one horrified mass of humanity.

The frightful clamor seemed to be coming from right over their heads and from all directions at once, a shrieking, clattering, thunderous roar such as never had been heard on earth before. To some it sounded like the yells and war whoops of attacking Indians. To others it was the last ding-dong of doom, announcing the arrival of Judgment Day. However, one elderly black man, wiser than his neighbors, was said to have protested that decision, arguing that the Day of Judgment could not occur at night. The general terror was increased when many villagers swore that they could distinguish particular names, like DYER and ELDERKIN (another local lawyer and militia colonel), reverberating, at intervals, across the heavens, as if in awful summons.

As the unholy uproar increased, citizens began to react according to their own peculiar lights. Parson White, who had been aroused by his Negro servant (one of the first to hear the sound as he returned home from some midnight frolic), did what came naturally. He rushed with his wife and children into the garden next to the parish house. There, among the bean poles and early peas, the trembling family fell on their knees and offered up an agony of prayer. From almost every house, old and young, male and female stumbled into the streets, many "in puris naturalibus" (i.e., buck naked), their eyes upturned, trying to pierce the palpable darkness around them.

Meanwhile, a handful of citizens less superstitious than the rest had concluded that the village was under siege by a large band of Indian warriors. Nothing daunted, these valiant villagers loaded their muskets and energetically pumped volley after volley into the murky gloom, until all their powder was expended. Several of the more daring musketeers were even bold enough to climb Mullin Hill, an elevation east of the village green, where they discovered that the sound did not come from the skies, as first believed, but from an area toward the foot of the incline, still farther to the east. None, however, dared to venture in that direction until the source of the noise could be determined for sure. They say that one member of this brave band, an elderly man named Stoughton, who had been rushing about simultaneously firing his rifle and brandishing a sword, was finally overcome by age and fear, and fell to his knees in noisy prayer. Taken altogether, it was not a pretty sight.

However, as the darkness slowly gave way to sullen dawn, the banshee sounds in the air seemed gradually to die away. As Windhamites of all persuasions slowly rose from their knees or hung up their muskets, they clustered in little groups to exchange questions or banded together to search the village perimeter for answers. In the light of day, it soon became apparent that no Indians had been in the vicinity the previous night, and since no one had been killed or died of a heart attack, the Day of Judgment had certainly not been at hand either.

It wasn't long, though, before the news began to get around that someone had discovered the awful truth, while riding down by Col. Dyer's pond, two miles east of the green, where the Follet family operated a grist mill. As people gathered there to witness the source of the previous night's panic, a curious spectacle was spread before them. Around the shore of the small mill pond and along the banks of the little stream that bubbled out of the pond to the south, lay the belly-up bodies of hundreds, maybe even thousands of bullfrogs!

It seems that the area had been in a state of severe drought for many weeks, causing the pond to be reduced to little more than a puddle. As the water became shallower and shallower, the heavy frog population was sorely affected. On the night of the horrible outcry, something must have finally snapped in the frog community. And as one after another the frogs desperately sought a few drops of water in pond or outlet ditch, they inevitably encroached on some neighbor's wet space. The result was a batrachian battle royal, complete with the anguished croaks of the dying, and little green casualties beyond any accurate body count. Owing, perhaps, to some peculiar state of the atmosphere, the horrible noise of combat appeared to the afflicted Windhamites to be directly over their heads. Thus, considering all the circumstances, it was not surprising that many distressing events occurred that night among the panicky people of the "village of bull frogs."

It is also not surprising that ever since that dark June night, Windhamites have been subjected to all manner of jokes and jests about bullfrogs. For years, no history of Connecticut was complete without some pun-laden or exaggerated description of the night the frogs put the fear of God into the folks in Windham Center. For example, in his *History of Connecticut*, the Rev. Samuel Peters, a notorious inventor of "facts," in an effort to improve his account of the battle, set the croaker casualty list at over five million! Popular poetasters, too, have waded in with such rhymed inventions as "A True Relation of a Strange Battle Between Some Lawyers and Bull-Frogs Set Forth in a New Song, Written by a Jolly Farmer of New England"; a 44-verse ballad called "The Bull-Frog Fight," published in the *Boston Museum* in 1851; and the Rev. Theron Brown's humorous "Epic of Windham," read at the town's bicentennial celebration in 1892. The great frog fight even served as the basis for a riotous 1893 operetta, *The Frogs of Windham*, which, they say, must have been excruciating not only to those who witnessed a performance, but also to the descendants of those who played leading roles in the original plot. The operetta featured a dozen major solo parts, several extensive dances and a cast of seventy performers, including Indians, frogs, local folk, Gypsies and even a fanciful English nobleman.

Yet, while some Windhamites may have felt the mortification passed on by their ancestors and the words of a hundred jingling verses, the majority of townspeople have come to terms with their untoward celebrity, even to the point of turning it to some advantage. The infamous Frog Pond (for so Col. Dyer's mill pond has been called since that dismal night in 1754) has been prominently marked by the local D.A.R. chapter with a huge granite boulder and bronze tablet commemorating the frog fight legend. When the Old Windham Bank issued its own notes back in the nineteenth century, the directors thought it entirely appropriate that their paper "greenbacks" should be embellished with the likenesses of two grumpy Windham "greenbacks," fresh from the Frog Pond.

Historians have also reported that the architects who drew the plans for the present Windham Town Hall made provision for two ample granite slabs in front, each designed to support a massive granite frog. However, whether tender feelings or tender purses prevailed, the sculptured frogs never materialized and the slabs remain today unencumbered by croakers. But, though modern visitors to Town Hall are not greeted by groaners at the gates, yet one reminder of Windham's genuine affection for the frog lives on: in the center of the official Seal of the Town of Windham squats a baleful bullfrog.

Considered together, the missing Town Hall frogs and the permanent town emblem would seem to confirm the mixed sentiments about the Windham frog fight expressed in a venerable verse on the subject:

> Some were well pleased, and some were mad,
> Some turned it off with laughter.
> And some would never hear a word,
> About the thing thereafter.
> Some vowed if the De'il himself
> Should come they would not flee him,
> And if a frog they ever met,
> Pretended not to see him.

The Church of Bacchus

ALTHOUGH IT HAS been more than a hundred years since the evaporation into legend of Eastford's "Church of Bacchus," time has not completely dimmed the folk memory of this unusual "congregation" and its eccentric founder, Ephraim Lyon. According to tradition, about the year 1820 Lyon hit upon the idea of "organizing" into a more or less formal association all of those citizens of Eastford who were known to worship — as Lyon himself obviously did — Bacchus, the Roman god of wine. Patrons of the grape (or "drunkards" as they were called by believers in the temperance heresy) from such other area towns as Ashford, Chaplin, Pomfret and Hampton were also said to have been enlisted in the mother church by the remarkable Lyon.

Membership in the Church of Bacchus came neither by invitation of the founding father nor even by the voluntary requests of prospective worshippers. Rather, Ephraim Lyon took it upon himself to enter eligible members on the church rolls, kept elaborate (but secret) records of the congregation and proclaimed to all who would listen that he was totally immersed in his work. He also maintained that his own capacity for leadership could only be proved by demonstrating his capacity for liquor, and he dedicated himself religiously to that task as well.

Since the only qualification for membership in brother Lyon's church was a reputation for excessive drinking, it was said that he had a brimming bowl from which to dip new members. There were some reports that as many as a thousand people from Eastford and surrounding towns swelled the church rolls during its peak years. While most of the members were said to be male, the leader of the Bacchanalians must have been an early believer in affirmative action. They say his aggressive searches for qualified candidates uncovered enough women to quiet any charges of sexual discrimination against the church. Once entered upon Lyon's church record, a member could only be removed by going on the wagon. An excommunicated member who had been stricken from the roll was immediately reinstated, however, if word reached the minister that he or she had resumed the habit.

As might be expected, residents of the community were not particularly pleased with the presence in their midst of Ephraim Lyon and his den of inebriate communicants. Active temperance people were outraged, ordinary non-drinkers were scandalized and those citizens inclined to an occasional sip from the cup that cheers were fearful of having their names added to the rolls of the Church of Bacchus. Although the universal dislike and dread caused frequent threats on the life of Ephraim Lyon, nothing deterred him from his purpose (whatever that was), and for a period of some twenty years he managed to escape assassination and dedicated himself to his priestly duties. At one point, they say, his wife became so alarmed over the repeated threats on her husband's life that she discovered and burned the church records. However, the clever Lyon soon reconstructed the rolls from memory and hid them so well that neither his wife nor anybody else ever found them again. It is said that during the life of the church, Lyon revealed the official records to a selected few members of an inner circle of bonafide alcoholics. After all, even in such an unorthodox church, something must be kept sacred!

The Church of Bacchus went out of existence when Ephraim Lyon died in 1840, but not before its founder was memorialized in appropriate ceremonies. According to one member of the church in very good standing who attended, the celebrants and their posterity would probably never forget the stirring occasion. And while it is ironic that the name of Lyon (not Ephraim but General Nathaniel) is revered today in the town of Eastford, it is even more ironic that the town is one of the few in Connecticut to remain steadfastly "dry."

Two Tales Of
the Insurance City

WHILE SOME SHORT-LIVED marine and fire insurance
companies popped up in the port towns of Connecticut around
the turn of the eighteenth century, the first substantial
insurance firm was incorporated in Norwich in 1795. In the best tradition of
Connecticut caution, the Mutual Assurance Company of Norwich insured
only those known personally to its company officers. Needless to say, it
remained solvent — and small. To the high-rollers of Hartford, like the
Hartford Fire Insurance Company, incorporated in 1810, and the Aetna,
founded in 1819, fell the bigger risks and, of course, the potential for higher
profits or losses.

According to tradition, several remarkably similar cases of corporate
salesmanship not only solidified the position of Hartford based insurance
companies at times of maximum threat to their very survival, but also focused
the eyes of the nation on Hartford as the unchallenged insurance capital of
the United States, a position which, once established, has never been
relinquished.

On the bitterly cold night of December 16, 1835, a fire broke out in a
wooden building in the heart of New York City. With the temperature
hovering around seventeen degrees below zero and a gale-force wind howling
from the northwest, a loosened wildfire quickly spread through block after
block of Manhattan real estate. Before the great fire was brought under
control (by dynamiting a wide swath in the path of the flames), some seven
hundred buildings had been destroyed, with property losses estimated at
nearly $20,000,000.

A post rider brought news of the disaster to Hartford the following day, but details remained sketchy. Even if the area of destruction had been known to the officers of the Hartford Fire Insurance Co., a major insurer in New York City, no street maps or records existed in the home office to set forth corporate liability. One thing, however, was patently clear: some effective steps would have to be taken quickly to assess the extent of damage to insured properties and to make good on legitimate claims against the company.

Eliphalet Terry, president of Hartford Fire and a man with a well-deserved reputation as a shrewd businessman and canny salesman, came up with a plan of action. He called in the leading Hartford bankers, extracted from them a blanket promise to honor any checks he might write on behalf of his company and even pledged his own considerable private fortune as security. He then called a livery stable to send around a horse-drawn sleigh, bundled himself against the sub-zero temperatures and proceeded to make the 125-mile journey over frozen and rutted roads to the stricken city.

Once he arrived on the scene, Terry learned that most of the New York insurance companies had been bankrupted by the monster fire. While property owners whose buildings had escaped the flames muttered darkly about the shortcomings of fire insurance as an institution, owners of gutted structures wandered in despair through the smoking ruins. Sensing an unparalleled chance to strike a blow for the infant Connecticut insurance industry in general and for the Hartford Fire Insurance Co. in particular, Terry ordered a large soap box to be placed directly adjacent to some still-smoldering debris in the heart of the burned-out area. Mounting the makeshift stage, checkbook in hand, the doughty executive calmly declared that he was prepared to pay in full and on the spot all claims against his company. He proceeded to back his words with action.

Although it was later determined that Hartford Fire was liable for less than $65,000 of the multi-million dollar loss total in the great fire of 1835, the value of the good will and rush of new business which followed Eliphalet Terry's dramatic mission was beyond estimate. For it is generally agreed that the integrity of the young insurance industry and the firm establishment of that industry in the city of Hartford were secured by his legendary act.

In fact, so pervasive was the story of Terry's gutsy New York gesture that it inspired several repeat performances: by officials of the Aetna and Hartford Fire after a second disastrous New York City fire in 1846, and, again, by a prominent agent for Phoenix Mutual, another Hartford firm, following the famous Chicago fire in 1871. In the latter instance, after $140,000,000 worth of property had been reduced to ashes by Mrs. O'Leary's cow, it fell to Connecticut's Governor Marshall Jewell to play the Terry role in the devastated Illinois city. As the story goes, when notified of the Chicago disaster, the president of Phoenix wired Gov. Jewell, who chanced to be in Detroit on business. Since Jewell also happened to be a Phoenix director, the company asked him to go immediately to Chicago and authorized him to act in their behalf in settling claims. Given carte blanche, Jewell agreed to do so.

True to the Terry tradition, Gov. Jewell no sooner arrived in the Windy City than he availed himself of a large dry-goods crate and had it installed on the charred banks of the Chicago River. Clambering upon the crate and looking out over 3000 smoldering acres where once a city stood, he announced to a sullen, half-crazed crowd that the Phoenix was prepared to pay in full and on the spot for every loss insured by the company. They say the crowd cheered, then cried, then laughed by turns, as the Phoenix checks were distributed among the stricken multitude. From the upper windows of the Chicago Tribune building a huge placard appeared, proclaiming that the Phoenix of Hartford was paying its losses. Once and for all, insurance and the "Insurance City" had come of age.

PART III
Supernatural Legends

An Introduction

The following supernatural legends constitute the most homogeneous group of stories in this collection, since each tale is a supposedly factual account of an event or experience which apparently validates a superstition or substantiates a folk belief. While it is true that the host of supernatural creatures familiar to European legendry has generally not survived well in America, it is also true that Connecticut tradition has offered up at least one example of a legend featuring such staples of European legendry as vampires, witches, elves, the Devil, huge monsters, enchanted animals and ghosts and other revenants (returnees from "the other side"). Since the Nutmeg State seems particularly rich in stories about witches and ghosts, I have included several of the former and more than a few of the latter.

Among the ghost stories are two which have probably originated in relatively recent times. The various legends related to "Midnight Mary" Hart apparently began circulating no more than fifty years ago, although the tradition has become firmly established in the New Haven area only within the past two decades. While the returning ghost tale was known in both the United States and Europe by the turn of the century, the automobile element did not appear until the 1930s, thereby generating a new group of "roadside ghost" stories, of which "The Vanishing Hitchhiker" is a classic example. Thus, several "Midnight Mary" stories and a Connecticut variant of "The Vanishing Hitchhiker" — all transcribed verbatim from collectors' audio tapes — are included in this section to suggest the vitality of contemporary legendry, as today's storytellers adapt old motifs to new circumstances.

Hannah Cranna, the Wicked Witch of Monroe

ACCORDING TO LOCAL tradition, Hannah Cranna did not earn much of a reputation as a witch while her husband, Captain Joseph Hovey, was alive. Even as plain Mrs. Hovey, though, she may not have been on very good terms with her neighbors, because very soon after her husband's death, the rumors began circulating that she had some sort of hand in it. What happened was this: one fine evening, while in the prime of life, Capt. Hovey had gone out for a walk, from which he never returned. For some unexplainable reason, he had apparently become disoriented or lost his way in an area which he had known all his life, and ended up toppling over a cliff. As searchers brought in his body the next day, several of them mumbled that Hannah Cranna (just when Mrs. Hovey assumed this strangely witch-like name is uncertain) must have placed Hovey under some sort of spell. Otherwise, they said, he never would have taken the plunge.

Hannah did little to discourage this sort of talk and, if we can believe the many stories that still circulate among the people of Monroe and vicinity, perhaps even stimulated the belief in her supernatural powers. For example, having already built a heavy reputation for cursing neighbors who failed to keep her well-supplied with free food and firewood (and doing very well by the gimmick, thank you), she chanced one day to stroll past a farmhouse where some freshly-baked pies sat cooling on the kitchen window-ledges. Hannah marched up to the door and asked the farmer's wife for one of the pies. Having recognized her visitor and recalled her reputation for casting effective spells if crossed, the housewife chose a small pie and offered it to her. "No way," said Hannah. "I want *that* one," she shrilled, pointing to the largest pie on the shelf. At that, the brave baker put her foot down. "That's my husband's favorite kind," she stated, firmly, "and you shall not have it." Hannah Cranna turned on her heels and stomped out the door, fire in her eye and a curse on her lips. Let us hope the farmer enjoyed his pie, because his good wife, somehow, was never able to bake another one.

Then there was the case of Hannah's forbidden trout brook. Unlike all the other fishing waters in the area, the stream which ran through the widow Hovey's property on Cutler's Farm Road (or maybe it was Turkey Roost Road) in Monroe had been declared off-limits for fishing by the owner. Since the creek was known to contain bank-to-bank "brookies," however, one brave sportsman finally decided to risk Hannah's wrath for just one shot at landing some of these beauties. Unfortunately, she caught him in the act and laid upon him a curse which not even the fisherman's prayer could disarm. Later, they say, he had to find another hobby, for that angler never caught another fish.

Possessed of a touch like that, the temptation was to flaunt it. And that Hannah Cranna did, to the point where people began to seek her out for favors. But Hannah was a hard case. She absolutely refused to cast spells on request unless the supplicant professed complete faith in her and her powers. But, if someone were willing to express such homage, she could work unbelievable magic. Once, for example, a farmer came to the wicked witch to seek her assistance in saving his withered and dying crops. Desperate for an end to the killing drought, the farmer willingly laid his soul at her feet in exchange for Hannah's intercession with the rain gods. "You got it," she promised, "before daybreak." Promptly at midnight, the first rain in weeks began falling.

In her later years, Hannah Cranna was attended by a pet rooster named "Old Boreas." Neighbors claimed that Boreas always crowed precisely at midnight with such uncanny accuracy that they set their clocks by his call. They said, however, that the wonder rooster's death hastened the end for his owner. After Boreas crowed his last, Hannah held an impressive candlelight burial service and then went into deep mourning for her late companion. A few days after burying her feathered friend, Hannah informed a neighbor who had come by to comfort her that she, too, was about to die. She then began to give the startled man explicit instructions about her own burial. "The coffin must be carried by hand to the graveyard," she insisted, "and I must not be buried before sundown." She died the next day.

Although her neighbors were inclined to carry out her wishes, a heavy snow storm began the day she died, and by the time it ended, the snow was too deep to permit hand-carrying Hannah's body to the cemetery. Instead, the mourners strapped her onto a sturdy, horse-drawn sled. But as the sled pulled away from her house and started up the hill to the graveyard, the straps must have somehow come loose, for, lo and behold, the casket fell off the rear of the sled and slid all the way down the hill to her doorstep! Fearing a similar accident, the attendants next secured the plain, board coffin to the sled with heavy chains. To make doubly sure there would be no more slip ups (or downs), several men — braced against the elements with considerable "anti-freeze" — sat on top of the coffin. This time, the sled had scarcely started to move before Hannah's casket began to shudder and shake so violently that the men were thrown to the ground. If the horses had not halted, the chains probably would have snapped from the strain.

The mourners decided at this point to carry out her original instructions, though the way was almost impassable on foot. And, luckily, by the time the bearers made it to the cemetery, the sun had gone down. Congratulating themselves on finally getting the old witch under ground, the funeral procession moved slowly back through the snow after the burial services, too slowly, as it turned out, to save Hannah Cranna's home. As they reached the top of the hill overlooking the departed sorceress' house, the empty bungalow burst into flames. It burned out of control until nothing was left but a smoking cellar-hole, fit monument, no doubt, to the wonder-working woman whose simple stone in the Stepney Town Cemetery reads:

HANNAH CRANNA, 1783-1859-60
WIFE OF CAPTAIN JOSEPH HOVEY

Midnight Mary

*J*UST INSIDE THE entrance to sprawling Evergreen Cemetery in downtown New Haven, a massive, modern-looking, pink granite tombstone stands in marked contrast to its smaller, grayer, Victorian neighbors. Even more distinctive than the stone, however, is the inscription, a concise tale of death's unexpected arrival in the midst of life, headlined by a mystifying assertion which many have read as a challenge or a personal warning. Upon a polished, elongated oval covering most of the otherwise rough-hewn marker is carved this cryptic story: AT HIGH NOON / JUST FROM, AND ABOUT TO RENEW / HER DAILY WORK, IN HER FULL STRENGTH OF / BODY AND MIND / MARY E. HART / HAVING FALLEN PROSTRATE: / REMAINED UNCONSCIOUS, UNTIL SHE DIED AT MIDNIGHT, / OCTOBER 15, 1872 / BORN DECEMBER 16, 1824. In larger letters, cut in bold, black relief, curving over the top half of the oval, appears the haunting proposition that THE PEOPLE SHALL BE TROUBLED AT MIDNIGHT AND PASS AWAY.

This striking monument to the memory of Mary E. Hart, known universally — and for obvious reasons — as "Midnight Mary," has inspired the folk imagination to such flights of fancy that Midnight Mary has become the central figure in what is probably contemporary Connecticut's liveliest supernatural legend tradition. Caught in the spell of story variants ranging in content from a premature burial and witch curses to ghost hauntings and unexplained accidents, scores of the curious have been attracted annually to the Hart gravesite, while Midnight Mary admirers from nearby Yale

University have made a motion picture featuring her storied but elusive spirit.

Despite the active and widespread circulation of Midnight Mary legends in oral tradition, almost nothing is known about the historic Mary E. Hart. There are those who claim that their research into nineteenth-century documents has disclosed that she was, at the time of her death, a rather ordinary, hard-working, almost anonymous machine-stitcher and corset maker, who was born in New Haven and lived quietly in the Winthrop Avenue neighborhood of that city until she died, at the age of forty-seven. The same researchers also report that the circumstances surrounding her sudden demise were entirely unremarkable, as was the immediate cause of death: apoplexy (the Victorian term for what would be called today a massive cerebral hemorrhage or "stroke"). However, as far as can be determined, none of these "facts" has ever been verified by trustworthy scholars.

If anything, reliable information about Mary Hart's pink granite tombstone and its provocative inscription is even harder to come by. According to one tradition, the Hart family was so anxious to have their Mary given the kind of notice in death that she had never enjoyed in life that they ordered the impressive marker and invented the enigmatic words carved upon it. If notoriety was what they wanted, the monument has probably burnished Mary's memory beyond their wildest dreams.

But, in fact, no one really knows who erected the stone, when it was set in place or why the strange words appear on it. When asked about its history — as he often is — Patsy F. Santoro, Evergreen Cemetery's superintendent since 1969, merely shrugs his shoulders and says neither he nor anyone he knows can remember as far back as 1872. But he will tell questioners that the marker looks almost new because he persuaded a local monument dealer to refinish it, without charge, around 1970. The cemetery's star attraction had been looking a bit the worse for wear, he thought.

Of all the legends about Midnight Mary which circulate today in oral tradition, probably the one most widely-known recounts a tale of live burial. It has been reported that not only New Haven youngsters and area college students — the most numerous bearers of the Midnight Mary tradition — have kept the story alive, but also that older residents of the Winthrop Avenue neighborhood where Mary Hart lived have been active in perpetuating the legend. According to those who know "the facts," Mary E. Hart did not have a "shock" on that October day in 1872, but was struck down by a rare disease, undiagnosed back in those times, which gave its ultimate victims only the *appearance* of death. Blinded by grief and apparently convinced by midnight of the same day that Mary had indeed departed, the family called the undertaker in and he hastily went about his funereal work, including burying her body in Evergreen Cemetery.

During the night following her interment, however, Mary's aunt had a terrible dream in which she saw her late niece writhing about in her coffin, clawing at the satin liner and moaning piteously for help. Could a terrible mistake have been made? Was her beloved Mary, in fact, still alive? It did not take long for the family to check on the validity of the vision. They ordered the grave reopened and the coffin removed for inspection. When the heavy lid was finally raised, a ghastly sight met their eyes. Mary was now unquestionably dead, but it was also plainly evident from the grotesque position of the body cramped in the agony of struggle, that her death had been hard — and *very* recent. To cover their mistake and ease their anguish, the story concludes, the family erected the magnificent monument with the weird warning and plausible but false death story inscribed on it.

Another tale known to many in New Haven may originally have been related by an 80-year-old Winthrop Avenue resident who swears to its veracity because he was involved in the incident. As the elderly informant tells it, he answered a knock on his front door one night and upon opening it, was greeted by a pleasant young man with a question: had the middle-aged woman he had given a lift to the previous night gotten in safely? The youth quickly added that the rather disheveled woman had been hitchhiking on Davenport Avenue, and after he picked her up, she told him that her name was Mary and that she was trying to get home. She had given the address of the informant's house, the young man said. He had dropped her off at the door and now was simply checking on her well-being. Although the homeowner had to inform the puzzled visitor that no one named Mary lived there, he later became convinced that the mysterious hitchhiker was Midnight Mary. Her grave in Evergreen Cemetery lay directly across the street from his house. (Folklorists would call this legend "Midnight Mary Meets The Vanishing Hitchhiker.")

Far and away the greatest number of legends involving Midnight Mary recall the disastrous consequences of "defying the curse" presumably chiseled on Mary Hart's monument. Known and retold by generations of young people in New Haven, each story incorporates the popular belief that Midnight Mary was a witch whose restless spirit continues to wreak vengeance upon those who fail to heed her tombstone's warning. Typical of the "consequences" cycle is the following account, taped by a 19-year-old South Central Community College student and life-long New Haven resident, in 1972:

The story that I'm about to tell you now is one in which three young people went to Midnight Mary's grave one night and walked on her grave and disturbed it.

234

You know she had been accused of being a witch and before she died she claimed that anyone who shall come and try to strike her grave shall die at the stroke of midnight. Well, seven years later, at the stroke of midnight, the exact day that they were there, one youth was found with his throat ripped open. Seven years after that, the second youth was found with his throat ripped open. Seven years after that [the other] youth was found with his throat ripped open, like someone had just slaughtered it away.

Another story which I have heard is about three sailors one time [who] were reported missing. After an investigation, their hats were found at Midnight Mary's gravesite. Supposedly, the way the story goes is that they had gone to Midnight Mary's grave and had heard something and they were frightened. When they ran away, they had to jump over the fence, but they got caught on the fence and they were stabbed by the spiked fence. [I don't know if] this is fact. This is only what I've heard. It should be noted that the wrought iron fence, with its spike-tipped palings, which completely surrounds the Evergreen Cemetery has held a special fascination for Midnight Mary legend-tellers. Many of the stories about those who defy the curse, conclude, like the one involving the three sailors, with the contemptuous disturbers of her grave impaled — usually through the throat — on the fence or gate.

Another group of legends about midnight intruders at Mary's grave tell of terrible accidents or strange disappearances which have followed close on the heels of such bold defiance. Two teenagers, for example, are said to have remained at the gravesite overnight to prove their courage. The next day, so the story goes, one was killed in a traffic accident, while the other later fell down a flight of stairs and was seriously injured. On another occasion, according to tradition, a horse and wagon made the mistake of passing by the main gate at Evergreen Cemetery one night, at the stroke of midnight. Witnesses claim that they watched both cart and horse slowly sink from view, as if in quicksand, never to be seen again. Similarly, two fraternity pledges from Southern Connecticut State University, sent at midnight to Mary's grave to make rubbings which they were then to sleep on the rest of the night, simply vanished. Their parents had difficulty accepting the loss.

Perhaps the most widely-believed legend of this sort, however, recounts the tale of two young men who set out one night to stand vigil at Midnight Mary's grave, hoping to see her ghost arise from the tomb at the witching hour. As midnight approached, one of the intruders could stand it no longer and hastily departed over the wrought-iron fence, carefully avoiding the spear-like palings. His companion, however, stayed on, thus apparently sealing his fate. When, in the morning, the lad who had taken early leave of the cemetery failed to meet his friend at a prearranged spot, he told his story to the police, who immediately began an investigation. A search of the cemetery quickly turned up the dead body, rigid in fright, with the cuff of a pant-leg caught tight by a thornbush. Everyone agreed from the evidence that he had been literally scared to death.

So what of the accidents, the disappearances, the injuries and deaths? And what of the message on the pink granite slab of Mary E. Hart? Coincidence? Curse? Hardly a week goes by when someone fails to put such questions to Patsy Santoro at the Evergreen Cemetery. He always has the answer for those who come, often from a great distance, to see and wonder at the legendary grave of "Midnight Mary" Hart. "All I know," says Santoro, "is what I hear."

The Black Dog
of West Peak

BOASTING THE HIGHEST elevations within twenty-five miles of the Atlantic coast south of Maine, the ancient lava flows known as the Hanging Hills rise steep and dark behind the city of Meriden, casting the old silver-making center into perpetual afternoon gloom. For years, the three distinct mountains in the range have provided hikers with the most challenging trails in central Connecticut, while the summit of West Peak, the most westerly of the hills, rising more than a thousand feet above sea level, has long been a mecca for lovers of panoramic vistas. Picnickers and campers have been attracted by the region's deep gorges and clear waters, like those of beautiful Lake Merimere, and, drawn by strange rock outcroppings, unusual geological formations and varied mineral deposits, geologists, too, have found this craggy country a profitable place for exploration and study.

However, such somber names of local geographical features as Black Pond, Misery Brook and Lamentation Mountain give some hint of the troubling shadow that has darkened the Hanging Hills for as long as people can remember. For death, often sudden and violent but almost always "accidental" — has periodically stalked these mountains, touching victims in such alarming numbers that it has made the local folk wonder. Even in recent years, when a new name has been added to the casualty list, old-timers around the area tend to shake their heads knowingly. "It's the dog, again," they say. "The poor devil must have seen the Black Dog once too often." Then the haunting legend of The Black Dog of West Peak will be told and retold, much as it was generations ago, much as it will be, no doubt, generations hence.

Over a very long period of time, they say, many who have visited the Hanging Hills have seen the dog: a short-haired, sad-eyed, rather nondescript beast of vague spaniel ancestry. One man who had encountered the dog while hiking in the West Peak area described his color as not exactly black, but more like that of "an old hat which has been soaked in the rain a good many times." With his wagging tail and friendly ways, the little fellow could hardly be distinguished from a thousand others like him — except for three extraordinary things. No matter whether he has been observed in the snow of winter or the dust of summer, he has left no footprints; and though he has frequently been seen to throw back his head and bark vigorously, no sound has ever been heard. But last and foremost, it is said of him, "If a man shall meet the Black Dog once, it shall be for joy; and if twice, it shall be for sorrow; and the third time, he shall die."

While at least a half-dozen deaths have been attributed by the folk living under the Hanging Hills to third meetings with the Black Dog, the most authentic stories about the fabulous creature were told by one W. H. C. Pynchon and published in the April-June, 1898 issue of *Connecticut Quarterly*. A geologist from New York who had come to the mountains around Meriden to examine the unusually accessible rock formations, Pynchon did more than anyone else to confirm and perpetuate the legend of The Black Dog of West Peak, which was apparently already a part of tradition long before his arrival on the scene. His account is well-remembered, even today.

On a beautiful spring morning, Pynchon said, he set out with a horse and buggy on the rough, dirt road that wound along past Lake Merimere to the summit of West Peak. Just as he reached the end of the lake, he noticed beside the road a great outcropping of gray rocks. He reined in his horse, got down from the wagon seat and began to examine the odd formation. It was there that he first saw the dog, standing atop the highest boulder, wagging his tail and appearing friendly in every way. When Pynchon was again ready to continue his journey, he was not displeased to find that the small black dog had decided to accompany him, trotting along behind the buggy as the geologist made his way over West Peak and then down the other side of the mountain into Southington. It was, thought Pynchon, a pleasure to have such a fine companion, as he drove through the lonely woods on that lovely day.

After taking a leisurely lunch at the tavern in Southington, Pynchon was surprised to see his little canine companion waiting patiently for him beside the buggy. As the New Yorker made his way back toward Meriden over the same route he had followed that morning, stopping occasionally to examine interesting geological features, the dog continued padding along behind or sitting quietly nearby during the scientist's rock stops. Finally, just at dusk, they reached the odd gray formation where the geologist had first picked up his companion for the day. Looking behind for his good friend, Pynchon only managed to see a shadow disappearing into the darkening woods beside Lake

Merimere. Though he whistled and called for a time, he would see the black dog no more that day.

It would be several years before Pynchon once more returned to Meriden. When he did, he brought with him a close friend, another geologist, to share his studies and his delight in the natural wonders of the Hanging Hills. No stranger to the area, Pynchon's colleague had scaled West Peak many times before and looked forward to seeing once more the mountainous country he loved so well. However, Pynchon remembered that on the night before their West Peak climb, as they sat before a roaring fire in their Meriden lodging place, his friend had told him of seeing a strange little dog on two of his previous visits to the Hanging Hills. The New Yorker immediately knew from his companion's description that this must have been the same animal which had befriended him on his earlier excursion over West Peak.

When the two men began their ascent of West Peak the next day, the sun was bright but the air was cold; and since it was February, ice and snow still covered the ground. They chose to climb through a gap between two great cliffs below the summit, a route made difficult in many places by the slippery footing and the chill winds gusting through the cleft. As they moved upward, Pynchon said, he was struck by the drama of black, volcanic rock pinnacles sticking up through the snow. Since the gap through which they were climbing was always dark, even on the sunniest days, Pynchon recalled that somehow the words of the Twenty-third Psalm crossed his mind — *Yea, though I walk through the valley of the shadow of death* — and a shiver not entirely related to the chilly weather ran through his body.

As the climbers approached the top of West Peak, they stopped to rest briefly before attempting the last leg of their ascent. Then, looking up toward the summit to gauge the distance they had yet to go, they saw him, the same small black dog each had met before, standing on the highest ledge, wagging his tail — and barking noiselessly. Anxious to greet their little friend, the geologists began their last push to the top, too carelessly, perhaps, in the case of Pynchon's colleague. Suddenly and quite unexpectedly, he lost his footing on the ice-covered rocks just below the summit. Before Pynchon could grab him, he was gone, sliding and smashing against the side of the cliff, to his death on the rock pinnacles hundreds of feet below. Once more the prophecy had been fulfilled: it was the third time the hapless victim had seen the Black Dog and the second time for Pynchon, who was, of course, filled with sorrow at the loss of his companion.

Although that ended Pynchon's account in the *Connecticut Quarterly*, it wasn't quite the end of Pynchon's story. Apparently undeterred by his friend's accident and his knowledge of the Black Dog's curse, the New York geologist made a final visit to Meriden, to retrace, it is said, the exact same route he had followed with his late friend. Someone else had to write the conclusion of Pynchon's story, because this climb would be his last. It ended when he plunged hundreds of feet to his death, landing in approximately the same spot where his friend had landed on that fatal day in February, a few years earlier. Had he seen the Black Dog? No one will ever know, of course, but for W. H. C. Pynchon, the fifth person within twenty-five years to lose his life among the crags and cliffs of the Hanging Hills, it would have been a third time.

The legend of The Black Dog of West Peak did not end with the death of geologist Pynchon by any matter of means. Over the years, many hikers in the region of West Peak and Lake Merimere have reported seeing the friendly little animal who leaves no footprints and barks without sound. Each sighting, they say, has been followed by great joy or great sorrow, even as the prophecy decrees. And each time some unfortunate soul suffers a fatal fall from the cliffs of West Peak — as did an experienced young alpine climber on Thanksgiving Day in 1972 — old-timers again shake their heads and repeat the ancient litany: *once, it shall be for joy; twice it shall be for sorrow; and the third time, he shall die.*

Haunted Gay City

WHILE IT MANAGED to survive, after a fashion, for some eighty years, Gay City was never, as its name seemed to suggest, either a center of metropolitan merriment or a tiny version of San Francisco. In fact, the twenty or thirty devout, hard-working families who first settled the "city" on the Hebron-Bolton town line probably would not have recognized the name. That's because the settlement planted in 1796 by Elijah Andrus and a band of devout followers from Hartford was long known as "Factory Hollow," until feuds, wars, liquor, fires and legends of murders and ghostly hauntings finally transformed the small community on the Blackledge River, below Still Pond, into a permanent ghost town in the 1880s.

Not until 1953, when the area where Factory Hollow once stood was turned over to the State of Connecticut for use as a state park, did the Gay City name become firmly attached to the place. There was an irony in this, too, since it was descendants of the powerful Sumner family, which for years battled the Gay family for village domination, who decreed that the state use the Gay name for the new public recreation area. So, though "Factory Hollow" or "Sumnertown" it should have been, Gay City — with all the possibilities inherent in the word "Gay" — it is, today.

If the traditional stories about the settlement are credible, there was trouble, right there in Gay City, almost from the beginning. Within four years of the founding, Elijah Andrus had abandoned his followers to the not-so-tender mercies of the rocky soil, steep terrain and utter isolation of the dark gorge of the Blackledge, just as the first frame houses and muddy streets began to appear. No one knows why Andrus departed, but tales persisted for years of feuding and fighting among the group of Methodist zealots which he had led into the wilderness. In 1800 John Gay was officially appointed "president" of the colony, while the Rev. Henry P. Sumner took Andrus' place as spiritual leader. John Gay and his brother Ichabod apparently shared with Sumner the responsibility of administering the community's affairs, though the relationship between them was never cordial.

According to legend, alcohol was the principal factor contributing to Gay City's next upheaval. Some say that it was part of the group's religious practice and others claim that it was an inducement to attend the compulsory twice-a-week services, but whatever the reason, all male members of the community were served hard liquor when they attended the frequent meetings for worship. Rum may have improved attendance figures, and it may even have encouraged spirited participation in the religious services, but legend has it that the booze did very little for the peace and tranquility of the religious gatherings. As the drunken brawls and blasphemous language of the male parishioners contributed more and more to the general civic unrest, a number of the first families of the colony packed up and left Gay City, resettling in the Hockanum River region of East Hartford and Glastonbury, and along the banks of the Connecticut River to the south. By 1804, the colony had reached a turning point.

John Gay and the remaining families decided that the survival of the struggling community depended on some sort of economic stimulus, something to bring jobs and income to residents whose interest in the colony was flagging, and maybe even inspire new population growth. Their answer: a mill for the manufacture of woolen cloth. So, after choosing a site about a quarter of a mile down river from Still Pond, the Gay City folks, aided in the back-breaking enterprise by outside laborers recruited from neighboring towns, began construction of a woolen mill.

Huge foundation stones, some weighing over a ton, were moved to the site on ox-drawn sledges, while a dam and canal were constructed to divert water from the river to run the huge, overshot wheel which operated the mill. The work was finally completed after many months, despite the defection of at least one of the laborers. According to a traditional story, this workman refused to have anything to do with building a canal in which the water "ran uphill" (as, indeed, it seemed to do). Proclaiming that it was "doing the Devil's work" to contribute to an "un-natural" stream of free-flowing water, he laid down his shovel, walked off the job and never came back.

The mill began operation under the name William Strong and Company around 1810 and, for a brief time, provided a welcome boost to the Gay City economy. Much of the wool used in the manufacturing process came from locally-raised sheep, while Hartford and other nearby towns provided a ready market for the cloth. Then came the War of 1812, the British blockade of shipping and a recession — inspiring decline in commerce. The Strong mill failed. Although Henry P. Sumner purchased full control of the factory and continued the business as the Lafayette Manufacturing Company, a disastrous fire in 1830 finished for all time the production of woolen cloth in Gay City. At least the venture may have preserved the village for several decades beyond its time.

Several years after the cloth factory burned, Dr. Charles F. Sumner, son of Henry P. Sumner, erected a new mill — this one for the manufacture of rag paper — near the site of the old woolen mill. Run by several generations of the Sumner family, the paper mill inspired a modest revival in Gay City, as well as a folk misconception about the operation which has persisted to this day. Because so many buttons have been found over the years at the site of the old paperworks, people believe that the place was a button factory. Actually, the buttons came from the scrap rags used in the paper-making process.

Even with the success of the Sumner paper mill, however, Gay City's days were numbered. The last members of the Gay family had left after the woolen mill fire. Other founding fathers and mothers were dying off, and young people were moving out of " The Hollow" to seek economic opportunities elsewhere. Then the Civil War carried off many of the village's young men, most of them never to return. Old homes stood vacant or deserted because death had removed the last resident. Finally, the paper mill met the same fate as the old woolen factory, burning to the ground in 1879. Gay City as much as died with it.

While students of the printed record may find in the succession of documented disasters sufficient causes for Gay City's untimely demise, folks around Hebron claim that the village would have survived longer if it hadn't been for the terrible murders — and the hauntings which followed them. They still tell, for example, about the unfortunate old jewelry peddler who was murdered and robbed of his wares, perhaps by a village charcoal-burner, shortly before the beginning of the Civil War. The sudden disappearance of the popular travelling salesman aroused many suspicions in the community, until a human skeleton, identified as the peddler's remains, was found in a charcoal pit on the edge of the village. Apparently the killer had tossed the body on the coals in an effort to destroy evidence of the crime. Although an investigation followed the discovery of the bones, the murderer was never brought to justice and the crime remains unsolved to this day.

Other versions of the story identify the victim as either a circuit-riding preacher who made the mistake of passing through Gay City one night or a drover returning home after successfully selling his cattle, killed for the contents of his fat purse. But peddler, preacher or cattle-dealer, the ghostly skeleton of the murdered man was seen on numerous occasions in the years following the crime, hovering over the dead charcoal pit, bones shining in the moonlight, apparently in vengeful search for a killer who would remain forever unpunished.

Legend also reveals a second murder in the Gay City of pre-Civil War days, one which, in its own grisly way, must have been more shocking than the peddler's slaying. According to tradition, the victim was the teenage assistant to the village blacksmith. It seems that the hapless lad turned up a few minutes late for work one day, and when he entered the smithy's forge, his angry boss went after him with a butcher knife.

Some say that the blacksmith carved up the tardy boy quite thoroughly, including the lopping off of his head, while others merely report that the assistant was slashed to death. In any event, the blacksmith made sure that the youth would never be late again. Despite the apparent open-and-shut nature of the crime, however, neither the blacksmith nor anyone else, as far as records reveal, was ever brought to trial in the slaying. As in the case of the jewelry salesman, the murder remains unsolved after more than a hundred years. Perhaps that is why folk legend has reported for years the presence in Gay City of the ghostly figure of a young man moving rapidly through the overgrown tangle of woods, bushes and vines, as if hastening to some appointment for which he seems to be always late. Sometimes, they say, in his obvious agitation, the restless spirit quite literally holds his head in his hands!

Now, on a sunny, summer's day, as swimmers splash in the cool waters of Still Pond and an occasional hiker tries the narrow trail that melts into the deep woods along the Blackledge River, Gay City's cellar holes and burned-out factories sleep with history. But wait for a calm, moonlit night, old-timers warn. Then sometimes the sound of drunken voices can be heard rising from "The Hollow" or a ghostly specter can be seen flitting through the trees, as if on an important mission. For when darkness shrouds the haunted town, they say, Gay City lives once more.

The
Jewett City
Vampires

*A*CCORDING TO TRADITIONAL stories still circulating in the eastern part of the state, belief in vampirism was not only current in nineteenth-century Connecticut, but at least one family living in the Jewett City section of Griswold translated their beliefs into grisly action. It should be noted that the New England brand of vampirism had little relation to the Transylvania-style version of the superstition popularized by novelist Bram Stoker in *Dracula*. Rather, the local belief was related to the conviction that some pre-deceased member of a family remained "undead" and returned from the grave to "suck the blood" from still-living relatives, thus causing their mysterious, untimely deaths. Almost always the belief tended to surface with successive deaths at an early age of members of the same family, from such ill-understood and abnormally feared diseases as "consumption" (tuberculosis), cancer and pernicious anemia.

The Jewett City vampires were all members of the Ray family, who are known to have lived in the area through most of the nineteenth century. The family consisted of the father, Henry B. Ray (1796-1849), and mother, Lucy (Downing) Ray (1791-1861), and five children, Henry Nelson Ray (1819-?), Lemuel B. Ray (1821-1845), James L. Ray (1823-1894), Elisha H. Ray (1825-1851) and Adaline Ray (1827-1897).

As the record shows, the first member of the family to die was the second eldest son, Lemuel, in March, 1845, at the age of twenty-four. Next to go was his father, Henry B., who reportedly died of consumption four years after Lemuel had been laid to rest (so they believed). But then, only two years after his father and six years after his brother had died, 26-year-old Elisha followed them to the grave. Clearly, the male Rays were being X'ed at an alarming rate.

As the story goes, the family patience ran out in May of 1854, when one of the two remaining sons of Henry B. Ray, the eldest, Henry Nelson, was stricken with dread tuberculosis and seemed ready to die at the age of thirty-five. Taking matters into their own hands, so to speak, on the night of May 8, accompanied by a few understanding friends and neighbors, the remaining healthy members of the Ray family entered the Jewett City burial ground on Main Street, shovels in hand and matches at the ready. Acting on the conviction that Henry Nelson Ray's seemingly fatal illness was caused by his brothers' emerging from the ground and draining the blood from his veins, the determined little band dug up the bodies of Lemuel and Elisha and burned them on the spot. Although father Ray may also have been suspected of participating in the ghoulish practice, something — perhaps filial respect — apparently spared his body from the flames.

Unfortunately, there is neither a gravestone nor any document to confirm the date of Henry Nelson Ray's death. But since there is a date of death (either on a marker in the Jewett City Cemetery or in the Griswold town records) recorded for all the other members of the family, it is entirely probable that Henry Nelson survived his "fatal" illness of 1854. The young man who caused his family's vampire panic may well have lived to a ripe old age. If so, the surviving Rays were undoubtedly convinced that their anti-vampire "medicine" had saved his life.

Ghost of The
Benton Homestead

WHILE THE *Connecticut Vacation Guide*, a directory of attractions published biennially by the Tourism Division of the Connecticut Department of Economic Development, has for some time recognized the Daniel Benton Homestead in Tolland as "a celebrated 'ghost' house," not everyone in the picturesque suburban community is happy with the "official" designation. Of course, almost everyone in town *has* heard stories about the mysterious apparitions and eerie events which have occurred there for years. But the more zealous guardians of the Homestead's historical decorum shun such "superstitious gossip," and roll their eyes heavenward when questions arise about a resident phantom. Still, they say, some very sober and reliable people have reported seeing and hearing things at the old manse which cannot be explained logically, and, well, maybe....

If ever an ancient house cried out for periodic visitations by shades from the past, it's the Benton Homestead. That is not to say that it *looks* like a haunted house, since the 1720 colonial cape, with its long ell in the rear, is clearly more early New England than late Charles Adaams. Rather, the unusual historical events that have taken place within the Homestead's ancient walls have been of the romantic sort which inspire legends, including a few of the supernatural variety. For example, because of its close proximity to the old Boston post road, the house was used in 1777 to quarter twenty-four Hessian officers, part of the large contingent of mercenaries who had surrendered to the Americans after the British defeat at Saratoga and were being marched across Connecticut toward Boston, for shipment back to

Germany. The Hessian prisoners are said to have enjoyed their stay in the smooth, stone-floored basement rooms at the Benton Homestead. Some say that vestiges of their complimentary graffiti (now undecipherable) can still be seen, carved in the darkened ceiling beams of their temporary home. Also, tradition still holds that more than a few of the Hessians liked the Tolland area so much that they were not among those present when the rest of their comrades finally moved on to Boston.

Even more conducive to legend-making than the story of the Hessian prisoners is the tragic tale of love and death which began to unfold at the Benton Homestead late in 1776. Of the three grandsons of Daniel Benton who served in the Revolutionary War, two died as a result of imprisonment, while the third, Elisha, was captured by the British and sent to one of their notorious prison ships, lying in New York harbor. There, like so many others, Elisha Benton contracted smallpox, probably as a result of his British captors' deliberately issuing clothing or bedding contaminated by the disease. Unlike most of his fellow sufferers, however, Elisha did not die on the plagued prison ship, since he became part of a general exchange of prisoners and was sent home to Tolland prior to his death.

Now, before his enlistment in the Revolutionary Army, Elisha had fallen deeply in love with a young Tolland girl named Jemima Barrows. Jemima returned his affection and the two plighted their troth. But for some reason now lost to history — perhaps because Jemima was almost twelve years younger than Elisha — the Benton family vowed that the marriage would never take place. This caused a serious rift in the otherwise close-knit clan, according to the story. Indeed, it is probable that young Benton signed up for military service in the hope that his absence from home and the passage of time might heal the family breach and change their minds about his marrying Jemima.

As might be expected under the circumstances, Elisha Benton's homecoming was greeted with mixed emotions by his family. As glad as they were to see him again, he was in a seriously weakened condition and wracked by a disease so contagious and frequently fatal that his mere presence became a terrifying threat to everyone around him. Since only those who had survived smallpox and had thus acquired immunity to the disease could safely care for a victim, the family faced a real dilemma, since none of them had ever had it. No doubt their relief was great when Jemima Barrows, the girl who had been faithful to Elisha through all the months of his absence and her ostracism, offered to nurse the critically-ill ex-soldier.

So, Jemima was shut away with Elisha in the special "dying and borning room" next to the keeping room, to tend the needs of her dying sweetheart.

Mercifully, her vigil lasted only a few weeks, for on January 21, 1777, Elisha Benton became, at the age of twenty-nine, the third of Daniel Benton's grandsons to die as a result of British incarceration. Since it could not be carried through the house for fear of contaminating the place, his body was removed through a window opening onto the back lawn. He was then buried on one side of the carriage drive at the west side of the Homestead and a plain stone marker was placed on his grave.

Though she had spent only a few weeks with Elisha as he lay dying, that was time enough for his brave nurse to catch the dread disease which killed him. On February 28, 1777, only five weeks after her fiancee's death, smallpox claimed the life of Jemima Barrows. She was one month short of her eighteenth birthday. In recognition of her heroic assistance in their son's final days, the Benton family agreed to bury Jemima near her sweetheart, in the west yard of the Homestead. But since they had not been married, the bodies could not lie side by side, according to contemporary burial custom. So Jemima was interred only a few yards away from the resting place of her sweetheart — but with the carriage road separating her grave from his. Thus have they been, apart in death as in life, to this day.

It is not clear just how long stories about a supernatural presence in the Benton Homestead have circulated, but the tradition was certainly alive during the period when Florrie Bishop Bowering owned the house. A beloved personality in the early days of WTIC Radio, Miss Bowering purchased the property, following her retirement, from the estate of the last Benton to live in it, and devoted much money and effort to restoring the Homestead to its eighteenth century appearance. Here she lived with a maid and handyman for thirty-five years (1934-1969), entertaining lavishly and carefully protecting everything she had inherited from the past.

Although there is no record of Miss Bowering's reactions to the odd occurrences and unusual noises which were said to have been common in the house during the Benton years, they say that on many occasions her maid witnessed the appearance of a young girl dressed as a bride, wandering through the house, crying. In fact, the sound of weeping was evidently heard so often that the maid became "almost accustomed to it." She assumed that the ghost was the restless spirit of Jemima Barrows, searching the house for the departed Elisha — and grieving over his loss. On another, later occasion, an overnight guest in the house reported a similar experience: "I was asleep in the front bedroom when the sobbing started. It was after midnight when it roused me. I was immobile 'til it stopped."

Many informants, particularly people who have served as guides in the Benton Homestead since it was given to the Tolland Historical Society in

1969 and subsequently opened to the public, have reported a variety of mysterious happenings in recent years. Several, for example, have experienced what they call "vibrations," unaccompanied by sounds or sightings of any kind. One of the docents from the Tolland Historical Society who had taken her dog with her to the Homestead to keep her company said, "I went into the summer kitchen with my dog, but she would not go into the dining room. I picked her up and carried her into the sitting room. She seemed to be all right until we got to the parlor. Then she again refused to move."

Another woman, also a member of the Tolland Historical Society, insisted that she be permitted to go upstairs to the second floor of the Homestead, an area closed to the public and generally off-limits even to the volunteer hostesses. Since she refused to take "no" for an answer, the curious local historian was finally given permission to climb the very narrow stairs to the upper chamber. Reported a friend who was with her: "She pranced up the stairs, but within a very few minutes she crept down again, with the comment, 'There were vibrations up there. I never want to go there again.'"

Many have reported hearing footsteps or other unexplainable noises in the house. For instance, a neighbor who was sleeping alone in the dining room was awakened by footsteps, but said that she "was not frightened." She got up, checked the house inside and out, but when she found nothing amiss, went back to bed. On another occasion, neighbors staying at the Homestead while their own house was being renovated were entertaining a guest, when they had a strange experience. "The fireplace in the living room was glowing," reported the informant, "and we were enjoying resting and talking about a great deal of nothing, when our visitor said, 'What is that?' We listened to footsteps coming from the east door down the hall. A little thump, light footsteps, then nothing. Our visitor left within fifteen minutes." The same informant also told of a snapping sound, like a branch being broken, coming from an unused fireplace. "We checked the flue and outside," he said, "but could find nothing. It was uncanny. Was it our good friend, the ghost? And he was our good friend. He did nothing to harm us, but he does keep us and all our friends verbally occupied."

Recently, a Homestead hostess told about an incident that happened while she was showing a reporter from a local newspaper around the house and explaining the history of the place. When they reached the front bedroom, the reporter asked if the stones in the fireplace had come from the property. Before the guide could reply, they heard three loud knocks — one, then a pause, then two more in rapid succession, repeated several times — as though something were answering "yes" to the reporter's question. At the same time, the hostess' watch jumped ahead an hour and twenty minutes, something she did not realize until she got home and found that she had cut short her tour of duty that day. The reporter, however, had left even earlier!

While most of the accounts of ghostly manifestations are connected in the minds of the story-tellers with Jemima Barrows, some traditions validate the notion that a male spirit — either the ghost of Elisha Benton eternally seeking union with the sweetheart denied him in life or the shade of a Hessian soldier experiencing again a place where he had been happiest during his lifetime — also haunts the Benton Homestead. For example, neighbors have on several occasions during violent thunderstorms seen the lights in the vacant house go on and off, heard voices raised as if in supplication and observed the distinct figure of a man in the uniform of a Revolutionary soldier come to the front door. There he stands for a moment, his hands stretched out before him in an apparent searching gesture.

Another experience with a male apparition was reported by a woman who, with her husband, was an overnight guest in the Homestead. While their hosts slept in the second floor bedroom, the visiting couple was obliged to sleep in the living room. When the hosts came down to breakfast the next morning, their female guest told them this story of ghostly encounter:

I awoke and saw a man's legs at the head of the sofa. A hand suddenly covered my mouth. I said to myself, 'Oh, you joker. You are trying to prove to us that there is a ghost in the house. I'll fix you. I'm not afraid.' It began to get hard to breathe and I thought, joke or no joke, this is too much, and pushed the hand away. Then I spoke out loud, very loud: 'What are you up to?' With no sound, everything — legs and hands — vanished. I got real close to my husband, who was sound asleep, and felt a little better. This report seems to be the only one, incidentally, in which the ghost has appeared in any way threatening. There seems to be no explanation for it. Certainly, the informant had none.

When Ed and Lorraine Warren, the psychic investigators, visited the Benton Homestead, they, too, were said to have encountered a male manifestation, a man dressed in colonial garb (not a military uniform) and surrounded by a blue light, who came to them in the dining room. It was the Warrens' feeling that this was the ghost of a glass blower from the European continent who had gone to Ohio and there committed suicide. The Warrens speculated that he might have been one of the Hessian soldiers once held prisoner in the Homestead who had stayed behind when his comrades-in-arms left for Boston, found his way west and there encountered insurmountable problems. His spirit had returned to the place where he had known happiness during his lifetime, they said, interpreting the aura of blue light as a positive sign.

Of all the stories about strange sights and sounds reported over a long period of time by a variety of first-hand observers, perhaps the most bizarre of them all was told only a few years ago to the chief docent at the Benton Homestead by a well-known architectural artist and photographer. He and his sister, a writer, were collaborating on a professional assignment at the Homestead when they encountered difficulties:

My sister and I went to the Benton Homestead to get some pictures for a project on which we were working. The sun was in the right place. Clouds were just perfect. Ideal August weather promised us perfect pictures. We started at the west lawn [where Elisha and Jemima are buried] with the Polaroid and aimed at the full side of the house. Click. Swish. The picture ejected. 'Oh, well,' I thought, 'something went wrong.' Next picture: click, swish — no picture. Click, swish, for the next six pictures, with an odd feeling growing that something was wrong. But what?

We decided to try the other camera. That had just been checked at the dealer's. Holding the camera, we found that it twisted in our hands and the light meter went wild. We still tried, and aimed at the west side of the house. The upper windows seemed to glow with an odd light. Although we were attacked with a wild sort of laughter, we decided to quit trying for the day. We went at a later day and got the pictures we wanted.

Like the puzzled photographers, local historians have found that developing a clear picture of more than two centuries of life at the Benton Homestead is not always easy. Sometime, perhaps, they might just have to adjust their focus in order to admit a few wandering wraiths to the panorama. Such a "die and let live" attitude could exorcise those vagrant spirits forevermore.

The Green Lady of Burlington

*T*HE PRESENCE OF a benign and beautiful female ghost haunting the town cemetery in rural Burlington has been verified not only by the many area residents who have sighted her in the past thirty years, but also by Ed and Lorraine Warren of Monroe, Connecticut's best-known and most indefatigable ghost hunters. Known throughout the Avon-Burlington-Simsbury region as the "Green Lady of Burlington," this restless spirit always appears in the form of a greenish mist, but with a well-defined body and a soft, pretty face lighted by an enigmatic smile.

Perhaps because of her generally happy features, quiet ways and non-threatening actions, stories about the Green Lady usually contain some imaginative explanation of her continuing presence in the town cemetery and speculation about her identity. Also, because she may be Connecticut's most boring ghost, her legends are almost always endowed by the story-teller with elements of violence or catastrophe, using motifs well-known by folklorists to "migrate" from one supernatural legend to another. So far as they can be reasonably established, however, her identity and motivations remain a total mystery. She just materializes unexpectedly, glows green for a time, smiles her sweet smile and then disappears.

Like most ghost stories, tales of the Green Lady of Burlington are most prominent in the legend repertoire of young people ranging in age, say, from early adolescence through the mid-twenties. This age group has been both active in seeking out the ghostly figure in green and in passing along accounts of her appearances. The versions of the Green Lady legend printed below were all told about twelve years ago by a student at Eastern Connecticut State College (now University), who, in characteristic fashion, was not an eyewitness to any of the things recorded in the stories. Rather, he had *heard* them from others and then tried to repeat what he had heard as accurately as possible.

The legends are set down here exactly as the student informant tape-recorded them, because with all their grammatical slips, digressions, repetitions, abrupt shifts in subject matter and gaps in continuity, they illustrate well the style of oral story-telling. In short, they reveal what legends really sound like at the point of transmission, before some writer has intervened to pretty them up for a reading audience. Even so, a reader of these verbatim transcripts should be able to get to know the Green Lady of Burlington and to sense the fun of immediate participation in the traditional lore she has inspired.

This is a story that concerns a lot of the people around Burlington, Connecticut. I don't live too far from there. I live in Simsbury. Most of the people around the area know the whole story. People have kept clippings, newspaper clippings, about it, since this has been going on a hundred years now. It happens at a gravesite in Burlington. It's near a dump and it's in the backwoods. It's a well-known place to go. It's closed off now. The police patrol the area and they have a fence around it, and people that are caught in the graveyard were persecuted [sic] by the police department. Of course, with so many deaths in the graveyard and people getting killed, murdered and so forth, they had to close it off for security sake. I've been down there about twice.

The story that I've heard is that the lady who used to live near the graveyard — and this happened in the 1800s — was drowned. There's a swamp or small lake near a house there (or a pond) and she was drowned mysteriously. I don't know if her husband had done it or someone in the area. Supposedly on her grave, she does have some remarks, but I don't quite remember what they were. Something about if you disturb her grave, she will haunt you, or whatever. She'll haunt you until she comes back — or something like that.

But she is supposed to be green. It was a swamp area and when she had risen from the swamp, she was covered with this green slime. It looks like a green mist. Kids have been in there. There's a house right next to where she used to live. There's no lights of course. It's a back road. It's a small cemetery. And there's a story, if you were caught around her grave, something will happen. Quite a few people have seen her.

* * * * *

There's numerous stories about the graveyard and this is just a story about what happened to two or three kids — two kids, as a matter of fact — that were in the graveyard. They were playing around the graveyard and they got startled and scared. There's two huge oaks in front of the graveyard and you can drive your car into the graveyard. They drove their car in the graveyard and they must have gotten so scared they didn't know what they were doing, apparently, and hit one of the oaks and they were killed instantly.

* * * * *

The house is right near the graveyard that she [the Green Lady] used to live in and if you pass near there, there's her portrait in the window! There's only one light on in the house and that's a light on the portrait. Of course, they never have the shade [drawn]. The shades are always open and the picture may be seen from the road. She was buried right near the swamp.

* * * * *

This story concerns the Green Lady, also. My brother was in there [the graveyard] once. It was about midnight or afterwards. It was in the early morning. He was in the graveyard with some of his friends. Out of nowhere a guy, apparently, with a lantern had chased them from the graveyard, screaming. Of course, they didn't wait to find out what did happen. But they did run. That, of course, is an unknown story, too. It may have been her husband or someone. I don't know. He has supposedly gone, like, mad. Also, if you bring a girl with you into the cemetery, the precaution you're supposed to take is to cut the girl's fingernails beforehand, 'cause the Green Lady may possess her body and turn on you. And this is also another story that goes along with her.

So, there are some of the things that they say about the Green Lady of Burlington. Just remember, if you ever chance to be driving along that back road in Burlington by the town cemetery and see a lighted portrait in a window of the house nearby, don't turn in at the graveyard before clipping your fingernails. And if you do happen to come face to face with the misty-green ghost, watch out for those oaks when you leave. After all, the lady really means no harm.

The Black Fox
of Salmon River

F ED BY THE sparkling waters of smaller streams with such
picturesque names as Blackledge River, Pine Brook, Jeremy's River
and Fawn Brook, the Salmon River flows down from Marlborough
and Colchester, along the borders of East Hampton and East Haddam and
finally empties into the Connecticut River, just below Haddam Neck.
Meandering through deep gorges, past sleepy little towns like Leesville, under
heavily wooded slopes and over several old mill dams, the Salmon, according to
experienced judges of riparian beauty, is just about the prettiest little river in
Connecticut.

Back in the days when Indians were the only inhabitants of the wilderness
drained by the Salmon River, they called it the Tatamacuntaway, a name so
long forgotten that even the earliest records fail to show it. But however it was
designated, the lovely stream provided the native Americans with some of the
best fishing waters to be found in all of Connecticut. In addition, the woods,
meadows and wetlands of the Salmon River basin created such an attractive
habitat for wildlife that the Indians often travelled many miles to hunt the
abundant game and birds which helped feed and clothe their families.

In the late seventeenth century, when the first whites discovered the
hunting and fishing paradise of the Tatamacuntaway, the Indians were
willing to share their knowledge of the area and to pass along their ancient

skills to the newcomers. The Englishmen were particularly enthusiastic about the seemingly inexhaustible supply of sea-run salmon yielded up by the easy-flowing river with the hard-pronouncing name. As the whites became proficient at taking the swift silver-sides from the stream, the salmon became a staple of the local settlers' diet and was soon honored with a river-naming by the grateful English fishers. Though both the Indians and the fish have long since disappeared, the Salmon River it has been to this day.

During those early years, too, the white hunters who ranged the hills in the company of friendly Indians began to hear from their native guides a strange legend, a story so compelling and yet so tragic that they scarcely knew what to make of it. Along the banks of the Tatamacuntaway, the red men said, there lived a black fox endowed with mysterious powers never seen in another animal. The fox had a coat so thick and sleek that whatever hunter chanced to see the beautiful pelt had an immediate and overwhelming desire to possess it. However, the Indians claimed that as many times as one of their fox-haunted hunters had sent an arrow winging toward the heart of the jet-black beast, none had ever found its mark. Instead, each arrow would seem to pass directly through the animal's body and emerge on the other side without causing any effect whatsoever.

Then, they said, the magical fox would begin to run, luring the frustrated but fascinated hunter into a lengthy chase, often punctuated by additional shots from the archer — but always with the same strange results. Such was the obsession with killing the black fox, however, that no amount of failure could ever discourage the hunter from continuing the hunt. Rather, each futile shot and each unsuccessful chase seemed to strengthen in the hunter a passion to bring down the enchanted quarry once and for all.

Sometimes, the Indians said, their bemused braves would return from a two or three-day chase after the fox so exhausted they could hardly move, but never too tired to recount in great detail their amazing adventures with the ghostly animal. At other times, the red men were saddened to say, some hunters who had set out to find and kill the darkling creature were never again seen on earth. Each mysterious disappearance, the Indians believed, could be attributed to the whimsical, indifferent but alluring spirit dwelling within the black fox of Salmon River.

On first hearing the legend, white hunters merely laughed in disbelief. There was probably no truth at all to it, they said, because Indians were forever making up stories such as this to explain those things which they found otherwise unexplainable. But, even if there were some marvelous phantom fox prowling the banks of the Salmon River, the Englishmen had supreme confidence that their powerful muskets and shot would succeed where the Indians' fragile bows and arrows had failed.

Nevertheless, when the reports came in from the first white gunners who actually saw and fired at the legendary black fox, they, too, contained the familiar ingredients of the red men's stories. First would come the uncontrollable desire, then the rifle shots passing through the ghost-like body without effect and, finally, the futile, almost overpowering chases over miles of rough terrain, ending in babbling frustration or — in the cases of those few who never returned from the hunt — tragic destruction. As time went on, the bitter truth of the black fox of Salmon River was accepted by the whites who inhabited the fertile valley as it had been by the red hunters before them: covetousness warps — and sometimes even kills — the human animal.

More than a hundred years after the last Indian had passed from the Salmon River hunting and fishing grounds, and not long before the last Atlantic salmon would run up the languid stream to spawn, the legend of the black fox was evidently still a living tradition among the white residents of the mid-Connecticut River valley. For it was from this tradition that Hartford poet John G. C. Brainard drew inspiration for one of the most popular verses published in his *Occasional Pieces of Poetry*, in 1825. Entitled "The Black Fox of Salmon River," Brainard's poem recaptured much of the mood and mystery of the original legend and probably did much to perpetuate the tradition far beyond its time. It ended, peacefully, with this:

> *And there the little country girls*
> *Will stop to whisper, and listen, and look,*
> *And tell, while dressing their sunny curls,*
> *Of the Black Fox of Salmon Brook.*

Debby Griffen

NOT MANY YEARS after the founders of Simsbury had rebuilt their frontier settlement after the disastrous 1676 Indian attack, there lived alone on the fringe of that village, under the dark shadow of West Mountain, a singular woman named Debby Griffen. Tall and spare, her long face dominated by terrible, piercing eyes, Debby always resisted the friendly advances of her Simsbury neighbors and gave notice to all that she just wanted to be left alone. Since she never volunteered anything about herself and no one in town ever got close enough to learn about her history, Debby Griffen remained for years a mysterious — and somewhat disturbing — curiosity. Even a prominent family in town with the same surname absolutely denied any kinship with the solitary Griffen.

According to those who occasionally witnessed her comings and goings, Debby spent much time in the woods and fields, gathering wild herbs, mushrooms and berries or hunting small game. She always carried her hunting rifle with her and was said to be capable of shooting a squirrel between the eyes at fifty yards. Her skilled marksmanship was yet another reason why her Simsbury neighbors gave Debby Griffen a pretty wide berth. There were times, of course, when she did come into the village for basic supplies, but since she always brought with her a great bundle of exceedingly fine linen yarn to exchange for provisions, her excursions into the town only increased the people's suspicions. No mortal hand, they said, could spin such gossamer thread as Debby Griffen brought in for barter. Could she be guided by some supernatural power?

Then, too, stories circulated about the strange happenings in and around Debby's cabin in the woods: black cats with enormous yellow eyes prowled about the premises and a huge, gray gander strutted up and down the entry path, hissing and squawking at strangers foolish enough to come near, an unlikely protective spirit.

As a matter of fact, there were some in Simsbury who suspected that Debby's guardian gander was possessed of a downright evil spirit. That belief was more or less encouraged by stories such as the one told by two young men who were returning one September evening from a militia training exercise. As they passed by the Griffen cabin, they heard "strange, unearthly noises." Suddenly, they reported later, Debby rushed from her cabin door, leaped upon the back of the giant gander and the two of them flew off down the valley into the gathering dusk. Since the two lads who witnessed Debby's flight had been known to linger, after a day of training, at the widow Hoskins' tavern, there were some who scoffed at the accuracy of their account. But knowing Debby's reputation, others were perfectly willing to accept the young men's report.

In the end, the truth about Debby Griffen was revealed in an incident that culminated in her death. It all began on a balmy Sunday in late April when Eleazer Hill went to open up the meeting house for services. On the way, he was so distracted by the beauty of the surroundings that he failed to heed the cry of a little bird which followed him along in the trees over his path, chirping, "You'll find trouble. You'll find trouble." When he reached the church and unlocked the doors, Hill was stunned by a scene of wild disorder inside. The chest containing the sacramental vessels had been opened and its contents scattered about the floor. After things were hastily set to rights, it was discovered that a valuable cup was missing. When they arrived for meeting that day, the parishioners were visibly upset as they learned of the sacrilegious mischief done in their house of worship. "Theft" was the subject of Deacon John Slater's sermon that day.

That Sunday night six volunteers gathered at the home of Deacon Slater to draw up a plan for solving the crime and catching the culprit. It was agreed that two of them, both militiamen, would stake out the meeting house, hoping to witness a repeat visit by the thief. Sure enough, not long after Captain John Higley and Sergeant Peter Bull hunkered down in bushes near the meeting house door, they spotted a tall figure in a gray dress with a white kerchief walking warily down the hill toward the church. Without a doubt, it was Debby Griffen. As they watched in amazement, Debby climbed the steps to the meeting house, approached the front door and disappeared in a wink — through the keyhole! And before the startled men could collect their thoughts, Debby popped right back out through the keyhole, a silver communion plate in her hand, and turned up the hill and out of sight.

By the time Higley and Bull started after her, Debby had a good lead on them. But from time to time they got close enough to see their quarry throw her hands above her head in such a way that the communion plate gleamed in the faint light of a half moon. Finally, the chase ended as Debby reached the shore of Three Cornered Pond. As she halted for a moment at the edge of the lake, Sergeant Bull raised his rifle to his shoulder and fired. A soldier whose marksmanship was known throughout the colony, Bull did not miss. He later reported that he put a hole through Debby Griffen so large that he could look through it and see moonlight reflected off the water behind her. Thoroughly ventilated but still belligerent, Debby thereupon clasped the communion plate in her hands, raised her arms above her head and with one enormous leap, threw herself into the pond. Naturally, she quickly sank from view. The rest of the volunteer band had arrived on the scene just in time to witness Debby's final dive. While some were inclined to congratulate themselves for so successfully closing the case, Sergeant Bull was heard to mutter, over and over, as they made their way back home, "Thou shalt do no murder."

Today, almost three hundred years after the shooting and sinking of Debby Griffen, Three Cornered Pond probably looks pretty much the way it did on that fatal night. It is one of those ponds that has no known inlet or outlet, and though many have tried, they say its depths have never been sounded. Even so, reports have persisted for years that on bright, moonlit nights a faint gleam — as if from a silver plate — can be detected in the unplumbed depths of Simsbury's Three Cornered Pond.

The
Headless Horseman
of Canton

ONE BRIGHT FALL morning in 1777, a lone French horseman departed from Hartford, headed toward Saratoga, New York, by way of the Hartford-Albany post road. At Saratoga, a rag-tag American army led by Benedict Arnold and Horatio Gates, along with several units of French troops, was at that time laying siege to a superior force of British regulars and Hessian mercenaries under General John Burgoyne. Since the French were sticklers for paying their soldiers on time and in cash, the rider's mission was very important to his superiors: he was to deliver the silver and gold packed in two heavy saddlebags — the month's payroll for French officers at Saratoga — to the army in the field, as quickly as possible.

The sky was starless when he reined in his mount at the Horsford Tavern in Canton, where he planned to spend his first night on the road. He stayed for a while in the tap room, chatting with the "barnacles" who always hung out there, yarning and gossiping. Then, saddlebags under his arms, he climbed the stairs to the sleeping quarters. That was the last anyone would ever see of the paymaster or the payroll.

As soon as it was apparent that the courier would not arrive in Saratoga, the French authorities launched an investigation into his whereabouts. Tracing his journey as far as Canton was easy enough, but there the trail unaccountably ended. Although the tavern owner insisted that the Frenchman had departed "safe and sound" early the next morning, it was, as one Canton historian put it, "probably heavenward, for no evidence of lateral travel was ever found." However, there was no more proof that he was dead than that he was still alive. The Frenchman and his payroll had simply vanished!

Naturally, there was a strong suspicion that a murder and robbery had taken place, and that the tavern-keeper was the one who had killed the paymaster for his gold. Yet, despite the rather unsavory reputation of the suspected man, nothing whatsoever was turned up to link him — or anyone else — with a crime. So, as time passed, interest in the paymaster's fate waned, the Americans took Saratoga, the unpaid French officers went on to other campaigns and Canton gradually settled back to normal, after all the excitement.

Not until many years later, following a fire which burned the Horsford Tavern to the foundation, was new interest in the old mystery sparked — by a grisly and disturbing discovery. There in the smoldering ashes of the hostelry, searchers found the bleached bones of a human skeleton, complete, except for the skull! Although no one would ever make a positive identification of the body, most of the folks living around Canton were pretty well convinced that the grim find had finally closed the books on the case of the missing French paymaster.

It wasn't long, however, before their convictions turned to certainty. A reliable Yankee farmer excitedly reported seeing the ghastly phantom of a headless horseman ride out of the mists of the Farmington River valley and head west along the old Hartford-Albany post road, his cape flowing out behind him and his horse's eyes ablaze with a strange light. This was only the first of a number of sightings of the headless rider over the years, with each witness breathlessly recounting the same details: the horseman always galloping west at a furious pace, along the same dark stretch of road; the flowing cape; the horse's bright, wild eyes; the observers' horses shying or bolting at the sight of the spectral figures.

Even in modern times, the headless horseman rides, frightening motorists along Canton's rural roads, sometimes even causing a startled driver to veer into a ditch to avoid "hitting" the frantic phantom. They always say that the beams of their car's headlights shone right through horse and rider, making them almost invisible, until, suddenly, car and horseman seemed about to collide. They never do, of course. No, folks in these parts have simply resigned themselves to the sight of the hapless French paymaster eternally riding toward Saratoga with his precious payroll, even though he was clearly unable to keep his head about him.

The Vanishing Hitchhiker

A S THIS MAN *is driving along Route 148 in Chester, he sees this girl hitchhiking; so he picks her up. She gets in the back seat of the car. She doesn't say anything, but directs him where she wants to go by her hand movements. He brings her to this house, and he gets out of the car to help her, but she's gone. Just disappeared!*

So he goes up to the house and this old lady answers the door. He told the lady what happened. The lady said, "I know. That girl is my daughter. She was killed in an automobile accident six years ago down at the intersection where you picked her up. She keeps trying to get home." "How could that be possible? I picked her up and she got in my car." She said, "Believe me, she's dead." The mother went over and showed him a picture of her daughter. It was the girl he picked up. She really was dead.

PART IV
Colonial Legends about Indians

An Introduction

The five stories which follow probably originated during the early years of the English settlement in Connecticut and have in common either an all-Indian cast of characters or, more often, the white storyteller's concept of Indian characters' relationships with the European settlers. It should be emphasized that these legends are the creations of whites, reveal the attitudes of the white settlers toward native Americans and almost all have parallels in other parts of the United States where European settlers had to cope with an Indian population that was seldom friendly towards them.

Legend of
Lake Pocotopaug

WITHIN THE NATURAL bowl formed by the gentle slopes of Meshomesic ("great rattlesnake") Mountain to the north, Baker Hill to the east and Clark's Hill to the west, lies placid, temperamental Lake Pocotopaug ("divided pond"), East Hampton's flawed jewel. Here, centuries before Governor and Mrs. William O'Neill built their home beside its waters, before the summer cottages and the bell factories, even before old Adrian Block explored the great river which curled in close, a few miles to the southwest, the Wangunk Indians found the fish and game so plentiful that they could almost forget the wiles of Hobomoko, their omnipotent and terrible-tempered Great Spirit.

Under the leadership of the grand sachem, Sowheag, and his local chieftain, Terramaugus, the Wangunks pitched their wigwams on the shores of Lake Pocotopaug and on the Twin Islands that sit like emeralds at the center of the lake. From their "long house" three miles north of Pocotopaug the braves ranged the woods to track and slay the fox, deer, bear and small game so abundant there, while from the crystal lake itself they harvested the bass and pickerel, swarming in endless plenty. They say that if ever there was an Indian equivalent of the Biblical "land of milk and honey," it was Lake Pocotopaug and the forests touching its shores for miles around. Through all the seasons, the Great Spirit smiled upon the Wangunks.

But one day tragedy came, all unexpectedly, to the Wangunk tribe. One of their braves drowned when his canoe capsized on Lake Pocotopaug at the height of a brief, fierce summer thunderstorm. It was almost inconceivable to the Indians that one so skilled in the use of canoe and paddle, so strong at swimming through the roughest water, could possibly perish during a brief squall on the small pond. Their religion taught them that nothing which occurred in the natural world — or to human beings — was a matter of chance or mere accident. Hobomoko must have recognized some wrong-doing, some evil not recognized by them, which caused him to reach out in the midst of that storm and snuff out the life of one of the tribe. Hobomoko was displeased, they feared.

Their alarm soon turned to panic when a second, and then a third member of the tribe lost control of their canoes on the turbulent waters of the lake and failed to reach the shore safely. There could now be no doubt that the hand of the Great Spirit had overturned those canoes and dragged the swimmers to their watery graves. Grief and fright blended together as the Wangunks looked heavenward and called out to Hobomoko to be merciful, for they knew not the reasons for his wreaking vengeance upon them. But Hobomoko was deaf to their pleas. Soon after the drownings of the heartiest braves, a terrible plague swept through the villages of the Wangunks, taking the strong along with the weak and the young as well as the elderly. The wigwams were full of the dead and dying — and terror stalked the shores of Lake Pocotopaug. In such a crisis, they decided, some means must be found to appease the mighty Hobomoko, to cause him to lift his yoke of horror from the suffering tribe.

His people having prevailed upon him to call together a tribal council, Terramaugus gathered all of his men, young braves and elders alike, under a great oak tree beside the waters of Lake Pocotopaug. As twilight fell, suddenly the Medicine Man of the Wangunks made his dramatic entrance into the circle of braves around Terramaugus and sat directly before the solemn chief. Then Terramaugus, tall and dignified and sad, arose to speak. In words both pained and eloquent he reviewed the awful events which had brought suffering and fear to his once prospering tribe.

It must be, he said, that the great Hobomoko is angry and is seeking retribution from the Wangunks for some failure or affront of which they have no knowledge. Why has he spread so much death and disease among his people? What can be done to appease the wrathful god and cause him once more to smile upon the unhappy tribe? Perhaps the wise Medicine Man could find both answers to these questions and some means by which the Wangunks could be delivered from disaster. No sacrifices, vowed Terramaugus, would be too great, if Hobomoko would but lift his scourge. With that, he resumed his seat.

After each of the braves in the circle had stood, one by one, and given his firm pledge to carry out whatever demand the angry god might make, Terramaugus rose once more, and addressing the brightly painted and feathered shaman before him, said, "You have heard our words, Gitchetan. Now go, with your chants and incantations, and commune with the Great Spirit. Find out, we implore you, why he is angry. If you discover that he is bringing a curse upon our heads for some misdeeds, learn from him in any way you can what we may do to gain his favor once more. You have heard our promise: whatever Hobomoko wishes will be our command."

Slowly Gitchetan arose, made his way through the council circle and disappeared into the woods, now black with night. As the men waited in tense silence, their faces looked haggard in the dancing light of the fire which now burned at the center of the ring, and no sound broke the stillness but the call of a loon, far out on Lake Pocotopaug. After what seemed an eternity, the distant thump of a drum and the weird chanting voice of the Medicine Man announced the imminent arrival of the priest. Soon Gitchetan emerged from the shadows and returned to his place in the circle, facing Terramaugus. The Wangunk braves rose to their feet, as they waited with sinking hearts for Hobomoko's word.

Gitchetan began with a long recitation of his approach to Hobomoko, recounting in great detail the ancient ritual, ending with mystic drum beat and incantations, through which he was able to communicate with the Great Spirit. Then, as he reported the great displeasure of Hobomoko and his thunderous demand for sacrifice, the Medicine Man's voice quavered and lowered almost to a whisper. He paused, seemingly unable to go on. Then arose Terramaugus, his body shaking in anticipation, and challenged the shaman to speak without fear: "Give us Hobomoko's word, O, Gitchetan. We are all ready to hear and obey." But when the Medicine Man replied, the words cut like a knife in the hearts of Terramaugus and every man in the circle. "The Great Spirit," he said, "requires the sacrifice of the fairest daughter of this tribe in the waters of Lake Pocotopaug. Your daughter, Na-moe-nee, O, Terramaugus, must die."

Scarcely able to conceal his feelings, the chief was silent for a time and only a throbbing at his temples revealed the rapid beating of his heart. His beloved daughter or the salvation of his people? Such was the choice facing the leader of the Wangunks. After a brief time, however, the chief raised his hand for silence. His decision was nobly rendered: "The will of Hobomoko will be carried out." So saying, Terramaugus slowly left the council circle, spoke no word to anyone and, with head held high, walked off in the direction of his wigwam.

There, though it broke his heart to do so, he awakened Na-moe-nee, and taking her by the hand, led her through the trees and out along the path that followed the north shore of the lake to the hill overlooking the northeast bay. As they walked, Terramaugus explained to Na-moe-nee the events that had taken place earlier that evening: the tribal council, the Medicine Man's talk with Hobomoko, the terrible sacrifice demanded by the Great Spirit. Only the chief's sense of commitment to his people and his fear of Hobomoko's wrath permitted him to reveal all to his daughter.

Na-moe-nee's reply was as noble as her father's vow. Accepting without self-pity her role in removing Hobomoko's curse from her people, she told her father that she felt fortunate to be chosen as the one who would deliver the Wangunks from evil. "I am willing to do this thing at once," she said, "if only Hobomoko will bring relief sooner to our suffering tribe." Terramaugus nodded sadly, and motioning to his daughter to follow, proceeded to pick his way around the head of the lake, until he reached the top of the ledges on the east shore of the inlet. Finally, father and daughter stopped at the summit of the steep cliff. Na-moe-nee asked her father to tie her hands and feet with heavy thongs, lest her will to live inadvertently foil her selfless act of mercy. Then, after stepping to the very edge of the precipice, she suddenly hurled her body forward and plunged into the unforgiving waters of Lake Pocotopaug. Hobomoko could smile once more upon the Wangunks — and he did.

From the moment the lake closed over Na-moe-nee, the disasters which for so long had beset the tribe, ceased. The records show that not a single death by drowning ever again took a Wangunk brave. Indeed, the benevolence of Hobomoko was even extended for several hundred years to the white men who began to settle the hunting grounds of the Wangunks soon after Na-moe-nee's death. Not until December 8, 1885, when a young man named Jeremiah D. Wall drowned when he fell through the ice while skating, was the peace of Hobomoko broken. But, of course, that was a long, long time after the last of the Wangunks had disappeared from the shores of Lake Pocotopaug.

The Nipmuck
Fishing Fires

*B*EFORE THE FIRST white settlers found their way into the
rolling hills and quiet valleys of easternmost Connecticut, the
Nipmuck Indians claimed the region's ample forests as their
private hunting preserves and the teeming Quinebaug River, with all its
tributaries, as their special fishing waters. Though they were a gentle people,
the Nipmucks stood ever ready to protect this bountiful land which they knew
the Great Spirit must have created for them alone. Especially were they
vigilant for signs of the fierce and warlike Narragansetts, who often struck
swiftly and stealthily from their territory to the south and east, in what
today is the state of Rhode Island.

The central link in the Nipmuck security network was a fortified area
atop a 625-foot height-of-land, only a mile or so from the center of what would
one day be the town of Thompson. From the summit of this hill (now called
"Fort Hill") the tribal lookouts commanded a fifty-mile view of the wooded
slopes stretching away for nearly 300 degrees around the horizon. Other tribes
found it difficult to mount a surprise attack on a people so well protected.
However, according to a legend still known in the area today, neither their
fine fortress on the hill nor all their strongest braves could save the Nipmucks
from an eerie sort of Narragansett "attack," which the local tribe brought
upon itself and which has continued, some say, to the present day.

Tradition holds that there once was a period when the Nipmucks and the
Narragansetts were not blood enemies. It was not a time of perfect peace,
perhaps, but there was a kind of truce, permitting interchange between the
tribal neighbors and some sharing of hunting lands and fishing streams.

One day, during the height of this era of good feeling, a Nipmuck fishing
party on the Quinebaug River met a group of Narragansett hunters heading
home after a successful foray into the local forests. The Nipmucks, too, had
enjoyed a splendid catch. They were especially proud of their plentiful supply

of river eels, a creature they regarded as a great delicacy. On the spur of such a happy moment, the Nipmucks asked their Narragansett brothers whether they would like to join them in a feast. They could share some eels, pass the pipe around and maybe exchange some tips on hunting or fishing or raising maize. The Narragansetts would be delighted, they said.

Well, everything went smoothly through the first few courses. Good-natured banter accompanied the herbed mushrooms. Some outrageous hunting and fishing yarns were spun over the squirrel and rabbit stew. But when the Nipmuck braves proudly presented their famous baked eels to their guests from Rhode Island, all conversation abruptly halted. The eels, according to Nipmuck custom, had been cooked and served, undressed. The Narragansetts, to a brave, took one look at the steaming, unskinned eels — and refused to touch them. Never, they said, should an eel be prepared in such a fashion. No Narragansett would think of serving an eel to a friend — or even an enemy — until it had been properly dressed.

Thus began an argument between the "dressed" and "undressed" factions which grew hotter and hotter. The Nipmucks were indignant at their guests' refusal to eat such good food, freely offered, while the Narragansetts insisted that their hosts' cooking was barbaric and insulting. As tempers rose, inhibitions dropped. Within a very short time, the happy feast turned into a general melee, with locals and visitors wrestling on the ground, grunting and groaning, as each side sought to convince the other of the superiority of its tribal cuisine.

Unfortunately, however, things quickly got out of hand. Some Nipmuck hothead split the skull of a Narragansett brave with his tomahawk. Another local Indian sliced a guest open with his filleting tool, then another, and another. Pretty soon, all of the usually benign Nipmucks were engaged in a murderous orgy. Before the killing ended, all but two members of the hapless Narragansett hunting party lay dead on the ground, surrounded by the remains of the controversial meal. Somehow, a couple of Narragansett hunters managed to escape the carnage and return home to Rhode Island to tell the incredible story. Not surprisingly, the Narragansetts vowed vengeance.

Once the bodies of the Narragansetts had been disposed of, the cool light of reason began to dawn on the Nipmuck fishermen. Since Indian belief held that any guest, even an enemy, must be treated with respect as long as he remained on the hosts' home ground, it was painfully obvious to the Nipmucks that they had broken a taboo which would invite the wrath of the Great Spirit.

What the Nipmuck fishing party did not expect, however, was what they got. On the very night of the fatal eel bake, and continuing from that time on, they witnessed an array of slowly moving blue and yellow lights hovering over the site of the massacre and up and down the length of the Quinebaug valley. These ghosts of the slaughtered Narragansetts, they feared, would haunt them forever. So a frenzy of guilt and supplication overcame the frightened Nipmucks. With beating drums and mournful cries, they confessed their terrible transgression to the Great Spirit — and begged for mercy. Call off the glowing Narragansett phantoms haunting their fishing waters, they pleaded. But the Great Spirit was unmoved, and the eerie lights continued their dance of retribution for as long as the Nipmucks remained in the land.

Even after the white man came to the region, they say, the colonists heard the drums and chants of the Indians, sounding from time to time through the hills and valleys of northeastern Connecticut. Then did the settlers shutter their windows, bolt their doors and huddle close to their fireplaces, for they, too, had seen the ghostly fireballs swinging over the local wetlands — and were afraid. Even today, some claim that the Nipmuck fishing fires burn every seven years, as the angry ghosts of the murdered Narragansetts still seek their Nipmuck killers.

Some skeptics, of course, explain the glowing lights along the Quinebaug as nothing more than "swamp fire," the result of gasses released by rotting vegetation. But for many others who now walk the land where once the Nipmucks roamed, the ghost fires are moving reminders of some redmen who came to dinner long ago and never left.

Legends of
Lake Alexander

Between Five Mile and Quinebaug,
While sounding through rockye Vales loud and hoarse,
From every Hill and Meadow Bog
Receive Supplies, and onward bende theire Course;
Enclosed around by Graves and various Trees,
With Shore of Sand and Skye of Blue,
Lake Mashapaug douthe meete oure View!

> — Anonymous verse fragment found in the
> garret of an eighteenth-century house

ALTHOUGH THE LINES above may be unremarkable for their rhyme and meter, right down to the exclamation point at the end they do convey that sense of admiration which Lake Mashapaug in Killingly has apparently stirred in viewers since ancient times. Long renowned for its scenic surroundings, beautiful margin of sand beach and crystal clear water, Mashapaug — or Lake Alexander, as it has been called since early in the English settlement — has served the residents of Killingly and the surrounding area as a place of refreshment and recreation from Indian days to the present. Indeed, so great has been the hold of Lake Mashapaug / Alexander on the folk imagination, that two legends, one of Indian ancestry describing the origin of the pond and the other an English tale about Nell Alexander, after whom the lake was named, have survived to this day.

As the local Nipmuck Indians told the earliest English settlers, the lands and waters of the Quinebaug valley had always been good to them. They had always found plenty of game in the woods, and fish in the local ponds and rivers. So prosperous had the people become, in fact, that one day the tribal leaders decided they should do something to celebrate their good fortune and to thank the Great Spirit for his benevolence. So after several tribal council meetings, a time was fixed for a general powwow, that peculiar Indian get-together which featured eating, drinking, smoking, singing, dancing and other activities designed to bring pleasure to body or soul.

The spot chosen for the powwow was a sandy hill, or mountain, covered with tall pines, which rose from the place where Lake Alexander now lies. Once the celebration got started, there seemed no stopping it. For four consecutive days the men and women of the tribe powwowed themselves with reckless abandon, hardly pausing to catch a breath, much less get any sleep. But all the time the party roared on, the Great Spirit watched — with growing concern and indignation over some of the things his earthly subjects were doing. Finally, at the end of the fourth day of celebration, the Indians' god had seen enough. So much lewd and lascivious conduct, he thought, deserved punishment of the severest sort. Accordingly, the Great Spirit found a way to end the orgy with a vengeance.

While the red people in enormous numbers capered and cavorted on the summit of the sand mountain, suddenly it began to give way beneath them. Slowly at first, then more and more rapidly, the hill sank beneath the surface of the earth to a great depth below. Then from the deep underground rivers, the waters rose, higher and higher, until they covered everything except what had been the highest peak of the former partying place. So, too, did the newborn lake cover all the sinful revelers, except one "good old squaw," who occupied the hilltop still showing above the waters, a place known today as Loon's Island.

Whether or not the Indian tradition has any basis in fact is difficult to say. However, it can be reported that for more than a hundred years after the last Nipmuck disappeared from the Quinebaug valley, if the day were bright and the surface smooth and unruffled, the huge trunks and leafless branches of gigantic pines could occasionally be seen beneath the waters in the deepest part of Lake Alexander. It was always a sight to make people reflect.

* * * * *

The man for whom Lake Alexander (or Alexander's Lake) was named was truly a legendary figure. A poor boy from Scotland who came to America on a ship loaded with a great number of emigrants, Nell Alexander parlayed an extraordinary, not to say legendary piece of good luck into a fortune, before finally settling in Killingly, on the shore of the lake called Mashapaug, in 1720.

As the traditional story has it, toward the end of the seventeenth century the ship that brought Alexander and the other Scottish emigrants to America landed them all in Boston. They say that just before he left the ship, Nell spied a gold ring lying on the deck, picked it up and put it in his pocket. Although it is said that he made every effort to find the owner of the ring —

he was an honest lad, though poor — no owner was ever found. At length, Nell claimed finder's rights to the valuable piece of jewelry.

Since he had been so fortunately and unexpectedly enriched, Nell Alexander's first stop after coming ashore in Boston was a pawn shop. In return for the ring, he obtained from the pawnbroker sufficient funds to purchase a goodly supply of household merchandise — pots and pans, tinware, clocks, tools and notions — with which to begin an itinerant sales business through the streets of Boston and Roxbury. As he was an enterprising young man, honest, personable and hard-working, Alexander prospered as an urban peddler to the point where he began to accumulate considerable wealth. Then, of course, he sought to do what so many people with assets have always done: invest in real estate. But before he left Boston to accomplish that goal, Nell Alexander returned to the pawn shop where he had left the golden ring only a few short years before, and redeemed it.

Now, with his lucky charm in hand, he was ready to move to the state whose name was synonymous with "Yankee peddler" and to pursue his business without threat of financial embarrassment. After a few years of constant activity, he had acquired sufficient funds to purchase a plantation of 3500 acres, more than half the area in the town of Killingly. From the day he moved into his home on the shore of the lake which would bear his name, Nell Alexander brought honor to himself, his home town and the itinerant peddling profession. In an era when Yankee peddlers were widely despised, Alexander must have been a very special person.

And what of the ring that started Nell Alexander on the road to success? According to historian John Warner Barber, writing in 1838, "The gold ring was transmitted as a sort of *talisman*, to *his only son Nell*, who transferred it to *his only son Nell*; who is now living at an advanced age, and has already placed it in the hands of *his grandson Nell*; and so it will continue from *Nell to Nell*, agreeable to the request of the *first Nell*, until the 'last knell of the race is tolled!'" Or, it could be said, until the last time Nell's story is told.

Lillinonah's Leap

WHEN THE ENGLISH colonies in New England were very young, there was hardly an Indian between the Hudson and the Penobscot Rivers who did not know about Chief Waramaug, the great sachem of the Pootatuck tribe of western Connecticut. Not only was he respected far and wide for his courage, wisdom and charismatic leadership, but also admired by all for his magnificent hilltop headquarters overlooking the Housatonic River, not far above the present town of New Milford. Called "Waramaug's Palace," the structure was said to have been at least twenty feet wide and a hundred feet long, a "long house," indeed, and unquestionably the largest Indian building ever constructed in New England.

Made from bark and logs which had to be carried for many miles (mostly up hill) on the backs of the artisans who built it, Waramaug's Palace was famed both for its architectural grandeur and its ornate interior decoration. It is said, for example, that the walls of the cavernous main council chamber were covered with colorful paintings of the chief, members of his family, his councilors and judges, while smaller apartments were adorned from floor to ceiling with pictures of all the beasts, birds, reptiles and insects to be found in the land of the Pootatucks. The best Indian artists, many loaned to Waramaug by the chiefs of distant tribes, labored for months to complete the unique administration building and museum of primitive art.

As proud as Waramaug was of his imposing palace, he was even prouder of the light of his life, his lovely daughter, Lillinonah. Taught from birth to cultivate those virtues most revered by her father — compassion for one's fellow man, loyalty to family and tribe and sensitivity to the beauties of

279

Nature — Lillinonah was, at the age of eighteen, a young woman whose humanity matched her grace and beauty. From near and far the young braves came, as moths to the flame, to pay homage to Lillinonah — and perhaps win her hand in marriage. But first, of course, each had to pass muster with old Waramaug, and that was no simple matter.

Now it happened that on a cold and wintry day, as Lillinonah was out walking in the woods high above the swift rapids of the Housatonic, she came upon a handsome young white man wandering aimlessly through the forest, stumbling occasionally and falling to his knees before rising once more and continuing on. It was obvious to the Indian maiden that the man was sick with cold and fever, weak of body and confused of mind. With pity in her heart for the suffering stranger, she offered to assist him back to the village of the Pootatucks, where he might find rest and treatment for his illness. When the white man nodded his assent, she slowly walked him to her home, though he had to lean heavily upon her for support, lest he collapse in the effort.

Although the elders of the village did not approve and did nothing to help her, Lillinonah nursed the stricken Englishman through all the rest of the long, cold winter, seldom leaving his side. As spring came to the encampment of the Pootatucks, he was well along the road to recovery, thanks to the care of his attentive nurse and the good medicine which she had provided. With the blossoming of the mountain laurel on the banks of the Housatonic, love, too, bloomed in the house of Lillinonah. As the beautiful daughter of Waramaug gazed with undisguised affection into the eyes of the man whose life she had saved, she saw that he returned her adoration with unaffected ardor.

When summer came, the two young lovers finally decided that they must go to Chief Waramaug, for a love as deep as theirs must be consummated by marriage. The great sachem's reaction, however, was as they both expected: he was very angry. With all the eligible Indian suitors for miles around still beating a path to her door, how dare Lillinonah ask for his blessing on a union with a white man, an unknown stranger whose culture was so different from her own? Was it not true that the paleface despised the Indians, regarding them as little better than the savage beasts of the forest? No, said Waramaug, never would he sanction Lillinonah's marriage to such a man.

But Lillinonah refused to eat or drink. Her once lovely face turned sallow and she began to shrink before the very eyes of her distraught father. As summer waned, the once beautiful daughter of Waramaug became a pale shadow of her former self, so great was her pain and powerful her will. Finally, although he still regarded marriage between his daughter and a white man as a burden almost too heavy to bear, Waramaug relented. Reluctantly, he consented to the marriage of his beloved Lillinonah to the man she had found lost in the woods on that long ago winter's day.

Before the marriage could take place, the betrothed couple agreed, the fair young man should return to his own people, to let them know that he was still alive and well, and to tell them of his plans to wed Lillinonah and live for the rest of his life in the company of the Pootatucks. Both lovers realized that his people would urge him not to go back to his lovely Indian princess. They would remind him that there were plenty of young English women in the colonies just looking for a husband as attractive as he was. What right had he to wed a dusky maid from a foreign and inferior race? But he promised Lillinonah that no argument would ever persuade him to break their vow to marry. After one final winter with his own people, he would return to Lillinonah — in the early spring. Sadly, he took his leave.

The autumn passed, and winter, too, and as the first green began to show in the hickory and oak along the Housatonic, Lillinonah bedecked herself with the wild flowers of the forest as she waited in happy anticipation for her lover's return. But summer came and went, the reds and yellows of autumn showed bright on the trees, and still the young Englishman had not come back to the land of the Pootatucks. Lillinonah no longer sang a joyous song. There were no more flowers in her hair. Wan and listless, she wandered through the woods, her eyes red-rimmed from weeping, searching and hoping against hope that she had not been forgotten.

Chief Waramaug watched sadly as once more his daughter's health began to fail and her usually happy disposition to turn morose under mounting waves of despondency. Perhaps, he thought, he might bring her back from the brink of deep depression if he could only interest her in a young man of her own race. So, unknown to Lillinonah, Waramaug arranged a marriage for her with Eagle Feather, one of the brightest, most promising braves in the Pootatuck tribe. Surely, such a fine youth as he, could give Lillinonah something to live for.

But word reached Lillinonah of her father's arrangement with Eagle Feather — and she reacted immediately. Down on the shore of the Housatonic River, now rapid and swollen with the heavy rains of autumn, she climbed into a canoe and shoved off into the teeth of the roaring current. As the canoe was carried faster and faster toward the turbulent waters above the dangerous falls of the river, Lillinonah tossed away her paddle and sank back in the bottom of the canoe to await her fate.

Then, high on a crag jutting over the river just above the cataract, she saw him! Her lost lover had not forgotten. Even above the roar of the water she heard him call her name. She stood in the canoe, waved her arms and screamed for help. Though he knew his chances of saving his beloved were slim at best, the young Englishman did not hesitate for a moment. He leaped from the overhanging bluff and plunged into the whitened water, just as Lillinonah's canoe struck a rock in the middle of the river and capsized, spilling her into the frothy current. Swiftly as he could, he swam to her side and clasped her body to him. Alas, neither realized that it was already too late. Still wrapped in loving embrace, the doomed pair disappeared into the boiling falls and were crushed to death as they were hurled to the rocks in the broad pool below.

They say that when the battered bodies of the star-crossed lovers were finally found, they were still locked in each other's arms. Noble, even in deepest mourning for his lost Lillinonah, Chief Waramaug ordered that his daughter and her white lover be buried side by side, contrary to Indian tradition, on the top of a hill overlooking the narrow gap of the Housatonic River now known as Lover's Leap. And when old Waramaug finally joined his ancestors many sad years later, legend says that he, too, was laid to rest near the ill-fated couple.

Though the tragic life of Lillinonah ended centuries ago, her legend will never be forgotten. Any Connecticut map will show that the wide portion of the Housatonic River which stretches for miles below the narrow rapids where the lovers met their deaths is, to this day, still called Lake Lillinonah.

Legend of Samp Mortar Rock

HIGH ABOVE THE surrounding countryside some two or three miles north of Fairfield center there is a precipice about thirty feet high, where a long, glacial outcropping terminates. The cliff has always been called "Samp Mortar Rock," after the excavation in the shape of a mortar which nature scooped from the granite at the summit. The mortar-like hollow is large enough to hold at least a half-bushel of corn, and there is a tradition that the native Indians did use it for pounding their corn (known as "samp") as late as the first English settlements.

In the beautiful valley south of the rock, according to ancient legend, lived a small tribe of Mohicans, numbering perhaps fifty in all, led by their chief, Onee-to. Onee-to had but one child, a daughter named Tahmore, who was as bright and beautiful as the sunlight. Yet, though many a love-struck brave came to Onee-to's home to court Tahmore, she rejected every one.

One day, Tahmore ventured into the woods with her bow and arrow to shoot birds from which she would pluck feathers to decorate her hair. On the way back to the village, she was suddenly confronted by a large panther. Quickly, she set her last arrow in her bow, pulled the string and struck the animal a death blow. As the panther lay dying, it sent forth a horrible, piercing shriek. Now it also happened that the twenty-year-old son of a recent English settler was in the woods nearby, hunting with his powerful dog, when he heard the panther's death-cry. Thinking someone was in distress, young George (for such was his name) hastened toward the horrible sound and quickly arrived on the scene.

On the ground he saw the huge beast with an arrow through its heart, but he also noticed in a tree nearby another big cat, perhaps the mate of the dead panther, prepared to spring at a beautiful young Indian woman. She stood before the animal, helpless but unafraid, staring into the burning eyes. Acting quickly, George raised his rifle and fired one fatal round. With his dog administering the final touches, the second panther soon fell dead. Tahmore knelt at George's feet and with words and gestures which could not be misunderstood, thanked him for her deliverance. Touched by her charm and grace, young George lost his heart to her on the spot.

As Tahmore turned to leave, he caught her by the hand, saying, "Will not the beautiful maiden tell me her name, that I may see her again; and may I accompany her to the tent of her father?" The Indian girl agreed and they returned to her village hand-in-hand. After hearing what had taken place in the woods, Onee-to grasped George's hand, thanking him for his kindness. The chief also agreed to give Tahmore as George's bride. George and Tahmore awaited happily for the day they would be joined forever.

Meanwhile, only a few miles from Samp Mortar Rock and Tahmore's village lay the great swamp of Sasco, where there lived a dwindling band of Pequots, with their once-powerful chief, Sassacus. These were the last of the Pequots who had fled along the Long Island Sound shore, pursued by English forces under Captain John Mason, after their main encampment at Groton had been brutally destroyed in 1637. Now it so happened that the fugitive chief had been out foraging in the woods where Tahmore and George had met and had secretly witnessed the killing of the panthers. Struck by Tahmore's beauty, the noble Pequot fell in love with her. Each evening, for many days after, Sassacus returned to the place where he had seen Tahmore, hoping to meet her and tell of his adoration. One day, it happened.

Although Sassacus was hidden from her view as he watched Tahmore pause in the clearing, he was so struck by her loveliness that he uttered an involuntary gasp, startling the maiden. She turned to flee, but he sprang forward, grasping her by the hand. He poured out his love to her and urged her to become his bride. But she replied, "Tahmore will be your friend, but she can never live in your tent, for Tahmore loves another." Angered by her reply, the spurned Sassacus clutched at his knife — just as George, along with his dog and Chief Onee-to, came on the scene. As the terrified Indian woman dashed into her lover's arms, Sassacus darted into the encompassing forest, vowing revenge on the one he could never wed.

The next day Tahmore sat upon Samp Mortar Rock pounding corn for the evening meal, her soul happy, for her wedding date had now been set. The ugly events of the previous day were far from her mind. As Tahmore sang quietly at her work, the tawny figure of Sassacus crept silently through the small bushes on the ridge behind her. Suddenly, a huge eagle flew screeching from the brush where it had been startled from its nest. When Tahmore turned to watch the eagle's flight, she spied Sassacus, knife in hand. Her escape cut off at the rear, there was nothing else for the courageous Indian maiden to do to avoid Sassacus' revenge but leap from the top of the cliff. Luckily, the thickly-matted grass at the base of Samp Mortar Rock cushioned her fall. She survived without injury and fled back to her village.

But Sassacus was not through. A few days later, as Tahmore waited in her tent for George to arrive, the Pequot chief appeared with news that struck fear in her heart. "Your lover is my prisoner," Sassacus informed her. "If by tomorrow's sunset you do not become my bride, I will tear out his heart and roast it for my supper. In the great swamp of Sasco, he is guarded by my trusty warriors. You have heard my decision. Now you must make yours." With that, Sassacus returned to the dismal swamp.

It did not take Tahmore long to make her decision. She hastened to the headquarters of the English forces sealing off the Pequots' escape routes from the swamp of Sasco. After she told Capt. Mason about Sassacus' white prisoner and warned him that George faced immediate execution, the English commander sent his troops into the swamp with orders to rescue the unfortunate captive and shoot all the Indians. The mission was accomplished successfully as far as George was concerned and with deadly efficiency in the case of Sassacus and his remaining followers. The "Great Swamp Fight" on July 13, 1637, saw the total destruction of the Pequots.

About the Author

Raised in the land of such legends as Jesse James, "Dizzy" Dean and Mark Twain (St. Louis, Missouri to be exact), Dave Philips has been a tongue-cutter in a shoe factory, a chicken plucker, a clothing salesman, a merchant seaman and a lobster-house waiter. He was also a professor of English at Eastern Connecticut State University for twenty-eight years, retiring in 1990.

A graduate of Haverford College and The Johns Hopkins University, he teaches American literature, folklore and writing courses at Eastern, and developed — with his students' field collection projects — an archive of Connecticut lore and history, now a part of The Roth Center for Connecticut Studies at E.C.S.U.

Dave shares his affection for Connecticut with the State of Maine, where he has a saltwater summer retreat and where for more than thirty years he was a book reviewer and contributing editor for *Down East* magazine. He has also been an associate editor and editor of *Connecticut History*, journal of the Association for the Study of Connecticut History.

In retirement, Dave continues to be an active participant in local and regional affairs, as an official and member of many boards and committees. As a popular professional storyteller, he has given over a hundred performances before historical societies, library groups, clubs and schools throughout Connecticut.

Among those things which he cherishes most, Dave includes his wife, children and grandchildren; the St. Louis Cardinals baseball team; the fieldstone walls and patios he has built around his house; and good stories of all kinds — in approximately that order.

Notes and Sources

The following list includes additional notes or commentary on some chapters of the text, as well as a record of the principal source(s) of information for each chapter. Sources are identified here by numbers corresponding to the reference numbers used in the Bibliography, followed, where appropriate, by the number(s) of the page(s) which yielded the information.

Example: *The Charter Oak*
Source: 2., pp. 48-50.
This notation indicates that information from pages 48-50 in Marguerite Allis' *Connecticut Trilogy* (Bibliography reference number 2.) was utilized in constructing the legend of The Charter Oak.

While all sources actually used by the author are recorded here, it must be noted that in the case of virtually every legend, additional sources of information – some presenting variant details – also exist. In short, when it comes to telling legends, no single text is definitive and each new retelling will have its own unique integrity.

1   *"The Old Leatherman"*
Sources: 14., pp. 178-185; 40., pp. 69-71; 53.; 54.; 61., pp. 3-12; 69.; 74.; 87.

2   *Israel Putnam*
Sources: 4., pp. 438-440; 6., pp. 231-232; 8., pp. 270-272; 19., p. 436; 21., pp. 98-103; 33., p. [39]; 38., pp. 85-97; 39., pp. 214-220; 46., pp. 23-27; 48., p. 95.

3   *Perry Boney*
Source: 39., pp. 144-159.

4   *Chauncey Judd*
Sources: 4., pp. 186-187; 19., p. 398; 23., pp. 126-128; 45., pp. 45-47.

5   *Gurdon Saltonstall*
Sources: 2., pp. 262-263; 19., pp. 338-339; 25., p. 44.

6   *Abel Buell*
Sources: 4., pp. 531-532; 6., p. 163; 19., p. 357; 25., p. 69; 27., pp. 115-116; 43., pp. 64-67.

7   *"Mother" Bailey*
Sources: 8., pp. 279-280; 19., pp. 157-158; 23., p. 66; 43., pp. 104-105; 46., p. 32.

8   *Elmer Bitgood*
Note: In addition to a verbatim transcript of an audio tape interview with several informants, the source listed below contains references to two published articles on Elmer Bitgood: Champlin, Richard L., "Li'l Elmer Bitgood: the Facts and the Legend." *Yankee*, June, 1968, pp. 87, 134-137, and Phillips, Prentice. "No Leopard Skin for Elmer." *Providence Sunday Journal*, 1 March 1970, [no page given].
Source: 85.

9   *"Old Gard" Wright*
Sources: 21., pp. 83-84; 75.

10 *Lorenzo Dow*
Sources: 4., p. 546; 8., pp. 291-294; 14., pp. 96-99; 23., p. 238; 39., p. 161; 81.

11 *Capt. S.L. Gray*
Note: According to "The Confederate Captain and the Well-preserved Whaler," an article by local historian John A. Johnson of Manchester which appeared in the June, 1982, issue of *New England Senior Citizen / Senior American News* (pp. 18-19), the name of Gray's ship was spelled incorrectly on his tombstone (it was the *James Maury*); the *Maury*'s home port was New Bedford; Capt. Gray died on March 24, 1865, 400 miles from Guam, probably from "inflammation of the bowels"; and there was no contact between the *Maury* and the *Shenandoah* until late June, 1865. The one common element in both the legend and the historical record seems to be the burial of Capt. Gray in a cask of "spirits." The Gray case is a striking example of the curious ways in which "the folk" both garble and preserve history as they pass along stories in oral tradition.
Sources: 19., p. 413; 83.

12 *Jemima Wilkinson*
Note: For a comprehensive biography of this legendary figure, see: Wisbey, Herbert A. *Pioneer Prophetess*. Ithaca, NY: Cornell University Press, 1964.
Sources: 4., pp. 478-479; 14., pp. 312-314; 19., pp. 366-367; 39., pp. 264-269; 46., pp. 28-31.

13 *"The Old Darn Man"*
Sources: 8., pp. 287-291; 21., pp. 80-83; 46., pp. 38-40.

14 *Rufus Malbone*
Sources: 21., p. 98; 75.

15 *Uncas*
Sources: 2., pp. 182-183; 4., pp. 295-297; 6., p. 223; 13., pp. 31-39; 23., p. 243; 79.

16 *"First Lady of Connecticut"*
Source: 4., p. 112.

17 *The Rev. Bulkley's Advice*
Sources: 2., p. 101; 4., p. 305; 8., p. 102; 19., p. 445.

18 *George Washington's Horse*
Source: 19., p. 121.

19 *Noah Webster's Reply*
Note: The author has heard that virtually the same anecdote has been told about Dr. Samuel Johnson (1709-1784), the great British lexicographer, writer and critic. It is possible that it has also been related about every notable dictionary-maker who ever lived.
Source: 2., pp. 228-229.

20 *Silver Hill*
Sources: 6., p. 241; 23., pp. 111-112.

21 *Rhodes' Folly*
Note: William Haynes notes in his *Stonington Chronology, 1649-1976* (Chester, CT: The Pequot Press, 1976, p. 45) that another version of the legend says that a severe storm wiped out Rhodes' Folly island and everything on it. Indeed, the island does not exist today. However, an old stone foundation topped by a flashing beacon, located just off the western tip of Sandy Point (island), is still known today as "Rhodes' Folly" or "The Folly." Source: [Haynes' *Stonington Chronology, 1649-1976*, as noted, above.]

22 *Bride's Brook*
Note: The name of the stream is often given as "Bride Brook" and at least one source (33.) records the bride's name as Mary Metcalf.
Sources: 2., pp. 141-142; 6., p. 118; 8., p. 250; 19., p. 363; 23., p. 59; 33., p. [10].

23 *Lantern Hill*
Sources: 19., p. 371; 23., pp. 246-247 .

24 *Devil's Den*
Sources: 4., p. 440; 49.

25 *Devil's Hopyard (and other Diabolical Places)*
Sources: 19., p. 359; 45., pp. 7-8; 49.; 68.; 86.

26 *Silver Lane*
Sources: 6., p. 116; 21., p. 66; 23., p. 184; 25., p. 43.

27 *Sachem's Head*
Sources: 2., p. 256; 4., p. 216; 6., p. 142; 19., p. 340; 23., p. 47.

28 *Town of Bozrah*
Source: 25., p. 14.

29 *The Charter Oak*
Sources: 2., pp. 48-51; 17., pp. 421-426; 45., pp. 31-34.

30 *Dudleytown, Cursed Village*
Sources: 7., pp. 1-22; 19., p. 468; 39., pp. 183-193; 40., pp. 312-315; 46., pp. 45-47; 55., p. 44.

31 *"Swamp Yankee"*
Sources: 26., p. 159; 57.

32 *The Church Stove War*
Sources: 2., pp. 87-88; 8., pp. 407-409; 19., p. 195.

33 *The Dark Day*
Sources: 4., p. 403; 19., p. 296; 31., pp. 111-113.

34 *Laddin's Leap*
Sources: 19., p. 331; 23., p. 4; 38., pp. 227-235.

35 *Yankee Doodle Dandies*
Sources: 6., pp. 218-219; 8., p. 273; 19., p. 267; 27., pp. 167-168; 46., p. 13; 56.

36 *Legends of Pirate Gold*
Sources: 2., pp. 20, 139, 272; 4., pp. 23-24; 6., p. 82; 9., p. 101; 19., pp. 216, 269, 340, 348; 20., p. 18; 21., pp. 46-47; 23., p. 43; 33., p. [4]; 41., pp. 72, 90; 44., p. 168; 45., pp. 38-40; 51., pp. 11, 13; 82.

37 *The Phantom Ship of New Haven*
Note: For an interesting analysis of the disastrous effect visited upon the fledgling colony's economy by the loss of the "Great Shippe," see: Dzikas, Joan A. "The Phantom Ship: Great Dream for New Haven's Future."*Journal of The New Haven Colony Historical Society*, Winter, 1978, pp. 2-13.
Sources: 2., pp. 231-232; 4., pp. 161-162; 8., pp. 179-180; 17., pp. 417-421; 19., p. 226; 31., pp. 38-40; 46., pp. 5-6.

38 *The Winsted Wild Man*
Note: In addition to the Winsted "Bigfoot" there have been reported sightings of a similar type of creature in at least four other Connecticut towns: Colebrook (1895), Trumbull (1969), Bridgewater (1970) and Ellington (1982). Walter Brundage of New Britain is Connecticut's premier wild man watcher.
Sources: 19., p. 425; 63.; 64.; 84.

39 *The Hessian Husband Kidnappings*
Source: 76.

40 Barkhamsted Lighthouse
Sources: 19., pp. 425-426; 23., p. 159; 45., pp. 21-22; 47., pp. 30-31, 76-79.

41 Escape from New-Gate Prison
Sources: 5., pp. 202-212; 27., pp. 120-126; 31., pp. 102-104; 43., pp. 153-176.

42 Legends of Mt. Riga
Sources: 4., pp. 489-490; 6., p. 244; 7., pp. 43-60; 19., pp. 420-422; 25., p. 178.

43 XYZ
Source: 71.

44 The Irving-Johnson Murder
Sources: 72.; 83.

45 The Lonely Death of Capt. Smith
Note: "Small Pox and Three of Its Victims," a paper presented by Margaret H. Talbot of Andover, to the Andover Historical Society on March 14, 1976, included an historically accurate account of Capt. Smith's final days. It is interesting to note the ways in which the folk legend is at variance with history.
Sources: 19., p. 391; 25., p. 3; 48., pp. 95-96.

46 The Moodus Noises
Sources: 4., pp. 526-528; 8., pp. 180-183; 17., pp. 427-431; 19., pp. 404-405; 34., pp. 169-181; 43., pp. 142-152; 45., pp. 23-25; 48., p. 94; 58.; 89.

47 The Atlantic's Bell
Sources: 59.; 60.; 80.

48 The Sunken House of Gardner Lake
Source: 77.

49 Norwich's Barrel Burning
Sources: 6., pp. 221-222; 27., p. 213.

50 The Tell-Tale Apples
Sources: 6., pp. 129-130; 19., p. 539; 25., p. 53; 40., pp. 156-158; 45., p. 30; 73.

51 The Windham Frog Fight
Note: A revival of the 1893 operetta The Frogs of Windham was staged on August 24-25, 1983, as part of the 150th anniversary celebration of the City of Willimantic (part of Windham). It was much applauded by S. R. O. audiences, but the author—who enjoyed it immensely—noted that the libretto had almost nothing to do with the famous legend. It really did not matter.
Sources: 4., pp. 446-447; 8., pp. 183-185; 17., pp. 436-438; 19., p. 392; 21., pp. 60, 62-64; 23., p. 257; 24., pp. 13-23; 27., pp. 252-254; 31 ., pp. 74-76; 48., pp. 94-95.

52 The Church of Bacchus
Source: 48., pp. 126-130.

53 Two Tales of the Insurance City
Sources: 6., p. 150; 19., p. 173; 27., pp. 228-229.

54 Hannah Cranna, The Wicked Witch of Monroe
Sources: 55., p. 41; 78.

55 Midnight Mary
Sources: 50.; 62.; 67.; 70.; 84.

56 The Black Dog of West Peak
Sources: 6., p. 179; 19., p. 400; 25., p. 179; 45., pp. 53-54; 65., pp. 153-161.

57 Haunted Gay City
Sources: 7., pp. 23-42; 66., pp. 112-123; 81.

58 The Jewett City Vampires
Source: 52.

59 Ghost of the Benton Homestead
Sources: 30.; 88.

60 The Green Lady of Burlington
Sources: 55., p. 44; 84.

61 The Black Fox of Salmon River
Sources: 17., pp. 439-440; 34., pp. 35-42.

62 Debby Griffen
Source: 90, pp. [3-5].

63 The Headless Horseman of Canton
Note: Although this legend seems to have disappeared from local tradition, it was evidently still circulating in the 1930's when field workers for the W. P. A. heard it from live informants in Canton. The late L. K. Porritt, one of the most prolific writers on the history and lore of the Farmington River valley, apparently failed to mention this legend in any of his articles about paymasters travelling the Hartford-Albany post road. Perhaps this retelling will revive the headless phantom.
Sources: 19., p. 427; 27., p. 255.

64 The Vanishing Hitchhiker
Source: 84.

65 Legend of Lake Pocotopaug
Sources: 6., p. 115; 19., p. 405; 23., p. 226; 25., p. 42; 34., pp. 3-22; 45., p. 9.

66 The Nipmuck Fish Fires
Note: John W. Barber's Connecticut Historical Collections (Ref. No. 4.) records a somewhat different version of this traditional legend (p. 428). The site of the fatal eel bake is Danielson, rather than Thompson, and the "fishing fires" are not mentioned. Instead, forever after the fight, no grass ever grew on the place of battle.
Sources: 19., pp. 536-537; 45., pp. 4-5.

67 *Legends of Lake Alexander*
Sources: 4., pp. 431-432; 19., p. 534; 21., p. 79; 23.,
p. 269; 25., p. 68; 45., p. 3.

68 *Lillinonah's Leap*
Sources: 6., p. 211; 19., pp. 452-453; 23., p. 82; 45.,
pp. 12-13; 46., pp. 3-4.

69 *Legend of Samp Mortar Rock*
Sources: 4., p. 356; 19., pp. 352-353.
[Also, paper by Cecile Parent, included in C. F.
A. 82.]

Following is a list of source materials consulted in the preparation of this book. It is divided into four sections, as follows:

I.   Books and Pamphlets.
II.   Periodical Literature.
III.   C. F. A. (Connecticut Folklore Archive) Materials. (These consist of audio tapes and / or transcripts of audio tapes included in student folklore collecting projects, in the collection of The Center for Connecticut Studies, Eastern Connecticut State University.)
IV.   Unpublished Documents.

Contrary to standard bibliographical practice, all entries have been assigned reference numbers in order to facilitate the identification of sources listed according to such reference numbers in the "Notes and Sources" section of this book.

I. Books and Pamphlets

1   Abbott, Katherine N. *Old Paths and Legends of New England.* New York: G. P. Putnam's Sons, 1903.

2   Allis, Marguerite. *Connecticut Trilogy.* New York: G. P. Putnam's Sons, 1934.

3   Ayer, A. D. "Old Darn Coat." In *A Modern History of Windham County, Connecticut.* Vol. II. Chicago: The S. J. Clarke Publishing Co., 1920.

4   Barber, John Warner. *Connecticut Historical Collections.* New Haven, CT: Durrie & Peck and J. W. Barber, 1838.

5   Barber, Lucius I. *A Record and Documentary History of Simsbury.* Simsbury, CT: The Abigail Phelps Chapter Daughters of the American Revolution, 1931.

6   Bixby, William. *Connecticut: A New Guide.* New York: Charles Scribner's Sons, 1974.

7   Blanchard, Fessenden S. *Ghost Towns of New England.* New York: Dodd, Mead and Co., 1960.

8   Botkin, B. A., ed. *A Treasury of New England Folklore.* New York: Bonanza Books, 1967.

9   Brooks, Lillian Kruger. *A History of Haddam Neck.* Haddam Neck Genealogical Group, 1972.

10 Browne, G. Waldo. *Legends of New England.* Manchester, NH: Standard Book Co., 1925.

11 Brunvand, Jan Harold. *The Study of American Folklore: An Introduction.* 2nd. edition. New York: W.W. Norton and Co., 1978.

12 Brunvand, Jan Harold. *The Vanishing Hitchhiker.* New York: W.W. Norton Co., 1981.

13 Caulkins, Frances Manwaring. *History of Norwich, Connecticut.* Chester, CT: The Pequot Press, 1976.

14 Coffin, Tristram Potter, and Hennig Cohen. *The Parade of Heroes.* New York: Anchor Press / Doubleday, 1978.

15 Cothren, William. *History of Ancient Woodbury, Connecticut, from the First Indian Deed in 1659 to 1872.* Woodbury, CT: William Cothren, 1872.

16 Crofut, Florence. *Guide to the History and Historic Sites of Connecticut.* 2 vols. New Haven, CT: Yale University Press, 1937.

17 Drake, Samuel Adams. *A Book of New England Legends and Folk Lore.* Rutland, VT: Charles E. Tuttle Co., 1971.

18 Early, Eleanor. *A New England Sampler.* Boston: Waverly House, 1940.

19 Federal Writers' Project of The Works Progress Administration for The State of Connecticut, Workers. *Connecticut: A Guide to Its Roads, Lore, and People.* Boston: Houghton Mifflin Co., 1938.

20 Ford, George Hare. *Historical Sketches of the Town of Milford.* New Haven, CT: Tuttle, Morehouse and Taylor Co., 1914.

21 Griggs, Susan J. *Folklore and Firesides in Pomfret, Hampton and Vicinity.* Danielson, CT: Ingalls Printing Co., [1950].

22 Hand, Wayland D., ed. *American Folk Legend: A Symposium.* Berkeley, CA: University of California Press, 1971.

23 Heermance, Edgar L., compiler. *The Connecticut Guide: What to See and Where to Find It.* Hartford, CT: Emergency Relief Commission, 1935.

24 Higbee, Lillian Marsh. *Bacchus of Windham and The Frog Fight.* 1930 (Privately printed 2 3-page pamphlet. No place of publication or printer listed.)

25 *Highways & Byways of Connecticut.* Hartford, CT: Case, Lockwood and Brainard, 1947.

26 Larned, Ellen D. *History of Windham County, Connecticut.* Volume II. Chester, CT: The Pequot Press, 1976.

27 Lee, W. Storrs. *The Yankees of Connecticut.* New York: Henry Holt and Co., 1957.

28 Mills, Lewis Sprague. *The Story of Connecticut.* West Rindge, NH: Richard Smith Publisher, Inc. 1958.

29 Mitchell, Edwin Valentine. *Yankee Folk.* New York: The Vanguard Press, Inc., 1948.

30 Needham, Helen L. *The Daniel Benton Homestead.* Tolland, CT: The Clinton Press of Tolland, 1980.

31 Newton, Caroline Clifford. *Once Upon a Time in Connecticut.* Boston: Houghton Mifflin Co., 1916.

32 Niven, John. *Connecticut Hero: Israel Putnam.* Hartford, CT: The American Revolution Bicentennial Commission of Connecticut, 1977.

33 Prendergast, William J. *Exploring Connecticut.* Stonington, CT: The Pequot Press, 1965.

34 Price, Carl F. *Yankee Township.* East Hampton, CT: Citizens' Welfare Club, 1941.

35 Roth, David M. *Connecticut: A Bicentennial History.* New York: W. W. Norton and Co., 1979.

36 Sellers, Helen Earle. *Connecticut Town Origins.* 2nd ed. Chester, CT: Pequot Press, 1973.

37 Shepard, Odell. *Connecticut Past and Present.* New York: Alfred A. Knopf, 1939.

38 Snow, Edward Rowe. *Legends of The New England Coast.* New York: Dodd, Mead and Co., 1957.

39 Sterry, Iveagh Hunt, and William H. Garrigus. *They Found a Way.* Brattleboro, VT: Stephen Daye Press, 1938.

40 Stevens, Austin N., ed. *Mysterious New England.* Dublin, NH: Yankee, Inc., 1971.

41 Stowe, Nathan. *Sixty Years' Recollections of Milford.* Milford, CT: Village Improvement Association, 1917.

42 Tallman, Marjorie. *Dictionary of American Folklore.* New York: Philosophical Library, 1960.

43 Todd, Charles Burr. *In Olde Connecticut.* New York: The Grafton Press, 1906. Reissued by: Detroit: Singing Tree Press, 1968.

44 Verrill, Alpheus H. *The Heart of Old New England.* New York: Dodd, Mead and Co., 1936.

45 White, Glenn E., ed. *Folk Tales of Connecticut.* Meriden, CT: The Journal Press, 1977.

46 White, Glenn E., ed. *Folk Tales of Connecticut, Volume II.* Meriden, CT: The Journal Press, 1981.

47 Wheeler, Richard G., and George Hilton. *Barkhamsted Heritage: Culture and Industry in a Rural Connecticut Town.* Barkhamsted, CT: Barkhamsted Historical Society, 1975.

48 Webster, Clarence M. *Town Meeting Country.* New York: Duell, Sloane and Pearce, 1945.

II. *Periodical Literature*

49 Donohue, John, and Michael Petersen. "Devils in Connecticut." *The Hartford Courant Magazine,* 21 July 1974, p. 12.

50 Friedman, Henry. "New Haven's Underground." *New Haven Advocate,* 4 October 1977, p. 1.

51 Grant, Ellsworth. "Welcome to Folderol Island." *Northeast Magazine* (of the *Hartford Courant*), 8 May 1983, pp. 8-15, 22.

52 Hileman, Maria. "Reporter's 'Stakeout' Puts Bite on Vampires." *Norwich Bulletin,* 31 October 1976, p. 24.

53 Hornstein, Harold. "In The Footsteps of The Old Leatherman." *The New Haven Register,* 4 June 1972, p. 1B.

54 Hornstein, Harold. "Preserving The Leatherman Legend." *The New Haven Register,* 9 January 1977, p. 4B.

55 James, Stuart. "Spine-Tinglers for Halloween." *Connecticut,* October 1976, pp. 41-45.

56 Lacy, John. "Doodling on Yankees." *Hartford Courant,* 29 March 1975, p. 2.

57 Lacy, John. "'Swamp Yankee' was Indeed a Term Meant to Disparage." *Hartford Courant,* 30 April 1982, p. A21.

58 Lehr, Dick. "Seismic Detective Solves 'Moodus Noises' Mystery." *Hartford Courant,* 19 October 1981, pp. A1, A3.

59 "Loss of The Atlantic. Further Particulars." *Hartford Daily Courant,* 1 December 1846, p. 2.

60 "Loss of The Steamer Atlantic and Many Lives." *Hartford Daily Courant*, 30 November 1846, pp. 2-3.

61 Masters, Al. "Strange Riddle of The Old Leatherman." *The New England Galaxy*, Winter 1973, pp. 3-12.

62 "'Midnight Mary' Has Many Visitors." *American Cemetery*. March 1970, p. 3.

63 O'Brien, Joseph A. "The 'Wild Man' May Be Back Again." *Hartford Courant*, 28 July 1972, 3rd edition, p. 20.

64 O'Brien, Joseph A. "Strange Creature Frightens Couples." *Hartford Courant*, 28 September 1974, 1st edition, p. 12.

65 Pynchon, W. H. C. "The Black Dog." *Connecticut Quarterly*, Vol. IV, No. 2 (April-June, 1898), pp. 153-161.

66 Redford, H. Phyllis. "Gay City: Connecticut's Ghost Village." *Yankee*, November 1968, pp. 112-123.

67 Ross, Mary Jo. "The Legend of Midnight Mary Lives On." *Journal-Courier*, 23 May 1979, pp. 1, 3.

68 Ryerson, Charlotte. "Halloween in Devil's Hopyard." *The Gazette* (Old Lyme), 21 October 1976, pp. 1, 14.

69 Sandahl, Eric P. "Mystery Still Conceals the Identity of Meriden's Legendary Leatherman." *The Meriden (Conn.) Record*, 22 July 1948, p. 1.

70 Seder, Eugene. "Ghost of Midnight Mary: Haunting Legend of Death." *The New Haven Register*, 31 October 1975, p. 9.

71 Smith, Timothy B. "The 80-Year Mystery of a Man Called XYZ." *Hartford Courant*, 30 March 1980, p. 41.

72 Snow, Sandy. "Mystery Surrounds Man Accused of Murder, Suicide More Than 100 Years Ago." *Norwich Bulletin*, 2 January 1977, p. 32.

73 "Tricia." "The Rood Apple." *The Chronicle* (Willimantic), 3 November 1973, p. 11.

III. *C. F. A. (Connecticut Folklore Archive) Materials*

74 Anderson, James, and Paul Levaseurr. "The Old Leatherman." C.F.A. No. 61. 1971.

75 Blanchard, Margaret, and Susan Brierton, Pauline Deragon and Barbara Cook. "Stories on Stones." C.F.A. No. 70, 1971.

76 Blejewski, Barbara. "Farmington Valley Folklore." C. F. A. [uncatalogued], 1974.

77 Bloom, Helene. "Bozrah Burial Legends." C. F. A., [uncatalogued], 1974.

78 Brigham, Glenn, and Noreen Bienkowski. "Legends of Monroe, Connecticut, and The Legend of the Indian Well, Shelton, Connecticut." C. F. A. No. 125, 1974.

79 Chamberland, Linda. "Folklore of the Norwich Area." C. F. A. No. 24, [1970].

80 Del Monte, John. "The Legend of the Ship, 'Atlantic.'" In "Folklore of Gravestones: in New London, Connecticut." C. F. A. No. 122, 1973.

81 Gallo, Francesca, and Judy Kubran. "Gay City – Connecticut's Lost Village." C. F. A. No. 41, 1970.

82 Kamarowski, Joanne, and Sharon Smeaton. "Ghost Hauntings of Connecticut." C. F. A. No. 118, 1973.

83 Kovach, Glenna M., and Robert G. McKinney. "Unusual Burials of Eastern Connecticut." C. F. A. No. 108, 1971.

84 Manroel, Peter. "Midnight Mary and Tales of Terror." C. F. A. No. 107, 1972.

85 Saari, John. "Legend of the Bitgoods." C. F. A. No. 56, 1971.

86 Vozek, Joanne. "Devil's Hopyard." C. F. A. No. 63, 1971.

IV. *Unpublished Documents*

87 Bates, Elmer H. "The Old Leather Man." Unpublished four-page typescript, in the collection of the Silas Bronson Library, Waterbury, Connecticut.

88 Brown, Yvonne (Mrs.). "The Daniel Benton Homestead" and other unpublished papers written by and in the private collection of Mrs. Brown.

89 Roelants, Rod. "The Matchitmoodus Noises." Unpublished essay, American Folklore course, Eastern Connecticut State College, April 25, 1966. Typescript in possession of David E. Philips.

90 Templeton, Laura. "Five Legendary Connecticut Witches." Unpublished essay, American Folklore course, Eastern Connecticut State College, May 11, 1982. Typescript in possession of David E. Philips.

Index

White House, Washington, D.C., 58, 143
White Plains, NY, 37
Whittier, John Greenleaf, 158
Whittlesey, John, 79-80
Wilcox, *Old Man*, 190
Wild Man, Winsted, CT, 175-77
Wilkinson, Jemima, 84-89
Willey, Hiram, 128
William of Orange (*King*), 141
William Strong and Company, Gay City, CT, 243-44
Winchester, CT, 175
Winchester Firearms Corporation, New Haven, CT,
    193
Winchester Road, Winsted, CT, 175
Windham, CT, 132
Windham Center, CT, 215, 217
Windham County, CT, 33, 36-37, 73, 90-91
Windham Frog Fight, 113, 151, 215, 217
Windham Town Hall, Windham, CT, 218
Windsor, CT, 167-68
Windy City *see* Chicago, IL
Winsted, CT, 175
Winsted Herald, 175
Winthrop, John, 98, 119, 137
  grandchild
      Winthrop the Younger, 137
Winthrop Avenue, New Haven, CT, 233-34
Woodbridge, CT, 26
Wooster, David, 44-46, 48
Wooster's Tavern, Middlebury, CT, 46
Worcester, MA, 171, 204
Wright, Phineas Gardner, 71-74
Wyllys, Samuel, 137, 139-41
  spouse
      Ruth, 140
Wyllys Hill, Hartford, CT, 141

XYZ Legend, 192-94

Yale University, New Haven, CT, 38, 49, 93, 232-33
Yankee Doodle, 165-66
Yantic River, Norwich, CT, 99
Yates County, NY, 86-87
Yeti, *see* Abominable Snow Man
York State Dutchman, 188